ALSO BY LAURA TRENTHAM

Kiss Me That Way

LAURA TRENTHAM

St. Martin's Paperbacks

This is a work of fiction. All of the characters, organizations, and events portrayed in this novel are either products of the author's imagination or are used fictitiously.

KISS ME THAT WAY

Copyright © 2016 by Laura Trentham.
Excerpt from *Then He Kissed Me* copyright © 2016 by Laura Trentham.

All rights reserved.

For information address St. Martin's Press, 175 Fifth Avenue, New York, NY 10010.

ISBN: 978-1-250-07763-9

Our books may be purchased in bulk for promotional, educational, or business use. Please contact your local bookseller or the Macmillan Corporate and Premium Sales Department at 1-800-221-7945, ext. 5442, or by e-mail at MacmillanSpecialMarkets@macmillan.com.

Printed in the United States of America

St. Martin's Paperbacks edition / June 2016

St. Martin's Paperbacks are published by St. Martin's Press, 175 Fifth Avenue, New York, NY 10010.

10 9 8 7 6 5 4 3 2 1

This book is dedicated to my parents
who have supported me through all of life's
ups and downs and in-betweens.

Acknowledgments

My journey as an author has been circuitous. A very early love of reading was inspired by my parents who are great readers. I remember tagging along with my mom who was (and still is) very active with my hometown library. Back in the days of card catalogues and stacks and stacks of books to get lost in, I discovered Victoria Holt and Mary Stewart and Phyllis A. Whitney and so many other wonderful authors who fired a lifelong love of romance. My parents never censored my reading (thank goodness!).

A detour through engineering and a couple of kids later, I got an itch. Without telling anyone, I started writing a book. The itch turned into an obsession. I finished one and immediately started another and another and another. I never thought anyone would want to publish them, much less someone besides my mom would want to read them! I'm glad I was wrong.

Thanks to all those old-school romance books and to my parents who let me devour them!

Chapter One

A jangle woke Monroe Kirby. She opened her eyes to a dark shadow standing over her. "Mama?"

The figure didn't answer. Monroe pushed up on her pillow and rubbed her eyes with the heels of her hands. Her sleepy confusion turned into a strangling dread with the sound of a zipper being lowered.

Sam was in her room. She could make out his broad shoulders in the black T-shirt he was wearing when he and her mama had stumbled in drunk from their night on the town. His pants were peeled open, a white vee of underwear at eye level, the bulge something she understood in an abstract way.

"Monroe-girl, I'm here to tuck you in." Sam Landry's sugared drawl veered toward an outright slur.

She pulled the sheet higher. "N-no thanks, I'm good."

"Ah, come on, now. I'll play nice." He ripped the pink candy-striped sheet out of her hands and whipped it to the footboard. She drew her legs up, trying to make herself small.

"I don't want to play with you." She looked from him to her open door. A long way. Could she make it by him to the bathroom? It was the only room with a lock, although not a strong one.

"Don't lie. I've seen you looking at me." He stroked her cheek with one hand while his other burrowed inside his underwear. Her head seemed to detach itself from the panicked mass of nerves that was her body.

Out. Could she get out? Could she get him out? "I think I hear Mama."

He shifted and listened, swaying on his feet. "I don't hear nothing."

"Could you check? And then . . ."

"I knew you wanted it." She couldn't see his smile, but she could feel it.

As soon as he turned the corner out of her room, she sprang up. How long did she have? She closed her door and struggled to push the bureau in front of it. One hand slipped off and her shoulder struck the sharp corner. She bit off a cry. Setting her forehead against the top, she rubbed at the pins and needles pain shooting from shoulder to hand until it receded. Seconds ticked off. The tears she fought were less about pain and more about frustration and fear.

Putting all her one hundred pounds into the motion, she pushed once more, gritting her teeth. The bureau inched forward with a loud squawk of wood on wood. The small victory fueled a burst of adrenaline. Inertia was on her side. They'd learned about inertia and momentum in her eighth-grade science class just that week. She'd never thought to put the knowledge to practical use so soon.

The *clomp* of boots echoed in the long hallway.

Her heart shot into overdrive. Didn't people gain superhuman strength under stress? Her hands shook and her knees felt mushy. She took a deep breath and shoved. The bureau slid a few more inches. She checked her progress. She'd only managed to move it halfway in front of her door.

The door slammed open a few inches, cracking against

the bureau. A little scream escaped her throat, and she jumped backward. A rose her mother had given her after her last ballet recital, dried and pinned to the back of her door, fell to the floor, the delicate petals crumbling.

"What the hell, Monroe?" Sam's voice retained the slur but lost the cajoling tone. "Let me in."

She backed away, looking around for someplace to hide. But the thought of sliding under her bed or huddling in the corner of her closet seemed childish and stupid. Sam would find her, drag her out, and do the things he promised with his eyes, things she didn't want to do with anyone, much less her mama's boyfriend.

He slammed the door against the bureau again, shoving it back enough to get his head through the crack. It was only a matter of time before he would be able to slip inside. "Come on, girl. I told your mama I would take care of you."

"G-go to hell." She'd heard her mama yell that phrase enough at various men, her father included, to know it carried some weight. "I'll scream."

Not bothering to camouflage his anger, he slammed the door against the bureau a half-dozen times, the bangs like gunshots. Each one made her flinch. "Your mama is passed out in bed, sweet thing. Let me in. You want this."

A warm breeze snaked through her cracked window, fluttering the curtains. The white cotton of her nightgown tickled her legs. The universe giving her a hint. She ripped the curtains open and slid the window up, the whine quieting Sam.

She looked over her shoulder, her gaze clashing with his. The moonlight streaming into the room revealed a good-looking forty-something man. His face was all over town on his insurance agency ads. A toothy, too-charming smile turned his lips, and he gestured her closer with two fingers.

She turned back to the window and punched the screen out in a fluid motion. It clattered to the roof of the covered porch.

"Aw, hell no. You get back over here and let me in. You don't want me to hurt you, do you?" He banged the door against the bureau again.

She threw her leg over the sill. He had jammed his upper body through the crack. The look in his eyes sent her out the window, clinging to the sill. She dropped and landed on the covered porch next to the screen. The gritty black roofing tile scraped her palms and knees. She peered over the short side of the porch roof to the bushes below. Logically, she knew it couldn't be more than fifteen feet, but all her body knew was she was getting ready to fall.

She lowered herself over, the edge of the gutter biting into her belly. The prickly leaves of the bush brushed her toes. Her arms shook with the effort, her fingers numb, her palms sweaty and stinging from cuts.

"Monroe! Where you at, girl? Come on out now. You're being silly." Sincerity laced his voice.

A shot of doubt stilled her, dangling over the edge, her muscles screaming. Was she being silly? He was the adult after all. But where her mama was desperate and trusting, Monroe had seen too many men come and go from their lives. Some were nicer than others, and some, like Sam, were too nice. The way he stared at her barely there breasts and skinny legs made her uncomfortable. What did she trust? Him or her instincts?

Mentally counting to three, she took a deep breath and let go. She hit the bush and pitched backward, landing on her back with her legs in the air, her nightgown bunched above her white cotton panties. Her lungs burned. Her panic had nothing to do with Sam and everything to do with the clamor of her body for oxygen.

Her lungs switched on, and she allowed herself five

seconds to just breathe, in and out, in and out, until she'd stopped wheezing. Rolling over onto her hands and knees, she listened. Sam was shaking bushes on the far side of the yard where her old, rotting play set stood, one swing swaying in the warm breeze. The kind of breeze that carried the scent of the ocean even though it was a hundred miles away.

She couldn't stay and play cat and mouse with him in the fenced-in yard. Holding her nightgown to keep it from flapping like a white flag of surrender, she scampered around the pool through the door at the back of the fence and hesitated.

She had nowhere to go. Her father was in the Caribbean with his new family, and if she showed up at Regan's house her best friend's parents would have questions Monroe would be too embarrassed to answer. Hearing the crack of a branch and Sam's voice get closer, she ran into the unknown.

Cade Fournette snuck through the night under the full moon. If the Cottonbloom, Mississippi, police chief picked him up again for trespassing, he would end up in jail for sure. His last chat with Chief Thomason had not gone well. The man's condemnation had lit a fire under Cade's pride. A couple of insults about the sheriff's excess weight and minuscule intelligence had resulted in a wrenched arm and bruised ribs.

Cade's nighttime poaching activities were becoming riskier now that he was on the chief's radar, but his family needed to eat, if not eat well. Anyway, he never emptied the nets, only took enough crayfish to make a couple of decent meals. His rabbit traps were a boon for everyone. Cottonbloom, Mississippi, took pride in its prize tomatoes and the mayor wouldn't want a rabbit herd destroying its reputation. Really, he was doing everyone a favor. That particular argument hadn't made a dent in the chief's stony demeanor last time.

Cade slipped in the mud down to his metal skiff hidden in the tall reeds close to the bank. He froze in a crouch, listening. All he could hear was his own heart beating, but the hairs on his neck stood on end. Not much scared him these days, except for thoughts of getting taken away from his family and put somewhere he couldn't protect them.

Had the police found his boat? Was the chief waiting? Should he run? No more than ten seconds passed.

"Who's there?" a little girl's voice called out, trembling behind the facsimile of bravery. "Leave me the h-hell alone, Sam."

He duckwalked closer, parted the reeds, and peeked through. A figure in white huddled on the far seat of his skiff. Her knees were pulled toward her chin, her hands clenching and unclenching around the sides.

He'd seen her around Cottonbloom a time or two, although he couldn't recall her name, if he ever knew it. She was his sister's age or thereabouts, but with the attitude of a Mississippi deb. One of those girls who were bred to know their place in the world and with a glance would recognize he wasn't part of it. What the hell was she doing out on the river?

Self-preservation had been his constant companion the last few years. Best all around if she didn't see him. Then, there'd be no one to squeal to later. No one would believe a Louisiana swamp rat over a well-to-do 'Sip. He eased the reeds back together and took a step back, his boot squelching in mud.

"Don't come any closer. I-I have a gun." Any hint of bravado was gone from her voice. She sounded straight up terrified. He looked through the reeds again. She was half out of her seat, the skiff rocking slightly in the shallow water. The girl reminded Cade of a rabbit, half-trapped and ready to gnaw its foot off to escape.

What if Tally needed help and he wasn't around? He looked up to the moon and mouthed a curse. The wave of protectiveness had him pulling off his ball cap and rising out of his crouch, his hands in front of him. Although he didn't see any sign she actually had a gun, this was Mississippi.

"It's all right. I'm not going to hurt you, girl. Name's Cade Fournette."

"D-don't come any closer or I'll . . ." She looked around her feet.

"I don't keep any sort of weapons in my boat. Unless you want to hit me upside the head with a paddle."

"This is your boat? I'm sorry. Do you need it?" The girl looked torn about what to do. Politely give up her hiding place or hunker back down.

A huffing laugh escaped him. "We can share for a while if you want. I have a sister named Tallulah. You two look about an age. What . . . Thirteen or so?"

"Yes." The girl nodded like a bobblehead but still looked ready to throw herself over the side in a bid for escape.

"She loves to come out on the river with me. Sometimes I even let her drive the boat." Lies. Tally hated the river. Said it reminded her of too many sad things. He tried on a smile.

Unlike Cade, the girl was used to trusting people. Her shoulders rounded with a shuddery sigh, and she plopped back onto the seat. Her hair appeared almost white in the moonlight, her features delicate, and when she tucked her hair behind ears that stuck out a little her face took on an elfish quality, cute and innocent.

He hauled himself onto the opposite seat, folding his

legs into a modified crisscross-applesauce. He'd learned when to be big brother, father, uncle, or friend. This girl needed a big brother.

"What's your name?"

"Kirby. Monroe Kirby."

"Are you an international spy like . . . Bond, James Bond?" His joke was silly, but it worked. A giggle spurted out of her. "What're you doing out here so late, Monroe?"

"What are *you* doing out here so late?"

He barely managed to keep his reaction contained to a quirk of his lips. He was glad that whatever had happened, the girl retained some spunk. The river that divided Mississippi from Louisiana also divided the town of Cottonbloom. At one time the town had been united, but for the past fifty years the sides faced off across the river like two sentinels on guard. And Cade, being a Louisiana swamp rat, shouldn't be this far upriver.

"I asked first. Who is Sam and why are you scared of him?"

She tensed again, fear masking her face. Her knees and legs were scraped, her bare feet streaked brown with mud, her hands scratched and dirty. Her ruffled white nightgown looked childish—she was in eighth grade if she and Tally were the same age—but her finger- and toenails were painted hot pink.

"You can trust me. I promise," he said softly.

A chorus of bullfrogs filled the silence. She didn't flinch away from his gaze as some people did. Something passed between them, something almost electric that put Cade on alert. Not attraction—he wasn't a pervert—but a sort-of understanding he couldn't explain.

As if a door unlocked, words poured from her. Not just about what had happened that night, but about her mother's descent into alcoholism, her parents' divorce, her shame. The more she told him, the angrier he became. It seemed things on the Mississippi side of Cottonbloom weren't always brighter than on the Louisiana side. Bigger houses, more money, same problems.

"What should I do?" She tucked her hands between her knees, the ruffles on the front of her nightgown waving in the breeze.

"Your mom is passed out?"

She nodded.

"This Sam fella has been sleeping over regular-like?"

She bit her bottom lip, but her chin wobbled. She nodded again.

"How about this? Let's go up on the bank to get away from the skeeters, and I'll clean up your scratches. When the sun comes up, I'll see you home."

"What about Sam?"

Innocence was fleeting, and Monroe was a kid. A kid who reminded Cade painfully of Tally, but as long as he was alive Tally would be safe. Monroe had no one.

He considered stalking to her house and de-nutting her mother's boyfriend, but that would only scare Monroe worse and get him thrown in jail faster than a hiccup. Instead, he banked his rage, knowing it would be there when he needed it.

"I'll handle him later. Make sure he doesn't bother you again."

Whether she heard the darkness in his voice or not, she didn't ask him how he would accomplish it. She held on to that much innocence at least.

"Thank you, Cade." She smiled, the action lighting her from the inside, turning her from cute into something beyond pretty, something like the flash of summer's first firefly or a shooting star. Then, it was gone, and he blinked, wondering if it had been his imagination.

He tucked the first-aid kit from the skiff under his arm and helped her up the slippery bank with a hand under her knobby elbow. She sat with her back against a cottonwood tree and talked while he cleaned her knees and palms and dabbed on antiseptic. She was too young to edit herself, and by the time the first streaks of sun lit the sky he knew her favorite foods, bands, color. He also knew her dreams and goals and fears.

Shockingly, he shared a few of his secrets, too. Things he tried to protect Sawyer and Tally from. The charity Cade had been forced to accept at the food bank since his parents had been killed by a drunk driver. A different sort of shame than Monroe's, but just as cutting. The medicine he'd stolen from the pharmacy when Tally's cough got so bad over the winter. Even though Monroe couldn't help him, she seemed to understand him, and in that simple act his burdens and shames were lessened.

With the branches of the tree swaying in the warm sea-infused breeze, he and Monroe watched the stars fade into predawn light. Handfuls of white bolls dotted the freshly harvested cotton field on the far side of the river. It wasn't until pink streaked from the ground that she spoke again. "Cade, please don't tell anyone."

"You could go to the cops." Even though he didn't trust the law to treat him fairly, surely it would protect someone like her.

"I can't. Then everyone would know."

He wanted to tell her it wasn't her fault, but he understood how hollow the words would sound. He'd heard enough platitudes like that to last a lifetime. "I won't tell. And you won't tell anyone about me, either?"

She took his hand and squeezed. "I would never."

He'd never met a teen girl who could keep a secret, but he could only nod. They walked side by side through the grassy field, entering her yard through a narrow door in the back of her fence. Her house was enormous by his standards. The chlorine of the pool pungent but not unpleasant. He'd never played in water so blue and clean. The murky river was his swimming pool.

He wrapped a hand around her skinny upper arm, all bone and tendons and tender flesh. Heat flashed through his body at the thought of her trying to fight off a grown man. "Can you get in the house? Where's your room?"

"Mama keeps a key under the flowerpot around front." Monroe pointed to an open window on the second floor, the drapes swaying with the wind. "That's my room. I think I can squeeze past my bureau."

He stifled a curse. A miracle she hadn't broken her neck. "Go around the front. Run straight to your room and give me a thumbs-up. Remember what I told you?"

"Jam the back of a chair under the door handle whenever Mama brings a man home."

"Right. I know you're tired, but you go to school today, you hear?"

"I will." She took a step away, then whirled back and threw herself into his chest, startling him. His arms came around her automatically to return the hug. She felt as delicate as a baby bird. "Can you come back upriver sometime?"

He should say no for a multitude of reasons. No one would approve of their association for one thing. For another, getting caught would be catastrophic to his family. "Next full moon. Meet me under the cottonwood tree."

"Thank you, Cade." Her voice was muffled against his shirt.

"Go on, then." He let her go and nudged her toward the house. She ran, looking over her shoulder several times. He waited until she came to her window and gave him the signal. After she'd closed her window and drapes, he stood there, nurturing his rage.

He was going to be late for work and lose out on precious wages. Not to mention the fact, he hadn't actually gotten any poaching done. He circled to the front of the house and settled under an oak tree across the street, trying to stay hidden. Any of the snobby 'Sips along the street could call the police and accuse him of loitering.

An hour later, a man in a well-fitting suit came out the front door of Monroe's house. Cade muttered a curse. He should have guessed Monroe's "Sam" was in fact Sam Landry, a prominent insurance salesman with advertisements all over both sides of the river. He was good-looking in a smarmy Sears catalog model kind of way. Now Cade knew Sam's toothy white smile and perfect hair hid a special kind of depravity.

Cade was on him before he had a chance to unlock the blue BMW in the driveway.

"What the—?" The man's voice was more outraged than fearful.

Cade looked up and down the street. Deserted. He slid a knife out of his boot, the handle worn to fit his hand. With an arm across Sam's chest, he set the tip at the crotch of the other man and pushed him against the car door.

"You messed with the wrong girl, Mr. Landry."

The man's mouth went slack, his eyes bloodshot, his pores still exuding the scent of liquor.

"Monroe is a friend of mine. You hurt her, and I'll take it personal. Real personal. You want to go to jail for molesting a child?"

"I didn't touch that girl." Sam shoved at Cade's arm, only managing to move it a couple of inches.

While Cade was only seventeen, he'd physically gained a man's muscles and had conditioned himself to harness his fear. He couldn't afford to back down from anyone. "Only 'cause she ran off."

The man stopped fighting him, his voice oozing charm and good humor. "You got it all wrong, boy. She's trying to get me in trouble. Doesn't want me to marry her mama.

Plus, she's got a little crush on me. Bad combination. You know how these young girls can be. Silly and impressionable."

Monroe hadn't seemed either to him. "I'm more inclined to believe her than you, mister. Especially considering I can still smell liquor on you."

The man's face tightened and his body jerked against Cade's arm. "I know you. You're a Louisiana swamp rat. You think the police will believe you over me?" This man was used to being in charge, used to being heard, while Cade did his business in the shadows.

"Probably not." Cade held the man's gaze and let the tension build in the silence. "How about I dish out swamp rat justice then? I'll cut your shriveled little balls off and feed them to a wild hog. You'll be singing soprano in the church choir the rest of your days."

"You wouldn't touch me."

Cade bared his teeth in the mimicry of a smile. He pushed the tip of his knife through the wool fabric of the man's suit pants, twisting and sliding the blade until a gaping foot-long hole revealed a pair of pink-and-blue-striped boxers.

Cade amped up his redneck accent. "I'd enjoy guttin' you and throwin' you to the gators."

Sam's throat worked, but no sound emerged. A man walking a high-stepping white poodle with a ridiculous pink bow came into view two houses down. Cade needed to wrap this up before the 'Sip called the law.

"Let me tell you how this is going to go down. You're going to break it off with Monroe's mama. You're going to move out of this house. And if I ever see you hanging around, you and I are going to take a little trip out to the swamps. Got me?"

Sam jerked his head, his mouth twisted. Cade removed his arm, slid the knife back into his boot, and walked away in one smooth motion. In the light of day, he couldn't traipse over other people's property back to his boat. It would be a hot, hour-long walk back to where he'd left his truck. At best, he'd miss half his shift and half his pay. At worst, he'd get fired and come home empty-handed.

Looking over his shoulder at the grand white house, he smiled. Either way, it had been worth it.

Chapter Two

Standing at a high counter, Monroe Kirby made notes in her last client's chart and rotated her ankles. It had been a long day. Ms. June, the office scheduler, bustled over, her nursing clogs squeaking. "I have a walk-in patient. Can one of you take him?"

Monroe propped herself on her elbows and massaged the back of her neck. "It's nearly five, and I have to meet my girls at the gym. Can you take him, Bart?"

Bartholomew Jones rubbed a hand over his cropped Afro and smiled one of his 120-watt smiles. "I would, Monroe, but it's Dana's birthday. If I'm late, I'll be one of your clients tomorrow. With a wrung neck."

Monroe returned his smile in spite of the inconvenience. No matter how stressful or busy they were, Bartholomew brightened everyone's day and made working as a physical therapist at Cottonbloom Therapeutics fun. It was his gift, and she'd never regretted coming back home to join his practice. She was tired, but any client deserved to be put through their paces with a smile on her face and encouragement in her voice.

"I'll shoot Tally a text and let her get the girls started. Hopefully this guy is cooperative. Records?"

"Doesn't have any."

"Paperwork?"

"He's filling it out in room two. Although he didn't look happy about it. Mr. Fournette brought him in, and they were arguing like two polecats in a sack."

"Was it a work-related injury?"

Sawyer Fournette managed an auto-parts manufacturing plant over the state line in Louisiana. If the injury had happened on the job site, there were government-mandated regulations to follow.

"Didn't mention it, and I can't imagine the kind of language they were using is appropriate for the workplace." Ms. June's ruddy cheeks shaded darker. "If I had to hazard a guess I'd say they were related. Does Mr. Fournette have a brother or cousin?"

Monroe's heart ramped to sprint-like levels even though she hadn't taken a step. Her mouth dried and every nerve ending seemed sensitized. She walked past Bartholomew and Ms. June without another word.

Had her stomach dived to the floor in nerves or anticipation? She hadn't felt like this since her first week practicing. Could it be that Cade Fournette had stepped foot back into Cottonbloom?

The last time she'd seen him had been during her freshman year of college. Ten years ago. She'd gone to a second-hand clothing store on the Louisiana side of the river to look for a party costume. The theme was white-trash wedding—not her choice.

Her social circle assumed the store would be bursting with overalls and daisy dukes. Giggling and teasing, they'd flipped through racks of flannel shirts and indestructible work pants. She'd separated from the group, embarrassed at their behavior, although she couldn't pinpoint why.

That's when she saw him. Standing not a dozen feet away with two shirts draped over his arm and staring right back at her. Internally everything kicked into a higher gear, yet she was frozen with her hand still on the shoulder of a shabby corduroy jacket.

She hadn't seen him for months and never in the daylight. Not since the end of her senior year of high school. He'd been distant that night, wishing her luck in college and brushing a kiss across her cheek. The first time he'd ever done such a thing, and when the darkness swallowed him she'd sensed a door closing. Sure enough, he hadn't come back to their tree even though she'd waited every full moon.

Something had happened to him over the recent months. A new hardness around his eyes made him look even older than twenty-three. A spark of something flew across the short distance. He nodded once. An uncontrollable urge to wrap her arms around his waist and lay her cheek against his chest came over her. She'd missed him.

She'd taken a step in his direction, but he'd set the shirts down and walked away. The door at the back of the store jangled and made her flinch. In the seconds that followed, she wondered if she'd imagined the brief electric connection or if she'd even imagined him. Then, her best friend, Regan Lovell, had snaked an arm around Monroe's waist and pulled her back into the giggling fold of girls.

He had moved to Mobile, Alabama, by the time she'd come home for Christmas break a few weeks later, and if he'd set foot on either side of Cottonbloom since, she hadn't heard. And as attuned as she was to news of him, she would have heard.

Anxiety bubbled under her nerves. Was it even him? Some instinct—maybe closer to hope—told her it was. What had happened to him? How badly was he hurt? She rubbed her lips together, peeled them into a fake smile, and opened the door.

The man who sat in the chair seemed too big for the small exam room. Not overweight or even bulky, he had an energy that seemed to press outward, seeking an escape. Her gaze skated down his body, her mind trying to take in and process everything at once. The air around them seemed to vibrate.

He registered as a stranger, yet her gut twisted with a strange familiarity. Big, callused hands twirled a scarred wooden cane between his knees; rubber-soled lace-up boots were on his wide-set feet. His thick black hair was in need of a cut, and at least two weeks' growth of dark beard was flecked with wiry steel. His shoulders were broader and his chest thicker than she recalled. His eyes transfixed her. Dark green and intense and holding all her secrets.

"Good Lord. Kirby. Monroe Kirby. All grown-up." His deep voice had acquired a rough edge as if the years had chipped at it. His gaze was as busy as hers, and she adjusted the lapel of her white coat.

"You remember me." God, she sounded like a starstruck teenager. She followed his exploits as best she could. The last splash he'd made was in a business magazine highlighting successful entrepreneurs, but the article had focused on his thrill-seeking adventures as much as his engine design company.

"Hard to forget a damsel in distress on a hot September night." His eyes narrowed as if trying to dissect her.

Did he remember every moment they'd spent together over the years as she did? Probably not. His life was bigger and more exciting than anything she could imagine in Cottonbloom. Now that it was obvious he wasn't seriously injured, perhaps she should mimic the tease in his voice. Pretend his return wasn't rocking her world.

"Well now, Mr. Fournette, what brings you back to Cottonbloom?" Instead of a friendly tease, a defensive edge snuck into her voice. The loneliness of waiting under the cottonwood tree for him night after night made an unexpected appearance.

"Insanity," he said dryly, and looked toward the window where drooping pink crepe myrtle flowers blocked the view of the parking lot.

"I didn't think you'd ever come back home." A tangled web of emotions crept into her voice.

The intensity of his green gaze transferred to her. "Sawyer showed up in my hospital room on the warpath. Apparently, a well-meaning bystander fished out an old emergency card and had him thinking I was dying. While I was still hopped up on painkillers I let him convince me to take a vacation. In Cottonbloom."

With the initial shock fading, she noticed other things about him. Under his beard his face appeared gaunt, and dark circles ringed his eyes.

"You're looking worse for wear."

"I'm feeling it."

"I don't have your records. What happened?"

"Short version? Toppled off a cliff."

"A cliff? Were you shoved off by a scorned woman?"

His lips twitched. "Hardly. Decided I wanted to climb El Capitan. Tried it. Didn't go as planned."

She blinked a few times. Somehow it didn't seem to matter she hadn't seen him in a decade. The sarcasm in her voice masked a very real and inappropriate concern. "You woke up one morning and thought, 'Hmmm, I think I'll climb the most dangerous rock face in the world'? How long did you train?"

"I've climbed for years around the Pacific Northwest. And, actually, there are much more difficult climbs in France and Spain, but I couldn't afford to take time off work."

"That's supposed to make me feel better?" Her voice

rose and echoed in the linoleum-and-steel-covered exam room.

"I didn't know you cared." His smile was bemused.

"I don't." Reflex shot the words out. "I mean, it's not that I *don't* care. Tally is a good friend of mine and . . ." She couldn't think of another lame reason she was lecturing Cade Fournette for doing something that was none of her business. She wasn't his sister or his girlfriend. Fate had thrown them together, and while he'd become her lifeline, she'd only been a little kid to him. That's all. "I wouldn't want you to die or anything," she finished weakly.

"That's awfully nice of you to say." He relaxed back in the simple waiting-room-style chair, his feet sliding farther apart in a typically male stance, one elbow propped on the armrest, his index finger tracing his smiling bottom lip.

In that instant, she was primally, uncomfortably aware of him as a man. A man who looked like he knew what to do with a woman in bed . . . or out of it for that matter. She'd entertained fantasies, of course, but they'd been confined to hugs and kisses. Innocent. He was knight in shining armor material. Not down and dirty lover material. But she was a grown woman now, not a naïve girl.

She dropped her gaze from his mouth to her clipboard. The words made as much sense as Mandarin Chinese. "I assume you're staying with Sawyer?"

"For now."

"Does Tally know you're home?" She raised her gaze again but focused on his hands.

"Course she does."

Monroe wanted to march over to the gym and give Tally a good shake. Of course, it's not like Monroe had ever confided in her. Monroe had never confided in anyone except Cade. Tally had no idea what Cade had done for her, and her interest might seem weird and borderline stalkerish without the facts.

Focus. She needed to focus. A professional wouldn't think about how his beard made him look rough and rumpled and sexy, like an action star trying to go incognito. A professional wouldn't notice how big his hands were or the fact that they were nicked and calloused and as rough-looking as the rest of him.

She glanced down at her paperwork again. "Did you break your leg?"

"Thank God, no. Overextended my knee and strained some apparently useful tendons. The orthopedist said it would heal on its own, but physical therapy would speed the process." His voice didn't reflect any of the angst and confusion running rampant through her. And why should it? Her strong reaction was only spurred by the remnants of a childhood crush. Reality would stamp it out.

"When did this happen?" Her voice was solid, brisk even. *Better.*

"Couple of weeks ago."

"Am I to assume you haven't seen a PT yet?"

"Figured I could rehab it on my own."

"And how's that working out for you?" She cut her eyes to him under her lashes. It wasn't unusual for people—especially men—to disregard their doctor's instructions for physical therapy.

"Not so good. I pushed too hard and made things worse." His lips quirked but fell into a frown. "Anyway, my leg's not the main problem. It's my hand." He held up his left hand, palm up.

"Ohmygoodness." Monroe set the paperwork aside and took his hand in both of hers. A four-inch-long gash ran from the meaty part of his thumb toward the base of his pinky finger. It had been a jagged, deep cut, the resulting scar thick and raised and angry. She ran her thumbs along either side, and he flinched. "Does it hurt?"

"Constant pins and needles, tightness, lack of grip strength."

"How did it happen?"

"A safety bolt came out and I grabbed at whatever I could. Caught the sharp edge of a rock. Sliced my hand, but it wasn't clean. Got infected." He turned the full force of his green eyes on her, and she rocketed back in time. The tease left his voice, leaving desperation and a hint of pain. "Can you help me?"

"Cade," she whispered his name on a sigh. Hearing herself, she cleared her throat and tucked an escaped piece of hair behind her ear. "I mean, Mr. Fournette—"

"No, call me Cade. I don't think I could ever call the little girl I met under the cottonwood tree Miss Kirby." He shifted on the chair. "Or are you something else now? Are you married?"

Her ringless left hand pulled into a fist around her lapel. "No. Not married."

"Good." A smile tugged at his mouth, at once disarming and mischievous.

Was he flirting with her? Her stomach tumbled, her knees shaky. Men occasionally asked her out after one of their sessions or flirted to the point of making things uncomfortable. Monroe had learned how to ice her demeanor to discourage forward behavior. But Cade was different. Special. And now her client. It would be dangerous to let a childhood infatuation color their professional relationship.

She dabbed her lower lip with her tongue. "Take off your pants, Cade."

Chapter Three

Her husky, sexy-as-hell near whisper shot through him like lightning, setting all his muscles at alert. Was she flirting? Was he? And why had the confirmation of her single status settled like a ball of warmth in his chest? What did it matter?

Only the fear of disappointing Tally and Sawyer—again—had kept Cade from driving to the airport already. He'd let Sawyer bully him home knowing he needed something from Cottonbloom. Closure. Once he found it, he'd be gone.

Seeing Monroe walk through the exam room door left him feeling off-balance. Even without a name tag on her coat, he'd recognized her. Her hair had darkened from near white to an ashy light blond and was swept into an updo of some sort. Wispy pieces had escaped and framed sharp cheekbones that cut away the babyish features he remembered, but her eyes were the same—the endless blue of the gulf on a summer's day.

The last time he'd met her under their tree, plans for his departure were in motion. His forced exit from

Cottonbloom was the low point of his life. Worse even than when his parents had died. Mostly because he had let his family down. Not that he'd had the stomach to confess why he was leaving Cottonbloom to Sawyer or Tally or Uncle Del. As much as Cade had needed a new engine for his boat, stealing was stealing. He supposed the ultimatum from the Cottonbloom, Mississippi, police chief instead of charges was a blessing, but at the time the humiliation and shame had felt worse.

He hadn't told Monroe about attempting to steal the engine or about his plans to leave Cottonbloom that last night. Instead, he'd let her talk about college and the endless possibilities stretching in front of her. Her optimism bled into his desolation and offered a small measure of hope. He could picture the woman she'd become and a longing had come over him.

In the small exam room, past and present collided, and he wasn't sure what part he was supposed to play. Big brother didn't fit anymore, and he was glad of it. She knew more about his past than anyone, if she remembered, yet they weren't friends, either. Something else entirely seemed to be blooming between them.

He worked the button of his jeans open with his right hand and fell back into a superficial tease. "What if I'm not wearing underwear?"

She tucked an escaped piece of hair behind her ear once more. A nervous gesture she probably wasn't even aware of. He made his money by reading a boardroom.

"Excuse me?"

"You told me to take off my pants."

Her gaze dropped to where his legs were spread wide in the chair, the top button of his jeans loose and the zipper easing down a few teeth. The heat building between them made him worry—hope—his pants might combust and fall to ash around them.

"Good Lord, how old are you?" She rolled her eyes, tossed a wad of cloth in his lap, and lowered the window shade. "Put on a gown and sit on the table. I'll give you a minute to disrobe."

Damn, he enjoyed the sass in her voice. Most women either pandered to him or were too intimidated to be themselves, and honestly, he didn't go out of his way to put people at ease. They either wanted to be around him or didn't. He found himself alone more often than not.

Thank God she hadn't actually been coming on to him, because the struggle to get his jeans off with his aching knee and one good hand was very real and extremely unsexy. By the time he'd kicked them off, wrapped the gown around himself, and scooched on the table, he had broken a sweat.

She rapped on the door, cracking it open enough so he could hear but not see her. "Decent?"

"As much as one can be in a hospital gown."

She closed the door behind her, her mouth curved into a smile, but it seemed wholly professional and polite. "Lay down please."

He maneuvered his legs up, grimacing and swallowing back a groan.

Her head was down as she made notations in a thin file folder. "You lied to me. You are wearing underwear."

The unexpectedness made him chuckle, the pain in his leg taking second stage. When was the last time he'd bantered playfully with a woman? Maybe never. "No. I said, '*What if* I'm not wearing underwear?' And you shouldn't be peeking. It's shockingly unprofessional, Miss Kirby."

Her smile changed, and even without being able to see her eyes he knew it was a real smile this time. She set the file aside. "Try to relax while I evaluate you."

He tried, but her prodding made him yank his leg out of her hands more than once. When she worked his kneecap in circles, he grabbed her upper arm in an unspoken bid for her to cease and desist.

Her hands quit their torment and massaged his tight calf muscle. He relaxed his grip on her arm but didn't let her go. Through the layers of her clothes her arm was taut and strong.

"I'm sorry, but I need to understand what I'm dealing with," she whispered.

"I'm sorry I fell off a cliff." He was going for a joke, but it fell flat considering his voice was hoarse and pain filled. "Can you fix me?"

She harrumphed, but a smile lit her eyes. "According to Tally, you're a hermit curmudgeon who is humorless and insufferable. In short, unfixable."

He raised his head, the paper under him crinkling. "Humorless?"

"*That's* what you take exception to?"

"I'll have you know I honed my sense of humor with years of Monty Python and *Saturday Night Live* sketches." He'd found the dusty videos in a box tucked in the corner of the charity store. The silliness had been a welcome distraction from the grind of his everyday life in Cottonbloom. The rest of Tally's assessment hit too close to the truth.

She laughed. The low, husky sound somehow made him feel immeasurably better. "I'll get you a temporary brace for your knee and develop some exercises that will have you back to your old self in no time."

"What about my hand?" He held out his left hand, and she cradled it in both of hers, prodding the scar tissue and testing his grip strength.

"Are you right-handed?"

"Yep. But I need both hands to do my job. Right now I'm having a hard time holding a wrench."

"You still work on engines? I thought you designed them."

"How did you know that?"

"Tally told me."

"I didn't realize the two of you had become close." In his mind, Monroe had been set apart from his family and everyday life. She'd been the keeper of his secrets. Was she still?

"Have you forgotten how small a place Cottonbloom is? She was bragging about your company and your place in Seattle."

"Bragging?" Another surprise. His relationship with his sister had gone through a freeze after he'd left. They'd only reconnected when she'd choked her pride out and asked him to invest in her gym. He'd considered the money a gift, but she sent him payments the first of every month.

"She's proud of you." Monroe glanced up from her examination of his hand to flash him a smile that was like a punch in the chest.

She refocused her attention on his hand and rattled off instructions his brain followed automatically. Her features were delicate and pretty, the classic Southern belle, and her hands were small compared to his, her fingers thin but strong where they kneaded his palm. He couldn't tell much about her body through her white medical-type coat, but she appeared slim and moved with an innate grace as if she was completely comfortable in her skin. Nothing like the doe-eyed, gawky girl he remembered.

"It's really a matter of loosening the scar tissue and giving your nerves a chance to heal themselves." Monroe set his hand down, glanced at her watch—a sporty plastic type—and closed his file.

"Late for a hot date?" Instead of jokey, his voice veered sharply aggressive.

"Something like that. Let me get your brace." She was

back in less than two minutes and strapped the brace on his knee, checking the fit. "You can get dressed. I'll tell Ms. June to work you into my schedule tomorrow. Any objections?"

She raised her eyebrows as if she expected him to protest. Honestly, with the fit he'd thrown in their waiting room when he realized what Sawyer was up to, Cade surprised himself by saying, "None at all."

"Good. Wear athletic gear. Unless you want to be traipsing around in your undies." She winked before backing out of the door.

The flirty tease in her voice and eyes was more intimate than mere acquaintances and certainly didn't register as sisterly. In fact, the entire encounter held an intensity and intimacy he usually did his best to avoid. A vibrant energy swirled around her like a tornado, and when the door closed he was left reeling in the aftermath, mentally and emotionally.

By the time he'd dressed, made an appointment, and limped out the door with the borrowed cane from his uncle Delmar, Monroe was nowhere to be seen. Why wouldn't she have a hot date—she was a beautiful woman—and what gave him the right to care?

She was a sliver of his past. A weak, scared kid who'd needed a champion. Her mother had liked to troll through the bars on the Louisiana side of the river, and he'd made it his business to know who she was hooking up with. A word or fist dropped here or there had kept a few scumbags looking for something easy away. Once Sam Landry married and moved away Cade had relaxed his vigilance. Yet even then, he'd continued his monthly treks upriver to make sure Monroe was safe.

She'd rarely crossed his mind during his busy days over the last decade. The work ethic he'd developed by necessity in his youth had carried into life away from

Cottonbloom. Yet something about all the nights they'd shared talking under the full moon had drawn him back to Cottonbloom more times than he could count in his dreams. He always woke restless and yearning for something he couldn't name.

Testing the knee brace, he walked down the street toward the stream that acted as the state line and had effectively segregated the town. In his grandparents' day, Cottonbloom had been one town, sharing a school system and town center. A disagreement involving fishing and harvesting rights had split the old guard of city leaders and broken the town across the river. The south side became Cottonbloom Parish, Louisiana, and the north side remained part of Mississippi.

Monroe's practice was on the Mississippi side of Cottonbloom, full of doctors, lawyers, and professors. His home lay on the Louisiana side, full of blue-collar middle-class workers—factory men, mechanics, fishermen.

Besides the two-lane steel bridge for cars, a wooden bridge for foot traffic had been erected since he'd last been home. Black graffiti marred the side, but a riot of flowers decorated the Louisiana riverbank. His heart swelled. His mother had loved her flowers. The wilder the better. Their front garden had been a colorful chaos of blooms.

He limped across the bridge. Clear and fast-moving, the stream bisected their town and then turned southwest, flowing through Cottonbloom Parish and eventually intersecting the Mississippi River.

The row of brick storefronts facing the river from the Louisiana side were of the antique and gently used clothes variety, whereas the shops on the Mississippi side were higher-end boutiques and specialty shops. Each side had called their road River Street, making mail delivery a crapshoot. The smell from Rufus's Meat and Three had his stomach jumping. He'd dined in five-star restaurants around the country, but none of their chefs came close to matching Rufus's magic with a smoker.

Tally's gym lay on a street perpendicular from the river and directly off River Street. Starting with traditional aerobics and strength training, she'd expanded into martial arts and self-defense over the last year, taking over two more storefronts and giving the Louisiana side of the city an economic boost. She'd turned down his offer to help financially with the expansion, and another year would see his initial loan paid in full. If she bragged about him, he was equally as proud of her—even if he hadn't had a chance to tell her yet.

He was regretting his decision not to swallow his oversize pride and text Sawyer for a ride. His stomach churned but not from hunger this time. The slight breeze that had sped down the river and mitigated the heat was cut off by the buildings, leaving the air stagnant, the humidity smothering.

A middle-aged woman in tight spandex pushed through the door of Tally's gym. A burst of air-conditioning welcomed him inside. He leaned a hip against the front desk and took the weight off his bad leg.

Behind the desk Tally put down the papers she was sorting. "You look like hell warmed over. Come sit before you collapse."

He didn't argue. Plopping down on a metal folding chair, he stretched his leg out and massaged his knee.

She joined him, her mouth tight. "Did you seriously walk all the way over here? Sawyer's going to have a fit when he goes to pick you up and finds you gone."

"How about you text him for me? You can give me a lift back, can't you?"

"You scared of Sawyer, big brother?" Her face sparked with a familiar tease, and the tension across his shoulders eased.

Cade made a *phish*ing sound. "Please. I'm not scared of anything anymore. But Sawyer and I are getting on like two crawdads trapped in a bucket."

She bumped his shoulder with hers. "It'll get easier. Can I get you a drink?"

"I would kill for a whiskey."

"I can do Coke."

"Jack and Coke?"

"Just Coke, you lush." Tally walked off, presumably to retrieve him a plain Coke.

A self-defense class was in progress on the matted floor. A bunch of youngish women gathered in the far corner.

The semi-circle parted to reveal a woman in tiny black shorts and a tight red top with straps crisscrossing defined shoulder blades. A long blond braid swung when she stepped forward and kneed a dummy in the crotch. She slow-motion punched its nose with the heel of her hand. Then, she quickened the pace, performing the combination move several times in succession. On the final hit, the dummy's head bounced across the floor and the girls dissolved into high-pitched giggles.

Tally plopped back in the seat next to him and held out a can. He took it with his left hand, the icy metal helping dampen the tingles of firing nerve endings. His gaze never left the woman on the mat.

She could have posed for a fitness magazine. Although toned, she was shapely, with long legs and arms. Her movements were reminiscent of a choreographed dance rather than a fight sequence. She bent over to retrieve the dummy's head, her backside high in the air. He swallowed, pretty sure if someone wanted to draw him as a cartoon character his eyes would be bulging comically.

When she turned, it took a few blinks for her face to come into focus. The sweating can slipped out of his numb fingers, a good amount of Coke spilling over his crotch before he could right it. Their gazes clashed briefly, and without taking his eyes off her he asked, "What is Monroe Kirby doing here?"

"She teaches a self-defense class. She's a double black belt in jujitsu and karate, you know."

"How was I supposed to know that?"

Monroe's attention was back on the giggling girls, so Cade transferred his to Tally, who sat with a Cheshire cat smile, examining her dark-purple-painted fingernails.

"Gee, I don't know. Come visit more often? I assume you were Monroe's late add-on. I didn't get a chance to grill her."

"Why didn't you warn me?"

"Should I have? Didn't realize you two were so well acquainted."

Ironic that he'd said almost the same thing about Monroe and Tally. "I barely knew her." He used misdirection in licensing negotiations all the time without a twinge of misgiving. With Tally, the half lie left bile climbing up his throat. He took a sip.

His sister's "uh-huh" seemed to convey deep meaning. What, if anything, had Monroe told her about them?

Monroe was looking over her shoulder at him, but as soon as their gazes met she spun around, her braid flicking. She stood beside one of the girls and drilled the movements. He shifted on the chair, unable to tear his gaze away. "Did she say something about knowing me?"

"Nope. Just like you've never said anything about her. But she's asked about you. More than a couple of times. Like she was fishing."

The picture he'd held of Monroe Kirby broke, and he wasn't sure how the pieces fit back together or if they ever would.

"Every eligible bachelor on both sides of Cottonbloom is pursuing her," Tally added.

He grunted. "So what, about five men?"

Tally barked a laugh. " 'Bout that."

Time for a subject change. Thinking of multiple men chasing Monroe had him putting finger-shaped indentations in the aluminum can. "Sawyer said you're dating Heath Parsons."

"*Was* dating. Definitely past tense." She still watched Monroe, but her eyes had narrowed and a frown drew her face down.

Tally was more like him than he cared to admit— distrusting and wary. Neither of them had inherited their father's optimism and natural good humor. Or the little of it they carried in their DNA had been stamped out during the struggles of their childhood.

Cade and Tally understood each other bone deep. They were realists, not dreamers. Sawyer was the one who looked and acted like their father. Being around Sawyer was a wistful reminder of what Cade had lost.

"Did things end badly?" If Heath broke his sister's heart, then Cade wasn't above still acting like her big brother.

"*He* took it badly. I'm fine." More hid behind her words, but before Cade could question her further she shifted to face him, brows up and a speculative look in her green eyes. Eyes nearly identical to his. "A doctor or lawyer might be considered the pick of the litter in a small town like Cottonbloom, but if a more interesting dog came sniffing around and wanted to mark his territory . . . who knows?"

While life circumstances had forced him to drop out of high school, he didn't qualify as an idiot. Tally needed to work on her avoidance tactics, but he would let it go. For now. "First off, I'm not sure how I feel about you equating the male species to urinating dogs. Second, what makes you think I'm remotely interested in Monroe?"

Tally shot him a you've-got-to-be-kidding-me look punctuated by a huffing eye roll. "You've barely taken your eyes off her since you walked in; I'd say the interest is there."

Heat crawled up his neck. Being called out for eyeballing Monroe—by his sister, no less—induced a teenage-like embarrassment.

"But I'd only suggest you pursue something with her if you're sticking around for more than a week. *Are you?*" Old resentments sharpened Tally's words, the last two like daggers.

Leaving Cottonbloom and his family had been hard, but building a successful life away from everything and everyone that dragged him down—including his family—had ultimately saved him. How could he explain that when he'd always protected her from how desolate and difficult things had been?

Maybe she'd understand the taint of shame that had dogged him. He hoped she'd forgive him. He would tell her, but not now, not in a crowded gym. It seemed they were taking turns dodging uncomfortable subjects. "What's got Sawyer all wide-eyed and stressed-out? Is something going on at the factory? Or does it have to do with the responsibilities of parish commissioner?"

"It's this festival business."

"What festival? He's been tight-lipped and tense since our flight back from Seattle—I figured he was pissed at me—but I heard him on the phone with someone talking about Regan Lovell. And not kindly."

"Oh, he's pissed at you all right, but you're only a small part of his troubles. Regan Lovell went and got herself elected mayor of Cottonbloom, Mississippi, last year."

Cade whistled low. No wonder Sawyer was walking around looking like the four riders of the apocalypse were nipping at his heels. Sawyer had dated the Mississippi beauty queen on the down low in high school. Her parents considered the Fournettes the worst sort of swamp rats— poor, orphaned, and without any decent connections. Their uncle Delmar certainly didn't qualify.

Sawyer had been forever borrowing Cade's truck or boat to head upriver to her house. Cade assumed Regan got her thrills by sneaking around with Sawyer. Not long after Sawyer headed to LSU and Regan to Ole Miss, they'd broken up. Cade had been secretly glad the relationship was over. Some things weren't meant to be, and Sawyer and Regan had been doomed.

Monroe was leading the girls through some yoga-like stretches, her body contorting, her backside back in the air. He shifted on the seat and took a sip of Coke to wet his Sahara-like mouth.

Tally's voice penetrated his fog. "Word got around that *Heart of Dixie* was offering a magazine spread and funds for a big civic project to the best small-town festival in the South. Sawyer had already been chewing on the idea of a weekend-long block party, and the competition gave him reason enough to pull the trigger. Well, Regan did the same. Intentionally or not, the folks at *Heart of Dixie* stoked the fire by insisting the Louisiana and Mississippi festivals take place the same weekend."

The magazine's ruthless streak didn't surprise Cade. It was a business, and the rivalry would make excellent copy. "Please. Totally intentional. Our towns' history isn't a secret."

"Now we have Sawyer planning a crayfish festival and Regan planning a tomato festival, both for Labor Day weekend. Tensions are higher than I've seen them. Ms. Effie says this is what it was like right after the town divided."

"Ms. Effie?"

"My neighbor. She's part of the Quilting Bee."

The Quilting Bee was both a circle of ladies from both sides of the river and a store on the Mississippi side of River Street. The ladies had gathered there for as long as Cade could remember, making quilts for anyone in need and gossiping.

"As you'd imagine, people are picking sides faster than fleas jumping off a drowning dog's butt and Sawyer and Regan are locked in an epic battle of good versus evil." This was the Tally he remembered—smart-mouthed and irreverent.

"I'm not so sure I'd classify Regan as evil. She's more a rich little spoiled girl wanting someone else's plaything."

"How would you know? You haven't been around in so long, she might have made a pact with the devil and sprouted horns." The edge of bitterness in Tally's voice drew his gaze off Monroe. His sister toyed with the end of her long, dark ponytail.

He tamped down the urge to defend himself. "Who planted the flowers along the bank?"

"Sawyer. Obsessed with them. He turns into a cranky old man if he catches someone stepping on them or, heaven forbid, picking one."

A well of emotion choked him, his words emerging as a near whisper. "They're beautiful."

"He's been after all the businesses along River Street to spruce up their storefronts, hoping once we draw some tourists in they'll come back for . . . I don't know why they'd come back actually."

"Old Rufus's Meat and Three is amazing. Or at least it was a decade ago."

"It still is, although I'm pretty sure he's using the same fry grease as he was when you took off."

Again, her jab hit below the belt. "Listen, Tally, you need to understand—"

Monroe's class broke up, and Tally stood up, cutting him off. Several of the girls gave Monroe quick hugs before retreating in clumps to the locker rooms. Her steps toward him and Tally seemed tentative.

"Monroe! I don't suppose you could do me a solid?" The demeanor of a mouse playing with its food hid underneath Tally's relaxed stance.

"Of course. Especially since you covered for me earlier. What's up?"

"I have another class coming in, and my poor brother overdid it walking all the way here from your office. Could you give him a lift to Sawyer's?"

He reached over and pinched the back of Tally's leg, an old childhood trick he'd used to keep her quiet in church when she was a kid. She sat back down and grabbed his hand in both of hers in an apparent show of love, while she bent his pinky finger down and milked it. He yanked his hand away.

Monroe leaned over and touched the knee of his bad leg, the top of her workout top gaping to reveal the curves of her breasts. "Of course I can. You can take walks, but don't push yourself so hard. Not until I give you the go-ahead anyway."

"If you're sure it's no trouble?" His easy acceptance had nothing to do with marking his territory. Monroe was not his territory or anything else for that matter.

His BS meter exploded. This new, all grown-up Monroe fascinated him, and she meant something to him; he just couldn't figure out what.

"No trouble at all. You ready?"

He stood up and tested his leg. The rest had done him a world of good, the pain a dull throb instead of a piercing jab, and the brace helped more than expected. Yet when she tucked herself under his shoulder, her arm around his waist, he didn't insist he was fine. Instead, he leaned into her, a soft breast pressing against his side. He took a deep breath. Her vanilla-sweet scent made him want to lean closer to discover its origins.

Her hand brushed his stomach, fluttered off, but returned, her fingertips lightly tracing the dip in the middle. Goose bumps rose along her arm. Was she affected as he was?

Entwined, they walked into a wall of heat—thick and pungent and heavy with memories. The air seemed almost a living entity that roamed Cottonbloom inciting violence and passion. The crisp, low-humidity Seattle air never seemed so dangerous or to hold any portents. Maybe that's why he'd settled there.

A silver Mercedes pulled to a stop on the wrong side of the street, close to them. The driver's window rolled down on a whisper. "Monroe!"

The man behind the wheel wore an expensive suit, his jacket still on despite the heat but his tie loosened. The buzz of an AC working overtime sounded over the soft purr of the engine.

"Well, hello there. What're you doing over here?" She dropped her head to see inside the car. Was this one of the dogs in pursuit?

"Business at the precinct. Are you interested in grabbing dinner? Pizza, if you want casual," the man said.

Monroe looked at Cade as if surprised to find him still hanging on to her like a barnacle. "I'm helping a . . . friend home. Cade Fournette, this is Andrew Tarwater."

Cade dipped his head lower and looked more closely through the car window. Yep, now he recognized the squinty eyes and smirk.

Andrew-fucking-Tarwater had been Cade's adversary, first on the football field and then for the long painful eight months he'd worked third shift bussing tables at a late-night diner. After his parents had been killed, he'd taken any job available for a high-school dropout, which wasn't much. Andrew and his posse had frequented the place after drinking at college bars with their fake IDs and turned Cade's life into a fresh hell. Their unvarnished taunts and laughter fed his resentment and anger.

If Cade was at all a gentleman, he would drop the pretense and allow her to ride off in the Mercedes if she wanted. His arm tightened around her shoulders, pulling her closer. "Good to see you again, Andrew."

"I didn't realize you were friends." Monroe looked back and forth at them.

Friends. Cade suppressed a guffaw.

Andrew piped up. "We both played quarterback our freshman year. Cade here was good. Might've had a shot at a scholarship if . . . well, if he hadn't dropped out."

Cade wasn't sure if the dig was intentional or not. "I heard you followed your daddy into law."

"That's right. Tarwater and Tarwater. You come see us if you get yourself in legal trouble while you're home." Andrew shuffled in his dash before his hand extended out the window with his card between his index and middle fingers.

Cade squeezed his hand into a fist. Punching the local lawyer in the face would likely require legal representation. "I can find you if I need you."

The card disappeared back into the recesses of the car, but the thousand-watt smile remained on Andrew's face. "I heard you turned into some inventor of some sort. Makes me think of crazy Doc Brown in *Back to the Future*. Is that about right?"

"Except for the fact I make way more money." Cade hated that he stooped to mention money. Andrew Tarwater was like chiggers under his skin.

"Do you hawk your stuff on the Home Shopping Network? Invent anything I've heard of?" Maybe the man was

trying to make small talk, but the hint of condescension—
and Cade had grown up hearing the tone often enough to
become fluent—set his path forward.

"My stuff is too complicated for you to understand." He
dropped his lips close to Monroe's ear and whispered, "I
need to get off my leg."

She tilted her head, exposing the line of her jaw to his
lips. He breathed her in, narrowing the sweet scent to the
heat of her neck and chest.

She directed her words toward Andrew. "Maybe another time."

"Sure. Not a problem." The man ran a hand through
streaked blond hair that Cade guessed wasn't entirely natural. "You haven't forgotten Mother's cocktail party, have
you? She has something real special planned."

"Of course not. I'll text you sometime soon." Monroe's
dismissive tone wiped the smile off Andrew's face while
the satisfaction of winning brought a smile to Cade's.

Cade let Monroe maneuver them a few steps down
the sidewalk. Andrew hadn't moved. Over his shoulder,
Cade nudged his chin and barely kept his middle finger
from popping up from behind Monroe's back. "Later, Tarwater."

Any pretense of politeness on Andrew's face was gone.
Cade didn't care. He wasn't home to make friends and sing
"Kumbaya."

The testosterone-driven nuances of the exchange didn't
seem to register with Monroe. She waved down the street.
"I'm the black SUV at the end."

Only a couple of years old, the car was well kept and
clean, inside and out. With his arm still around her shoulders, he pretended to lose his balance while easing onto
the seat and pulled her into him, between his legs.

He was playing dirty. It's the only way the world worked
for people like him. The Andrew Tarwaters of the world

could traipse up the ladder on their family name, money, and looks. Cade had scraped and clawed his way out of poverty, dragging his brother and sister with him, doing his best to protect them by fair means or foul. He hadn't wanted Sawyer and Tally to end up jaded and manipulative. Like him.

Monroe fell into his chest. Her mouth brushed over the hair of his beard. What would her lips feel like against his neck or, even better, on his lips? He hoped the spark between them wasn't a figment of his imagination. Her hands came between them, and she pushed on his chest. He dropped his arm from around her, but she didn't immediately retreat.

"You're in denial." Her soft voice sent skitters up his spine.

"About what?" He said the words slowly, wondering if she'd caught him at his game.

"You think you can push yourself until you're in control of your body again. It's not going to work that way this time. You need to concede to my expertise in order to get what you ultimately want."

"And what's that?"

Her blue eyes stared straight into his with a measure of truth no one but Tally and Sawyer was brave enough to dish out.

"You want everything to be the way it was before your accident. You want your life back. You want to be out of Cottonbloom."

A day ago—hell, two hours ago—she would have been correct on all counts, but now right or wrong, logical or not, he wanted one thing even more: her.

Chapter Four

Between the summer heat and his muscular body pressed against her, Monroe felt like she was on the surface of the sun. His beard had tickled the side of her face, and she'd nuzzled into him before her mind could rein her body in. He smelled amazing, all spicy, yummy man. She probably stunk from a long day's work and sweat.

She pushed off him, adjusted her spandex top, and swiped the back of her hand over her forehead. Climbing behind the wheel, she cranked the engine, the AC still set for max after her quick trip from the office to the gym.

Sawyer Fournette's house was less than ten minutes away. He could have bought a bigger, nicer house on the Mississippi side of Cottonbloom. Instead, he'd opted to buy an older traditional farmhouse with a wraparound porch. It was secluded, sitting squarely in the middle of at least fifty acres. He kept the land around the house cleared but was letting the remainder revert to wilderness.

Tightening her hands on the steering wheel, she kept her gaze fixed on the road but was uncommonly aware of the man only a few feet away. Cade remained silent, and she gave up trying to think of something not silly to say.

She slowed once they hit the bumpy ruts on Sawyer's un-paved driveway, but he seemed more pensive than in pain, his index finger tapping the top of the cane.

"Tally said you have two black belts and teach self-defense." His voice was low but carried over the AC noise.

She treated his statement as a question. "I offer a class free of charge for high-school girls. Tally lets me use her gym at no cost. Most of them don't have the money to join."

"That's nice of you."

"I don't want those girls to be afraid. Not just of strangers, but the boys—men—in their lives. Mississippi and Louisiana have some of the highest crime rates against women in the country. Mostly from boyfriends and husbands."

A few beats of silence passed, and she glanced over to find him staring at her. "Do you do it because of what happened that night?" he asked.

She whipped her head back around to stare at Sawyer's house in the near distance. Memories rushed back along with the doubts she carried like chains. Her heart expanded in her chest. Cade was the one person who might be able to dissect truth from imagination. Yet a decade was a long time. She was different, and so was he.

"I'm surprised you remember."

"Why wouldn't I remember?"

She pulled to a stop. A red-and-gray truck was parked under a willow tree in the front, its limbs offering partial camouflage. Grass grew tall around its deflated tires. Rust pocked the tailgate, obscuring the *DODGE* lettering, and a bird had built a nest where the cab met the bed. The abandoned truck made for a melancholy picture.

"I was young, and you were—seemed—so much older, wiser."

"I don't know about wiser."

"You didn't say good-bye." She hadn't meant for the words to come out at all, much less with such vehemence.

"Excuse me?" The coldness in his voice rivaled the AC.

She considered backtracking, laughing off the strange accusation, but as soon as she met his eyes her path was set. She'd learned at a young age how to keep her own counsel, how to protect herself. While she was friendly and polite to everyone, she didn't trust anyone. It made true friendships hard and relationships impossible.

But with Cade she'd never censored herself. It was the way it had always been with him. Old habits she'd never shaken. "You left Cottonbloom without telling me. Without saying good-bye. I want to know why."

"It was complicated." He broke eye contact, dropping his gaze to where his hands fiddled with the cane. "You were a good kid in a bad situation. Like Tally and Sawyer."

"Weren't you a good kid in a bad situation?"

He shifted toward her, bracing a hand on the dash and laying his other arm over the back of her seat, invading her space. She didn't retreat. His intensity spurred her heart rate into an erratic gallop, yet she wasn't intimidated. Perhaps it was only echoes of the past, but he made her feel safe, even when he was the one she should be scared of.

"I grew up fast and tough." His voice contained more than a hint of warning.

"You were nice to me," she said softly.

"Don't fool yourself into thinking I'm nice. I wasn't then, and I'm sure as hell not now."

He ran a callused finger down her cheek, the rasp igniting her nerve endings like a flint. His hand continued south and wrapped itself in her braid, the slight tug on her scalp sending shivers through her body in spite of the sun bearing down on the truck. Her nipples felt tight, and she hoped her tight sports tank masked her sudden, inexplicable arousal.

He pulled her braid, forcing her toward him. She didn't fight him. He dropped his face next to hers, his coarse beard hair caressing her cheek, his mouth close to her ear. "If I see something I want, I go after it and get it by any means necessary."

"How very Machiavellian." She tried a laugh, but it came out more like a stuttering sigh. His scent hooked her even closer, and her lips grazed the outer rim of his ear.

He pulled back, his green-eyed gaze roving her face. She returned the favor, noting the faint brackets around his mouth, the crinkles at his eyes, the thick beard. A full-grown man. Yet was he so different from the boy in the boat?

"Ovid." The movement of his lips jammed the cogs of her brain. The word made no sense. Her confusion must have been obvious, because the mouth she stared at tipped up in the corners, deepening the grooves. "The Greek philosopher Ovid, not Machiavelli, actually wrote: *The end justifies the means.*"

"Ovid. Of course." Apparently, Monroe had slept through that philosophy class at Ole Miss. The fact that high-school dropout Cade Fournette was quoting Ovid made her wonder what other mysteries she might uncover if she went digging.

Just when she was ready to grab a shovel, he released her braid and slipped away. His limp was less pronounced as he took the stairs holding the cane parallel to the ground. Although he'd physically released her, she felt bound to him in some other fundamental way, incapable of tearing her eyes off him until he disappeared behind Sawyer's front door. Even then, she sat, unable to drive away for a long minute.

How could the simple brush of Cade's finger ignite a fire when other men left her cold? As her arousal ebbed, she realized something else. She'd just been manipulated by a master. He hadn't explained why he left.

She spent the evening going through the motions of her life, eating when her stomach growled and heading to bed when her eyes felt heavy. A few short hours ago, her life had been tidy and predictable and boring. Cade Fournette had spun her into chaos.

Chapter Five

The next day, her mind still wandering in the fog of past and present, Monroe spent her lunch hour eating a sandwich and window-shopping on the Mississippi side of the river, trying not to think about her next client—Cade—and failing miserably.

Her stomach protested every bite of sandwich and she gave in, tossing it half-finished into one of the fancy metal trash cans the town had installed. The footbridge over the river drew her. The longer she stared into the water the calmer she became.

During the summer months, Cottonbloom's river classified more as a stream, fast moving but shallow. During storms the current quickened and surged to the edge of the banks, but flooding was rare. The water-cooled breeze made being outside bearable.

Checking her watch, she left the serenity of the water to meander back to the office. A midnight-blue cocktail dress displayed by a headless mannequin in Abigail's Boutique window caught her attention. The skirt was knee-length and flared prettily, but the neckline plunged in a deep vee in front. An arm looped through hers, startling her.

Regan Lovell stood at her side, at least three inches taller than Monroe in her heels. "You should get it. Classic and sexy. Exactly your style."

"I do like it. Where would I wear it, though?"

"How about the cocktail party the Tarwaters are throwing for the upper slice of Cottonbloom? Pretty sure Andrew would approve of the view."

"Andrew and I are not dating."

"Not yet." Regan waggled her eyebrows, but the teasing only made Monroe uncomfortable.

"Not ever." After a night tossing and turning and thinking of Cade, Monroe knew deep in her gut she had something to settle with him before she could move on with anyone else. She wasn't sure how to explain the intense connection, especially since Regan had no idea Monroe's and Cade's pasts had intersected.

"Good Lord, you don't have to sound so excited the best-looking man in Cottonbloom County wants to impress you."

"Impress me how, exactly?"

"The cocktail party? The fund-raiser?" Regan looked as confused as Monroe felt.

"What are you talking about?"

"The cocktail party is doubling as a fund-raiser for your girls at risk group. Didn't Andrew tell you?"

A throb kicked at her temples. "Why would the Tarwaters do that? I had no idea they even knew about the girls."

Regan made an "are-you-serious?" chuff. "They probably didn't until Andrew informed them. Pretty sure Andrew will expect thanks in the form of many dates. Plus, Mrs. Tarwater gets to act the high-and-mighty do-gooder."

"You think Andrew is trying to buy my affections?"

"More like make you feel obligated to go out with him. The Tarwaters like having people in their debt."

How did her life become so complicated over the course of twenty-four hours? She jabbed a finger toward Regan. "I'm not going out with him."

Regan held her hands up. "Hey, don't poke the messenger's eye out. If you don't want to go out with him, then don't. Although I don't understand what's wrong with him."

"He doesn't do it for me."

A memory of Cade leaning close to her in her SUV, his hand wrapped in her braid, his breath skating across her cheek, flashed in her head. She rubbed her forehead, trying to banish the image. Cade had nothing to do with this. Her antipathy toward Andrew had been present long before yesterday.

"I should tell him to cancel, right?" she asked.

Regan slipped an arm through Monroe's and they stepped in tandem back toward Monroe's office. "I don't know. He's manipulating you in a jerky way. I don't see why you shouldn't go along with the fund-raiser. The money is for an excellent cause. You aren't signing a contract to date him. It's for the greater good, right? Very Machiavellian."

"Ovid."

"Excuse me?"

A laugh welled up, but she stifled it. "Nothing. I don't know; maybe you're right. I could use the money, that's for sure." While she could teach the girls self-defense, low self-esteem and zero confidence were the root causes of girls getting into abusive relationships. She needed to augment her classes with weekly counseling sessions, which weren't cheap.

"Of course I'm right."

Silence fell between them as they strolled. Regan cleared her throat. "Listen, since we're talking about obligations and such, I could use a favor."

"Does this favor in any way involve Sawyer Fournette?"

Regan stutter-stepped. "How—*why* would you think that?"

"I don't know, maybe because lately you've been obsessed with the festival in general and Sawyer Fournette in particular."

"Obsessed? That man . . ." Regan swallowed the rest with a huge sigh. "I have to give credit to Sawyer for one thing; people love his block parties. If we win, *Heart of Dixie* will finance the entire riverside project and we'll be able to compete with him. It will be gorgeous."

"Why do we need to compete with the Louisiana side?"

Regan stopped, turned them around, and gestured at the view in front of them. A line of trendy shops including Abigail's Boutique, Regan's home interior studio, and the Quilting Bee, faced the row of antique stores, used-clothes stores, and Rufus's restaurant over the river. Each brick front was painted a different color—blue, red, purple even—giving a homespun, kitschy charm to the Louisiana side. The stately redbrick façades and placard signage gave the Mississippi businesses a high-end feel. Both sides had their appeal.

"Our towns are heading in two different directions. Cottonbloom, Louisiana, is stuck in the past, while Cottonbloom, Mississippi, is ripe to flourish, not die like other small towns. We have to stay progressive, and the riverside project is one way we can stay a step ahead without costing the taxpayers."

"Isn't the festival costing the taxpayers?"

"A minimal amount for a huge gain. Even if we don't win, every business downtown will reap the benefits if things go well. And that's where I need your help."

Monroe couldn't deny the rally-the-troops enthusiasm in Regan's voice. "What do you need?"

"Talk up the festival to your patients. Sound enthusiastic.

I need some word-of-mouth advertising. And if something should come up, I can count on you in a pinch, right?"

The vagueness in Regan's voice had Monroe staring at her best friend trying to get a read on her intentions. Throughout their childhood, Regan had always been the ambitious one; Monroe, her accomplice. Worry shadowed Regan's brown eyes, and she twirled a piece of strawberry blond hair that had escaped her updo in an old gesture of anxiety.

Monroe touched Regan's forearm, stopping the motion. "You can count on me."

Her assurance garnered a small smile, and for the rest of the walk they talked about which shows they were binge watching and books they were reading.

They were less than a block from Monroe's office when Cade climbed out of the driver's side of Tally's black sedan on the other side of the street and jaywalked toward them. Dressed in athletic shorts and a blue T-shirt, he had a duffel bag looped over his shoulder. He'd left the cane at home but wore the knee brace. His limp gave him a John Wayne–like gait, and his beard only added to the rough-and-ready sexy vibe pinging like a radar signal.

Monroe's twist of emotions for a man she knew yet didn't was profoundly confusing.

"Lord help me, is that who I think it is?" Regan asked.

"Cade Fournette is back in town recovering from an injury. And—" Monroe checked her watch "—he's my next client."

"Geez, he's gotten bigger and even rougher looking if that's possible. He always scared me a little," Regan added the last part on a whisper.

Cade's path intersected theirs a few feet from the door to the PT offices.

"Afternoon, ladies." Steel girded his voice.

"Cade, you remember Regan Lovell, don't you?"

"I could never forget the girl who broke my brother's heart."

"*His* heart? He's the one—" Regan puffed with a deep breath before deflating. "It's not important now. You're on board with the fund-raiser, right?" She pointed a finger toward Monroe.

"For the greater good." Monroe pumped a fist.

"That's the spirit." Regan's sweet tone bordered on fake. "Welcome back to town, Cade. I'm sure with Monroe's help you'll be feeling better in no time. She's the best PT in Mississippi." Regan strode back toward the river and her interior design studio.

"What kind of fund-raiser do you two have planned?" Cade asked as Monroe led them into the offices.

"It's Mr. and Mrs. Tarwater. Andrew too, I guess. They're hosting a cocktail party slash fund-raiser for my girls at risk program." She snapped her fingers. "Hey, I'll get Tally an invite since she was instrumental in getting the whole thing off the ground."

He didn't acknowledge the offer. An awkwardness descended. Her attempts at small talk stalled. She affected a professional attitude even though inside she was confused. She demonstrated each exercise before making him perform a set. One exercise followed another. Twenty minutes in, the uncomfortable vibe had eased.

Sweat crawled from his forehead into his beard, and his shirt was damp. "Dang it, woman. Are you sure this is helping and not slowly, tortuously killing me?"

Her laugh died when he raised his shirt to wipe his face dry. His stomach was well-defined with a tempting trail of dark hair. A silvery scar tracked from his ribs around his side, stopping an inch above the waistband of his shorts.

Her hand was out before she considered her actions. With a light touch she traced the scar, faded but still raised.

A mark he'd never lose. "Was this from one of your epic adventures?"

"No." He covered her hand with his, but instead of brushing her away, he trapped her hand against his warm skin. "It happened a long time ago."

He dropped his hand and his shirt. Although his warm, smooth skin beckoned further exploration, she pulled her hand to her chest in a fist. "How old were you?"

"Sixteen. Mom and Dad had died a few months earlier, and I was out looking for food. Heard something out in the dark. I went running like it was Bigfoot and tangled with a barbwire fence. It made me pay." Although he tried to sound jokey, she could imagine his fear.

"Did you go to the hospital?" The cut must have been deep to leave a scar after all these years.

"Naw. Uncle Delmar stitched me up." He rubbed a thumb over the scar on his palm. "I swear he did a better job of it than that ER doc did on my hand."

She refused to bite on the subject change. "Obviously, you went back out again or we wouldn't have met."

"Had no choice." He rolled his shoulders. "What's next?"

While he'd shared some of his troubles with her on those full-moon nights, now that she was an adult she wondered how much he'd kept to himself. Questions she'd been too young to formulate burned, one above all others. Had anyone taken care of him while he was taking care of everyone else?

"Do you rock climb El Capitan–like faces on a regular basis?" She'd done some research on the Internet and watching the videos of elite rock climbers gave her vertigo. And if he was attempting to summit El Capitan he was elite—or crazy.

"Go big or go home, right?"

"In the South that generally refers to hair, not climbing sheer faces of rock."

His smile was a brief flash of white in his beard. "I've heli-skied and hang glided and rock climbed for years. The thing on El Capitan was a freak accident."

"I'm not getting you better so you can go back and kill yourself, am I?"

"Will you quit as my PT if I say yes?" All laughter was gone from his face, the sudden seriousness tilting her off-balance. "All that stuff has become kind of a compulsion, I suppose. Not sure I can stop."

"Why do you really do it? Are you trying to prove something to yourself or this town? All that stuff doesn't matter. You were born here and you'll always be welcomed back to Cottonbloom."

"I don't think either side of this town would welcome me home with open arms even if I were the president."

"Certainly not if you ran as a Democrat."

A beat of silence passed before he burst into laughter. Belly laughs that filled the room and made her join him for the joy of watching him.

Finally, his laughter subsided, but not his smile. "In a way, Cottonbloom is refreshing. No apologies or hiding its jacked-up social hierarchy and bigotries. They are clearly marked and on display." The slight disdain in his voice galvanized her pride.

"We have our faults, but this is a good town." She poked him in the shoulder. "Both sides of the river. And while the rest of the country has drifted further apart with wealth inequality, Cottonbloom has actually closed the gap."

"You sound like you like it here."

His green eyes probed. His experience with the town had been tainted with grief and responsibility.

"I wouldn't have come back here after college if I didn't." She dropped her gaze to the speckled linoleum floor. The truth was more complicated and nothing she wished to discuss.

"How's your mama?" he asked as if reading her mind. His soft voice attempted to strip away the years, but she'd spent most of her life covering for her mother.

"She's fine." It wasn't a lie. At the moment, she was sober and even holding down a job. "Come on; we have a few more stretches to get to before we run out of time."

They finished up in relative silence except for the heavy breathing involved. As he gathered his things, he said, "For the record, I don't do all that thrill-seeking stuff to prove something to this place."

"It's for the adrenaline rush, then? I've heard it can be addictive." She made a note in his file.

He stepped in front of her, and she looked up, clutching the file to her chest. His warmth drew her closer, her body swaying. His light touch on her arm froze her. Goose bumps rose. She waited, sensing that any prodding from her would silence him. His long, slow breath made her understand how difficult this was for him.

Like that night so long ago, she slipped her hand into his. Even though she'd touched him throughout their session, positioning his body and stretching his limbs, the contact of their hands was more intimate, more important, casting back to long-ago promises.

"Part of why I took risks was the exhilaration of experiencing freedom. But I think a bigger part was trying to eradicate fear."

"I remember." Every word of their conversations had been carved into memories.

He tensed. "What do you remember?"

"What you were most afraid of."

He pulled his bottom lip between his teeth, broke eye contact, and gave a shake of his head. She wanted to cup his cheek and force him to look at her. Instead, she squeezed his hand.

He was quiet for a long moment, and she worried she'd

overstepped. Finally, he spoke, his voice scratchy. "Every night I lay awake and schemed to keep my family together. The state would have put them somewhere I couldn't protect them."

"Cade." She breathed his name on a sigh, drawing his gaze to hers.

Even after the years, the success all three siblings had achieved, a torturous fear reflected on his face. That's what he'd tried to leave behind on the rock face, in the sky, on a mountain, but he couldn't. It would be like ripping off a piece of his soul.

Hadn't she done the same in her own way? Black belts in jujitsu and karate, constant training to stamp out her own fears. Had it worked? She trusted her abilities to defend herself, but in her nightmares she was powerless against the creeping terror and doubts.

"You can't cut those sorts of memories out of your head. If you did, you wouldn't be . . . you." Her words echoed with a hollowness off the sterile floor and walls.

"Some people might say that's a good thing." His voice had hardened and the vulnerability and affinity between them vanished. He extricated his hand and opened the door. "I get time off for good behavior, right?"

"You need to continue to stretch and work your leg and hand even on your off days."

He nodded and walked out, his gait looser and his limp less noticeable. His excellent overall physical condition meant he wouldn't need many more sessions before he would be close to a hundred percent. Then what? No doubt he'd hightail away and probably flip Cottonbloom the bird on the way out of town. A full, exciting life awaited.

What would her life have been like in some other town in some other state? More fulfilling? Lonelier? It was a useless road to travel. She tried to put Cade Fournette out of her mind while she focused on her last client and failed.

* * *

Cade wandered back over the bridge to his side of Cotton-bloom. Restlessness pervaded his mood, but not the kind that sent him climbing the nearest cliff. While he couldn't qualify the feeling, without a doubt Monroe was the cause.

Bees darted through Sawyer's wildflowers. Who would have thought Sawyer had such a wide sentimental streak. He snapped one of Sawyer's flowers off, closed his eyes, and took a breath of the sweetness. The sorrow that welled up was tempered by a strange happiness. His mother lived on in the flowers and his father would live on in the old Dodge truck. Cade had moved the rusting hulk to Sawyer's garage.

The internals were in better shape than the frame. There wasn't much to those types of trucks. The mechanics were simple, and the truck was released before every-thing went computerized. Every spare moment he had would be spent on getting the truck running. It had become an obsession.

Rufus waved from the front of his restaurant. As Cade approached, Rufus wiped his hands on a stained formerly white apron, a gold-and-purple LSU emblem emblazoned across the front. Cade's heart grew in his chest.

Rufus had been the first one to give him a job. It had paid next to nothing, but Rufus had let Cade take home leftovers. For a while the Fournettes had eaten well, but the need to bring in cash had forced Cade to find some-thing else. Still, it hadn't been uncommon for Rufus to press food into Cade's hands whenever he had wandered by the restaurant in those first tough months.

"Heard you were back. Del keeps me up on the news. You're a big shot, I hear." Rufus's voice sounded like it had been infused with river rock. All the years working his smoker had taken a toll.

Words failed Cade, so he threw an arm around the other man's shoulders and gave him a half hug. Rufus was lean and a good five inches shorter than Cade. He had the skin of an aged outdoorsman, leathery and wrinkled. The comb-over he'd maintained a decade ago had been buzzed short, leaving the top of his head as bare and brown as an acorn.

"I've traveled the country sampling barbeque. None of it came close to yours. You got some fresh back there?" Cade dropped his arm and stepped back. The unusual show of emotion on his part was another surprise.

"Actually, I'm getting ready to pull my smoker around for our little party."

"What little party is that?"

"Why, your welcome home party, of course."

"What are you talking about?"

"Del called me this morning. It won't be as big as one of our regular block parties, but we'll get up to some fun, and I've got the food covered." Rufus retreated back into the restaurant, and Cade followed. Nothing had changed, except the addition of more autographed pictures of LSU football players lining the walls.

"I don't want a party." A thread of desperation sharpened his words.

Rufus's laugh was smoky and rough. "Exactly why no one told you about it. Tally was supposed to knock you out and drag you along if necessary. We can call it a get-together if it helps. A get-together with welcome home cupcakes."

His frustration was offset by a warm fuzzy feeling and a shot of dark humor. A forced-home welcome party. Without being asked, he helped Rufus set up the smoker and carried out folding tables and chairs. By the time they were done, people were showing up.

Tally strolled down from the gym and gave him a hip bump. "Didn't even put up a fight. How unlike you."

"I was ambushed." Still, a smile he couldn't quite stem lightened the words.

An older lady with bottle-red hair and a grin carried a plastic bin filled with cupcakes. Tally gave the woman a hug. "Cade, this is Ms. Effie, my across-the-hall neighbor."

"Nice to meet you, ma'am. Tally's told me all about you." Besides Monroe, he got the impression Ms. Effie was one of Tally's only friends.

"She'd told me about you, too, young man. I was acquainted with your parents. Your mama made the best deviled eggs in Cottonbloom. People loved to see her coming at the church potluck."

Cade's smile came easy and natural. It felt strange. "I remember. She was like the pied piper of deviled eggs."

Ms. Effie patted his arm and laughed. He'd been hugged and patted and touched more since he'd been home than in his many years in Seattle combined. The distance that separated people in Seattle was absent in Cottonbloom. Maybe because everyone's lives intersected at some point, like interlocking threads creating cloth.

By the time Rufus whistled for everyone's attention, fifty or more people milled along River Street, laughter punctuating the conversations. Rufus quieted the crowd and got everyone to bow their heads for a brief prayer. The men whipped off hats.

Most of the people Cade recognized. They had been fellow church members or fishing buddies of his daddy or master gardeners like his mother. His second-grade teacher was there and clapped her hands when he greeted her by name.

He took the lemonade Tally offered, the sweet-tartness reminding him of summers long gone. "I can't believe how many people came for me."

"Rufus did offer free barbeque," she said dryly. "And Ms. Effie's cupcakes are wickedly good."

"True, but—"

"Ohmygoodness." Tally was staring over his shoulder, her face the definition of shocked.

"What is it?" He tried to turn, but she grabbed his arms.

"For Pete's sake, don't look." She used him as a shield and peeked around his arm and murmured, "I can't believe it's really him."

"Who?"

"I think that's Nash Hawthorne, but he looks . . . different."

Cade shifted and, as casually as possible, looked behind him. Sure enough, a man who somewhat resembled the boy who'd grown up down the river from their house stood on the outskirts, the setting sun outlining him. The Nash he remembered was the classic one-hundred-pound weakling. This man, while he had the same rumpled brown hair and glasses, was over six feet and at least two hundred pounds.

"Pretty sure that's him," Cade said. "You two were inseparable until everything went to hell." Nash's mother had succumbed to cancer, and their parents had died within a short amount of time. Cade couldn't recall what had happened to Nash after that.

"Yeah. We were best friends." The soft, vulnerable note in her voice drew Cade's attention.

"Why don't you go talk to him? See what he's been up to."

"No. Too many things have changed. I doubt he even remembers me. Listen, you don't mind if I duck out early, do you? Lots of stuff to do in the morning." She was backing away before he even answered. He watched until she disappeared around the corner, wondering how worried he should be.

The sound of Delmar tuning his mandolin distracted Cade. The sound brought back memories of lying in their trailer and hearing his uncle play and sing from his porch. The river had seemed to amplify the songs.

Delmar launched into a song about love and loss and coming home, his eyes closed, every part of him lost in the music. The crowd stilled, the emotion in Delmar's voice connecting all of them.

A sense of notching in place like a puzzle piece filled him with disquiet. He wasn't staying, didn't want to belong anywhere, much less Cottonbloom.

Delmar's voice trailed into nothing. Heartbeats passed when no one moved, then, as one, the crowd erupted. Delmar smiled and started another tune.

"He's amazing."

Cade startled. Monroe was beside him, her voice filled with wonder. She was still in her work clothes.

"He is," he said simply.

The look she cast him was both shy and teasing. "Hope you don't mind that I came? You didn't mention it, so I wasn't sure you wanted me here. Tally texted me after you left."

"I want you here." He was slightly embarrassed at how vehement he sounded. "I didn't know about it until I walked over here after our appointment. Got stuck setting up for my own party."

Another haunting song filled the evening air. Although low conversations took place all around them, he and Monroe stared at each other. It should have been intensely uncomfortable. Instead, it was just intense.

When the song ended, he said, "Let's take a walk."

He didn't wait for an answer and grabbed two cupcakes on his way down the street. Once they left the chaos behind, he handed one over. She took a bite and moaned. His gaze shot to her face. Although the pleasure wasn't sexual, arousal flickered in his body. She licked a dab of icing off her upper lip.

"Ms. Effie made these, didn't she?"

"How'd you know?"

"Tally brings them to the gym on occasion." She glanced back at the people. "Should you be wandering away from your own party?"

"No one will miss me. I have a feeling my Louisiana brethren search for any excuse to throw a block party."

Her laugh made him smile. She forced them to walk slowly. He didn't plan to complain. At the end of River Street stood the abandoned Cottonbloom Park. Two swings hung from the rusted metal A-frame in the dilapidated playground. The overgrown skeleton of a baseball field stood in the distance.

Part of him was afraid she'd bring up their earlier conversation, but the simplicity of the moment must have affected her as well. After testing the strength of the seat and chains, Cade gestured to the swing. Monroe sat and swayed from side to side, the chain squeaking from disuse. He gave her a push. Her hair was up, but the motion sent wispy pieces around her face. Three more strong pushes had her flying high, and he limped back around so he could see her face.

She leaned back and tilted her face to the sky, her eyes closed. The swing slowed, the squeak growing dimmer. With a laugh, she jumped out of the seat to land close to him.

"That was fun. It's been years since I was on a playground."

A whistle cut to him. His brother was making wild hand gestures. "If Sawyer embarrasses me, I'm going to put him in a headlock later."

"Maybe he's planning on giving a heartfelt speech about what you mean to him."

Cade barked a laugh. Not likely. The two of them hadn't managed to be more than civil with each over since he'd been back. When he'd moved the truck into the garage, the civility threatened to crumble into outright hostility.

The closer he and Monroe drew to the crowd, the more he slowed, partly because of his knee and partly because he wanted more time with her. "Are you sticking around?"

She checked her watch. "Actually, I have some stuff to take care of."

Did her stuff involve Tarwater? It shouldn't matter, because Cade had no claim on her. It mattered. "All right, I'll see you at our next appointment then."

"Don't rush things with your leg." She wagged a finger and backed away.

A group of men who were contemporaries of his father gathered around him and Sawyer to reminisce and blocked Cade's view of her. By the time he got the chance to look, she had disappeared across the river.

Chapter Six

The next day, unwilling to examine the feeling of something missing from her day, Monroe pulled up to Sawyer
Fournette's house and parked behind Tally's car. She
hopped out of her SUV, smoothing a hand down the front
of her sleeveless white blouse and tucking her still-damp-
from-the-shower hair behind an ear.

Instead of a June afternoon of bearable heat, a hellish
inferno more typical of August had come calling. A deep
breath was impossible with the maxed-out humidity. She
retrieved her purse from the backseat and tucked the invitation inside.

Her mission was to hand-deliver Tally's invitation to the
Tarwaters' cocktail party. Though Tally had never made
her nervous, she had seen her an hour ago at the gym, and
the compulsion to shower and dress up before dropping by
for a visit was new.

The logical assumption was that Cade had everything
to do with her erratic behavior, the flip-flop of her stomach, and her fidgety hands. Accepting the truth as being
ill-advised still didn't stop her from walking over the
gravel to Sawyer's back door.

She knocked on the door. No one answered. She knocked again, cracked it open, and called out, "Tally? Something smells good enough to eat."

She'd already stepped inside when Sawyer Fournette popped his head into the small foyer. "Hey, Monroe. Tally took my truck to the grocery. Come on in."

She forced a smile, her steps hesitant. In high school, because he and Regan had dated, they'd hung out with Monroe occasionally, but his breakup with Regan had destroyed any bridge to friendship under construction. Monroe always got the impression Sawyer tolerated her because of her friendship with his sister but didn't trust her as far as he could throw a dead raccoon because of her friendship with Regan.

But rudeness wasn't part of her DNA, and she followed him into the kitchen. Gumbo bubbled in a big pot on the stove while steam puffed out of a rice cooker. Sawyer propped a hip on the counter and crossed his arms over his chest.

The only trait Sawyer shared with Cade and Tally was the intensity in his eyes, although Sawyer's veered toward a softer hazel. Otherwise, his sandy blond hair, handsome, open face, and ready grin were his own. He was Mr. All-American. The man should be in a baseball uniform and carrying an apple pie at all times. Everyone loved Sawyer, which sent Regan careening further into madness.

"What brings you by the house? Regan send you to check up on my festival plans?" Sawyer asked in a friendly-enough voice, but the underlying competitive spirit had her muffling a smile and turning the invitation to the fundraiser in her hands.

"She's too wrapped up in her own plans to give yours much thought." Regan was doing more stewing over Sawyer than she had in years, but Sawyer sure didn't need to know that.

He harrumphed and gave the pot a stir. He wore khakis and a white undershirt. A plaid button-down hung on one of the cabinet handles. After taste testing a little gumbo, he jabbed the wooden spoon in her direction. "I've got big things in the works. Big. Things. You tell Regan that."

"I'm really not involved, Sawyer. I mean, I'm not even heading up any committees."

"I got the Cottonbloom, Mississippi, marching band. It's a done deal."

Monroe gasped. Regan was going to be madder than a wet hen. She'd already penciled in the marching band for her parade. "How'd you manage that?"

"Got old man Bancroft to donate some instruments." The smile on his face was Cheshire cat meets Hannibal Lecter.

"Well played." Her lips twitched.

"Terrible pun." He shook his head, but a genuine smile lurked at the corners of his mouth. "I need that prize money."

"What civic project are you throwing in the ring?"

"I want to revitalize Cottonbloom Park. Revamp the playground and the baseball field. Turn it into some-place people can gather with their kids. Maybe restart the Cottonbloom intramural league. That would be good for both sides, don't you think?" As with Regan earlier, it was hard to deny the fire and passion in his voice.

"That's a fabulous idea." And it was. Within walking distance of River Street, the park had spiraled into disre-pair, the money to maintain it funneled into fundamental projects like road repair. Before the town separated, area businesses would play baseball against each other for brag-ging rights. The older people on both sides of the river still talked about those days with a smiling nostalgia.

He gestured toward the white envelope she held. "You dropping something off for Tally?"

"Invitation to a fund-raiser for my girls at risk program."

"Not sure you'll get her into a cocktail dress, but maybe I can drum up some money to donate."

"That'd be great. I want to expand the services I offer into counseling."

The conversation waned, and Monroe looked out the back window. Two bays of the hulking metal garage out back were up and the long shadow of a man moved.

"I'll get out of your hair." She shuffled backward toward the door.

"You can leave that on the table if you want."

She looked down at the invitation and back up to the window. Cade emerged from the garage and riffled in a metal toolbox on wheels, disappearing back into the garage with a long metal object.

"I'm going to check on my patient." When Sawyer looked confused, she added, "Your brother."

Sawyer's gaze razored through the window, his body growing taut. Tension enveloped the small kitchen. "I'm surprised he's still around. I figured I'd wake up one morning to find him gone."

"I've only met with him twice, but he seems determined to get his hand better."

"So he can head back to Seattle at the earliest opportunity no doubt. Not sure why he agreed to come home. He shook off this town—and us—and I can tell he hates being back. He's been at it with our daddy's old truck almost since he landed."

She wanted to respond to the bitterness in Sawyer's voice. Tell him how Cade had worried over him so long ago. Worried about keeping him safe and fed, worried about his grades and girls, worried about the pain he hid behind his ready smile. She didn't say anything and escaped out the back.

The sun had dropped to the top of the trees, but the heat

hadn't abated. The air had surrendered and lay heavy and dense and unmoving. Bugs swarmed in pods that darted back and forth with one mind. She waved a hand in front of her face to ward off the gnats.

The opposite bay doors had been opened, too, giving the garage a barn-like feel. The sun shone through the back, and she shielded her eyes with a hand. Cade was hunched over the engine compartment of the rusted old red-and-gray truck, elbow deep in hoses and metal. Country music played from a portable speaker sitting on the cab. His blue jeans were faded and ripped at one knee, and his white cotton T-shirt was half-tucked. Both were dirty.

Cooler air circulated around her legs from two box fans set up to give some relief from the heat. When she was within ten feet, he straightened and propped his hip on the grill of the truck. "Well now, this is a surprise. Did you miss me so much you came out for a house call?"

She'd learned early on how to hide her truths behind a wall of confidence. No one had guessed that behind her smiles she wrestled with demons. But Cade seemed possessed with X-ray vision, her smiles no match for him. She reverted back into an unsure teenager confronted with her crush. She pulled at her blue-and-white-striped skirt. The inches of fabric between the hem and her panties seemed to shrink exponentially.

She made a few word-like noises before her tongue began working again. "Of course I didn't miss you. Next session, I'll see what I can do about your inflated head."

His smile was fleeting, and she had the feeling he wasn't in the habit of using it often.

"I came to give Tally an invitation to the Tarwaters' fund-raiser. Maybe you can talk her into going."

He used his shirt like a rag, black stripes of grease decorating the hem. "Let me see."

She held it out. His fingerprints dirtied the creamy parchment envelope as he pulled out the invitation written in black embossed letters. "*Mr. and Mrs. Tarwater invite you for an evening of entertainment and charity,*" he read in an exaggerated posh accent. "What's the entertainment?"

"I assume that's code for food and drink. If there's music, it'll be Frank Sinatra. Maybe the Eagles if things get wild."

"Sounds fun. Maybe I'll come if Tally doesn't want to. Represent the Fournettes." He tossed the invitation on top of a red metal tool cabinet with at least a dozen drawers, half of them open and filled with various nuts, bolts, and tools.

"It's black tie. Did you pack a tuxedo?"

He spun a wrench in his hand and grinned. This time his smile stuck around longer, as if muscle memory were kicking in. His bottom two teeth overlapped slightly, but otherwise his teeth were straight and white against his dark beard. "I expect I can rustle up something to wear. Uncle Delmar has a powder-blue tux with ruffles I might squeeze into."

"To see Mrs. Tarwater's face . . ." She laughed and came closer to peer at the engine compartment. "Are you going to get this old thing running again?"

He rubbed his hands down his jeans before nesting the wrench around a nut and tightening it. The muscle of his biceps flexed. She pulled at her skirt again.

"It was Daddy's." The simple words hid a wealth of feeling she could sense roiling behind his blank expression. She didn't answer but stood beside him while he worked, the silence between them strangely comfortable.

The tools seemed extensions of the long, dexterous fingers of his right hand. He moved with a grace and economy of motion that was hypnotizing. The effect was like watching an artist or musician at work. A hollowness grew in her belly, and her voice came out hoarse with a longing she couldn't identify. "You're good with your hands."

His head startled up. A slow, knowing smile lightened his face and he winked. "So I've been told."

What began as hero worship after he saved her from Sam had gradually turned into a teenage crush. The fantasies she'd harbored had been more along the lines of a Disney movie, unrealistic and innocent. Besides one quick brush of his lips on her cheek at the very end, they'd never kissed. She wasn't sure what she'd meant to him so many years ago or why he'd kept coming back upriver every full moon.

One thing had become painfully clear. Instead of withering over the years, her feelings had only lain dormant, breaking ground as blatant, very grown-up lust. Was he aware of the electric currents snapping around them?

She sashayed around him, and his head swiveled to follow her progress. Pushing a pile of papers aside, she scooched to sit on a stainless-steel desk and tried to channel the sexiness of a Victoria's Secret model when she crossed her legs.

He didn't react in any way.

"Tally told me you hold patents on some mechanical . . . thingamagigs." She didn't want to admit she'd pored over the magazine article she'd stumbled upon more than once. The accompanying picture showed him preparing to throw himself out of a plane. It bolstered the image of a man used to taking risks in all aspects of his life.

He buried himself back under the hood, his face in shadows, but a fair amount of humor threaded his words. "I prefer the more technical term, 'doodad.'"

She uncrossed her legs and swung them, a nervous energy pulsing with every beat of her heart. The edge of the desk bit at the backs of her thighs. Had his face moved the tiniest amount toward her? He straightened, polished his wrench on the bottom of his shirt, his gaze fixed north of her shoulders.

"You sell your patents to the highest bidder?" she asked.

"Actually, I license my designs. That way I retain rights and make money over the term of the patent."

"And companies are willing to pay to use them?"

"Darlin', they *fight* over my designs. My business partner and I play one against the other to drive the price up. We're ruthless. *I'm* ruthless." A warning was in his voice.

From what she'd read, he *was* ruthless. Maybe she should be scared. She wasn't. She was fascinated. "That's amazing. Where did you learn how to . . ." She shrugged, not sure how to finish. The facts of his past didn't seem to line up with the reality of the man he'd turned into.

"What? Negotiate or design engines?" He spun the wrench in his good hand over and over as if he was unaware of his actions, the habit so ingrained. "Daddy taught me the basics of car repair. Then, afterward . . . I learned real quick we couldn't afford a mechanic when things broke. It came natural. I may have dropped out of high school, but I made good grades. I could have gone to college, but I had to keep us together. Keep Tally's and Sawyer's lives as normal as possible."

What about your life? she wanted to ask. A hint of the desperation he must have felt threaded a now familiar defensiveness through his voice. She wanted to hop off the table and give him a hug.

"I read repair manuals in my spare time. Then, when Sawyer went to study engineering, I would flip through his books when he came home on weekends. By then, though, the theory wasn't as useful to me. I'd taught myself how to take any engine apart and put it back together. I could see how to make them better. So I did."

She had no doubt the simplicity of his declaration

masked years of hard work and sacrifice. "Why did you settle in Seattle?"

"I don't know. Maybe because it's the opposite of Louisiana. Cool. No gators or bugs big enough to eat you." His voice was teasing, yet the message was disconcerting.

The opposite of Louisiana. "Also no family."

"No family." Was he even aware of the hollow loneliness reflecting in his eyes? Then, it was gone and she wondered if she'd imagined it. His voice lightened. "Some might consider that a good thing."

Questions swirled. After everything he'd done for his brother and sister, why distance himself so thoroughly? But it was a different question that burned its way up her throat and out. "Do you have a girlfriend up there?"

"No one special."

"What does that mean?"

He raised his eyebrows, the corners of his mouth tilting into his beard. "Means I'm not a monk, but no woman is crying her eyes out that I'm not around."

She huffed, but the answer satisfied her. Her cotton skirt was scrunched around her upper thighs and she wiggled, pulling the hem down. This time she was positive his gaze dropped to skim down the length of her legs. The temperature rose a few more degrees.

"I should go."

"Actually, I could use your help." He opened and closed his bad hand. "I've been working for two days straight and can barely feel my fingers. But I'm so close to firing her up."

"Cade, I swear." She slid off the desk, took his hand, and massaged her thumbs along his palm. "What did I say about pushing yourself too hard, too fast?"

"I can't help it if I like it hard and fast." While the innuendo was clear, a self-deprecating humor kept him from sounding creepy.

"How old are you? Twelve?"

"The heat is deep-frying my brain cells. Apparently, I'm reverting. Even had a fight with Sawyer earlier about the truck." Cade's smile morphed into a grimace. "I can't damage my hand any worse, right?"

She hesitated, sensing the set-to with his brother loomed bigger in his worries than he wanted to admit to her. With that added to the odd hostility in Sawyer's voice earlier, she surmised the Fournette family reunion wasn't all hugs and happy tears.

"You won't make things worse, but I hate seeing you in pain." His hand jerked in hers, and her impetuously whispered words unscrambled themselves in her brain. God, was the heat dumbing her down, too? "I don't like seeing *any* of my clients in pain."

"You take your job pretty seriously, huh? Go above and beyond the call of duty?"

She should drop his hand yet couldn't unlatch her fingers, couldn't stop touching him. "What did you need help with?"

"I . . . What?"

She raised her gaze, slowly, deliberately, letting it linger on the broad expanse of his chest under the thin T-shirt, then onward to his neck where his throat muscles worked and to his mouth where his tongue dabbed the middle of his bottom lip. Air from the fan caressed her legs, fluttering her skirt. The syncopated whir settled into a hypnotic rhythm with the soft music. *Closer, closer, closer.*

"You needed me?" Her voice was husky, and she lifted her gaze the last few inches to meet his, the green as dark and beautiful as a magnolia leaf.

"I do need you." His whisper hooked her a step closer. His eyes flared and he cleared his throat. "I mean I need your help with my nuts."

"Your *nuts*?" She dropped his hand and startled back a step.

"Of the nuts-and-bolts variety." They both glanced toward his crotch. He scrubbed his hand over his head. Red tinged his cheekbones even as a small laugh stuttered out.

His smile lightened the mark so many desperate years had left and her lips mimicked his instinctively. She would put on a clown costume and hit herself with a cream pie if she could keep a smile on his face forever. She wasn't sure what that meant, but it couldn't be good.

"I'd be happy to help with your nuts."

A booming laugh exploded from his chest and triggered a landslide in her stomach. As his laugh reduced to a chuckle, he gestured her over. She stood facing the engine block. He moved up behind her, not quite touching her, but she was aware of him nonetheless, the hairs on the back of her neck reaching for him.

His arm came around her, his biceps brushing hers, the wrench extended. She took it out of his hand, the metal warm from his grip. He braced his hands on the truck's frame, caging her in. The rasp of his jeans on her bare legs had her shuddering a breath in and out. Even in her wedge sandals, he topped her by a few inches.

He pointed into the dark recesses next to a set of parallel hoses. "It's down there."

She stuck her hand in the crevasse and felt around, the wrench clanging in her clumsy attempt. "I'm not sure . . ."

He tucked himself right behind her and put his hand over hers. Everything about him overwhelmed her senses. His scent was car grease and sweat and soap. A combination she would have never thought was sexy, but he wore it well. So well, in fact, she turned her face to where his arm covered hers and took a deep breath.

His body branded her through the layers of cotton, hard and hot. Desire streaked through her body like the first cut of lightning before a storm. She wanted to drop the wrench and turn in his arms. She didn't. That sort of behavior went against her habit of staying safely removed.

Her dating history was sketchy at best. Sporadic dates with men who assumed her friendly yet distant manner was a version of playing hard to get. None of them had ever earned her trust, leading to a series of short-lived relationships. She hadn't been sorry to see any of them go.

"Do you feel it?" His breath caressed her ear, and she turned her head, wanting more.

God, yes, she felt it. Felt every inch of him, felt the powerful draw to him despite the years, felt her body spark. Was it simple lust or was something older, more primal, at work between them? Her instincts were trumping her ingrained habits.

"The nut is under my finger. Can you feel it? Fit the wrench around it, and I'll help you torque it." He turned toward her, putting them nose to nose. Black grease fanned from the corner of one eye and had settled into a long groove along his forehead as if highlighting the hard years.

"I feel it." Her whisper barely penetrated the heavy, humid air around them. Her brain instructed her to move, to do her job with the wrench. All she could do was stare at the way the coarse hairs of his beard perfectly framed his lips.

"Are you okay?" he asked.

She was as okay as someone emerging from a coma. Disoriented and confused. "I'm just peachy."

"All righty then." His lips quirked. "You ready to get on it?"

She startled, her butt bumping into his pelvis. "Get on it?"

"Torque the nut?"

"Yes, yes." Through sheer luck, she managed to seat the wrench around the nut. He made encouraging grunting noises that didn't help her concentration one little bit. When she gave him the go-ahead, he wrapped his good hand around hers and pulled.

"Excellent. That should do it." He backed away.

The air around her thinned and the pressure fell, making it easier to think rationally.

"Why don't you stay for dinner?" he asked. "You can hand off the invite to Tally."

"Not sure Sawyer wants me around."

The grease-streaked furrow on Cade's forehead deepened. "You and Sawyer feuding?"

"Not exactly. The dueling festivals have pitted one side of Cottonbloom against the other and your brother and Regan are the field generals."

"And you and Regan are still best friends, I take it."

"Since kindergarten."

"But you and Tally have become friends, too, right?"

She and Tally probably had more in common than she and Regan did. The biggest being neither one enjoyed heart-to-heart talks. Their friendship involved the gym, the girls at risk program, and superficial chats about pop culture and their unexciting love lives.

She shrugged an answer. "I love Regan, I do, but your brother knows how to make her lose her mind."

"Based on Sawyer's rants and his increased whiskey consumption, seems like she can return the favor. He wants that grant money from the contest."

"So does Regan. They both want the best for their sides of Cottonbloom." She refused to throw Regan to the gators, but she wasn't certain her friend's vehemence to produce a spectacular festival wasn't born out of years of nurtured hate toward the Cottonbloom Parish commissioner.

Cade held out a hand. "You're not Regan, so Sawyer has no reason to object."

Her lungs ceased moving air in and out as past and present blurred. She remembered Cade standing on the bank in an identical pose, younger, clean shaven, and undeniably the same. She also remembered the solace she'd found in the simple touch. The moment took on a significance far beyond an invitation to stay for dinner.

She'd touched him during their physical therapy sessions, and he'd been pressed against her, his hand around hers not two minutes earlier, yet her fingers trembled as she reached for him. His hand engulfed hers. He caressed the back of her hand with his thumb, and the rough calluses along his palm rasped against her skin. The electric sensations zinging up her arm shocked her lungs into an erratic rhythm.

He didn't speak or tug her toward the house. Maybe the seismic shift affected him as well. The silence was full of memories. Even the bugs had quieted. The green of his eyes darkened like clouds moving in from the horizon, and mysteries lurked behind the storm.

Chapter Seven

A shiver ran up Cade's spine in spite of the oppressive heat. With her hand in his, the two of them existed in a state of limbo he didn't understand. At eighteen she'd grown into an achingly pretty girl—one he'd started to think about as more than a surrogate sister—but the beautiful, complicated woman she'd become bemused him.

Although she was confident, hints of the vulnerability he'd first seen in her at thirteen were still there. She was in turns refreshingly honest and closed off. Her deflection about her mama the day before had not gone unnoticed. Calling her on it seemed dishonest considering he'd sidestepped more than one question she'd lobbed in his direction.

He wanted to know everything about her. Was her favorite color still green? Her favorite food still pizza? Had any other man come into her life and tried to hurt her? Had he succeeded? His hand tightened around hers as if he could protect her from her past.

"There you are!" Tally jogged into the garage but stopped short, eyeing the two of them.

The connection broken, Monroe pulled her hand out of

his and tried to smile, but he could see the strain. The moment seemed to have left her shaken, too. Good.

She shuffled backward a few steps, picked up the invitation, and held it out. "I was dropping this off for you."

Tally took the fingerprinted envelope from Monroe, but his sister's gaze stayed on him as she hummed an ironic affirmative. "Looks like someone already left their mark on it."

"I'm going to get cleaned up. Convince Monroe to stay for dinner, Tally," he said as if directing an underling. His sister wouldn't let that kind of crap slide more than once, but he needed a few minutes alone. He limped away but felt two sets of eyes on him the whole way. Sawyer's question about dinner necessitated a grunting answer before Cade closed himself behind the bathroom door.

He turned the water to hot, propped his hands on the counter, and stared in the mirror. He was looking at someone else. Someone who looked like him but wasn't exactly him. Not anymore. Or maybe he was closer to his real self than he'd been in years.

Had he ever joked and laughed and teased a woman like that? He smiled at himself in the mirror, looking even more like a stranger. Probably he should be embarrassed he'd faked needing her help to tighten that nut, but he wasn't. The feel of her body fueled desires he'd denied and squashed so many years ago when she'd been too young and innocent and he'd had nothing to offer.

Steam fuzzed out his reflection, and he stepped into the shower to scrub off the grime. When she'd walked in with the sun highlighting her extraordinary legs, his breath had lodged somewhere behind the lump in his throat. Her vanilla-sweet scent had inflamed his imagination—images scrolled of laying her over the metal desk ready to be devoured.

He'd come dangerously close to slamming his mouth

down on hers and putting his filthy hands under that flirty little skirt of hers. His past relationships had been business-like transactions, and he always kept the upper hand. His interactions with Monroe weren't remotely businesslike. An old feeling he thought he'd left behind years ago had stopped him. He felt unworthy.

He flipped the water to cold, the sting welcome. The uncertain, broken boy he'd been in Cottonbloom still existed, it seemed. Monroe was part of the past he'd tried to leave behind. She was his sister's friend, his physical therapist, and an old . . . Acquaintance? Friend? Neither fit. Her place in his life wasn't definable and seemed to be changing every minute he was in her company.

A knot tightened and grew in his chest the longer he dallied in the bathroom. Had she stayed or gone? Suddenly he was desperate to know. He pulled on clean jeans and walked into the kitchen barefoot, tugging a black T-shirt over his head.

His gaze caught her mid-laugh, standing at the sink with Tally. The electric connection that had formed in the garage arced the ten feet between them. With a long, slow exhale, the almost painful place around his heart eased. He didn't want to examine why her being here was important.

A pretty blush spread to her cheeks, highlighting her fair complexion. With her blue eyes and blond hair loose around her shoulders, she was a snapshot of innocence. But, seductive details shaded the simple picture— the edge of a lace bra peeking from her blouse, short skirt riding well above her knees, long bare legs and pink-painted toes.

He half-tucked his T-shirt into his jeans. "You stayed."

"Tally twisted my arm."

His sister barked a laugh but didn't comment further. Sawyer strode into the kitchen, their uncle Delmar on his heels. His uncle's rich voice cut through the small room, a few decibels too loud for comfort. "Cade, my boy! Could you come look at my engine tomorrow? It's acting up and I've got to get out on the river this week."

Delmar had been hard of hearing for as long as Cade could remember. His daddy had blamed Delmar's hearing loss on a mortar explosion in Vietnam.

Cade raised his voice. "Sure thing. I'll drive out to your place tomorrow afternoon."

"Don't want to put you out."

He made a scoffing sound. "Please. I have nothing going on besides physical therapy. It'll give me something to do. Maybe I'll have the old truck running by then, even though it'll look a mess. Rust has been eating it away."

A dish clattered on the stove, drawing everyone's eyes. Sawyer's mouth was tight, and a now familiar tension both linked and repelled them. Anger licked around Cade's chest. Sawyer had allowed the truck to turn into a wild animal sanctuary. What did he care if Cade drove it again?

Uncle Del clapped Cade on the shoulder with a gnarled hand that resembled the roots of the cypress trees in the swamps. The aroma of tobacco smoke distilled from Del's clothes even though he claimed to have quit a year earlier. The smell was oddly comforting.

He sidled to Monroe and put an arm around her shoulders. Cade expected her to cringe away, but instead she leaned into his uncle's hug and patted his shoulder. "I've missed seeing you around town, Del."

"You know how it is. City wouldn't let me off for the start of duck season, so I told them to stick it." Uncle Delmar's laugh stuttered in his unique way, making him easy to pick out of a crowd.

Raymond Fournette had been considered the successful brother, providing a solid middle-class lifestyle for his family. Like recalling an old movie, a conversation between his parents scrolled through his mind—his daddy urging his mama to be kinder, more patient, with Delmar because he couldn't help the drinking and erratic behavior.

Two quarter-sized scars courtesy of the Vietcong had faded into the wrinkles that drew his cheeks down. Delmar never talked about his deployment, but now Cade was older he understood his uncle bore more scars than what was visible.

Before Cade's parents were killed, he had been dismissive and more than a little embarrassed of his uncle. Delmar's thankfully brief stint as the Cottonbloom Parish Elementary janitor had been the worst.

Cade hadn't yet sunk to the depths where an animal from one of Delmar's traps was a godsend. Delmar hadn't held any real or imagined slights against Cade and shared what he could. Cade would forever be grateful.

Not taking his eyes off Monroe, he hooked a foot around one of the kitchen chairs and sat, stretching the sore muscles of his back. Sawyer's setup in the garage wasn't exactly ergonomic. He used the space to tinker on his cars, not as part of his paying job.

If Cade was staying longer, he'd enclose the garage, put in air-conditioning, and buy better equipment. The convenience of having the river as a testing ground in the backyard was huge. The gears of his brain turned in a direction that should have him wanting to hightail it to the nearest airport. He pushed the thoughts away, not dismissing them but storing them in the "if hell freezes over" file.

"Bartholomew has been talking about hiring some help. It would be cleaning and helping to file and such," Monroe said. "Come on down and talk to him about it if you're interested."

"That's mighty nice of you. I'll head over sometime soon." That meant Delmar might show up first thing in the morning or three months from now. His concept of time revolved around hunting and fishing seasons.

They fixed bowls of gumbo and took seats at their old round, scarred kitchen table. After the way Sawyer had let the truck molder, Cade was surprised he hadn't chopped the table apart for kindling. With the family back together for the first time in years, the talk turned to the past.

"Old Raymond could hit a squirrel at fifty feet with his slingshot. Never seen nothing like it before or since. And all the Fournettes can see in the dark. It's said one of our ancestors saved a witch-woman out in the swamps and she cast a spell for him."

Monroe laughed, but everyone else just nodded and her smile turned disbelieving. "Are you serious? All of you? Even you, Tally?"

"I can't see as well as the boys can, but better than most. Uncle Delmar's exaggerating some. It's not like we're cats or anything." She propped her chin in her hands, her eyes twinkling. Tally was as happy as Monroe had seen her in a long time.

"The Fournettes were born night hunters. We have a leg up on the competition." Delmar winked.

"I never knew that," Monroe murmured. She cast reassessing eyes toward Cade. He stared into his bowl of gumbo. There were lots of things she didn't know about him.

"You remember the night you tangled with that barbed-wire fence, Cade?"

He touched his flank, knowing exactly where the scar lay even if he couldn't feel it through the cotton. "How could I forget? Dangled there for a good half hour before you found me."

"You had me worried at first you didn't have the Fournette makings for being a hunter, but you impressed me. You turned out all right, Cade."

Everyone's eyes were on him, and he shrugged. No way would he admit how bone-deep scared he'd been that night. He hadn't seen the fence because he'd been looking over his shoulder, sure something was after him—animal, ghost, he'd never been sure.

He'd hunted and fished all his life, but that night was the first time it mattered. Catching something wasn't a matter of pride; it was a matter of whether he had something substantial to feed Tally and Sawyer the next day or was opening another can of pork and beans. He'd never hunted with that kind of desperation.

While he could see better than almost any man at night, to a sixteen-year-old whose imagination wasn't grounded by harsh reality yet, danger permeated the shadows. After Delmar separated Cade's clothes from the barbs, he'd continued with the hunt, even with the stinging pain in his side. He'd managed to bring down a buck close to dawn. There was no euphoric adrenaline rush, only relief and a numbing exhaustion.

Delmar had given him a shot of whiskey—another first—and stitched him up. Unable to keep his eyes open a minute longer, he'd skipped school that day, promising not to miss another, but invariably he had until he fell so far behind it was either repeat a grade or drop out. It wasn't long after dropping out he'd found Monroe in his boat.

A touch feathered over his bad hand. It was drawn into a tight fist on his leg, pain prickling along the nerve endings. His hand unlocked like she was the key, and she threaded their fingers together, her thumb massaging up and down his scar.

His anemic attempt at a smile fell as her blue eyes enveloped him. She couldn't truly understand his childhood—he didn't want to burden her with the depressing details—but she knew enough that he didn't have to pretend with her. In fact, she knew more than anyone—even his family.

"What do you think, Cade?" Sawyer asked.

Pulling his gaze from hers was like separating magnets. "What's that?"

"If you can get Uncle Del's motor fixed up, you want to head out on the river soon? Relive your past?"

It was the last thing he wanted to do. His past needed to stay put. While Cade was trying to come up with an excuse, Monroe's phone beeped. She pulled her hand from his and retrieved her phone.

"Come on; it'll be fun," Sawyer said.

Cade shot a quick glance in Sawyer's direction. Was this a peace offering or a test? He was caught in a foreign state of indecision.

"What d'you say, boy?" Uncle Del prodded.

Chewing on her bottom lip, Monroe sent a return text and slipped her phone back in her purse. Was it Andrew Tarwater? Jealousy gave Cade's words an unintended bite. "Sure. Whatever."

"We don't need you to come, you know." Sawyer's voice took on a childlike petulance.

Cade had failed the test and would have to work for some extra points. Pulling at the hair on his chin, he transferred his attention to Sawyer, even as he remained aware of every shift and sigh coming from Monroe.

"No, I want to come. The closest I've been to a boat or body of water lately is the tank we use to optimize engine designs."

Sawyer slumped in his chair and toyed with his spoon. "We'll hit all our old haunts."

"Dinner was amazing, guys, but I have to open the gym up in the morning." Tally pushed up from the table. "Will I see you tomorrow, Monroe?"

"Definitely. Will I see you at the fund-raiser?"

"Doubtful." Tally's laugh sounded like someone had told a bad joke. "Not really my crowd."

The clap of the screen door prodded everyone into action. Monroe rose, stacked the bowls, and carried them to the sink. Sawyer waved her off. "Cade'll wash up later, right, man?"

Sawyer chucked his head, and he and Uncle Delmar moved their discussion of fishing lures into the den.

"I can help clean up." Monroe rubbed her hands down the front of her skirt and fingered the hem. It only made him more aware of her legs and what lay underneath.

"Absolutely not. You've worked all day. Your feet must be tired in those shoes."

One corner of her mouth hitched as she cocked her ankle. "I didn't wear this to work."

Her gaze streaked up, and he noted the flash of consternation in her face. Had she just admitted to dressing up for him? His mouth dried. What was his play? Dating in Seattle usually included a fancy dinner and bed. A gentleman wouldn't throw her over his shoulder and make straight for a bedroom. A gentleman would . . . walk her to her car?

"Guess I'll be heading out then." She backed toward the door. He stepped around her and held the screen door open for her. "You don't have to—"

"I know, but I'm going to."

They walked in silence. The oppressive heat of the day had given over to a cooling night. She slid into the driver's seat of her SUV. He rocketed back in time, watching his laughing parents set off on their final date.

Before Monroe could close the door, he grabbed the steering wheel, his hand next to hers. "Will you text me when you get home?"

Surprise but also wariness came over her face. "I can take care of myself. I'm a black belt, if you'll recall."

He swallowed, not sure how to express the illogical need to know she was safe. He averted his gaze. A whip-poor-will sat a few branches up, his song haunting and full of loss. "It's not that. I saw you in action. But . . . what if a deer ran in front of your SUV or you broke down or something?" There were probably a hundred other people she would call over him if she needed help. Maybe even Tarwater.

She feathered her hand over his and gave a quick squeeze before reaching for her purse. "Sure, I'll text you. What's your number?"

Once she was ready, he rattled off the number, thankful she hadn't made him admit his fears aloud. The moonlight made her appear younger and more vulnerable, casting him back a decade. She cranked the engine. Still he didn't step away.

"Night, Cade."

His stay in Cottonbloom was temporary. He had no right to kiss her. Forcing his legs to move took Superman-like strength. "Good night, Monroe."

Her taillights were swallowed by the darkness in the tree line at the edge of the road. He stood there staring into the night until his phone beeped.

Made it home. Anytime you need help with your nuts, give me a call.

The building worry crumbled like a sand castle in his wave of laughter. He had no idea if she was flirting or not, the uncertainty nerve-wracking and exhilarating at the same time. A million cockleburs tumbled in his stomach. The whip-poor-will called again, this time his song mocking.

Chapter Eight

Two nights later, Monroe lay on the couch and stared at the ceiling fan going round and round in an endless loop with no forward progress—mimicking her thoughts. Cade had canceled their last appointment with no real excuse. Tally had only shrugged and rolled her eyes when asked. Now Monroe had his number, she'd started about twenty different texts, each one sounding more adolescent than the last.

Every time their paths crossed, another door unlocked between them, the way becoming darker and more confusing. He was different from her adolescent memories, yet under the gruff, sometimes distant, façade he wore she recognized the man-boy who'd protected her that night and come to her so many times afterward.

His insistence that she check in with him had been driven by a deep fear. A fear he refused to admit, and compassion had softened her knee-jerk reaction. She didn't need his protection anymore, but she could at least offer reassurance.

Her life seemed to hinge on that night, her trajectory forever changed. After that night she'd vowed never to depend on someone else—not even her mother. Especially not her mother.

Monroe had checked out self-defense videos from the library and taught herself Jackie Chan–style moves in the privacy of her bedroom. Even with the confidence they'd instilled, she'd slept with her door wedged shut whether a man was in the house or not.

After she and Regan had become roommates at college, Monroe had jammed a chair under the knob only once. Regan had been the picture of questioning surprise, and Monroe recognized how odd and irrational the habit had become. Still, it had taken a year before she'd slept soundly. Mastering jujitsu had added another layer of confidence and given her a new handle on her fears.

Her phone buzzed. Nerves spiraled from her stomach. She glanced at the screen, her hand trembling. Not Cade, but one of the girls from her program. Relief, disappointment, and worry collided.

"Hey, Kayla, what's up?" She sat up.

"Mon-Monroe?" Behind the girl's teary, shattered voice came the low buzz of voices and the occasional bark of laughter.

"What's wrong? Where are you?" She stood and stared into the empty grate of her fireplace, her senses attuned to whatever was on the other side of the phone.

A sob cracked through the phone, the girl's desperation and fear palpable.

"Everything is going to be fine." Monroe's words tripped over each other belying the mature calmness she was trying to project. She slipped on flip-flops and stumbled on the way out, banging her hip on the porch banister. "Tell me where you are. I'm coming to get you."

"The Rivershack Tavern." Kayla's voice was barely a whisper.

The bar was a local gathering spot on the Louisiana side

of Cottonbloom. Not seedy, but hardly high-class, it boasted dartboards, pool tables, and a bar stocked with ice-cold beer and mid-shelf liquor. But Kayla wasn't even eighteen and shouldn't have been allowed to step inside the bar.

"Are you with Dylan?"

Kayla had never been the most attentive or engaged girl in her program, but over the last month all she'd done was distract everyone else by gushing about her new boyfriend. Monroe hadn't gotten the impression he was any older than Kayla.

"I'm scared." She sounded close to collapse. "Oh, God, he saw me."

The phone disconnected.

"Gosh darn it," Monroe muttered at the blank screen.

She called Kayla back and squeezed the phone between her cheek and shoulder to start the SUV and throw it into reverse. The carefree, chipper voice asking her to leave a message was in stark contrast to that of the scared, tearful girl of seconds ago.

Monroe tossed her phone into the passenger seat and hit the gas. Every red light in town caught her, and she banged her fists on the steering wheel, muttering more colorful curses at each one. Her phone rang when she was two minutes from the bar, and she nearly bobbled it to the floorboard before answering.

"Are you okay? I'm almost there, sweetie. Hang on."

"What the hell is going on?" A deep voice slid through her.

Considering his radio silence the last couple of days, the fact that Cade was calling seemed a figment of her imagination. She checked the screen to confirm. "Sorry, Cade, thought you were someone else."

"Obviously. Who?" His voice bordered on angry. What right did he have to be angry with her?

"I don't have time to talk. Kind of have a situation to

handle." She pulled into the Rivershack Tavern's lot and parked on a section where the pavement had started to crumble into gravel.

"You have thirty seconds to tell me where you are and what's going on."

She chafed at the autocratic command. "The Rivershack Tavern. One of my girls needs me."

She disconnected, jumped out of the SUV, and called Kayla. Voice mail again. The phone vibrated, and Cade's name flashed on the screen. She ignored him, slipping the phone into her back pocket. He didn't need a physical therapist to deal with a bruised ego.

A bouncer occupied a stool outside the door and scrolled through his phone. A cigarette defying gravity dangled from his bottom lip. He looked up as she approached, his gaze sliding down her body suggestively, making her wish she'd taken two minutes to change out of her black short shorts and scooped-neck red tank top into something that was less "Buy me a drink and you might get lucky" and more "Mess with me and I'll kick your ass."

He took a draw of the cigarette, the smoke still in his lungs when he asked, "Got your ID?"

The bouncer's head looked like it sat directly on his shoulders, his short neck the same width as his head. The man must invest hours a day bodybuilding to achieve the bull-like shoulders and thick arms straining the T-shirt with the Rivershack Tavern's emblem across the chest.

She glanced toward her SUV, seeing her purse on the side table in her foyer in her mind's eye. She tried an ingratiating smile. "I'm nearly thirty and only here to pick up a friend of mine." She took two steps toward the door, but he grabbed her wrist, his hand hammy and damp.

"Not without an ID, sweetheart."

His use of the endearment wasn't charming; it was denigrating. She twisted her arm out of his hand with ease. His jaw fell, the cigarette landing at her feet. She stamped it out with a twist of her foot.

"The friend I'm picking up is underage, has been drinking, and is somewhere in your establishment crying while you waste my time. Now, how did she get in if you're so diligent about checking IDs?"

The man pulled a pack of cigarettes from his back pocket and chucked his head toward the door.

The room was awash in people. Men and women in factory uniforms mingled with those dressed in going-out kinds of clothes—sundresses and miniskirts for the women, nice jeans and golf shirts for the men. A smoky haze haloed the lights. Unlike on the Mississippi side of Cottonbloom, Sawyer hadn't managed to get a smoking ban to pass, which had only increased business, drawing people from both sides of the river.

Monroe might have enjoyed the welcoming, eclectic vibe if she hadn't crept into a dozen bars too much like this one to cajole her mother home. Sometimes she was a happy, compliant drunk. Sometimes she was a sad drunk, crying and huddled at a corner table. And occasionally she was a mad drunk, bitter at the hand she'd been dealt. Those nights had been the hardest.

Monroe was no longer the girl who felt inadequate to the task, and this bar wasn't filled with strangers. She slipped through the crowd, scanning for Kayla. A hand wrapped around her upper arm and forced her to a stop.

Sam Landry. He held a cigarette and hard-liquor drink in the same hand. Judging by his flushed face, he was at least three drinks in, maybe more. "Hey there, pretty girl, don't ever see you around the Rivershack. Your mama with you?"

Another set of worries tightened a vise around Monroe's

lungs. She broke his hold with an upward rap on his forearm, a simple technique. "Mother's not hanging out at places like this anymore."

"Is that what she's been telling you?" He guffawed. "She's still an attractive woman, and I never did get her out of my system. Now that Carla's dumped me, I need someone to keep company with."

"You are a pig." She didn't try to mask her disgust.

"Darlin', she's the one who was all over me last weekend wanting to rekindle things."

While Sam might have been baiting Monroe, she feared more than a nugget of truth lay in his declarations. Should she have told her mother about that night so many years ago? Now it was too late.

"Leave her alone." Her voice came out weaker, childlike, and she was frantic to shore up her defenses.

"Or what?" Hostility simmered on his face.

Confusion seeped through the cracks in her confidence. A couple of years after that September night, Sam had married and moved to Georgia. In his absence, she could almost pretend nothing had happened. But he was always waiting in her nightmares. When he'd moved back to Cottonbloom after his divorce and reopened his insurance office, old doubts had edged into her anger. Had she exaggerated the danger of the night in her memories?

The bar noise faded to nothing. Squatting in her memories, her terror of him reared up. "Or I'll tell Mother—everyone—what happened that night."

His expression flipped as if his face had two sides, like a coin. A nonchalant smile replaced the burning animosity, the change jarring. "What night? I have no idea what you're talking about. You had the biggest crush on me. Do you remember?"

He either lied to add to her confusion or believed the

lie. Did it matter? She wasn't here to face her own screwed-up past; she had to find Kayla.

"I don't have time to waste on you, old man." She walked away and scanned the room. Every second that passed notched up her anxiety.

"You looking for a pretty, dark-haired girl? Young?"

Monroe spun on her toes. A man had swiveled around on his stool at the very corner of the dark, scarred bar top, a beer bottle hooked between his fingers. Corn-colored hair was pulled back into a low ponytail and a snake tattoo trailed out of the sleeve of his gray T-shirt and down one forearm. More colored ink peeked from his other sleeve. He was a stranger.

"Maybe." Her tentativeness was born of mistrust. For all she knew, this could be Dylan. "Have you seen her?"

"She's been in the bathroom for a while now. Seemed upset."

Already on the move to the back corridor, she called over her shoulder, "Thanks."

She bypassed a half-dozen women to get to the women's restroom door. A middle-aged woman with smudged eyeliner and a too-tight T-shirt at the front of the line blocked her access to the door with an arm. "Hey, we all gotta go. No cutting."

"I'm here to pick up my friend." Monroe dropped her voice to incur some sympathy. "She's had too much to drink."

The wrinkles around the woman's liner-smudged eyes smoothed. "I was wondering. Poor thing. We've all been there, haven't we?" She waved Monroe into the cramped two-stall bathroom. Colorful graffiti decorated the walls and wooden stalls. A woman emerged from the right stall, so Monroe tapped lightly on the left.

"Kayla? It's Monroe. Are you in there?"

The lock jangled and the stall door creaked open.

Kayla's eyes and nose were red, any makeup cried off. The girl pulled her shoulder-length dark hair forward and played with the ends. The motion only drew Monroe's attention to Kayla's left cheek.

Women moved behind Monroe, from the toilet to the sink, but she was focused only on Kayla. Very slowly, Monroe reached forward and tucked Kayla's hair behind her ear revealing a nearly perfect red handprint on her cheek.

Fury, hot and wild, churned in Monroe's belly, sending fire through her body. "Did he touch you anywhere else?" She whispered through clenched teeth.

Kayla's chin wobbled and another tear slipped out. "He thought I was flirting with one of his friends. I wasn't, I swear, but he . . . slapped me. I called you, but he saw me and grabbed me up hard."

Her face fell, her hair swishing forward like curtains closing. Monroe brushed Kayla's hair back, barely touching the light finger-shaped bruising on her upper arm. It would look worse come morning. "You did the right thing by calling me and going somewhere safe."

"He didn't mean to hurt me. He only gets like this when he's had too much."

The implications of Kayla's justifications for her boyfriend's behavior filled Monroe with equal amounts frustration and despair. Everything she lectured about week after week hadn't changed Kayla's outcome. Was she fooling herself into thinking she was making a difference?

Monroe tightened her focus to the situation at hand. She pulled her phone out of her back pocket. "I'm going to call the police. You can press charges."

"No! I don't want anyone to see me like this."

Monroe recognized the shame. She was still covering up her mother's drinking for the same reasons.

"I've had a few drinks, too." Kayla's voice was tentative. "Won't a bunch of people get in trouble if the cops come?"

A bunch of people deserved to get in trouble—the bouncer, the bartender, Dylan—but that wasn't Monroe's priority. Her priority was to get Kayla somewhere safe. "Is your mom home?"

"Working second tonight."

The stream of women into and out of the bathroom hadn't abated. Monroe put her arm around Kayla's shoulders and guided her through the gauntlet at the door. Kayla stumbled a couple of times and leaned into Monroe.

She hesitated outside the bathroom corridor. The length of crowded bar they'd need to navigate seemed overwhelming. Somewhere in the crush was Dylan. And Sam.

A hand cupped her elbow and she startled. "Take her out through the kitchens." The blond man had come up beside her, and she allowed him to guide her back down the hallway, past the bathrooms, and into the kitchen.

He was taller than he'd appeared on the stool, his body lean. In the bright lights of the kitchen he looked younger, too, although life's experiences had etched a maturity on his face she was familiar with.

"The walking a-hole she was hanging with . . . You want me to keep him from following you?" He had to raise his voice over the music pumping from a grease-splattered stereo system sitting on a counter.

If Kayla weren't clinging to Monroe, she would have given the stranger a hug. "If it's not too much trouble, I would be forever grateful."

The man's gaze skated to Kayla, and he nodded once. "Back door?" he asked the fry cook.

The cook pulled a basket of fries out of boiling oil and nudged his chin toward racks of supplies. An industrial-size garbage can marked the exit. Monroe pushed the heavy metal door open, glanced over her shoulder to see the blond man disappear, and stepped outside.

A weak finger of light from a dimmed spotlight hanging on a gutter lit the alley. A Dumpster blocked one end while empty crates and liquor boxes were stacked in a makeshift wall in front of a line of pine trees.

The warm night exacerbated the smell of rotting food and skunked beer. Kayla lurched away, fell to her knees in the gravel, and threw up next to an empty keg. Monroe squatted next to her and stroked her hair back. Sweat dotted the girl's forehead, and her pale, clammy face served to emphasize the handprint.

Monroe rubbed small circles on Kayla's back as the girl's dry heaves settled. She tried to keep her voice from reflecting her inner jitters. "Kayla, sweetie, I need to get you out of here. Can you walk?"

Kayla nodded and Monroe helped her, sliding an arm around her waist. Before they made it a dozen feet, a twentysomething man with shaggy brown hair turned the corner, his hands stuffed into the pockets of his slouchy jeans.

Kayla turned from compliant into panicked. She grabbed Monroe's arm and pulled her back toward the kitchen door. The man was focused on Kayla. He was big, at least six feet tall and close to two hundred pounds.

The kitchen door had a pushbutton key lock on the handle. Kayla yanked on the handle and beat on the door. No way was the fry cook going to hear them over his booming music. Monroe accepted their fate before Kayla did. Dylan was already within ten feet of them. Monroe stepped forward and put herself between the man and Kayla. Like a missile acquiring its target, his focus remained on Kayla.

"I need to talk to my girl over there alone, so you need to get on, lady."

She wasn't weak like her mother. She was strong. She would protect Kayla. Her pep talk couldn't completely stamp out the fear. Breathing in through her nose and out through her mouth, she tried to ready herself, but her mind blanked.

"Move it before I'm forced to take care of you, too."

I told your mama I would take care of you. Words that haunted her dreams blurred into a monstrous reality. Something dangerous cracked open in Monroe.

"Yeah? Well, that's not going to happen. You must think you're a real tough guy, pushing women around." Sarcasm poured into her voice, concealing any trembly note.

He shifted his feet apart and pulled his hands out of his pockets to crack his knuckles. If she weren't afraid to take her eyes off him for a second, she would have rolled them at his clichéd intimidation tactics.

"You'd best keep outta my business."

"When you hit Kayla, your business became my business."

"You want some of what I gave her?"

Monroe attempted a calming breathing technique, but all the extra oxygen did was shoot aggression through her muscles. "Kayla is only seventeen. She shouldn't even be here."

"She was looking to screw my buddy, so I'd say she's old enough. And who was that blond dude? Someone else she was looking to hook up with?"

Kayla's tinny voice barely carried across to them. "I'd never cheat on you, I swear."

Dylan pointed toward Kayla. "I'll deal with you in a minute, slut."

Fury obliterated any caution. Monroe took two steps forward and shoved him in the shoulder as hard as she could. He fell on his butt; either he was drunker than he appeared or the adrenaline had given her strength. Rocking on her feet, she waited for his move. A mistake.

His scramble up was faster and more agile than she expected. Before she could react, he grabbed a hank of her hair and yanked her forward. A hundred needles jabbed into her scalp, bringing a sting of tears to her eyes.

Her training had been sterile and safe. She'd never had to actually fight someone off in an alley. Had never had to fight her own instincts to run, save herself.

His movements were like watching a video in slow motion. He raised his arm, ready to backhand her. Without consciously planning to, she blocked his punch. The contact was jarring and numbed her forearm and hand, but after hours of repetitive training her body knew what to do next.

She popped him on the bridge of his nose with the heel of her hand. He released her hair to cover his nose. Throwing her weight into his body, she swept her leg around his. The move dropped him to the ground again. His hand flailed and caught her jaw. She reeled backward into the brick wall. She was breathing hard, and the pain in her face edged stars into her vision.

Now was the time for flight. She grabbed Kayla by the wrist and pulled her in a run-walk toward the corner of the building, hoping for more light and more people. Crying, the girl stumbled along. Monroe barely stopped herself from yelling at her to move faster, faster. She risked a glance behind them. Dylan was up and weaving in their direction, his hand cupped over his nose. Her SUV was in the far corner of the crowded lot. They would never make it.

A man appeared, limping slightly and with his big body backlit. His face was shadowed, but of course she knew. Cade. She couldn't summon any sort of resentment at him being here. All she felt was relief.

Cade didn't say a word, didn't even make eye contact,

as she and Kayla slipped by him. His face was hard, the ferocity a revelation. Monroe stopped behind him and supported a trembling Kayla around the waist. The danger had passed like a storm, and as her adrenaline seeped away her muscles quivered under Kayla's weight.

She was safe with Cade. The knowledge was something she understood without question. Like the sky was blue or the Earth was round.

"Did you touch either one of these women?" Cade's voice thrummed with a threat.

Even Dylan sensed an alpha predator. He stopped fifteen feet from Cade. "The blonde shoved me."

"I'm taking that for a 'yes.' Only a coward beats up on women half his size. How would you do against me?"

"I could take you, old man." The snarling menace had faded from Dylan's voice, revealing a weak bravado.

"Give it your best shot." Cade gave a come-and-get-me gesture with both hands.

Dylan withered, smaller and younger than her impression at the height of her fear. If he hadn't been drunk, he might have done the smart thing and thrown himself on Cade's mercy. Instead, Dylan closed the distance between them and tried to land a blow. Cade blocked it with his left hand, threw a straight jab followed by a left uppercut. Dylan swayed for a moment before toppling like a cut tree.

Kayla broke free and knelt at Dylan's side. She ran her hands over his face, dabbing at the blood dripping out of his nose. Cade cradled his left hand to his chest, muttering.

Feeling suddenly unsure, Monroe sidled closer to him. "Let me see your hand. Does it hurt?"

"Yes, it effing hurts." He held out his left hand, and she took it in both of hers. Without her having to direct him, he made a fist and then spread his hand wide.

The bouncer approached, his bulked-up arms swinging wide from his body, his legs sticking out of too-long shorts and comically skinny by comparison. "Why's all hell gotta cut loose on my shift?"

Cade stepped forward. "What's up, Butch? How's your daddy been?"

"Cade Fournette? Dadgum, it's been a while." They exchanged handshakes. "Family's same old, same old. You should swing by the house. What's going on? Need some help?" With Cade, the bouncer was all sunshine and helpfulness.

"The d-bag on the ground was messing with these two ladies. Can you get him sobered up and home?"

"Sure thing. I tossed his buddies out for starting a fight inside not five minutes ago. Three against one." Butch hauled Dylan over a shoulder.

Monroe caught Butch's arm. "Hold up. Were they fighting a man with a blond ponytail?"

"That's the one. They got some good licks in, but the dude didn't want me calling the cops. He rode off on a motorcycle a couple of minutes ago."

When Kayla tried to follow Dylan, Monroe looped an arm around her elbow and steered her toward the parking lot. "I'm taking you home and staying until your mama gets off work. We need to talk."

Cade fell into step with them, and she glanced over, not sure what to say or do. "Thanks. I guess I'll see you later?"

"I'm following you. My guess is the punk will come to mad as a sack of crawfish and might come looking for one or both of you."

She took a breath, twingy pains shooting through her jaw. Even though needing his help encroached on her well-manicured streak of independence, she couldn't deny having him around would settle her nerves, because she'd already considered the same scenario. After weighing pride and common sense, she nodded. "All right, I'd appreciate that."

Chapter Nine

Tension flowed out of Cade's shoulders. He'd half-expected Monroe to tell him she didn't want him around. Or to tell him to go to hell for interfering. The fear and frustration that had overtaken him after she'd hung up on him still boiled close to the surface.

He'd been itching for a fight, but the kid went down with two blows. Of course, he hadn't considered the state of his hand on that left uppercut. The healing nerves shot pain all the way up his arm.

He'd parked his truck behind her SUV, effectively blocking her in. The Rivershack Tavern was packed. He'd wasted a good five minutes searching the bar floor for her, even sending a woman into the restroom to check. The relief at finding her with the girl around back had been tempered by the panic and determination on her face and the man following close behind.

Even with the threat gone, Cade settled a hand on her lower back and kept pace with her and Kayla. The girl stumbled, crying softly, Monroe's arm around her shoulders seemingly the only thing keeping her up. How the girl could waste a single tear on that abusive jerk was beyond him.

He limped ahead and opened the passenger door so Monroe could help the girl onto the seat. The interior lights illuminated the red slash of color covering her left cheek and jaw. Bile burned his throat.

Monroe closed the door and pulled her keys out of her front pocket. In her shorts and tank top and with her hair around her shoulders, she didn't look much older than the girl she'd rescued.

Before she could walk around to the driver's side, he grabbed her hand. "Did he hit you, too?"

She touched her jaw. "I knocked him off-balance and his hand got me on the way down. Collateral damage. I've been hurt worse training in the gym with your sister."

"This wasn't training." He dropped her hand to cup her nape and run his thumb along her jawline, tilting her face toward the flickering parking lot light. "Is the girl badly hurt?"

"Her name is Kayla. She'll be okay." Her voice wavered as if she wasn't quite convinced.

With his left hand still hooked around her neck, he pulled his phone out of his pocket. "I'm calling the police."

She grabbed his wrist. "No. She didn't want me to call. She's ashamed and embarrassed and I don't think she would end up pressing charges."

"You could do it."

She looked over her shoulder. The girl had drawn her knees up. Her face was hidden in her arms, but her shoulders shook like she was crying. "If I do, she'll never trust me again, Cade. Then who will she call if she gets into a fix like this again?"

"Why does it have to be you?"

The look she gave him made him feel like a selfish

a-hole, which was a perfectly accurate description of him the last few years.

"Why not me?" she said softly. "Someone has to stand up for these girls. Like you stood up for me."

Jesus, that night. That fateful night had come back around. But he wasn't the same boy he'd been then. He'd cut every tie to Cottonbloom, or tried to at any rate. Even his brother and sister had learned not to rely on him for anything more than making a monthly phone call and cutting a check.

Yet Monroe had taken on more and more until she was so tightly bound to Cottonbloom she couldn't move. Her mother, the girls, Tally and Regan, her clients. And him.

She slipped by him and slid behind the wheel, starting the SUV. Cade did the same and backed up so she could pull out first. Kayla lived in a lower-middle-class neighborhood miles from the river. Yellow pollen and grime streaked the white vinyl siding, but the porch was swept and a swing hung from the rafters, swaying slightly in the breeze along with a set of seashell wind chimes made by young hands.

Cade followed them inside. Monroe disappeared into the back of the house with Kayla, and he wandered into the kitchen. Riffling through the freezer, he pulled out a pack of frozen peas and covered his sore hand.

The house was neat, the kitchen spotless, and knick-knacks and pictures of a pretty woman and a girl at various ages covered every flat surface of the small den. No sign of a father. Could have been a bad divorce or could be he'd never been around.

He picked up the closest picture. Kayla, minus her two front teeth, sat on the bank of the river with an old-fashioned cane fishing pole, her gap-toothed grin infectious. His conscience twinged, and an old protectiveness reared. The murmur of voices came from one of the back rooms.

He retreated to the porch swing, the chains creaking under his weight. His hand had stopped throbbing, and he removed the bag of peas to do the exercises Monroe had taught him. He didn't know how much time passed before the front door opened.

"She's asleep and going to feel terrible tomorrow between the slap and the hangover." Monroe's step was hesitant.

"Come sit. We'll wait for her mama." He scooched down the swing.

She joined him, tucking her legs to the side, and massaged his hand absently, as if she couldn't help but give comfort to those around her even if she was the one hurt.

He shifted on the bench and tilted her face to his. "You sure your jaw is okay?"

"It hardly hurts now." Her voice thickened, and she sounded close to tears of her own. "From a couple of things she said just now, I don't think this is the first time he's knocked her around. I don't know what to do."

He tugged his hand free and wrapped his arm around her shoulders, pulling her into his side. She didn't fight him, notching her forehead into his neck and snaking her arm around his chest.

"You've done what you can, sweetheart." As hard as he worked and as much as he sacrificed, Tally and Sawyer never had what their friends had. His best times were doing something foolish like buying Sawyer new baseball cleats or spending money they didn't have to get Tally the brand of jeans everyone else was wearing. The looks on their faces had made the battle worth it. "It'll never feel like enough, but trust me, you're making a difference."

"Teaching them how to fend off a physical attack is one thing. How can I make them understand they deserve more than to be called names and pushed around?" She sounded more than physically tired. She sounded close to giving up.

Working two jobs, taking extra shifts, then hunting and trapping at night had left him in a constant state of exhaustion, but he'd done what he'd had to do, day in and day out, ignoring the creeping desolation. He searched for the right words and came up empty. "I don't have the answers, but you have to keep trying, right?"

"I feel like a hamster on a wheel. Working, working, working, and getting nowhere. Kayla was one of the first girls to join the group three years ago. Three years, Cade, and nothing I've done has changed the path of her life. Nothing."

"That's not true. She called you, didn't she? What if she hadn't had that lifeline? Would she have come out of that bathroom and gone home with that punk? Maybe things would have escalated even further. She knew she could count on you."

"I guess." Doubt riddled her voice. She pulled from under his arm and leaned forward, her elbows on her knees. "I need to get a counselor in on a regular basis."

"How much does one cost?"

"More than I can afford at the moment." A bitter note flavored her words, but determination swept it aside. "This fund-raiser is important. I could have a counselor in place by July."

Cade wanted to write a check and hand her the key to the next phase of her program. She'd never accept it from him. Not even to help her girls. It would make her too dependent on him.

"I don't want them to end up like me." Her voice was so soft, it took a few heartbeats for the message to register.

"What are you talking about? You're successful, smart, gorgeous, kindhearted. You're a saint compared to most people."

"I'm so not a saint." She began rocking them in a jerky forward and back rhythm. "You want to hear something insane? In a way, I'm envious of Kayla. Her ability to love with blind devotion. I think there's something seriously wrong with me."

Her confession was important. Not only because of the content but also because she was telling *him*. "Why do you think there's something wrong with you?" He kept his voice at a whisper.

"Because I can't . . ." She leaned her head back, her neck pillowed over his arm, her gaze directed into the darkness of the rafters. "I saw what love did to my mother. She believed whatever a man told her—good or bad. Whether it's that she's beautiful or worthless. And men say whatever they need in order to get what they want."

A darkness skated on the edge of her words. A darkness he recognized. He was the last person who should be lecturing her on love. "That's not love, Monroe."

"Well, it's all I know." Only the clinking of the seashell wind chimes broke the expectant silence. "Why did you come tonight? Not that I'm not grateful. I am. But why?" Other questions hung unsaid but understood. *What do you want from me? Are you using me?*

He swallowed. The games he'd played with women in the past seemed an immature pastime. He had been a user the last few years. Looking back made him feel like Flat Stanley—a cardboard cutout moving through life. The irony was almost laughable. Almost.

"When you hung up on me . . ." He took a deep breath. Was he seriously putting himself out there?

"You were mad."

"A little," he admitted. "But more than that, I was concerned. No, more than concerned. Terrified. I've spent years not worrying about anyone else but myself."

"That's not true. What about Tally and Sawyer?"

"After I left Cottonbloom, I wasn't around for them. Not like I should have been. I told myself they were better off without me. Told myself they didn't need me anymore. But being back . . ." He shook his head, not sure what to say. Like a tree transplanted from a desert to fertile ground, his roots were inching deeper and deeper by the day. Roots he'd hacked off years ago.

"The thought of you hurt, hurts me." The confession ripped from his chest, leaving his heart exposed and beating too fast. His name falling from her lips acted like a salve and the arm she wrapped tight around his chest a bandage. He dropped his face into her hair, soft and smelling of summer.

"I was scared tonight." Her voice trembled.

"It's all right to be scared. Bravery is about doing something even though it scares you." Once the words were out, he wondered if he hadn't directed them at himself as much as her. A reminder. He'd been brave once. He'd done things that terrified him because his family had needed him to.

The day he'd walked into the pharmacy and slipped the cough medicine into his pocket or the night he'd taken refuge in a gulley when it was clear he wouldn't make it home before a tornado-spawning storm caught him. Attending parent-teacher conferences even though he was still a kid himself, and a dropout at that. Walking into the food bank to accept charity for the first time. All terrifying.

Even though he'd built a company, become successful, he hadn't done anything truly brave since he'd left this place. Maybe that's what he'd been trying to recapture by climbing hand over hand up a sheer face of rock or jumping out of a plane, but like he knew every bend in the river, he knew none of his crazy exploits were true bravery.

Headlights blinded him like the flash of a camera. An older-model sedan pulled into the driveway. He'd been so caught up in Monroe, he hadn't even heard the car approach. He stood at the top of the porch stairs. A fortyish-year-old woman climbed out. He recognized her as a faded version from the photos in the den.

"Stacy." Monroe joined him. "Kayla is fine, but something happened tonight."

The woman quick-stepped to them, her gray factory uniform wrinkled and grease stained. "Ohmigod, was she in an accident?"

"Nothing like that. She called me from the Tavern."

"What was she doing there?" The shock in Stacy's voice was real and heartbreaking.

Monroe led the woman inside, glancing over her shoulder at him, the message clear. He was free to go.

Monroe rubbed her hands down her face and leaned against the old-fashioned wood paneling in the hallway. After Monroe imparted the events of the evening and her concerns about Dylan, Stacy sat on the edge of Kayla's bed and tucked her in like a child, brushing her hair back from her face.

Monroe leaned against the wall in the hallway, their murmuring drifting out in bits and pieces. Maybe Stacy's advice would mean more and go further than Monroe's. After all, she was as screwed up as Kayla in her own way.

Heat whooshed through her body and she pressed her hands against her cheeks. What did Cade think of her now? She had tried to keep things casual, but nothing had ever been casual with him. Her confessions on the swing had sounded crazy even to her own ears. She'd barely ever admitted those things to herself alone in the dark, much less said them aloud.

Stacy emerged from Kayla's room and Monroe straightened. Stacy's eyes were red and puffy, and creases bracketed her mouth, giving her a sad, weary look.

"Thanks for getting her home safe, Monroe." Stacy led them into her small kitchen, pulled a bottle of vodka out of the freezer, and held up two glasses.

Monroe waved her off. Stacy poured a good measure of vodka into one glass and took a sip. A sheen of tears came to her eyes, and her chin wobbled before she said, "I'll admit when you started that program down at Tally's gym I thought, 'A little rich 'Sip wants to sleep better at night.' But you've proven yourself a true friend to my little girl, and I appreciate it. I do."

"Dylan is trouble."

"I know. But if I tell her she can't see him, I worry that will drive her toward him and away from me." Stacy pulled out a kitchen chair and sat heavily, taking another sip.

Being a mother wasn't about making cookies and attending recitals; it was this. The hard stuff. Picking up the pieces of broken hearts and helping reassemble them, dealing with insecurities, teaching children how to stand on their own.

"You'll figure it out. I'm here if you need me." She squeezed Stacy's shoulder and backed away but stopped in the kitchen doorway. "Lock up tight after I go, all right?"

"I will." Stacy killed the rest of the vodka, the empty glass thudding against the table. The corner of her mouth drew up. "I have a shotgun in the closet if necessary."

Monroe stepped outside and heard the dead bolt flip and the rattle of the chain. Cade's truck was still parked behind her SUV. She wasn't even surprised.

The chains on the porch swing squawked as he stood. "How'd things go?"

"As well as can be expected, I suppose." Kayla was her

mama's burden now, and selfishly Monroe was relieved. She led the way down the porch steps, his footsteps sounding behind her. "You didn't have to stick around."

"I'm following you to your house to make sure you're safe."

Independence battled with a warm feeling of being taken care of. A new experience. A scary one. Did it make her seem weak? "If on the off chance Dylan shows up, I can handle him."

He stopped her at the curb between their vehicles. "No doubt, but take pity on me. I'll be worthless worrying about you if I don't see you home."

After a moment's hesitation, she shrugged and tried not to let the fuzzy feeling in her chest show on her face. "Well, come on then."

She slipped into her SUV and set off, uncommonly aware of his headlights and the grind of the old truck's gears behind her. As she got closer to her house, she grew more alert, her hands tightening on the steering wheel. Even though she didn't expect trouble, it was a relief to see her house deserted and dark, no strange cars parked on the street.

His truck rumbled off behind hers. She walked up to the driver's side as he got out and gestured around them. "See? No one here."

"I'll feel even better if you let me take a look around inside."

She should insist he leave. Instead, she chucked her head toward the front door. The truth was she wasn't ready to be alone.

Only the sound of the churning air-conditioning broke the silence of the house. Like a policeman in a movie, he checked all her rooms. Amusement had her biting her lip while she plopped onto her couch.

Cade was a big man, and his dark beard made him

appear that much more intimidating. No wonder Dylan had looked like he might wet himself when they'd faced down. He prowled back into the den, a note of aggression flavoring his movements. Yet he wouldn't hurt her . . . or any woman for that matter.

An idea flashed, and she moved to the edge of the couch at the surge of energy. Facing a flesh-and-blood man had been different from beating up body bags or flipping fellow martial arts students. There was a line never crossed in the gym that didn't exist in dark alleys.

"Discover anything?" she asked with fake casualness.

"You don't hang your towel up, your flip-flop collection might qualify for a world record, and a couple of rabid dust bunnies have taken up residence under your bed."

She laughed. She couldn't help it. "I wasn't expecting company."

"Good to know," he murmured, giving her a speculative look she couldn't interpret.

"What are you up to Tuesday afternoon?" The question burst out of her. She'd meant to ease into the conversation.

"Let's see. . . ." He silently ticked off items on his fingers, before letting his hands fall with a shrug and smile. "You know I have absolutely nothing going on."

"I don't suppose you'd like to help me out? It can be in place of your therapy at the office." The gym work would be as good as if not better than the exercises she had him do in her office.

"What kind of help?" Her enthusiasm apparently wasn't contagious. He sounded suspicious.

"I need a dummy, and you'd be perfect."

The look on his face was priceless—shades of shock and amusement and insult. She burst out laughing.

"A dummy, huh?" He sat so close her body tilted in his direction with the shifting of the cushion under his weight.

"Not like an idiot, but a real, live man to stand in for Bubba."

"Bubba?"

"The stuffed dummy I use with the girls at Tally's gym." She turned to face him, one leg up on the couch and tucked against his. "I realized something tonight. My training has been sterile. Always in a gym against inanimate objects or other students. There's been no sense of unpredictability."

"Let me get this straight. You want me to pretend to attack a bunch of young girls so they can practice kneeing me where it hurts the most and breaking my nose?" His dry tone put a damper on her excitement.

"Put like that, I don't suppose it sounds very appealing." She pulled a loose thread out of the corner of the cushion. "Forget it. It was a silly idea."

He slipped a finger under her chin and tilted her head up. "It's never silly to want to help someone. I'll do it, but my crotch is strictly off-limits."

She tossed her arms around his neck for a girlish hug. When she should have pulled back she couldn't, and the simple hug of gratitude morphed into something else entirely.

He smelled good. No, better than good, he smelled delectable. Like she wanted to sample him. She nosed into the wiry, tickling hairs of his beard. One of his hands drifted up her spine to cup the back of her head. He pulled away but didn't release her. His green eyes searched her face. She wasn't sure what he was looking for or what he found in her eyes. Maybe the same swirl of conflicting emotions she found in his.

She wanted to kiss him, needed to know. Needed to know if the fantasies she'd nurtured all these years were foolish. Her heart accelerated like hitting the first peak of a roller coaster as she leaned in and fluttered her eyes closed. She brushed her lips against his. The hand in her hair clamped tighter, holding her in place. The slight tug sent pleasure to every nerve in her body.

His lips were soft and dry. She pulled his bottom lip between her teeth and ran her tongue along the smooth flesh. His beard tickled her chin and her upper lip, the added friction undeniably arousing. He didn't deepen the kiss or push her away. A mewl of frustration escaped her throat as she threaded her fingers in his hair.

"What are we doing?" His lips moved against hers.

"I'm trying to kiss you, and you're sitting there like a bump on a log."

His chest rumbled an instant before he took control. He banded his arm tight around her and kissed her back. Alarms should have clanged in her head yet didn't. The trust she'd settled on him as a young girl had faded like a picture in the sun but hadn't disappeared.

The reality of Cade Fournette didn't disappoint. He didn't go too far, too fast; instead, he explored her lips, slowly, thoroughly, gently. The kiss was a seduction.

Usually, she had a difficult time shutting her thoughts down while kissing. Worries about what the man wanted or what she didn't want or even her patient list for the next day would steal her attention. She'd never understood the attraction of making out for hours.

She finally got it. With Cade, her body pulled the plug on her brain. It was too busy sending and receiving pleasure signals.

Time slowed. Each nip and brush on each other's lips marked the passing of the minutes. She twisted closer, more of her weight settling against him. His gentleness only threw tinder on the fire, making her frantic for more. More of his mouth on hers, his hands on her body, his body over hers, easing her ache. More of everything. Lost in the present, she forgot about the past.

He brushed his tongue across her upper lip, and she opened her mouth on a noise she'd never heard come out of her. Something close to a whimpery, begging moan. Their tongues tangled. She straddled one of his legs. Her knee pressed up against something hard that had her squirming.

He turned his face to the side but didn't shift her away. She nuzzled into the hair at his temple. His chest rose and fell with the same urgency hers did.

"Monroe, this is . . . crazy."

Not amazing, incredible, life changing, but crazy? The heat of passion took a detour into embarrassment. The kind that had her wanting a sinkhole to open at their feet. Or maybe an asteroid to hit the Earth.

She scrambled off him and stared toward her mantle. What had come over her? She'd never jumped on top of a man like that. "Sorry. I don't even know . . ."

"Don't be sorry. I've been thinking about kissing you since you walked into that PT room and told me to take my pants off."

She quit chewing her bottom lip and glanced in his direction. "Then why is this crazy?"

"Because of who you are and who I am. I've only been back a week and we barely know each other. Plus, you have to know . . . I'm not sticking around."

She veered from confusion to disappointment. His announcement he would be leaving Cottonbloom wasn't a news flash. A slow-festering thorn worked into her heart at the truth, but his other excuses rang false.

"What do you mean, who I am?"

"You were always too good for me. Sweet and innocent. I'm still a swamp rat. Nothing will change that."

The past defined her in ways she could name and in ways she was yet discovering. It seemed she wasn't the only one. Cade's past as the high-school dropout forced to accept charity haunted him even though he could probably buy the biggest, oldest house in Cottonbloom, Mississippi, if he desired.

They were at a crossroads, maybe the first of many. Past or present. Which would define them?

Bravery is about doing something even though it scares you. His words came back to roost on her chest, the pressure almost too much to bear. With reflexes honed in the gym, she was back in his lap, straddling both his legs and fisting her hands in his hair. She tugged his head back until they were face-to-face, her in the dominant position.

"I'm not sweet and innocent, Cade Fournette. You can lie to yourself all you want, but I know you better than anyone on earth. I know your secrets. And you know mine. If that scares you? Well, you need to man up and get brave."

His eyes flared. She'd surprised him. Heckfire, she'd surprised herself. Should she move from surprise into shock? Was *she* brave enough? She dropped her mouth back to his. This time he took control on contact. He flipped her and pressed her back into the cushions, his weight over her. His lips moved down her neck, sliding the strap of her tank top and bra over the curve of her shoulder, his lips following.

He gently bit the sensitive skin of her collarbone. Her breast ached for his mouth and he was close, so close. She arched toward him. He stopped, breathing hard, and propped himself up on his elbows over her. His green eyes were hypnotizing. If he took her hand, she would follow him anywhere, even to her bed.

"I should go." His voice was rough, and the press of his body informed her in no uncertain terms, he wanted her.

Pride edged out her bravery. She refused to beg, sliding her hands from around his neck to his chest and pushing. "Then go."

He rose quickly, and she was left to grab the cushion for balance. Cade was doing the smart thing. Her body argued fiercely that being smart was overrated.

"I'm not used to playing the gentleman." The thread of humor dissipated a portion of the sexual tension.

"What are you used to playing then?" She adjusted the strap of her tank and stood.

"A country boy who isn't afraid to get a little dirty." He pushed her hair over her shoulders, his fingers trailing over bare skin, igniting a path of need. "But you deserve more than that," he added in a whisper, moving to the door.

She considered shaking some sense into him or kicking his shin or jumping him again. None of it would work. Just like telling herself Sam had no power over her anymore didn't stop the fear each time he invaded her dreams.

Somehow she would have to show Cade that she wasn't the same girl he remembered. Or was a stronger version of that girl. A version who didn't need his protection. She needed him in other ways now. Ways she didn't understand herself. Not yet.

He had one foot out the door when she said, "We're still on for Tuesday afternoon, right?"

He hesitated but nodded. "Lock up after I'm gone, okay?"

Once she'd turned the dead bolt, she leaned against the door. While she was confused about the storm of emotions seething through her body and wondered about the future, there was one thing she knew with certainty—Cade Fournette had felt the same rush from their kisses as she had.

Chapter Ten

Monroe peeked around the redbrick corner of the dry cleaner to the other side of the river. Regan poked her under the ribs, making her flinch. "What are they doing?"

"Talking and looking at the wall. Sawyer is making grand hand gestures, and Cade is pointing at something." Monroe ducked back around to face Regan. "You know, you might want to consider glasses. And you're the one with the binoculars."

"I don't want to be obvious. What now?"

Monroe looked to heaven. Considering it was Sunday, maybe Jesus would take pity on her. She peeked around the side again. "Sawyer is hauling a big ladder over, and Cade is unloading what looks to be several gallons of paint from his truck bed."

"That mildewed brick wall is an eyesore. I'll bet he feels the need to do something to compete with our gazebo."

The framed shell of a gazebo stood in a common area on the Mississippi side. The beautiful riot of wildflowers on the opposite bank emphasized the barren mix of grassy weed and dirt on the Mississippi side. If Regan won the festival competition, her vision would turn the common area into the centerpiece of the town and a place to gather.

"What are they doing now?" Regan asked.

"Sawyer is fanning himself and . . . yes, he's stripping buck naked," she said in as serious a voice as she could muster.

Regan jumped out from behind the wall, the binoculars to her face. "He is not."

Monroe tried to contain her laughter. "Nope. But you seemed *real* interested in the possibility. By the way, that wasn't obvious at all."

Regan retreated, hidden once more. "Sawyer and I have been over for years. Yes, he was once an important part of my life, but people change. They grow up and let stupid dreams go and that's that."

Regan's voice held a vulnerability Monroe hadn't heard for a long time. Her friend generally went through life with a brash confidence that, depending on who was in her crosshairs, drew either admiration or annoyance.

Regan and Sawyer had ended things in an explosion whose aftershocks were still being felt. While they hadn't flaunted their relationship due to Regan's mother, people had whispered about them. The beautiful, rich Mississippi girl with the poor, yet ambitious, Louisiana boy, but like Romeo and Juliet, the ending was tragic.

Animosity had taken root in the burned-out ground, blooming since both sides of town had entered the magazine competition. Monroe feared the festivals would tear the towns further apart.

Regan pushed off the wall. "Here comes my hired help."

Delmar Fournette parked his truck on the curb. Monroe looked beyond him, but only a handful of people were out and none of them were headed in their direction with a toolbox except for Delmar. Monroe grabbed Regan's arm. "You didn't."

A calculating smile replaced any vulnerability on Regan's face. "He was happy for the work."

Monroe shook her head and peeked back around the corner. Sawyer and Cade had started on opposite ends of the wall, yellow spreading like the sunrise. Red would have been more practical, but already the wall looked brighter and added a splash of cheery color to the row of buildings.

The toolbox bumped Delmar's leg on every step, tools clanging and tinking. "Hey there, Monroe, Ms. Mayor."

Regan glanced at her cuff watch. "You're a little late, Mr. Fournette. We're already behind schedule."

Monroe gave Regan's ankle a little kick. If she'd been wearing pointy-toed stilettos like Regan instead of sneakers, her nudge might have made more of an impression. Monroe trailed after Regan and Delmar, listening with only half an ear to her instructions.

They stepped out of the shadows into the sun. Although it was hot, the air had shed its moisture sometime during the night, leaving things comfortable—as long as you didn't move around too much.

Regan grabbed her hand and pulled her back toward the street. "Let's grab something to drink and enjoy the show."

Monroe followed Regan into a small café that did major business during the week. Sundays were slow. Bigger cities lured residents away for shopping or entertainment on the weekends. The festival was the kickoff to what Regan hoped was a revitalization of downtown Cottonbloom. Since the beginning of her term as mayor, she'd offered incentives for new businesses to move into empty storefronts and encouraged the existing ones to spruce up.

Bypassing an iced coffee for an ice-cream cone of

butter pecan, Monroe strolled next to Regan toward the common area. Hammering echoed off the brick storefronts. While Monroe didn't approve of Regan constantly needling Sawyer, she couldn't deny it was entertaining.

"I had dinner at Sawyer's house the other night and—"

"What?" Regan grabbed her upper arm, perfectly manicured nails biting into her skin. "What did he say about me? I mean, about the festival?"

"He wanted me to tell you he booked the Cottonbloom, Mississippi, marching band for his parade. Got his boss to donate some instruments."

"Sneaky little jerk." Regan dropped Monroe's arm, walking faster. "How did he say it? Casually, like it was no biggie?"

"No, he was pretty much thumbing his nose and chanting, 'Nana-nana-boo-boo,' as jerks will do."

They sat on a buckling wooden bench at the edge of the common area. Regan was picking the polish off her thumbnail. Things must be dire indeed. "Next time you see him, tell him I got the Shriners. And their little cars and funny hats, too."

Monroe held her hands up. "It's not like I regularly hang with him. I was dropping the fund-raiser invitation off for Tally and ended up staying for dinner. A onetime thing."

"Mrs. Tarwater is outdoing herself with this shindig. She should be able to raise some good money for your girls."

An icky feeling she was using the Tarwaters burrowed deeper. The picture of Kayla crying over the boy who'd left his mark on her strengthened her resolve. "I had to rescue one of the girls from the Rivershack Tavern."

Regan gasped. "What happened?"

Monroe gave her an abbreviated version. The fact that she left Cade out of her story niggled at her conscience, but she wasn't ready to discuss the complicated range of emotions he instilled. Or maybe because she'd never told anyone about him; habits were hard to break. He'd always been her secret.

"I do appreciate everything Mrs. Tarwater is doing, but I hate wondering if they're expecting something to happen between me and Andrew." Monroe stared across the river at Cade.

"Look, you need the money. Go into this assuming Mrs. Tarwater is doing it out of the goodness of her heart."

"Ri-i-ight." Monroe drew the word out.

A beat of silence passed before they burst out laughing.

"It's not like you've been stringing Andrew along or something. The opposite in fact. You have nothing to feel guilty about. Take the money and put it to good use."

Regan was right. Monroe hadn't promised anything to Andrew. Even a lick across the ice cream couldn't counteract the sourness in the pit of her stomach. She'd considered dipping into her own savings, but that money was there for her mother.

Monroe was putting back money each month to pay for a highly recommended, ridiculously expensive residential program for alcoholics. The trick was getting her mother to admit she needed the help. So far, she had waved off any notion her "occasional overindulgences" were a sign of something more serious.

Regan didn't know how bad things were with her mother. No one did. And after what Sam had insinuated, Monroe's worry had escalated. Although nothing indicated her mother was bingeing again, she was a master of hiding it.

The sound of Delmar's tools and the occasional trilling birdsong filled the space with white noise. She raised the binoculars and focused on the men working across the river. Cade had put his paint roller down and was squirting water from a bottle into his mouth. His dark beard trailed down his neck, his red T-shirt a flag of color against the yellow bricks.

He glanced in her direction. His gaze bounced over her but snapped back, and he angled toward her. An invisible connection tugged her forward until she was sitting on the edge of the aged wooden bench. The draw to him was becoming stronger with every passing day. His hands went to the hem of his T-shirt. He wouldn't. Not in the middle of town.

He did.

"Sweet baby Jesus," she muttered, and blew a shuddery breath out.

She should quit staring at him through the binoculars. It was pathetic and stalkerish. Worse still, he could see her being pathetic and stalkerish. She pressed the binoculars tighter to her eyes and ignored the ice cream dripping on her hand.

His chest was phenomenal. Not jacked into ridiculous lines, but thick and muscled. Solid. Dark hair to match his beard shaded his pecs. His gaze bored into her with a challenge she wanted desperately to accept. Good grief, could he see not only at night but at crazy distances also?

"What do you see?" Regan squinted and reached for the binoculars. A brief tug-of-war ensued before Monroe gave them up. Regan looped the strap around her neck, took a swig of her iced coffee, and raised them. She jerked forward a few inches. "Mercy me. I can see why you've been panting after the man. Cade Fournette is hotter than a Mississippi brush fire."

"I have not been panting. That makes it sound real romantic, Regan. Geez." Licking her ice cream turned into a sensuous action. Was his skin salty from sweat? Even though sweet butter dominated her taste buds, her imagination was vivid.

Regan lowered the binoculars as she swiveled slowly to face her. "Romantic? So is this more than a lust fest?"

Monroe chuffed to cover her misstep and licked at her cone. "It's . . . something." She took the binoculars back as Regan hummed. With the strap still around Regan's neck, Monroe yanked her close until they were nearly cheek to cheek.

If anything, she had underestimated the beauty of the man. The white stripe of his underwear showed at the top of his slouchy elastic-waisted athletic shorts. She trailed her binocular-enhanced gaze up the line of hair along tight abs to his shoulders, broad and muscled.

His body shifted, changed stance, his singular focus transferring to his uncle working on the gazebo. Cade grabbed Sawyer's arm and pointed.

"They've noticed Delmar," Monroe whispered even though no one was around to hear. She slumped back on the bench, her body weak with aftereffects of the tension that had held her taut.

Regan grabbed up the binoculars. Monroe didn't need them to see Sawyer throw down his roller and stalk toward her and Regan.

"They're coming over." Regan whipped the binocular strap over her head and set the binoculars on the bench behind her.

Sawyer was over the bridge and in front of them in a few long strides. The air around him thickened like a storm cloud ready to unleash. He whistled and Delmar poked his head from behind one of the supports.

"What the hell, Uncle Delmar?" Sawyer threw his hands up.

"What's up, Sawyer? I like the yellow you picked." Delmar came over, hiking his tool belt up with one hand and waving his hammer toward the wall.

While Delmar and Sawyer volleyed back and forth and

with Regan nearly bouncing on the bench and clapping her hands at how well her plan to gig Sawyer was working, Monroe turned her attention to Cade.

He wiped over his face and down his neck with his shirt, leaving a damp stain on the red cotton, and tucked it into his shorts, the waistband pulling down another inch. He wore a common store brand. She was surprised they weren't Calvin Klein's.

"Low blow getting Uncle Delmar to build your little gazebo." His low, husky voice rippled through her like pebbles tossed into a placid lake.

"I'm just sitting here enjoying some ice cream. But hey, it's a job and Delmar is making money."

Her unattended ice cream dripped on her hand again, and she licked it off, her gaze rising to look at Cade beneath her lashes. His pecs flexed as he took a step closer. She stared at the line of dark hair bisecting his abs and crossed her legs.

"That looks good," he whispered, somehow imbuing the simple words with a wealth of sexual innuendo. Or maybe that was her hopeful brain's translation.

"Want some?" She held out the cone. Was it weird to offer someone a lick of your ice cream? The beats of silence and stillness made her decide it was very weird, but before she had time to retract the offer he leaned over and propped his hand on the back of the bench. Very slowly, he wrapped his other hand around hers and brought the cone to his mouth.

He took one strong swipe right across the top and then licked up the sides with systematic precision, finishing with a swirl. She clenched her legs together, her entire insides performing a jig.

She imagined him between her legs performing a similar alchemy. The hand under his began to tremble and her entire body flushed. With her free hand, she patted at the sudden sheen of sweat on her forehead. As his final shot, he cleaned a line of sticky ice cream that had dripped on her index finger with a long, slow pass of his tongue.

The clang of metal on metal penetrated her daze. Delmar was packing up his tools. "Sorry, Ms. Mayor, hate to see my nephew's shorts in a wad. Guess you'll have to find another handyman." He checked his watch, hummed, and muttered more to himself than to them, "Might have time to get a little fishing in."

Delmar headed back to his truck, whistling. Sawyer stalked over, and Cade straightened, letting go of Monroe's hand. Regan faced off with the brothers as if she wanted to wipe all Fournettes off the face of the earth by poking them in the eyes with her stilettos. Monroe rose but kept to the neutral zone.

"My shorts are not in a wad." Sawyer's voice was defensive. "But hiring my uncle was dirty."

Regan put on a falsely sweet smile that had won her numerous pageant crowns. "We agreed these festivals are for the good of our towns and have nothing to do with whatever ancient history we might share."

"But you . . ." Sawyer ruffled his hair, looking discombobulated. "You hired Delmar to pick at me."

"I needed someone good with their hands and your uncle needed a job. Now neither of us has what we need, thanks to you." Without looking in her direction, Regan said, "Let's go, Monroe."

Old loyalties were difficult to put aside, especially when their motto throughout high school and college had been "chicks before you-know-whats." Regan performed an about-face, which must have been difficult in her heels on the weedy grass. Monroe trailed behind her, throwing a glance over her shoulder at Cade.

With his arms crossed over his bare chest, he looked

intimidating, his biceps ridiculously jacked, yet something in his face spoke of amusement. He raised his chin in her direction, and she could have sworn he winked.

Her insides fluttered, and she turned around before she tripped and humiliated herself. Regan was speed-walking. As soon as they turned the corner, out of sight from the common area, she leaned against the brick wall and rotated first one ankle and then the other.

"I can't believe Sawyer thought I hired Delmar just to get a rise out of him."

"Hello?" Monroe tossed the rest of her cone in the trash and joined Regan against the wall, the rough bricks biting through her clothes. "You can lie to me, but don't lie to yourself. You poke at Sawyer like a toddler pokes at an anthill. You can't be surprised when he bites back."

Regan huffed and kept her gaze directed down.

Monroe chewed on the inside of her mouth and watched her friend kick pebbles with the pointy end of her black heel. "I know he hurt you, Regan, but it was a long time ago."

Regan had buried the details of what had happened between her and Sawyer. Considering Monroe had kept the reality of her mother's problems and her association with Cade to herself all these years, she'd never pressed Regan for the gory details, but the shell-shocked look on Regan's face when she'd walked into their dorm room had spoken volumes.

Regan had grown up with everything. She had been Miss Cottonbloom and the head cheerleader. She was popular and confident and sought after, if not a little spoiled. But from the moment her path crossed with Sawyer Fournette's during the annual Cottonbloom–Cottonbloom football game she'd only had eyes for him.

Monroe slipped an arm around the usually stoic Regan and squeezed her around the waist. "He was your first real boyfriend, and maybe he's sometimes a turkey whose tail feathers you want to pluck out one by one, but he loves his uncle and he loves his town."

Regan tensed. "I love my town, too. This festival is not some evil plan to get back at Sawyer for something that happened a decade ago." Her voice had taken on a more mayoral tone. "If the magazine hadn't insisted on Labor Day, I would have been happy to hold my festival a different weekend."

"So beating Sawyer wouldn't make you happy?"

"No. Winning the competition so I can move ahead with the improvements would make me happy." Regan rubbed a hand over her forehead. "I'm putting through a motion to raise property taxes."

"Is that necessary? Can't you wait to see whether you win the grant?"

"The money's not for the common area project. Roots are destroying the sidewalks. They need to be torn out, the roots pared down, and repaved. It's expensive, but if we don't fix it soon someone is going to break an ankle."

One of the charming aspects of downtown Cottonbloom was the stately trees that grew along River Street and up the spoke of the main perpendicular street Monroe and Regan were on now. The trees offered respite from the sun in the summer and provided color in the fall.

"Will the motion pass?"

"Don't know. Word's out about my plan, and I've already gotten a threat."

Monroe grabbed her arm. "What kind of threat? From who?"

"Anonymous letter."

"Did you take it to the police?"

Regan shot her a side-eye. "It's not the first time and won't be the last. It's harmless. Pretty juvenile actually. Someone cut out magazine letters and glued them on a page. My point is that Cottonbloom is my top priority. Not Sawyer Fournette."

The call of songbirds overhead filled the lull.

"Do you think I should apologize for hiring Delmar?" Tentativeness replaced Regan's mayoral stoicism.

The fact that Regan was even contemplating an apology was a miracle. "It would be a nice olive branch. Granted the band thing was pretty underhanded, but you have the chance to bury the hatchet. And I don't mean in his back. Make sure Sawyer, and everyone else, knows this is about making Cottonbloom better and not a personal vendetta."

"All right. I'll do it. Later, though. I have a feeling he wouldn't be very receptive at the moment. Anyway, I have to find someone else to finish the gazebo. Preferably for next to nothing. Any ideas?"

"Nash Hawthorne is back. If he doesn't know how already, the man can teach himself to do anything. He is a certifiable genius."

Regan tapped a finger against her lips, the polish picked away. "Think he'd do it?"

"Ran into him at the grocery and he said he wasn't teaching until fall. He's working on some research paper."

Regan pushed off the wall. Energy replaced her moment of vulnerability, but she seemed injected with a "fake it until you make it" vigor. "I'll text you later."

"All right," Monroe said to Regan's back, worrying over her in more ways than one.

Another peek at Cade wouldn't hurt. She poked her head around the corner and startled two ladies. All three of them let out gasps.

"Goodness me, you scared me, Monroe." Ms. Leora's voice wavered. A tremor had affected her hands and voice in recent years, making simple tasks more difficult for her. Her health was one thing that had drawn her nephew Nash home. Although she seemed as sweet as a can of pie filling, the woman cut an intimidating swath through Cottonbloom, Mississippi, society.

The lady with her, Ms. Effie, was Louisiana born and Ms. Leora's opposite. Ms. Effie's twinkling eyes, red hair, and penchant for Jane Fonda–era leg warmers and white high-tops were in direct contrast to Ms. Leora's sensible shoes and the Sunday dresses she wore every day of the week.

What they had in common was the Quilting Bee. Ms. Leora was the unofficial leader of a quilting circle. They were the old guard, the protectors of all things genteel and ladylike. Although their power was fading, those ladies held sway over the town, and Monroe always wondered what sort of gossip and seditious talk the old ladies got up to while stitching quilts for the needy.

"How're you ladies doing?" Monroe asked.

"I talked Leora into trying an iced coffee. So the world might be ending in a few minutes if you want to hang around." Ms. Effie's voice was full of teasing laughter.

"Coffee should be hot and tea iced. You're as bad as Nash, wanting to drink hot tea." The harrumphing quality of Ms. Leora's voice was tempered by a small hovering smile. She looked over Monroe's shoulder. "Did I see Delmar Fournette loitering in our streets?"

"He headed out for a spot of fishing, I believe."

"Sounds about right," Ms. Leora said tartly. "I hope Regan plans to finish the gazebo soon. It's an eyesore at the moment."

"She's looking for someone to finish it up." No need to mention Ms. Leora's nephew Nash was on the very short list of contenders. The Quilting Bee ladies were a vocal group and, to Monroe's surprise, hadn't thrown their support behind or against the festival. "What do you ladies think about the tomato festival Regan's planning?"

"It's exciting. To think we might get in *Heart of Dixie*. That's a big-time magazine right there. In all the doctors' offices." Ms. Effie's enthusiasm was infectious. To everyone but Ms. Leora.

"Cottonbloom is fine the way it is. I don't relish the crowds and noise and wild abandonment that the festival will bring."

"Wild abandonment? Cottonbloom isn't hosting an orgy." Ms. Effie laughed and elbowed Ms. Leora's arm. "Don't be such a fuddy-duddy. It'll be fun."

"Good gracious, Effie. Such coarse talk." Ms. Leora rolled her eyes but linked her arm through Ms. Effie's. "Well, come on; let's get this over with. Afternoon, Monroe."

Monroe murmured polite farewells as the ladies headed toward the coffee shop, their heads close. She stayed planted against the bricks like moss until the ladies were out of sight. Then, like the pathetic stalker she was, she peeked back around the corner, but Cade was gone, the wall half-painted and sad-looking.

Chapter Eleven

Cade pulled up to Tally's gym and followed a clump of high-school-aged girls through the front door. They veered toward the ladies' changing room like a school of fish. He propped his hip on the front desk and caught his sister's twinkling eyes.

"When Monroe told me you had agreed to be her real-life practice dummy, I didn't believe her." Tally looked ready to dissolve into laughter. A rare sight these days, Cade realized with a flutter of unease.

"How about we substitute 'volunteer' for 'dummy.'"

Her laughter bubbled out and the sound was so contagious, Cade smiled in spite of the reservations about his sudden altruism. The girls swarmed out of the changing room together, chattering. Kayla wasn't part of their number.

"I almost called and canceled," he said.

"Why didn't you?"

Monroe swept through the door full of apologies for being late. "Had to work in too many clients this afternoon. Seems like half of Cottonbloom has had some joint or other replaced this week. So sorry. I'm ready, though. Are you excited, Cade?"

Seeing the way her smile lit up her face was the reason he hadn't canceled. No way was he admitting that to Tally. "Extremely excited."

Monroe dropped her duffel behind the counter and bounded up to the girls waiting on the mat, clapping her hands and doling out hugs. Add the way her short shorts and tight workout tank hugged her curves while emphasizing her strength to the list of reasons why he hadn't canceled. And the way her ponytail brushed across her shoulder blades, wispy pieces of hair framing her face.

But it was mostly her smile. It seemed to produce its own gravitational pull. He slipped around the desk.

Tally punched his arm on the way by. "You sly dog. I knew you were going to mark your territory sooner or later."

"Shut it, Tally. You want to help me get the pads on?"

Tally strapped pads on his arms and legs and over his chest. Feeling a couple of miles beyond ridiculous, he walked up to the cluster of girls and tried his best to sound jovial and non-threatening. "I hope y'all are going to go easy on me."

Although they differed in height and hair color and weight, they seemed one entity, laughing nervously, none of them making eye contact with him. He smoothed a hand down his beard. To them, he was a creepy old man trying to lure them into his carpeted van down by the river.

Monroe clapped her hands twice. The girls' giggling faded into silence as they each took a seat on the mat. "Girls, this is Cade, Miss Tallulah's brother. He's going to make our sessions a little more realistic. Amelia, why don't you get us started."

A girl around the same height as Monroe but with frizzy red hair and a dozen constellations of freckles shuffled in front of Monroe. Amelia was spindly in the way young girls were, still a couple of years away from filling out.

Monroe stood behind her and whispered in her ear before stepping away. "All right, Cade."

He side-eyed Monroe with a hint of exasperation. "What should I do?"

"Grab her wrist. Try to pull her toward you like you're forcing her somewhere."

Great. Exactly like the creepy man by the river. Knowing this was important to her, he grabbed Amelia's arm and tugged her. The girl's eyes widened and she didn't fight his backward pull, bumping into his padded chest.

Monroe got close. "Think, Amelia. This is basic stuff. What have you learned about breaking an attacker's grip?"

The girl came to life. Before he could react, she had twisted her arm out of his hand and punched him in the chest with enough force to knock him back a step. Amelia walked back into the fold of girls as they cheered.

"Yes." Monroe paced in front of them and fist-pumped. "That was awesome. Who's next?"

Throughout the lesson, Monroe kept up a constant stream of encouragement as well as checking on his knee and hand. The session was surprisingly vigorous but not painful, and the hour passed quickly.

The girls headed to the changing room as a group of kickboxers took over the mat. Tally strolled over, fitting a microphone over her ear and tucking the sound pack into the waistband of her shorts.

"Great job, Cade."

"Thanks, Sis." He threw a padded arm around her and hauled her in for a half hug. She pushed him off the mat with a small laugh.

He stripped the padding off and took the water Monroe offered him. "I didn't see Kayla."

"Nope." A frown replaced her smile. "She hasn't returned my texts. I think she's mad at me."

"Mad? After what you did? My guess is she's embarrassed."

"You think?"

"Put yourself in her place. I remember Tally at seventeen. Forget sugar and spice and everything nice; she was tears and angst and melodrama."

"Maybe I'll ride out to her house later. I don't suppose you'd let me buy you dinner for helping out?"

He hesitated. Their kisses had unleashed a muddy, confusing flood of emotions in him. She'd wanted him. But why? Women usually pursued him because he was rich. The excitement of his lifestyle drew others. Monroe didn't seem to care about either. None of the others had ever really known him—he didn't allow that sort of intimacy.

Monroe had been a good girl 'Sip, and he'd been the troublemaking swamp rat. Was she satisfying her own curiosity about him? Acting out a fantasy, maybe? She knew he wasn't sticking around.

Her kiss had been a plea to be claimed. He could have gotten her naked. He could have satisfied his pent-up sexual frustration. But it would have broken some unspoken bond of trust between them. It would have hurt her. That he couldn't do, and that's what scared him. Monroe was different. Special.

He hid his inner turmoil behind a bland expression he'd perfected during negotiations. "Sure. What were you thinking?"

"How about the pizza place over on my side? It's laidback. You don't need to change." She pulled a T-shirt over her workout clothes.

He followed her across the river in his truck, found parking down the street, and marveled at the revitalization taking place in downtown Cottonbloom, Mississippi. He reached the front of the pizza place a few seconds before

Monroe and opened the door, gesturing her through. She grabbed a free booth and he slid in across from her. For a weeknight, the restaurant was doing steady business. The tables were half-filled and several people walked in to collect to-go orders.

"I'm impressed with the changes. Things were looking worn and run-down when I left."

"Things got worse before they got better. Regan has done a bang-up job encouraging new businesses to take root. I know the festival is a sore point, but she really cares about this town."

"I figured she ran for mayor for the attention and prestige. Kind of like a pageant for grown-ups."

Monroe's laugh made his insides feel warm. "Prestige? The only perk she receives is free coffee down at Glenda's and a seat in the lead convertible for the Christmas parade. Otherwise, it's mostly fielding complaints."

The waitress plopped two waters with lemon wedges on the table and pulled out an order pad. A frisson of something had him wiping his hands down his shorts. Surely it wasn't nerves? He hadn't been nervous for years. Hanging from a cliff face and leaping into the unknown were adrenaline rushes. Negotiating a million-dollar deal? Exciting. How could something as mundane as eating pizza with Monroe incite nerves?

They'd never eaten together. Never been on a date. Their meetings had been illicit. Cade remembered something. Something simple, yet the knowledge calmed the rush.

"You still like pizza with everything on it except onions?"

Her smile turned his insides from warm into gooey. "I sure do. I can't believe you remember that."

The waitress jotted down their order and disappeared. Cade propped his elbows on the table and poked his lemon wedge into his water. "Sawyer looks like crap. Being commissioner must be just as stressful as mayor."

"Probably even more so. Sawyer has the entire parish to handle, and there are different issues on that side. Harder issues in most ways. He and Regan had done a good job ignoring each other until they both entered the festival competition."

"I have the feeling me being home has only added to his troubles." He ran a hand down his beard and scratched at the stubble on his neck.

"Why do you think that?"

"I don't know, maybe 'cause he threw a hissy fit worthy of a *Housewives of Cottonbloom* reality show when I moved Daddy's truck to the garage to fix it up."

He glanced out the window. The truck was nothing special. Not old enough to be considered a collector's item, it looked downright decrepit next to the vehicles from the last decade parked around it.

A couple of springs were poking through the upholstery, the headliner was hanging down in one corner, and the AC still wasn't working. Cade didn't care. Seeing it slowly disintegrate had driven a spike through his heart. He hadn't been able to save his parents, but he could damn well save his daddy's truck. Sitting behind the wheel brought him a comfort he hadn't felt in forever.

"Isn't it technically Sawyer's truck? Did you ask if he wanted to help you fix it up?" She cut her clear blue eyes back to him and leaned onto her elbows.

"I'm the one that drove that truck, kept it running, so I could work. So he could finish high school, play baseball, go to college. He never offered to help me back then." The bitterness that ran from his heart to his mouth shocked him. Disgusted him. He had made sure Sawyer hadn't had to deal with the hardship he faced on a daily basis. He swallowed and looked out the window. "I didn't mean that."

The warmth of her hand came over his, their fingers

weaving naturally. Her touch provided a solace he didn't realize he needed until she offered it. "It's okay to be mad at the cards you were dealt, but you made something of yourself. Made it out of here."

Made it out. Forced out. Driven out. She didn't need to know that.

He had never felt normal. Like Monroe, he'd questioned whether he was capable of real love. The kind that made a man want to sacrifice everything to protect his woman. He was afraid he'd used it all up on his brother and sister. His heart bounced around his chest, trying to communicate in Morse code.

A familiar figure came down the sidewalk, the setting sun glinting off the highlights in his hair. Andrew Tarwater pushed the front door open and stepped straight to their booth. The look on his face would sour milk.

"Monroe?" Her name was accusatory. She snatched her hand away, her oversize T-shirt falling off one shoulder.

Cade clenched his hand into a fist. Was she embarrassed to be seen with him or was something serious going on between her and Tarwater or both? A resentment born of years fielding pitying looks and thinly veiled insults burned under the pleasant mask he forced himself to maintain.

"Hi, Andrew." The friendly welcome in her voice only stoked the fire.

"Father and I are working late on a case and he sent me down for a pizza. What are you two up to?" A jealous suspicion hid behind the question. Could Monroe hear it?

"Cade helped me out with my class this evening, and I thought a pizza was the least I could do." She favored Cade with one of her ice-melting smiles.

Andrew harrumphed like a grumpy old man. Someone from the front counter called his name, but he didn't move.

"Your pizza's ready," Cade prodded.

"I heard," he snapped in return. "Are you getting excited for the fund-raiser, Monroe?"

"Superexcited." The vagueness in her voice belied her words. "I appreciate your mother's kindness."

Andrew's jaw worked as he cast a glance toward Cade. "Yes, well, I've worked hard on the party as well. I've made sure the best of Cottonbloom will be in attendance."

Was it his imagination or was the smile she gave Andrew smaller and cooler? "Your interest in the girls at risk program is admirable. The money is going to a good cause, I can promise you that."

Andrew collected the pizza and walked out, decidedly more stiff than when he'd entered. She seemed to deflate.

"What's the problem?" Cade gestured toward the door.

"What do you mean?" She was fiddling with the end of her silky ponytail.

What *did* he mean? He was the one with the problem. The animosity he felt toward Andrew had a definite green tint.

"Nothing," he murmured as their pizza was delivered, steaming and aromatic.

The act of eating together eased the tension jumbling his emotions. He didn't bring up Andrew again and neither did she.

"I know you moved to Mobile first. Where did you go next?" she asked.

"I moved to a different port city every few months. Never had a problem finding a job with my skills. In fact, I found my reputation started to precede me. By the time I looped up to Maryland, an engine shop came looking for me." The corner of his mouth lifted.

"Weren't you lonely?"

"A little." The understatement wiped his prideful smile away. The first night in the cheap, dirty motel had been worse than his family's first night in the old trailer. At least then, Sawyer and Tally had been within calling distance. No one in Mobile knew him. No one cared what happened to him. The noise of a restless city had been jarring after so many years drifting off to the sounds of the river. He hadn't slept that night.

"But you moved from port to port? Never settling down?" Her blue eyes searched for the truth.

The truth was complicated. "You can't know what freedom felt like after so many years under a yoke."

"You eventually settled down in Seattle, though. What changed?"

"I was in Connecticut, and the guys around me had been working on rich men's engines for twenty, thirty years and they would die working on rich men's engines."

"You wanted more." It was a statement.

"I wanted more. I was used to working hard. I put in twelve-, sixteen-hour days and played with some ideas I had rolling around in my head. Engines with my mods were able to produce noticeably more horsepower. I started to get a lot of attention." He shot her a sly grin. "Men seem to think there's a correlation between their engine horsepower and the size of their junk."

Her throaty, husky laugh was like a shot of rich whiskey. "So men started to come see you for enhancements." She bracketed the last word in air quotes.

"Exactly. Eventually, a man showed up who was more a visionary than I was at the time. He encouraged me to file for a patent, and we became business partners. The rest is, as they say, history."

"Why didn't you stay on the East Coast? Why Seattle? Besides the lack of gators." She smiled around a bite of pizza.

"It's where my partner, Richard, was based, so I followed him out there."

Her brows bounced up as she chewed. "You don't seem the following type. What's this Richard fella like?"

At the beginning of their business relationship, Richard had been more mentor than partner. He'd taught Cade the jargon of the rich, how to dress, manners. Richard had treated him like a son and had never belittled Cade's lack of knowledge of his world.

"He's more than just a business partner. I count him as a friend." His phone buzzed with an incoming text and he glanced at the screen, debating for a second whether he could blow off his obligation to stay with Monroe. "I'm going to have to head out."

"Emergency?"

"Only if you consider a nighttime boat ride down memory lane with Sawyer and Uncle Delmar an emergency."

"You're not going—" she leaned forward and dropped her voice "—poaching, are you?"

He couldn't tell if she was worried for him or excited at the prospect. Questions rose again. Was she only interested in him for a different kind of thrill?

He met her halfway over the table, his mouth close to her ear. "With Uncle Delmar in charge, no telling what kind of mischief we'll get up to."

A flush raced up her neck and into her cheeks. Could he make her entire body flush like that? A picture of her naked and laid out on a bed flashed. He tried to shake the thought, but it was too late. It was as if his sudden hard-on had graffiti painted the image on his brain.

He leaned back, the distance not helping the state of his mind or body. "I can afford to hit the grocery store these days. I can buy this pizza, too." He pulled out his wallet and tossed cash on the table, more than enough to pay for the pizza and put a smile on the waitress's face.

"But this was supposed to be me treating you." Monroe tucked wisps of her hair behind her ear.

"You asking me to share a pizza with you was treat enough." He slid out of the booth and worked his knee.

She popped up and her gaze dropped. "You look stiff."

His mind veered directly into a middle-school arena, and he moved his hands in front of his pants. A second passed before he realized she was talking about his knee. He burst out laughing. The sound rang in his ears. "My knee's better. Only bothers me if I sit for too long."

They lingered on the sidewalk, their vehicles facing opposite directions. "How's your hand?"

"Some better. I've been doing my exercises, Miss Kirby, I promise." He opened and closed his wounded hand. "Gets achy if I try to use it for too long, and sometimes the pins and needles thing wakes me up."

"I can't do much for nerve damage, unfortunately, but the exercises will help with strength and endurance." She took his hand and massaged down the scar tissue. "There are some things only time can heal."

Their eyes tangled and her words seemed to encompass more than his hand. A lump settled in his throat, and the tingling along his palm grew into a burning sensation. "Yeah, well. I'll see you later."

He turned and walked away, knowing it was abrupt yet unable to bear another minute of her eviscerating stare. Too much wanted to pour out of him, too fast. The rumble of the truck engine drowned out any street noise, and he sat until her SUV turned the corner.

Chapter Twelve

Monroe tramped through the tall grass to the water oak standing like a lone sentinel in the field. Halfway between their childhood homes, the tree marked her and Regan's meeting spot growing up. Cursing herself roundly, she wished she could take back their earlier conversation. Her casual mention of catching a bite with Cade had led to her telling Regan about his planned nighttime boat ride with Sawyer.

Regan had been suspicious, but it wasn't until she called back in a tizzy, ordering Monroe to their tree, that she realized the severity of her misstep. Not only had she been roped into some kind of reconnaissance mission, but the feeling she somehow had betrayed Cade niggled her conscience also. What if the men were going poaching and Monroe had given them away? She wasn't sure what Regan would do if she got incriminating evidence against Sawyer.

Wearing black slacks and a dark-blue summer cardigan, Regan paced, looking ready to jaunt off to a Junior League meeting. Monroe's black leggings and dark-gray T-shirt were more practical. Movement under the tree caught her attention.

A man with rumpled brown hair and glasses leaned against the trunk, his hands buried in the pockets of his green cargo pants, his biceps bulging in the fitted black cotton T-shirt, a tattoo peeking out of a sleeve. An eight-inch knife hung from a belt holster. How had Regan roped Nash Hawthorne into her plans?

If it wasn't for his soulful brown eyes behind black-framed glasses, he could have passed for Special Forces instead of a newly hired history professor at Cottonbloom College. She had no doubt his classes would be extremely popular among the coeds. But to her, he would always be Nerdy Nash, the boy who'd been teased and ignored most of their childhood.

"Did Regan guilt you into this, too?" She joined him in the arms of the tree, the wind making the leaves shush around them.

"Ha-ha," Regan said. "He cares about our town and the festival, too."

Nash's thick brown eyebrows arched over his glasses. "She oh-so-kindly reminded me of the time she saved me from total humiliation in the cafeteria our sophomore year by letting me sit with you guys."

"Wow. Totally unprofessional, Regan. I'm appalled at the lack of moral fiber in our mayor." Monroe tutted but couldn't hold back a grin.

"Hush up. Did you bring the greasepaint?"

Monroe laughed, but Regan didn't crack a smile. "I offered as a joke. I didn't think you were serious. Anyway, I don't actually own anything that pertains to hunting."

"Well, never mind. We'll manage." Regan ducked under a low branch and looked toward the river, even though it wasn't visible in the gloaming.

"Do you know what the heck we're doing out here?" Monroe leaned toward Nash.

"She was muttering something about rabbits and Sawyer Fournette earlier."

"Hold up, Regan. Before Nash and I blindly follow you into Lord knows what, you have to tell us what's going on."

"After I got off the phone with you, I made some calls. After our little argument over his uncle, he put out extra traps."

"And his plan with these extra rabbits?"

"How devious would it be to release a colony of rabbits into Mama's garden? They eat their fill and are gone by morning. Or, even worse, they burrow down and reproduce."

Monroe sighed and rubbed her forehead. "Your leap from extra traps to tomato sabotage isn't logical. Tell her, Nash."

"I don't know. I've heard stranger things. Aunt Leora used to tell me stories about Mississippi men crossing over and cutting crayfish baskets. And Louisiana men would come over at night and raid gardens and traps. There's one story about a boat of swamp rats coming face-to-face with a party of 'Sips at the state line."

"What happened?" Regan asked.

"Both parties pretended jaunting around the river at midnight was perfectly normal and went on their merry ways. After that things settled down some."

"That was fifty years ago. Those men have mostly passed on. Sawyer isn't going to do something so juvenile and devious," Monroe said.

Nash chuckled. "Juvenile and devious but bordering on brilliant. It's like murder by icicle." Monroe sent him a questioning glance. "The evidence melts before anyone can point a finger. Or, in this case, hops off. Seriously, though, do you really need me here to scare off some rabbits?"

"No, I need you to take Sawyer *out* if we catch him creeping through here with his marauding bunnies."

"Take him *out*? I'm a professor. Not a hit man."

"Maybe not, but I mean, look at you." Regan waved a hand over his body. "You could beat him up, right?"

"First of all, Sawyer is in great shape. It would be a toss-up. Second, I'm not beating anyone up. This festival business has driven you around the bend, woman."

Regan threw up her hands. "Why does everyone keep saying that?"

"Because it's true," Monroe and Nash said at the same time, and then looked at each other, startled.

"One, two, three, jinx." Monroe popped Nash on the arm. It was rock hard. Regan was right. The man was in phenomenal shape. He wasn't Nerdy Nash any longer.

"I knew I should have stayed in Scotland," he muttered, looking up into the tree branches.

"How's Ms. Leora feeling?"

"Her shake is getting worse, but the doctor says there isn't anything to do about it. Part of getting older. She still insists on driving." Nash's sigh was heavy. His childless aunt Leora had taken him in after his mother had died of breast cancer, so his father could continue his high-risk, high-paying job as an oil platform supervisor in the gulf.

Dusk was upon them. Lightning bugs rose from the base of the tree to blink around their knees. Cicadas picked up their call, the noise ebbing and crashing like ocean waves. As the stars snuffed out the sun, the air cooled and the breeze picked up.

"I seriously doubt Sawyer has any plans on heading this far up the river. Anyway, Cade wouldn't join in his shenanigans," Monroe said.

"You guys are probably right." Regan's tone turned conciliatory. "I have a cooler with some snacks and drinks.

How about we hang out and reminisce? And if Sawyer happens by then we can have a civilized chat. Two city leaders who want the best for their respective towns."

Nash picked up the soft-sided cooler and dropped the strap over his shoulder. "All right, I'm in, if only out of curiosity and because I'm tired of hanging out with Aunt Leora and the Quilting Bee ladies. Every single one of them wants to set me up with one of their female relatives. Where do you want to set up camp?"

"In that grove of pines behind my parents' house? That'll give us the high ground and leave our enemy exposed," Regan said.

Nash gestured. "Lead on, Napoléon. Let's hope this isn't our Waterloo."

"That was an ABBA song, right?" Monroe asked, hoping he couldn't see her twitching lips in the dark.

He groaned as if she'd physically injured him. "Nineteenth-century Western European history? Duke of Wellington? Please tell me you're joking."

Monroe gave him a hip bump as they trailed behind Regan, who was making remarkably good time through the grass in her black ballerina flats. "I'm joking, but the look of horror on your face was totally worth it."

They set up under the pine trees, the needles thick on the ground. Nash sat on a stump while Regan and Monroe shared the quilt. Regan handed out beers. The night was clear, stars winking in the black sky. The full moon rose to their left, highlighting the grass wavering like water as far as she could see.

"So I heard you teach at Tallulah Fournette's gym?" Nash broke the silence.

Monroe twisted to see him. "I meet with a group of at-risk girls to teach them self-defense."

"That's cool." He picked at the label of his beer. "She still dating Heath Parsons?"

"She dumped him, thank the Lord. I never understood what she saw in him, but then again, I can only remember what he was like in school. Tally didn't have the pleasure."

Nash perked up like a hunting dog catching a scent. "Who's she dating now?"

"No one that I know of. She's not exactly forthcoming with information. Why? Are you interested?"

"What? Me? Of course not." His too-casual tone had her scooching around to face him.

"Really?" she asked dryly. Nash had never been a good liar.

"I remember her as a kid. Wondered how she was doing since I haven't run into her yet."

"She's either at the gym or she occasionally hangs out at the Rivershack Tavern. I keep trying to get her to come out with me, but she's never been comfortable over the line." Monroe rested her chin on her bent knees and tilted her face toward Nash. "Didn't you live on the river over the line before your mama passed?"

"Yeah-h-h." He drew the word out as he grabbed two more bottles. "Don't remember much about it, though. I'm going to stretch my legs and take a leak." He stood up, tucked one bottle into the pocket of his cargos, and headed into the trees, quickly swallowed by the darkness.

Regan held out another bottle, but Monroe shook her head. She hadn't taken more than a sip or two of the one she held. After seeing what alcohol did to her mother, she never overindulged. She'd spent her life holding full glasses of wine or bottles of beer for appearance's sake.

She lay back on the quilt, her head in pine needles. The tang of sap reminded her of the holidays, and a sense of melancholy crept up and surprised her.

"I used to meet Sawyer on the river." Regan's voice reflected a similar feeling. She stretched out on the quilt, putting them shoulder to shoulder.

"I didn't know," Monroe said softly. Regan's shoulder moved against hers.

"We had to steal our moments, and with as much as Cade worked, he couldn't get the truck too often. I remember sitting on the bank, straining to hear his boat."

The lump in Monroe's throat grew with her gathering tears. Monroe had done the same. She'd marked off the days until the next full moon on a calendar, her excitement building until dark. Sometimes she would wait hours until the soft putter of the boat engine prodded her heart into a sprint.

If anyone would understand, surely Regan would. Maybe she could help put those years into perspective. Maybe it was time to finally tell someone.

Regan shot up and grabbed Monroe's knee. "Did you hear that?"

Monroe propped herself up on her elbows to listen. The low croaks of the bullfrogs rose like a chorus. A large animal-like rustling popped her to sitting. "I heard something, too."

No sign of an approaching man or animal. Regan hissed Nash's name. No answer.

Regan pointed out into the field. "Head that way. Holler if you spot anything. I'm going to double back around to the garden fence."

She was gone before Monroe could mount an objection. The river beckoned like an old friend, and she took a step out of the trees toward what she couldn't see or hear but knew was there. The river represented a safe place, but in the darkness her fears populated the field between her and the water.

She stopped next to a wild, thorny rosebush. Its scent was cloying and at odds with the sense of urgency snaking through the night air, making her lungs work harder. Noises sounded in every direction, but when she turned to look nothing was there. Between Cade being home and her recent confrontation with Sam Landry, memories had frayed her nerves a little more every night in her dreams.

A twig snapped. Monroe swung around, not sure which direction the noise came from. A dark figure stood even with the tree line. She ran.

The water oak where she met Regan emerged as a hulking shadow in the darkness. Her heart pounded, the noise of her harsh breathing filling her ears. Her senses betrayed her, turning inward. She couldn't determine whether the figure chased after her or not.

Slowing as she came under the branches of the huge oak, she looked over her shoulder, seeing nothing. Taking one deep breath after another, she leaned against the trunk and pressed the heels of her hands against her eyes.

Why had she run? Now that she was away, logical thought resurfaced. Sam Landry didn't know she was out here. No doubt, it had been Nash and now he thought she was crazy. The adrenaline faded, leaving her knees trembling and weak. She was no braver than she'd been at thirteen.

A hand circled her upper arm. Her leg shot out, and she used the man's weight against him—for there was no doubt the big hand was that of a man—flipping him to the ground. Instead of her breaking his hold, the hand tightened around her arm and she tumbled down with him.

"I cry uncle." Cade. His black ball cap was cocked back on his head and greasepaint darkened the skin above his beard.

"Oh, God, don't tell me Regan was right?"

"Right about what?" There was a fake innocence in the question.

"What are you doing out here?"

"Why did you run away from me back there? Did you not hear me calling out?"

She hadn't, her panic too encompassing. "No . . . I didn't recognize you. I hate being scared." The admission gouged into a place she hadn't shared for years. Ever since he'd left.

"Sometimes being scared is a defensive mechanism that can save your life and running is the smartest thing you can do." A matter-of-fact truth born from experience was in his voice.

His absolution washed through her like a river baptism. "You don't think I'm weak?"

"Weak? Damn, woman, I've got at least eighty pounds on you. How did you drop me?"

It wasn't the answer to the question she'd been asking, yet she relaxed, not needing to fake the tease in her voice. "It's called leverage. Did you miss that science class?" The implication of what she'd said sent an embarrassed fire to her cheeks. "I shouldn't have—"

His bark of laughter sent a squawking bird into the night. "It's okay. And yes, I do understand the concept. It's just that you're tiny." He curled his hands around her hips, his fingers splayed on the outer curve of her butt.

His hands were hotter than the noonday sun. Suddenly she was aware of how big and hard he was underneath her. "Who's on top, big guy?"

"You are." His voice had deepened and roughened in texture. "I happen to love having a woman on top."

The conversation had taken on sexual shades. The tree branches left them in heavy darkness, blocking most of the moonlight. Something about Cade Fournette smothered the fear that had grown like weeds since her childhood. Weeds she couldn't seem to eradicate on her own.

She bent at the elbows, dropping her face over his, her

lips within an inch of making contact. His breath mingled with hers. The same courage she'd found with him once already welled up inside of her, urging her on.

He didn't wait for her move this time. He jerked on her hips and popped her forward. Her lips mashed into his, rocketing the kiss into the stratosphere.

She moaned and moved against him with a frantic neediness. She threaded her hands through his hair, her body falling fully into his. One arm wrapped around her back, and the other hand tangled in her hair, trapping her close.

His beard was both prickly and arousing, adding another element of tactile pleasure to the experience. Their tongues tangled, the act a battle of wills she was determined to win. He was as committed to success, and before she could launch a protest he rolled them and reversed their positions.

The weight of his body pushed her into the soft ground. She took a huge breath. The scent of sweet grass mixed with the nearby river and Cade's clean, masculine smell.

He took the advantage and kissed her with a savageness that made every nerve ending tingle. She normally didn't let a man on top of her, didn't like the position of weakness, the need to have an escape always on her mind. Nothing with Cade was normal. Everything felt new and the spine-tingling excitement didn't scare her; it only made her want more.

She arched against him and wiggled her hips against the undeniable erection he rocked against her. She hooked her leg over his, trying to pull him fully over her, but he was too strong and in control. She loved it.

One kiss melded into another, the heat between them explosive, ready to burn them to ashes. She tugged his shirt out of the waistband of his jeans and traced the puckered scar along his side. Any worries as to afterward splintered in the storm of their passion.

She broke their kiss long enough to whisper, "Cade. Please."

He dropped his lips to her neck, the hair of his beard sending shivers through her body, adding to her desperation.

He lifted his head, the breeze caressing where his lips had been. The darkness kept his expression a mystery. She suspected his long inspection meant his Fournette superhuman night sight was in full effect. What did he see? Memories that still resonated and connected them in a way she didn't understand? Or a simple need only he seemed to be able to satisfy?

Chapter Thirteen

Her eyes eviscerated him. Cut to his core. The one he feared was as black as an apple left to rot on winter's ground. The reckless passion that had exploded between them took him by surprise—again.

She'd gone wild on him, her kisses aggressive, her hands desperate. He'd wanted to take her, let her moans join all the wild animals' calls in the night, but when he looked in her eyes more than raw need shot into him. Whether he was seeing her truth or his he wasn't certain.

What he was certain about was that adding sex into their oddly twined histories would tangle them further, yet he wasn't sure he could deny either of them the pleasure. *When* he took her, it wouldn't be on the hard ground in the dark.

He brushed his lips over hers. A kiss filled with longing and regret and understanding. Then, he rolled off her to lie on his back. The full moon peeked through the dancing leaves. The night sounds filled the silence between them.

He wasn't sure how long they lay shoulder to shoulder. She broke the silence, her voice hoarse. "I'm sorry if I'm pushing you to do something you don't want to do."

The apology sounded rehearsed and stiff and utterly ridiculous. Had he not been kissing her back, grinding his painfully hard erection against her? He propped himself up on an elbow. A shaft of moonlight wavered over part of her face, leaving one eye bright and the other shadowed. That was Monroe—light and dark. Sweet and tough. Controlled and wild.

"I promise you're not taking advantage of me, Miss Kirby." He picked pine needles and leaves out of her hair. "As much as I love hanging out by the river in the light of the full moon with you, I'd rather continue this somewhere bug-free and not so itchy."

Her lips curled into a tremulous smile, giving her the look of an innocent. But she wasn't innocent anymore. She wasn't a little girl anymore. She was a woman. A fascinating puzzle of a woman he knew yet didn't.

She took his injured hand and pressed her lips along his scar. Tingles ran up his forearm. The gesture tossed a grenade into his chest, the detonation rearranging his insides.

"Monroe!" Regan's voice wavered across the distance.

"I should head back." Her lips moved against his palm.

He hoped he wasn't projecting his own regret into her voice. She stood and brushed at her tight black leggings, only managing to move the clinging debris around.

He rose, too, pain pulsing in his knee. The run to catch her had strained his healing tendons. "I'm headed back to the river."

Regan called again, this time with more urgency. Monroe cupped her hands around her mouth. "I'm fine! I'm coming!"

She looked toward a grove of trees at the edge of Cottonbloom, Mississippi's richest neighborhood and back at him. "Wait. Was Regan actually right? Were you looking to sabotage her mother's tomatoes?"

"I was along for the ride," he said as vaguely as possible. He'd dropped the two rabbits he'd been tasked with as soon as he'd spooked her, his priorities shifting.

Regan called again and Cade could imagine a foot stomp to go along with it. Monroe backed away from him. "Regan was planning to offer Sawyer an olive branch."

"Think he torched it."

Monroe's smile flashed before she turned and ran toward the grove of pines. The moon lit on her blond hair, making her run across the field look like something out of a fairy tale.

He waited until she was out of sight to begin his less magical limp back toward his uncle Delmar's flat-bottomed boat. His uncle and brother were arguing in low voices by the time he made it down the bank.

Sawyer stood, rocking the boat from side to side in the shallow water. "Where have you been?"

"Busy," Cade said shortly, his boots squelching in the mud. He claimed the narrow seat in the front and massaged his knee.

"You okay?" Sawyer asked. Delmar got the engine purring, and they set off in the middle of the river. The slight current pushed them home faster than their approach.

"I will be once I'm home with an ice pack and a beer. What happened to you? Regan catch you?"

"Rabbit handed. She jumped out of a bush wearing a damn cardigan and dress shoes screaming like the church was burning down. The rabbits went nuts, probably expecting her to rip them open with bare hands. And she might have if it wouldn't endanger her manicure."

"What did you do?"

"Dropped the mother-flipping rabbits and ran. She was on me like a crazed monkey. I had to pin her to the ground to settle her down."

"You look fine to me. How'd you manage to escape?"

"She stopped trying to maim me." Sawyer's voice turned vague and distant.

After an awkward amount of silence, it became clear Sawyer wasn't planning to elaborate and Cade glanced over his shoulder at their uncle. "What about you, Uncle Del?"

"Sawyer and Regan raised such a ruckus, I was able to walk right up to that pretty little garden and drop my boys right over the fence. Old Nash Hawthorne was standing there drinking a beer."

"Did he spot you?"

"Considering he offered me a cold one, I'd say so, but he didn't raise the alarm. Maybe he still holds a soft spot for his birthplace." Del pulled a beer bottle from the side pocket of his pants and uncapped it against the side of the boat.

"Did you get your pair into the garden, Cade?" Sawyer asked.

"Nope."

"Regan said Monroe was out there somewhere. You run across her?"

"Yep."

"A veritable fountain of information. As usual." The antipathy in Sawyer's voice had Cade sitting up straighter and leaning forward.

"What do you mean by that?"

Sawyer sat there for a moment before erupting like the top of a pressure cooker. "I got a call from some stranger about your accident. And only because you had me listed as next of kin on some ancient card in your climbing pack. Once you broke free from Cottonbloom, you broke free from me and Tally."

The exchange took a detour Cade hadn't anticipated. "If either one of you ever needed help, I was there."

"Sure. Free with your money and advice." Sawyer shook

his head and looked to the bank. "I don't even know you, Cade. Not really. I felt like I lost my brother, too, after Mom and Dad died."

Cade had closed himself off for a reason—to protect his little brother and sister. A knee-jerk anger sharpened his words. "Look, I'm home now—"

"For how long? Another week or two?"

"I'm planning to stay for a while." Until that moment he'd existed in a strange limbo between past, present, and future, but now the words were out he felt planted. He wouldn't lie to himself. Part of why he wanted to stick around longer than he'd originally intended was Monroe, but his siblings made the choice an easy one. "If you don't have any objections, I was thinking about getting one of my current projects shipped down. Maybe you could help me figure some stuff out considering you're the one with the fancy degree."

"I suppose that'd be okay." He sounded like Cade had offered to pluck his fingernails out one by one.

Their uncle either couldn't hear them or didn't want to involve himself. He deftly steered them downriver, avoiding the logs that could catch the motor blades. The enjoyment Cade had felt being back on the river had faded into a headache, Sawyer's accusations rubbing like sandpaper.

Cade had held Sawyer and Tally as they cried but never cried in front of them. He was the oldest and had to be the strongest. That didn't mean he hadn't cried into his pillow more nights than he could count.

He'd cried because he missed the way his mother had brushed his hair before school even after he was old enough to do it himself. He missed the way his daddy had patted his shoulder when he'd brought home his report card and the way the small gesture had made him swell with pride. He missed the ease with which life had flowed, one day much like the last, some better than others but none hard.

Their uncle brought the boat to ground close to where Cade had left the old truck. Sawyer hopped out and was up the bank before Cade maneuvered over the side with his sore knee. "Thanks, Uncle Delmar. You have any more trouble with the engine, you bring it around."

His uncle chucked his chin in acknowledgement. "Push me off, would you, boy?"

Cade watched his uncle disappear around the first bend, shoved his hands into his pockets, and joined Sawyer in the truck. By the time they got back to the house, Sawyer's aggression had turned pensive, his answers to Cade's probing questions monosyllabic.

Tally was inside, leaning against the kitchen counter and popping cherry tomatoes like candy. Sawyer ignored her greeting and disappeared up the stairs. Tally turned to Cade and put her hands on her hips. "What the heck happened?"

He shucked his mud-caked boots and stepped inside. "We got caught."

She covered her mouth with both hands, muffling her words. "By the police?"

If Chief Thomason had nabbed them, Cade would have fulfilled his youthful lack of promise in the chief's eyes. "By Regan Lovell."

"Lord have mercy." Tally pulled out two long-necked ice-cold beers and plunked them on the table. He limped to a chair, and without him having to ask she opened the freezer and rooted around. He caught the ice pack on her toss, laid it over his knee, and grunted, curving his bad hand over the top. The numbing relief was immediate.

She joined him at the table, and they sat in silence for a few minutes, drinking their beers. This was the first beer they'd ever shared. She hadn't been legal when he'd left, and the two times he'd flown her to Seattle for a visit he'd never thought about hanging out with her like a friend. Instead, he'd packed her days with sightseeing, joining her if he wasn't too busy.

Cade studied her from under his lashes. "Do you think I've been selfish?"

Without taking her eyes off him, she took a slow draw on her beer before setting it down with a thud. "How so?"

The fact that she hadn't come out with a *No way* or *Of course not* was answer enough.

"You should have gone to LSU."

Her attention transferred to picking at the bottle's label. "I wasn't like Sawyer. My grades weren't good enough."

"You could have gotten a track scholarship. If not at LSU, then somewhere smaller."

Tally was tall and agile and fast. She'd set several school records her senior year in cross-country, but she'd always blown off his suggestions of applying for an athletic scholarship.

"Maybe, but I wouldn't have been able to keep up with the schoolwork. Gracious, I could barely keep up in high school."

"What are you talking about? You're a math genius."

"One subject. My English composition teacher gave me a C minus out of pity. I should've flunked and not even earned my diploma. Social studies, history . . . I barely squeaked by any subject that required reading. Can I tell you something without you freaking out?"

He wanted to say no. Monroe had already twisted the supposed truths from his memories, and he had a feeling Tally was ready to shatter them. "Sure."

"I was diagnosed with dyslexia my junior year of high school."

He half-rose out of his chair, the ice pack falling to the floor. "Why didn't I know this? The school should have—"

"They did. I forged your signature on everything. Apparently, mine is mild to moderate, which is why it went undiagnosed so long." She huffed a sigh. "And I thought I was just stupid all those years."

He forced himself to sit, mostly because his knee throbbed. What he really wanted to do was pace and lecture and maybe beat up anyone who had made her feel dumb. That wasn't his role anymore. "Who said you were stupid?"

"No one had to tell me. I watched you and Sawyer read a book in one sitting when it would take me an hour to decipher a few pages. It was easier to not like reading, to find my own thing."

"Sports."

"The gym has been good. I'm not an idiot when it comes to business plans and money."

"You're not an idiot, period. Jesus, Tally, we could have gotten you more help. I see those services advertised all the time."

She shook her head and scraped the label off the sweating beer. "I checked into it. We couldn't afford it. Not without you working even harder, and I couldn't ask you to do that. You deserved to have a life outside of taking care of me and Sawyer." The magnanimous way she said it wove a sense of cowardice through the guilt.

"No matter what I'm doing or how far away I am, if you ever have a problem or need anything you can count on me."

Tally leaned over and gave him a one-armed hug. "I know. But Sawyer and I are doing fine. We don't want you to sweep into town to fix our problems. Let us help you and just . . . be our brother."

His mouth opened and closed. Not sure how to respond, he apologized even though he wasn't quite sure what he was apologizing for. For leaving? For coming home? For not trying hard enough? "I'm sorry."

"Nothing to be sorry for. Have you decided how long you're staying in Cottonbloom?" She turned her intense green eyes on him. It was like looking in a mirror.

"For a while yet." He gave her the same answer he'd given Sawyer, and once again his departure, which had seemed set on the end of the month, now fuzzed indistinctly into the future.

The conversation waned and she rose to toss her bottle into the recycling bin.

"There's something I have to tell you, too." His voice must have reflected his inner turmoil, because she sank back down, sitting forward.

"What?"

"I didn't leave Cottonbloom because I wanted to." The words grew heavier and harder to force out. "I left because Chief Thomason caught me stealing."

"Stealing what?" Her voice was flat.

"A boat engine from Mr. Wiltshire. Our engine had crapped out again, and I was sick of dealing with it. I should have sucked it up and fixed it, but I saw his row of boats and . . . I got mad and maybe jealous. What did one man need with a dozen boats?" The silence buzzed like white noise, but he was scared to look up.

"Why didn't you get thrown in jail?"

"Thomason and Mama were in school together. He let me go because of her. Made it clear how disappointed and ashamed she'd have been if she'd been alive. Told me to get gone and stay gone." A gash in the wood peeked from under his beer bottle. He and Sawyer had been messing around with pocketknives when Cade was about ten. He'd never seen his mother so mad.

"She'd have given you a good, long lecture and then a great big hug." Tally reached over and squeezed his hand. "Why didn't you tell us?"

He met her gaze, finding nothing but understanding.

Now that he had told her, he wondered how things might have been different if he had confessed years ago. "I don't know. Shame, I suppose. I had vowed to take care of you and Sawyer, and I royally screwed up. Some role model I was."

"You had to leave," she said almost to herself. "If you had told us we could have helped you."

"How?"

"I don't know. Sent you care packages or something." They both chuckled, but not in a comfortable way. "It felt like you abandoned us, Cade."

He heaved a sigh. "I know. And I did in a way. Once I was gone, I couldn't come back. Didn't want to. Out there—" he threw an arm wide "—no one knew me as a high-school dropout or a swamp rat. I had a chance to re-invent myself."

"I get it; I do. Sometimes I wonder why I stay." Tally's voice held a hint of the bitterness he'd carried around like lead weights. A brotherly worry had him taking notes.

"Is everything all right at the gym?"

"Everything at the gym is fabulous." She rose and squeezed his shoulder. "Have you told Sawyer?"

The sudden subject change registered as a deflection, but Cade wasn't sure if either one of them could handle exposing another secret. "Not yet."

"I'm heading back to my place. Unless you want me to stay as a buffer between you two."

Cade drank down the last of his bottle. "We don't need a buffer."

"O-kay," she drew the word out, and tossed her purse over her shoulder.

"Hey. Question."

She turned back with one foot inside and the other out. "Fire away."

"Monroe's fund-raiser. You going?"

"Heck no. It'd be like volunteering to be a human sacrifice."

"You mind if I use your invitation then?"

Her eyebrows rose, but she fished the parchment envelope out of her purse and sailed it across to him like a paper airplane. "Be my guest. Or Monroe's guest."

The envelope landed at his feet and still bore his grungy fingerprints from the afternoon she'd delivered it. He picked it up and tapped it against his lips. He would ask Richard to ship some more clothes, his tux included, and his latest project. Playing handyman for his family wasn't going to cut it, and the deadline for completing the design was fast approaching.

He checked his watch. With the time difference, Richard would still be up, probably enjoying an after-dinner drink. The phone rang twice before his deep, Boston-tinged upper-crust voice sounded on the other end. "Finally, you call. Thought an alligator might have eaten you."

"I haven't even seen a gator, I'll have you know." Cade smiled, completely at ease with the other man.

"I've been worried." Richard's tone turned fatherly.

"Is the Simpson deal not going well?"

"I'm not talking about the deal and you know it. It's going fine, by the way. How's the hand?"

"Better. Sawyer forced me to see a PT, and she's really helped."

"How's the fight going against your demons?"

The question scrambled Cade's mind. "What are you talking about?"

"Please. I know what drives you, even if you avoid talking about it. Now what can I do for you?"

"I'm going to be down here longer than I anticipated. I need you to ship me a few things."

Ice clinked against crystal. Richard was a connoisseur of high-end imported whiskey. "What kind of things?"

"I need my tux. The nice one."

Richard's laugh boomed across the thousand miles separating them. "Yes or no answer. Does this involve a woman from your past?"

Damn Richard and his telepathic abilities. "Yes, but—"

"I'll get it overnighted along with an assortment of other clothes. What else?"

If admitting a woman was part of the reason he was staying longer weren't bad enough, the next request might prove even stickier. "I'm bored. And Sawyer has a decent setup down here. I want you to ship down my latest project."

This time the silence was heavier and Richard's voice held no tease. "What's going on, Cade? Thought this was more a vacation than a relocation?"

"It's neither. It's a rehabilitation. I'm bored and need something to work on. You were after me before I left for El Capitan to wrap up this design. You should be thrilled."

"You're definitely coming back to Seattle by the end of the summer?" Richard didn't sound thrilled; he sounded worried.

"That's still my plan." His reassurance would have felt more solid if doubts weren't shooting holes in his words. "I would be an idiot to screw up what we've built up there."

"You would," Richard said with a hint of warning and another tink of ice.

"Will you see to sending the clothes and the latest design?"

"First thing in the morning."

"Thanks, Richard."

"Yeah, yeah. Don't get eaten by a gator." The phone beeped.

Cade tapped the phone against his chin, unease binding him. While he hadn't exactly lied to Richard, he certainly hadn't been as forthcoming as usual. It wasn't a matter of trust. Richard had proven himself loyal time and again. He had been Cade's guide into an alien world.

When the Cottonbloom's city limits sign faded in his rearview mirror, he'd assumed he'd also left the insular, divided mind-set of the town behind. But like the river mud caked on his boots, he only tracked it into the next city and the next. Even to Seattle.

The same socioeconomic barriers that had kept him apart in Cottonbloom threatened his success in Seattle. In fact, they were more subtle, more dangerous, because instead of being marked by a physical divide like the river, the roadblocks moved, snuck up on him, surprised him.

It was only when he'd learned to play dirty that the barriers no longer barred him from his goals. He played a cutthroat and ruthless game that would make even a banker gasp.

He had success. He had money. The elite welcomed him into their fold like he was born into it. Yet something was still missing, and he wondered if everything he'd learned so far would be of no use in obtaining the missing key to happiness.

It seemed to lie in the hearts of the people he cared about. His funny, fierce sister and his resentful, brilliant brother and his laid-back, irresponsible uncle. And Monroe. Too much seemed to hinge on her. Fear pervaded his unease. His well-guarded independence was being eroded like the river slowly, but surely, reshaped the land around them.

He sat there a long time, his usual decisiveness absent. When he finally went to bed, he opened the window and let the rich, loamy night-cooled breeze from the river sneak memories into his dreams.

Chapter Fourteen

Nerves had Monroe shifting on her strappy heels. Her feet would be hating life tomorrow, but right now the confidence the extra inches gave her was comforting. She'd gone back to try on the sexy cocktail dress in the shop window, and as soon as she'd seen herself in the mirror she'd done some mental calculations in order to justify buying it.

Andrew's eyes lit up when he'd met her at his parents' front door, but she hadn't bought it to impress Andrew. She'd stared at her reflection, wondering what Cade would think of it, and he wasn't even coming to the party. Another red flag that he had worked even deeper into her psyche.

Mrs. Tarwater, dressed in a floor-length beaded gown in gold, greeted her with a kiss that didn't quite touch her cheek. She bustled off to direct the caterers while Mr. Tarwater stood at the mantle with a whiskey, looking like he would rather be getting a liver transplant.

"I'm in charge of getting the bar organized. Will you be fine alone for a few minutes?" The sense of ownership and entitlement in Andrew's smile rankled, but she only gave him a tight-lipped smile drilled into her during hours of cotillion practice.

"I'll be fine." When he leaned in to presumably buss her cheek, she bobbed backward in an instinctive defensive move.

He gave her a funny look but headed off. The two-story living area had been turned into an open gathering area with buffet tables and a bar along the wall and a mini–dance floor in one corner.

If tonight went well, she could book a meeting space and get a counselor in on a regular basis to discuss a roundtable of issues facing the girls. All Monroe had to do was smile and talk up the program for a few hours. A small sacrifice. Her thoughts drifted back to Kayla. Still no word from the girl. Worry took up space in her stomach.

Regan swept in the front door in a little black dress that molded to her curves but covered her from neck to knees. "You went back and bought the dress." Regan hugged her, the delicate floral scent of her perfume enveloping Monroe.

"I wish I hadn't."

"Why on earth not? You look hot."

Monroe looked around, but Mr. Tarwater didn't seem interested in anything except emptying his glass. "Because Andrew assumes I wore it for him. I'm pretty sure he's considering this our first date. I feel like a fraud. Like I'm doing something dirty for the money. Like his mother is buying me for her son."

Regan sighed and waved her hand dismissively around the room. "Ultimately, this is not about you or Andrew. It's all about Mrs. Tarwater. I wouldn't be surprised if she wants you to name the group after her. The Tarwater Girls or some such."

"So I shouldn't feel guilty about this?"

"You're ensuring all these people will sleep better tonight knowing they've helped the less fortunate among us."

Regan's teasing cynicism held more than a seed of truth. "All you have to do is avoid being alone with Andrew the rest of the night, which should be simple. Then, next time he calls politely decline another date. Did you invite Cade?"

"I invited Tally, but she's not coming. Why would I have invited Cade?"

"He would have been a nice, big shield between you and Andrew. And although you were reticent about what went on after you disappeared the other night, you came back covered in greasepaint."

Heat rushed up her neck. "I didn't think you noticed."

"I noticed; I just didn't want to say anything in front of Nash."

Deflection was Monroe's defense of choice when avoiding topics. "What happened between you and Sawyer?"

"Nothing." Regan's cheeks flushed, making her light freckles stand out. "In more exciting news, guess who got pulled over for DWI?"

"I won't even hazard a guess."

"Sam Landry."

A wave of numbing tingles passed through her body. "When?"

"Last week sometime. Not a mile from the Rivershack Tavern by the Cottonbloom Parish police."

"What's going to happen to him?"

"No clue. I don't know if I even have the authority to force him off the town council. I got at least two dozen calls from concerned citizens." Regan air-quoted the last two words and injected a shot of sarcasm. "As if they really care about the town. They were sniffing after information. I suppose he'll be here tonight."

"He's invited?"

"He and old man Tarwater are golfing buddies, and he generally shows up to any social function with an open bar.

Now that he's back in town and single, he's got the look of a man on the prowl."

Ironic to think about Sam giving money to help her cause when in a twisted way he was the reason for its existence. She forced her mind to stay in the moment and not slip into the past.

The first guests arrived and cut off her and Regan's ability to have a private conversation. Andrew approached with a toothy, lopsided grin that Monroe supposed was boyish and charming but also seemed insincere.

"You look gorgeous tonight. Did I tell you?"

"Thank you. You're looking rather dapper yourself." That at least was the truth. Andrew was a good-looking man who wore a tuxedo with the ease of Cary Grant.

"Mother wants you to greet guests with us."

Monroe gritted her teeth behind her smile but allowed Andrew to guide her to stand between him and his mother. She wished for the power to teleport herself down to the edge of the river where the water flowing in the darkness would soothe her frazzled nerves.

Guests arrived in a steady flow over the next half hour. The buzz of noise increased to a near roar, echoing off the marble in the grand entryway. A tight, uncomfortable feeling in her chest grew, ratcheted higher every time Andrew placed his hand on the small of her back, his thumb subtly caressing the skin at the top of the low vee. Finally, after several minutes with no new arrivals and with her cheeks growing sore from her cartoonish smile, she excused herself for a drink.

Clutching a glass of chilled champagne, she nodded and made small talk with a slice of Cottonbloom's elite. She'd grown up with her feet firmly planted in this world, but it was like she was wearing a pair of shoes that were a size too small.

The woman she was making inane small talk with

wandered away to chat with a group of women surrounded by a pungent cloud of Chanel Nº5 and holding Gucci bags.

Monroe ducked behind one of the faux pillars, her untouched glass of champagne sloshing onto her hand. Maybe she needed some liquid courage. She took a too-big gulp. The champagne burned the back of her nose, and she put the glass on a nearby table.

"You look like you need another glass for survival's sake." The deep rumbly voice close to her ear startled her around. Her senses went into overdrive cataloging the man in front of her. Her ears had concluded the man was undoubtedly Cade Fournette, but her gaze roved over his neatly trimmed hair, clean-shaven face, and impeccably tailored tuxedo unconvinced.

No stodgy cummerbund or pleated white shirt for Cade. The man might be auditioning to play James Bond. He looked years younger and sophisticated without the beard. He was the sexiest thing Monroe had ever seen.

"Here." He held out one glass of champagne and took a sip of the other.

She took it like a robot, still blinking against the radiance of manhood in front of her. "I'm surprised you're not drinking a martini."

"Shaken, not stirred?" He smiled, his lips more expressive without the frame of hair. "The invitation did say black tie."

"Sure did," she said inanely while staring at his perfectly tied bow tie. Obviously not a clip-on. She tried to look away but only got so far as to notice the width of his shoulders in the black well-fitting jacket. "Is Tally coming, too?"

"Nope, but she sends her best."

The cologne he'd applied filtered through the air and drew her closer for a deep, shuddery breath. Her thong was

no match for the delicious spicy scent obviously formu-
lated to disintegrate women's underwear.

"What's wrong? You don't like champagne?" He'd finished his glass while she'd been staring at him.

"I don't drink." The ease with which the words came
out surprised her. Not that it was a deep, dark secret, but
she had gone through college and afterward with a cam-
ouflaging drink in her hand. It had seemed easier than
going into the reasons she was a teetotaler.

He hummed, took the glass out of her hand, and set it
down. "Because of your mother?"

People milled, not close enough to overhear but too
close for a discussion she didn't want to have in the first
place. She nodded, and he moved into her space. With him
near, it was easy to get distracted.

"You shaved." Without instruction from her brain, her
index finger trailed down his strong cheekbone and across
his bottom lip.

His eyes flared and his stance turned predatory, all
charm and good humor wiped from his face by her touch.
He looked like he might devour her right there in the
middle of Cottonbloom's finest. She was no mouse to his
cat. Maybe she'd jump him first, wrap her legs around his
hips, and beg him to find a horizontal surface. Or maybe
even vertical. Could he see the intent in her eyes?

Why was he here? Certainly not because he had taken
up her cause. Maybe to thumb his nose at the people who'd
never given him the time of day years ago? Maybe to prove
he was as good as they were? Or had he come for her?

She needed to steer them back onto solid ground and
out of the engulfing waves of desire flowing and ebbing
between them. She cleared her throat but still sounded unusually husky. "Why did you come tonight, Cade?"

Chapter Fifteen

He'd walked into the room, drawn to her like a ship seeking a safe harbor in the storm. Not that he was nervous exactly, but a chord thrummed off-key and disorienting in his chest. The sight of her calmed him. He'd grabbed two drinks and stalked her. From behind he took in the expanse of white exposed by the low plunge of her dress and the sexily mussed artful updo. Yet under the soft, seemingly delicate skin of her back was toned muscle.

He was a natural hunter, studying his prey, exploiting weaknesses, applying the necessary leverage to achieve his goal—whether it was to trap or annihilate. The mentality contributed to his success and solidified his reputation as a ruthless negotiator.

Monroe wasn't playing a game. Her gaze was hungry, and he found himself wanting to match her candor. Why pretend? This was what he'd come for. To see her. To have her see him. To show her he was as comfortable in this world as he was on the river. That he could compete with and beat the Andrew Tarwaters of the world.

"I'm here representing the Fournettes. That okay?"

"Of course. I just wasn't expecting . . ." Her gaze trailed down his body.

Her dismay made him smile, as had the reaction of the parking attendant who'd gotten the pleasure of parking the old truck. Cade was enjoying flaunting the juxtaposition of his youth and what he'd made of himself.

"You look beautiful. That dress should come with a warning label."

The blush suffusing her fair skin started at her chest and reached into her cheeks. And he could tell because the front plunged nearly as deeply as the back. The clutch pressed under her arm and the blue-stoned pendant that hung between her breasts discreetly emphasized the soft curves. He wanted to touch her but was afraid he wouldn't be able to stop.

"You clean up pretty well yourself," she said with a sultriness that was unbalancing.

The black Armani suit he wore had been tailored for him. Off-the-rack suits never had enough give to comfortably contain the breadth of his shoulders, and he'd learned from Richard that packaging mattered. Especially to the group gathered tonight.

"I occasionally get gussied up and paraded around to potential investors and companies interested in licensing my patents."

"Just how rich are you?"

Coming from any other woman, the question would have put him on guard and have him seeking the nearest emergency exit. But Monroe had tossed the question out with a vagueness that told him she didn't really care. It was simple curiosity.

"I have enough money to do what I want. Travel. Have fun."

"Like helping Tally get her gym off the ground?"

He clenched his jaw and debated whether to deny it.

Normally, he didn't have a problem twisting the truth to fit his agenda, but Monroe had awakened his long-dormant conscience and it loomed like a Titan in his mind. There was no doubt in his mind they were in negotiations. He just wasn't certain what was at stake. "She wasn't supposed to tell anyone."

"She didn't. Shockingly, *I'm* not a dummy." Her teasing drawl made him smile.

Something he never did during negotiations. This negotiation felt like the most important deal of his life. He never allowed any deal to become so important he couldn't walk away, yet nothing short of an explosion was prying him away from her right now. Alarms sounded dimly.

"Shockingly, I've noticed."

"What else have you noticed?" Was this how the phrase "undressing him with her eyes" originated? Because he could almost feel the tug on the knot of his black silk bow tie.

How far was she willing to take their flirtation in a room with her social peers? He tested her by letting his gaze follow the deep vee of her dark-blue cocktail dress. She didn't shy away. Her shoulders flattened against the pillar and her back arched in a pose of complete confidence and ease with her body.

The cut of the dress emphasized the shape and fullness of her breasts unmarred by a bra. A hint of her nipples peaked against the fabric made him achingly aware he could slip the dress off her shoulders and expose her to his eyes and mouth. He settled a hand on the pillar above her head and leaned closer, not touching her in any way. Her scent wove around him, sensual and alluring.

"I've noticed you're all grown-up and like to play with fire, Monroe."

Her gaze dipped as she played with the pendant hanging between her breasts.

His voice turned even huskier. "I can't stop thinking about the way you went wild on me down by the river."

Her eyes flared and her fingers stilled. He was honestly as surprised as she was to hear the words come out of his mouth. He'd laid all his cards on the table instead of protecting his trump.

"Maybe it was the situation."

"Which was?"

"You know, dark and dangerous."

The thought of another man on his back with Monroe straddling him and driving him insane with her kisses made Cade's teeth grind. "So you would have kissed Andrew Buttwater like that?"

"That is the most juvenile nickname I've ever heard," she whispered on a spate of giggles.

It had been completely juvenile. The old nickname had jumped from his head to his mouth. He'd learned early on to fight the Andrew Tarwaters of the world with words, not fists. Usually, his technique was more refined, but the man gigged Cade something fierce.

"You laughed," he said in a slightly embarrassed, defensive voice.

"Well, I've never claimed to have a highbrow sense of humor." She winked at him.

The feelings tumbling in his stomach as if they were in a dryer were disconcerting and unfamiliar. He took a deep breath and grounded himself by glancing around the room.

Andrew held court, surrounded by half the Junior League. Regan Lovell stood by the floor-to-ceiling windows, staring out into the dark, pensive and in her own world. Holding his drink in both hands and looking tortured, Mr. Tarwater had been cornered by the Church of Christ preacher and his wife, probably on the hunt for their own donation.

Cade recognized a few townspeople straight off, the

only visible changes a few more gray hair and thicker bodies. Some he couldn't name, although something about them would trigger recognition. Time had marched across Cottonbloom like Sherman's army.

"Everyone here is writing you a check for your program?"

"I suppose so. I'm grateful for anything, to be honest. I can teach the girls to defend themselves, but you saw what happened with Kayla. She's still not returning my texts. I worry something worse will happen."

"Worse?"

"Date rape is disgustingly common. Lots of times the girls blame themselves. They don't tell anyone. They think because the guy is their *boyfriend*—" she air-quoted the word "—that makes everything okay."

"Was it like that when we were growing up?"

"Can't you remember?" She graced him with a small smile. "You know, I always wondered if you had a girlfriend back then but was too shy to ask."

"I was too busy working, and with no extra money to take a girl anywhere nice. Anyway, I wasn't exactly a catch. The girls interested in a high-school dropout supporting two kids were on the desperate side."

He didn't mention the pang he'd felt when all the kids in his class went to prom. He was getting off a long second shift when girls in sequins and ruffles and boys in tuxedos and colorful vests had taken over his usual haunt. Their energy permeated the plate-glass window of the late-night diner, and Cade had sat in his truck, the engine sputtering, looking from his former classmates to his grease-lined fingernails and rough hands. He'd driven off and skipped dinner.

Her tone was still light, but it sounded forced. "I didn't date much, either."

Although discussing his love life had been off-limits

during their full-moon meetings, she'd sometimes talked about one boy or another who wanted to date her. At first Cade had felt protective, knowing how boys could be, but later on the feelings had been more complicated. He'd eventually stopped asking if she had a boyfriend, because picturing her with someone else had made him mad and resentful.

"Who'd you go to prom with?" If she said Tarwater, he would need something stronger than champagne.

Her lips twitched. "Regan made for a lovely date. Since she couldn't go with Sawyer, we went together. There was no one in my school I wanted to go with anyway."

"What if I'd asked you?" Why the hell had he said that?

She drew in a quick breath. "I didn't think you saw me like that."

"I didn't. It was a hypothetical question." He cleared his throat and took a step back, needing to put some distance between them. "I hope you can put my donation to good use."

"I appreciate you taking an interest. You saw firsthand why I need the money."

"Look, I feel bad for girls like Kayla, but don't mistake me for an altruistic do-gooder." His gravelly voice was full of warning and got her attention.

"What do you mean?" She narrowed her eyes on him.

"I don't take on causes."

Her head tilted, her look one of cautious confusion.

Did she really need him to say it? After years of watching her, protecting her, the words felt inevitable, and his voice emerged with a primal roughness. "I came for you, Monroe. I want *you*. You understand me?"

Underneath the coarse sentiment lurked something even more potent. Something he wasn't ready to acknowledge. Sex was simple and straightforward and the only thing he could honestly offer her.

Instead of acting surprised or outraged or even pleased, she hardened her expression into something he recognized as determination. He saw the same every morning when he looked in the mirror.

"What if that's not enough for me?"

A virtual gauntlet had been thrown, and Cade, for the first time in a long time, was at a loss as to his next move. What the hell did she expect from him? Promises of forever? Impossible.

He saw what he wanted and pursued it with the same single-mindedness that had kept his family together. If what he wanted was sex, he got it. End of story. He hadn't had any complaints. Not that he stuck around long enough for a woman to fill out a comment card.

Monroe certainly wasn't immune to him as a man. Maybe he could exploit that weakness. With her back against the pillar, a sense of false privacy emboldened him. "Your necklace is lovely. Perfect for the lines of your dress."

Starting at her collarbone, he trailed two fingers on either side of the chain, all the way to the pendant. He fingered the blue stone, letting the backs of his fingers brush the inner curves of her breasts. Her breathing hitched, and her skin flushed, the delicate scent of her perfume becoming stronger.

She whispered his name, and he looked from his hands to her eyes. He fell into their depths, the buzz of people muting into nothing. He recognized her blazing need, was sure she could see the same in him. But there was something else. Caution.

She covered his hand, her fingers soft on his work-dinged knuckles. He stopped teasing her and took her hand in his, threading their fingers in a symbolic gesture from long ago.

"Hypothetically speaking, Cade? I would have said yes."

The warmth that enveloped him had nothing to do with passion.

"There you are, Monroe." Andrew sauntered up from the side, and she dropped Cade's hand like she was ashamed. Hell, maybe she was.

Andrew slid a hand behind Monroe's back, and Cade puffed his chest out like a territorial animal. With as low as the dress plunged, the man was no doubt touching her bare skin. The thought was nearly unbearable.

Andrew's annoying fluorescent smile flickered. His gaze darted between Cade and Monroe. The man would have to be blind and deaf not to sense the undercurrents between them.

A fiftyish-year-old DJ in an ill-fitting tuxedo filled the empty space in the room with music. A Sinatra throwback brought a few couples to the middle of the great room and conversations swelled louder to compensate for the extra noise.

"Fournette. Excellent to see a Louisiana representative here, considering most of the girls Monroe helps are from your side of the river."

A sledgehammer began decimating every polite thought and word Cade retained, sending his mood meter to "ill." "Tarwater. I'm happy to support Monroe. And Tally."

"This problem is not confined to race or economics, Andrew. You know I have girls from both sides of the river," she said in a chiding tone that made Cade think she'd told Andrew several times already.

A wave of clapping crashed through the bubble isolating them from the rest of the party. A few people called Monroe's name.

"Mother wants you to say a few words. If you'll excuse us?" Andrew shot Cade a look that could maim. Cade held his eyes a beat longer than was comfortable and bared his teeth in the approximation of a smile.

Andrew guided Monroe to the bar area where his mother waited to hand her a glass of champagne. A speech followed. Her confidence was natural and commanding, yet Cade only half paid attention to her words of praise for the community and the listing of services she wanted to provide for the at-risk girls on both sides of the state line.

Andrew stayed glued to her side, a hand on her at all times as if she were either incapable of standing on her own or a flight risk. He stared at Monroe with a combination of puppyish devotion and very adult intentions. The man looked utterly charmed by her.

A smattering of applause marked the conclusion of her gracious speech. These people had come for a party and a tax write-off. While fundamentally they cared about stopping abuse, in reality they didn't have time to worry about it—unless it touched them in a personal way like it had Monroe.

Andrew cupped her elbow and leaned down to whisper in her ear. He was probably breathing in the sweet scent of her skin and admiring her breasts like Cade had done. Andrew guided her to the open area and twirled her into a dance. Cade fumed, stoking the hostility bubbling through his body like lava.

A waiter walked by with a tray of champagne. Cade grabbed a glass and tossed it back in two swallows. His tie was a noose, and he untied the bow and unbuttoned the top button of his dress shirt, letting the ends dangle.

Andrew's mother joined Cade at the pillar. He pried his gaze away from Monroe. Mrs. Tarwater required his full attention if he didn't want her to strike unexpectedly. Her smile was a warning. "Mr. Fournette. How good of you to come."

He didn't bother with a smile. He was here for Monroe. Even so, the compulsion to impress a bunch of folks who'd never given him a chance in hell of doing anything with his life weighed on his chest like a shovel full of river mud.

Mrs. Tarwater sipped a glass of champagne, the diamonds on her bracelet twinkling under the lights. She reeked of old money, good breeding, and expensive perfume. If she had been a hunting dog, she'd be a purebred pointer. Cade had always had an affinity for mutts.

"Mrs. Tarwater. It was good of you to put this fundraiser together."

"Yes. We adore Monroe." She tilted her head, looking up through her lashes. An old-fashioned glance labeled "How to Manipulate Men" in the 1950s Debutante Handbook. "Andrew is enchanted."

Cade's gaze shot to the dance floor where Monroe was turning the magic of her smile on Andrew. Something painful crimped his heart. Was she using him for a temporary thrill until she settled down with a man like Andrew?

Mrs. Tarwater continued sotto voce. "Your donation to Monroe's cause was very generous, Mr. Fournette, but I wouldn't want it to cause you undue hardship. If you want me to tear up the check, I'll make sure no one's the wiser."

Part of him wanted to spout his net worth, wanted to make it clear that he could outright buy their mansion if he wanted. The prideful part, the one that made sure his chin was up when he went to the food banks as a teenager, made him say only, "That won't be necessary. Now if you'll excuse me."

He turned his back on her and headed to the edge of the crowd. A man stood close to the bar and stared at him as if he'd like to slip a blade between Cade's ribs. A familiarity tinged the antipathy, and Cade riffled through his memories to place the middle-aged man. It didn't take long for the man to weave through the crowd toward him.

"Evening," Cade offered with the carefulness of baiting a trap.

"It was you, wasn't it? I saw you that night."

"You're going to have to be more specific, I'm afraid."

"You called the cops to pick me up."

"Not me, sir. And where did you say you saw me?"

The man's shoulders dropped and some of the animosity slipped off his face. "You don't remember me, do you, *boy*?"

Ignoring the blatant jab, he studied the man again. Cade had tried to keep a low profile in Cottonbloom during his youth, needing to stay out of trouble in order to keep Tally and Sawyer with him, but he'd obviously pissed this man off at some point.

The frisson of recognition coursing through Cade was like sticking his finger in an electrical socket. "Sam Landry. Thought you'd married and moved on to Georgia. When did you crawl back to town?" Fury that should have diminished over the past decade crackled between them.

Once the man had married and left Cottonbloom, Cade had stopped keeping tabs on him. His tuxedo was stylish and he'd been invited, so his life hadn't self-destructed. Unfortunately.

"You always were a rude little swamp rat." The ingratiating smile on Sam's face was for appearance's sake only.

His insult didn't faze Cade. He'd been called much worse. "Does Monroe know you're back?"

His lips curled in and he muttered, "Goddamn, Monroe. It was her."

Cade's back bowed and he took a step toward the man. "What are you talking about?"

"Monroe and I had a little chat at the Tavern the other night and then I'm pulled over by the cops? No way is that a coincidence."

Cade had been so focused on finding Monroe that night, he hadn't given anyone else at the Tavern a second of his attention. Now he wished he'd met up with Sam in the

Tavern's dark parking lot and not the bright lights of the Tarwaters' mansion.

"What'd they nail you for? Drinking and driving?" Sam's no response was answer enough. Maybe things weren't going so well for him after all. "Whether Monroe called the cops or not, you were the one who got behind the wheel. You expect people to look the other way?"

"I'm on the Cottonbloom city council. Got elected in the spring." He laid the fact down as if it were a get out of jail free card in Monopoly. Cade wouldn't be surprised if Sam made a run for Cottonbloom mayor next election cycle. The man possessed a snake-like charm and was still nice looking and trim. To many people, nothing mattered but the packaging.

How could Monroe face the man day in and day out? "I've not forgotten what you tried to do to Monroe years ago."

"You took the word of a young, impressionable girl who had a crush on me. Her feelings got hurt when I told her I loved her mama. If you'd given me the chance to—"

"You've told yourself that lie enough times, you actually believe it, don't you?"

"It's the truth." Sam's dark eyes flashed with uncertainty before blanking. "She got mad and ran off."

"Maybe she's come to terms with what you tried to do. I, however, don't have such a forgiving nature. You're hiding a bushel of trouble somewhere. Maybe I'll go looking."

"Are you threatening me?" The shocked wonder in the man's voice made him think not many people crossed Sam Landry.

"Yep. I believe I am." At that, Cade ambled off with a smile on his face. It never hurt to leave an enemy off-balance. Having ammunition at the ready in case he did something to hurt Monroe would be smart. Cade would make some calls. As arrogant as Sam seemed, he wouldn't have hidden his troubles too deep.

Monroe was still hobnobbing with Andrew Tarwater as her guide. After his confrontation with Sam Landry, old memories lingered in his mind like rotting fish. He stepped through the French doors and took deep breaths. The heat and humidity of the day had fallen into a cool, comfortable night.

His body thrummed with pent-up frustration. He might be in the most expensive clothes in the room and have signed the biggest check, but 'Sips like the Tarwaters would never see him as more than a swamp rat. Andrew led Monroe back onto the dance floor. Insecurities Cade thought long buried reared up.

Chapter Sixteen

Tension kept Monroe's body stiff in Andrew's arms as he shuffled her to the beat of the music. She enjoyed dancing, but not this kind. She enjoyed rocking out in her kitchen and singing into a spatula while she cooked. Dozens of sets of eyes bored into them. While Andrew seemed unfazed, every vein in her body felt like it had been shot with quick-hardening cement.

The interminable song ended, and she took a step backward, trying to escape Andrew's embrace. She bumped into Andrew's father, who'd been coerced onto the dance floor with his wife, looking about as happy as a cow headed to the butcher.

Monroe mumbled an, "I'm sorry," and pointed her feet toward her hiding place behind the pillar. She prayed Cade would be waiting. Mrs. Tarwater took her wrist.

"Darling, let's switch. I'll dance with my son and you dance with Bill."

Jean Tarwater wasn't a woman who accepted *no* as an answer. It's what made her a force for good and bad in the community. A piranha in the courtroom, Bill Tarwater sighed complacently, took Monroe's hand, and pulled her into a dancing stance. Her surprise at his easy acquiescence made her a pliable partner. Several other couples joined them. A sense of claustrophobia made her heart beat too fast.

Andrew caught her gaze and grinned over his mother's head. Monroe was a fraud. He believed he had a chance with her, but another man had set up camp in her head . . . and heart. Knowing Cade was somewhere watching her made this exponentially worse.

"My wife likes you. I can't say that she's ever felt that way about one of Andrew's girlfriends before." Even at a near whisper, Mr. Tarwater's voice held a hint of courtroom resonance.

She stutter-stepped. "Andrew and I are not dating."

He tensed, slowing their swaying movements, the hand at her back gesturing to the side. "Why did he and Jean plan all this then?"

"I assume because they wanted to support the expansion of my girls at risk group. It's very much appreciated by me and all the girls." The polite, stiff thanks was all she had to offer.

The incredulous glance he aimed in her direction made her feel a little too much like the accused on cross-examination. "My son is very taken with you. You're all I hear about at the office."

Andrew was polite and knowledgeable about the world. He was handsome and well-off. But he had never entered uninvited into her dreams at night. He had never made her feel the least bit like losing control.

"Your son is a fine man," she said in as honest and heartfelt a voice as she could muster.

"An evasion." Bill Tarwater chuckled, although little humor penetrated the sound. "A word of advice, Monroe?"

Not sure she wanted to hear, she nodded anyway.

"Men like Cade Fournette are users. He's been beaten

down too many times and tries too hard to prove he belongs with people like us. He doesn't belong and never will. If you take up with him, my son won't be waiting."

Anger burned away the layers of polite lessons. She had the urge to flip him on his back in the middle of the dance floor. What would Jean Tarwater think of her then?

Forcing her chin up and her eyes to meet his, Monroe stopped the shuffling dance and shook her arms free of him. "I'm nothing like you. Cade Fournette has nothing to prove, least of all to anyone here."

Not caring whether it was rude, she walked away and pushed through the crowd to their pillar. No sign of Cade. Had he given up on her and left? Tears stung. Alone. She needed to be alone. She continued on to the bathroom. Several chatting women were knotted in the hallway and had her changing course. The last thing she wanted to do was engage in a round of gossip.

The back wing of the house was dark and several degrees cooler than the body-jammed great room. Tiptoeing and feeling like an interloper even though no one had closed off the area, she pushed the door to a guest bedroom open and stepped from hardwood onto plush carpet. The room had the unused smell of mothballs and cleaner.

Air chugged from the vents. Hair tickled her nape and the air stirred against the bare skin along her front and back. A shiver passed through her, her nipples reacting to the sudden coolness.

"Tired of dancing?" Cade's deep voice startled her around. He'd propped his shoulder against the doorframe, his hands tucked into the pockets of his pants. He was lit from behind, his face a blank, dark space.

She couldn't determine from his flat voice whether he was upset or angry. With Bill Tarwater's comments fresh and painful, she flew at him and wrapped her arms around his neck, her heels bringing her within an inch of his mouth. Although he hadn't heard the vitriol, she needed to comfort him anyway.

"Wha—"

Her lips silenced the rest of his question. The champagne on his tongue was almost as intoxicating as his scent. The music from the great room drifted, muted and unrecognizable. As if slow dancing, he wrapped his arms around her and turned them enough so he could close the door, leaving them in silence, except for the ticking of a clock.

His hands roamed her bare back, slipping inside of her dress to brush the top curves of her buttocks. She pushed him backward against the wall. Infinitely stronger than her, he could have held his ground or taken charge at any point, but the fact that he let her lead only made her want him more. She was done listening to logic, done fighting her hunger for him. She wanted him.

Cupping her cheeks, he pulled his lips from hers. "And again you do the unexpected."

"Unwanted?" she whispered.

"Does it look like I'm protesting?" His breath puffed against her cheek before he kissed her once more, slipping his tongue alongside hers, before his mouth retreated once more. She tipped into him seeking more. He took her weight, bracing his legs farther apart, but evaded her mouth.

"I watched you dancing with Tarwater. What are you playing at? Is he the man you want to be seen with and I'm the one you're keeping for the dark?" A thread of emotion in his voice tied itself around her heart and bound her. Was he jealous? Hurt? Angry?

"Do you think I'm using you?" She pushed off his chest.

"You know I'm not staying long."

She did know. She just didn't want to think about the day he would walk away from Cottonbloom. And from her. "What are you getting at?"

"I think you get something from him you can't get from me and vice versa. He has clout in this town, but I'm the man that you want in the dark and in your bed, aren't I?"

"If you think all I care about is my standing in this town, why did you follow me?"

"Because I want you. That's why I came." Belligerence instead of seduction beat at his words. Underneath was a boy who did care what Cottonbloom thought of him. He hadn't always been the poor swamp rat sneaking around in the dark.

"All you want is sex?"

"If that's what you're offering." His voice softened, and he squeezed her hips and fit them together. "I can be rough and dirty and a little bit dangerous if that's how you want me."

Arousal flared even as the gentleness of his touch belied his coarse words. He skimmed his good hand from her hip to settle under her breast, his thumb running up and down the exposed skin in between. Her nipple puckered, begging for his touch.

"Is that what you want, sweetheart?"

Her body shifted toward his instinctively, seeking to anchor itself to him, needing to draw from his heat and strength. "Th-that's not what I want." Before the words were even out, she knew they were untrue, or at least a partial truth. Sex wasn't *all* she wanted. But she did want it.

"Don't lie to yourself or me." He dropped his lips to the shell of her ear and nuzzled. She grabbed the lapels of his jacket. "I could take you right here, right now, with the Tarwaters and all of crazy Cottonbloom a few rooms away. And I'd make it good, Monroe. I'd make your body sing. I'd make you beg before giving you everything you need. Then, you could walk back out into that damn party like nothing happened. No one would know the things you want to do in the dark with a poor, dirty boy from Louisiana."

Her body sang a song of longing and need. She wanted to stay in the dark with him the rest of the night, but there was something even more important she needed to do. With the effort of separating strong magnets, she pried her body from his, opened the door, and took him by the wrist.

"Come with me." Reality in the form of a crooning Michael Bublé song and the murmur of laughter-punctuated conversation drifted closer.

"What are you doing?" An edge of panic replaced his dark sexual tease. She'd thrown him off-balance. Good. Time for her to return the favor.

She led him back into the great room. The song changed to an eighties ballad she occasionally heard on the classic rock station and in old movies. While it wouldn't have been her statement song of choice, it would have to do.

She stopped at the edge of where a handful of couples swayed like they were reliving their high-school prom.

"You want to dance with me?" Incredulity but also a sense of wonder lilted his question. "In front of the Tarwaters and all of Cottonbloom, Mississippi?"

She answered by slipping her hand in his and squeezing. As if they had made a pact to jump at the same time, they moved forward on the same beat of music. She turned toward him, sliding her hands up the lapels of his tuxedo to link around his neck.

He tightened his arm around her waist and brought them closer than she'd danced with Andrew. "You sure you know what you're doing?" He splayed his fingers on her back, tucking them under the edge of her dress. She felt branded.

"I have no idea what we're doing; do you?"

His mouth tightened before he laughed softly and skimmed his smooth chin along her temple. "Not a clue."

Whispers and side-eye glances came from all directions. She'd be lying if she said she wasn't uncomfortable, but not because she was ashamed of Cade.

The song ended, and they stopped swaying yet stayed interlocked. The next song was faster paced, leaving them in limbo.

Cade tensed, sending a cold stare over her shoulder a second before someone tapped her arm.

"Could I have a moment, Monroe?" Although Andrew directed the question toward her, his gaze was pinned on Cade. The possibility of one of them throwing a punch seemed high. People on the dance floor weren't bothering to disguise their interest.

If only to defuse the situation, she smiled. "Of course. I'll be back in a second. Okay, Cade?"

He chucked his chin toward the pillar. "Sure. What-ever." Even though they stood close, distance shadowed his face and voice.

She allowed Andrew to guide her through a side door and into the garden. The cooler air was a welcome balm after the muggy great room. They stopped where the manicured lawn gave way to the field. The river was in the distance and the knowledge settled her nerves. If worse came to worst, she could hightail it into the night and seek the safety she'd always found on the river with Cade.

"What did you need to discuss?" she asked.

Andrew stepped closer and propped his hands on his hips, his bow tie askew. Sensitized to the smell of alcohol, she sniffed and confirmed her unease.

"What do you think you're doing?" Around her he'd always maintained a jovial front, but he'd inherited his father's courtroom demeanor.

"Not sure what you're talking about."

"My mother did all of this—" he flung a hand toward the house "—because I asked her to. She doesn't care about those girls any more than I do. And you go and embarrass me in front of everyone with that swamp rat."

Anger swept through her like a brush fire igniting. "Tell your mother to rip up the checks and return any donations. I didn't ask for any of this."

"What about us?" He settled his hands on her shoulders, his fingers moving in a near caress.

Instinctively she broke his grasp in an aggressive move intended to deter an attack. "There is no *us* beyond friendship. There never was and never will be."

Hurt and anger in equal measures marred his catalog good looks. She took a step backward, and he matched her retreat.

Moonlight shimmered over the dewy manicured gardens. The beauty and magic in the night air had an effect on Cade, but perhaps not the one the landscaper intended. The scene was set for lovers and somewhere in the shadows were Andrew and Monroe. If Cade came upon them in an embrace—or worse—he would drive himself straight to the nearest airport.

Voices carried from a back corner where high hedges concealed the tinkling of a fountain. On hunting feet he drew closer. Frustration strung the male voice tinny. "We're perfect together. Everyone says so."

"I don't feel *that* way about you. I can't help it." Monroe's voice carried more compassion than Andrew deserved.

"You haven't given me a chance to take you out. I can get a table anytime at the country club. I'm invited to every party in Cottonbloom. He can't compete with me." Tarwater's frustration morphed into determination and warning zinged up Cade's spine. Men out to prove something to a woman made poor decisions more times than not. It started on elementary-school playgrounds and continued until the coffin lid was closed. "Let me show you how good we could be together."

Cade stepped from behind the bush. Andrew gripped Monroe's upper arms, his face poked forward like a turtle's head out of its shell. Monroe's back was bowed, trying to avoid him.

"Get your hands off her."

When Andrew didn't immediately comply, Cade took two ground-swallowing steps and shoved him in the shoulder. Andrew stumbled back, letting go of her to catch his balance. Cade stepped in front of her.

Andrew's upper lip curled. "You always were a pathetic little swamp rat. You remember cleaning up after me?"

"Yeah. You always were an entitled prick."

"We aren't in high school anymore, Fournette. That's right, I forgot, you never finished high school." With his smirk in place, he transferred his attention to Monroe, who'd stepped from behind Cade. "You seriously want this—" he flicked a finger toward Cade "—instead of me?"

Cade's hands fisted, nerves tingling along his wounded palm. One more word and he'd punch a couple of Andrew's perfect teeth out.

Monroe wrapped her hands around one of Cade's biceps and squeezed. "Yes, I want him."

A good amount of the resentment and bitterness that had grown all evening escaped with his huge, sighing breath. Andrew didn't matter anymore. Cade transferred his attention to her.

He wanted to see the soft glow in her blue eyes. Instead, her expression had taken on that of a scolding teacher.

"You two deserve each other," Andrew mumbled on his stumbling way past them. Cade didn't spare him a glance and neither did Monroe.

"Do you mean it?" he asked.

"Of course I mean it. I don't say things I don't mean." Her voice was brisk with an edge of annoyance.

She didn't want Andrew Tarwater. She wanted to be

with Cade, and their dance had been the announcement. He had never experienced the feelings churning inside of him, couldn't even begin to identify them. It was a rush like he'd climbed the tallest rock face and stood on the dizzying edge of the world.

He grinned. She popped his shoulder with her fist. The unexpectedness of the move sent him back a step.

"What the heck, Cade? You did not help matters."

"You don't want him."

"No. But I would have handled the situation diplomatically—and about a million percent more maturely than you did. It's not like he was forcing himself on me. And—news flash—even if he'd tried, I would have had him curled into a crying ball of mush in about five seconds."

"I thought I was helping." He rotated his shoulder, the spot she'd punched smarting.

"What is it about Andrew that makes you crazed?"

Andrew, Monroe, the town as a whole, had turned him into someone he thought he'd left behind for good. Someone with the drive to prove he belonged, to prove he deserved someone like her. The crazy part was that he felt more alive than he'd been in years.

Maybe subconsciously he'd known coming back would expose a fault line; he just wasn't prepared for Monroe to set off the earthquake.

"You want me, and everyone knows it." He hadn't stopped smiling.

"Maybe I should reconsider." Her voice veered from exasperated to a full-out tease, and the hint of an answering smile quivered her lips.

He had no idea what his next move was. Throwing her over his shoulder and making tracks to the nearest bed would only cement his Neanderthal-ish behavior. They entered into an unofficial staring contest, except instead of abiding by playground rules, he let his gaze lick up and down her body, never blinking.

The breeze fluttered her skirt around her legs, giving him peeks of her toned, sexy thighs, and the moon lit the path of her bare skin from neck to below her breasts like a landing strip. She was unfazed by his blatantly sexual perusal and even took a step closer. The air took on an electric quality that was fast becoming familiar.

She startled as if stung. Flipping her clutch open, she pulled out a phone. The light of the screen emphasized her frown and the worried pull around her eyes. He went on alert. "What's wrong?"

"Nothing. It's probably nothing, but I've got to go." Her voice cracked, revealing a distracted worry. "I'll see you later, okay?"

She spun around, her skirt floating around her, and ran like Cinderella up to the house. Thunder cracked in the distance, and he looked to the west. Clouds encroached on the stars, snuffing the pinpoints of light. With Monroe gone, Cade could commiserate.

Instead of running the social gauntlet, he let himself out of the garden by a side gate. No one would miss him. The taillights of Monroe's SUV shone in the distance. She'd left in a hurry. Would it hurt to make sure she was safe?

Chapter Seventeen

Monroe's hands trembled on the wheel. Her mother's text had been nearly indecipherable. As telling as a slurred phone call. She parked behind her mother's old BMW in her childhood home's driveway. The bumper was crumpled on one end and rust was eating at a side panel. Once a symbol of status and now a symbol of decline.

She slid out of her SUV, feeling overdressed and underprepared for what awaited. After Sam's insinuations, she had been anticipating a phone call from her mother with a fateful dread. It didn't seem to lessen the shock and disappointment.

Monroe stared at the front door and gathered her courage, feeling more alone than she had in years. The spare key was under a flowerpot with sun-wilted pink petunias. She unlocked the door and replaced the key. Kicking off her heels, she threw the lock out of long-ingrained habit.

"Mother?" Her voice echoed with a tentative quality of youth.

Every step farther into the house tumbled her backward in time to her tumultuous childhood. Some memories were good. The weeks when her mother was between boyfriends, between binges, when all her attention was focused on Monroe. The smell of cookies would greet her after school, and they would watch movies or put puzzles together.

But many memories were tinged with fear and loneliness. The procession of men through her mother's life intersected hers. The nice ones never lasted long. It was the men like Sam who stuck, because they exploited her mother's fondness for alcohol and drama.

"Mother?"

"Up here." Her mother's voice was weak and tremulous.

Monroe took the steps two at a time. Light spilled out of the bathroom. Like in a horror movie, she tiptoed closer when every instinct urged her to turn and run from the monster.

Except her mother had turned from monster into a pitiable creature. She sat on the floor in front of the toilet, her tight pencil skirt riding up her thighs, dark blond hair straggling around her pale face.

Monroe flushed the vomit down the toilet and helped her mother stand. Treating her like a child, Monroe washed the trails of mascara off her face and helped brush her teeth. She led her mother into her bedroom, got her skirt and the tight undergarments off. Finding a T-shirt in one of the drawers, Monroe guided her mother's arms through the holes and tucked her into bed.

Since she'd never remarried, mostly out of spite, her mother had maintained her lifestyle on the alimony Monroe's father had anted up each month. But his court-ordered commitment had been fulfilled at twenty years. With the monthly support gone, her mother had been forced to work. Without a college degree or skills, she got a job as a secretary-receptionist at a doctor's office with Monroe pulling strings in the background. Although it didn't pay great, her mother had seemed happy. Monroe had thought she was finally in a good place.

Monroe sat on the edge of the bed and stroked her mother's hair back. At least her fall hadn't involved Sam Landry. "Who were you with tonight?"

"Friends."

"Where'd you go?"

"The Corner Pocket. Met a man. Seemed nice. Hot. Young. Kept buying me drinks."

Monroe closed her eyes and fisted her hands in her lap. The Corner Pocket was an almost cookie-cutter bar to the Rivershack Tavern, but on the Mississippi side. The crowd skewed younger with college kids and young professionals. The main draws were the pool tables and the drink specials. An alcoholic at a bar was like an overeater at a buffet.

"You know better than to hang out at the Corner Pocket."

"Got invited by a girl at work. Didn't want to be rude."

"I wish you'd come to the fund-raiser with me." Monroe spoke mostly to the universe.

After a pause, her mother asked, "Why do I do this?"

"Because you are an alcoholic, Mother."

"No, no. I'm not that bad. I'll be fine. . . ."

As her mother slipped into oblivion, Monroe tilted her mother's head to the side in case she vomited again. The hallway light tracked the deepening furrows along her mother's forehead and the fine lines at her eyes. Slight jowls were pulling at her cheeks, the plumped flesh of youth dragged down by time. When would she grow up? When would she finally admit she needed help? Monroe couldn't have her mother committed to the residential program. She had to attend of her own free will.

Exhausted in mind if not body, Monroe wandered to the other end of the house and into her old room. She stopped to trace the long scratches in the wood floor with her foot. A ritual she performed every time she entered. Like taking communion at church, she did it in remembrance.

Thunder rattled the windowpanes. The coming storm fit her mood, and she raised her window sash. Girlish pink diaphanous curtains billowed in every direction. The wind came in gusts and circled the room like an animal reconnoitering. The departing air pulled one curtain out of the window to wave like a flag while the other fought to get out, whipping around her legs.

Monroe took a deep breath. The humidity and pressure had increased over the last hour, the air ready to crack. This storm came from the west and smelled fresh. Not like the remnants of hurricanes that beat a path from the gulf, the rain retaining a hint of salt and the wind spawning tornadoes.

Leaning farther out the window, she let the wind buffet her. A raindrop hit her neck and slid down between her breasts. If the dress hadn't cost so much, she might run outside like a heathen to welcome the storm.

Lightning split open the sky, illuminating a dark figure under her window. Her hands tightened around the windowsill.

"This is private property! Leave before I get a gun!" The wind snatched her words and she couldn't be sure the man even heard.

The figure came closer. "It's only me." The deep voice and slight limp gave Cade away.

He was still in his fancy tuxedo shirt and pants, the jacket folded over his arm. The formality of the suit had tamped down his natural aggression, but with every piece of clothing he shed the real Cade was revealed. He was dark and a little bit dangerous, and she loved it.

Dear Lord, the man cast some sort of hypnotic spell over her whenever they were within ten feet of each other.

His gaze sliding up and down her body had nearly incinerated her in the garden.

"What are you doing here?" She leaned farther out the window, a raindrop marking a cool path down her back.

He wiped drops off his face. "Front door's locked and you didn't answer my knock. Wanted to make sure you were okay."

Lightning flashed, illuminating fast-moving dark clouds. "I'm not a kid anymore. I don't need you following me home and checking on me. Just like I didn't need you to step in with Andrew tonight."

He ruffled a hand through his hair, looking to his feet, before lifting his face again. "Dammit, I know that in here—" he tapped his temple "—but something happens in here—" he splayed a hand over the white of his shirt "—when I sense something is wrong. I can't seem to stop myself from charging in. I'd rather have you mad as hell at me than see you hurt when there's something I could do to prevent it."

Hard, stinging raindrops dissolved her exasperation like sugar. Part of her wanted to lay her problems bare to him, but it smacked of dependency. No one, not even Regan, knew how bad things sometimes got with her mother. Anyway, as he kept reminding her, he was leaving soon. Depending on him for anything was dangerous. She would handle things on her own like she always had.

"Everything's fine. My mother needed help, that's all. So you can go." She cursed the crack in her voice and shut the window before he could sense a weakness and exploit it.

Through the thin cloth of the drapes she watched him retreat. The rain fell faster now, pelting the gutters and obscuring her view through the window.

He was gone. It was better this way even if the urge to run after him had her gripping the window frame.

"Hey."

"Fudge!" Monroe whirled around, losing her balance and grabbing hold of one of the curtains. Cloth ripped, and her butt hit the sill. A man stood framed in her doorway like a figment from her nightmares. How many nights had she thrashed through a sweaty nightmare of a man standing over her or where she was unable to push the bureau in front of her door?

It took less than a second for her brain to align with reality, but the second seemed an eternity and it was too late to rein in her body's response. Her heart raced and her body trembled, her breaths too short and shallow to bring the panic under control.

She hated the instinctive fear she couldn't stem no matter how long and hard she trained. No matter how confident she was in her ability to defend herself. The same panic had overtaken her in the alley with Dylan and again in the field with Cade when she ran.

"Wow, you have such a dirty mouth, Monroe." Cade's amusement rubbed like sandpaper against her raw nerves. He strolled into her room, his jacket hooked over his shoulder with a finger, his hair slicked back from the rain. He was playing a part in an old Hollywood musical while she was in a B horror movie.

Then, in a blink, he tossed his jacket on her bed and put his hands on her upper arms. "What's wrong?"

The warmth of his touch jump-started her lungs, but she reacted instinctively, breaking the hold. He held both hands in front of him as if coaxing a scared animal but took up too much of her space. Her chest tightened even as her head chanted logic. Cade, this was Cade. He wouldn't hurt her. Her heart sped along like a runaway horse, wild and panicked. It didn't help that they were in her childhood bedroom. The scene of so many of her nightmares.

"You scared me. I thought—"

She closed her eyes, the scene as clear as if it had happened yesterday—Sam looming over her, his pants undone, his honeyed voice twisting her insides. A trembling spread through her body. Had it even been real? Dream or memory, it didn't matter anymore. She heaved in a deep breath.

"How'd you get in?" She cursed the telling shake of her voice.

"A rusty key under the flowerpot outside."

Tentatively, he reached out again, giving her time to protest. She should tell him to get out. She didn't need anyone to lean on. She'd performed this dance with her mother a depressing number of times. When he chafed his hands up and down her bare arms, she didn't push him away this time; she fell into him.

His rain-splotched white shirt stuck to various muscles along his chest and shoulders and dampened her cheek. Still sitting on the sill and with his hands caressing her arms, she draped her arms around his hips.

Her cheek pressed against his breastbone, his heart thumping in her ear. Hers sought the same rhythm, slowing its cadence. His scent was a combination of subtle cologne and fresh rain.

She stood, but an outside force not yet identified by scientists held her against him. She moved her hands to his chest, flattening them on either side of his heart. He kept up a gentle, soothing caress along her arms. Heat built in her belly.

He made her forget why she was here and what she was trying to hide. She skimmed her lips along his jaw to his mouth. The kiss was slow and toe curling. His hands trekked over her body. One delved into the open back of her dress. Her bare skin ignited. She pulled his shirt from his pants and slipped her hands underneath. Despite the dampness, his skin was hot.

His back muscles shifted under her hands, and she skimmed her fingernails across the planes. He hissed and dropped his mouth to her neck, biting her gently. One of his hands pulled at her skirt and slipped under. The roughness of his fingers, the scar across the palm, rasped up her thigh until he cupped her bare buttock. She squirmed. The raging storm added to the primal undercurrents.

He hummed. The sound vibrated the nerves along her neck and sent tingles through her body. "This dress is dangerous. I've wanted to peel it off you all night."

The extravagance had been money well spent. He removed his hand, and the skirt fluttered against her bare skin. A soft mewl of protest escaped. She needed his big hand on her again. It seemed he was only moving on. He slipped one shoulder strap over the curve of her shoulder, kissing along its retreat.

The fabric pulled across her breast. He tipped her backward over his arm, her balance upset enough she clutched at his upper arms. He trailed his fingertips down the front of her dress, one breast nearly exposed. Her back arched, her body begging him. She wanted him to rip the expensive dress off her.

Something outside banged against the house startling them both. The heart of the storm was over them. The wind came in great gusts and whistled its way through cracks in the window.

He slid her shoulder strap into place and kissed her again, this time with less passion and more regret.

"Is your mom down the hall? How is she?"

"Fine." She didn't want to think about her mother. She wanted to be selfish. He turned his face, and her lips landed on his cheek.

"Last thing I want is to get caught with my pants down by your mama."

"She won't be bothering us. Promise."

She slipped her hands back under his shirt, but he took her face in his hands and forced her back enough so their gazes met.

"You need me to help you get her cleaned up or into bed?" His calm understanding made her wonder if he made a habit of putting middle-aged puking women to bed.

"How'd you know?"

"I remember."

The denials and excuses she trotted out for everyone else were worthless with him. "She made it to the toilet this time, and I got her in bed."

He massaged her nape, the action more comforting than any trite expression of sympathy.

"I can handle her. I've done it for twenty years now," she said weakly.

"Just because you can doesn't mean you should have to, Monroe. Has she tried AA?"

"She can't—or won't—admit she has a problem. She'll go for weeks without drinking. This time she made it a few months before she went on a binge. Every time I'll think, this is it, she's going to stay sober. And every time I get a call or text."

The feeling of having someone to lean on literally and figuratively lowered her defenses. His arms came around her, and she laid her head on his shoulder, looking to the wall where the edges of an old poster curled. This time the hands on her back offered comfort and support and nothing more.

"What about rehab?"

"I saved up a few thousand to cover the costs of a nice one up in Jackson, but she refused. Said people will make assumptions."

"Haven't people already guessed?"

"Maybe. She covers well, laughs it off. It's not like she stays drunk twenty-four-seven." Frustration poured out of her. He continued to rub her back. She let out a shuddery breath, letting more of her weight fall into him.

"Doesn't make her less of an alcoholic."

"I know." She hesitated only a moment. "It's all about maintaining a certain image with her. She had to get a job now the alimony has run out, but she tells everyone she's doing it for fun. Something to get her out of the house. Sometimes I wonder if I let her wake up on the bathroom floor in her own vomit she'll finally admit she has a problem. Isn't that awful?"

"Sounds pretty normal to feel that way if you ask me. Anyway, you'd never not be there for her."

"She wasn't always there for me." Her voice cracked, and his arms tightened around her. She took a shuddery breath. "I'm saving to send her to a fancy treatment place in Arizona. Somewhere gossip won't be an issue. They recommended at least a month stay, preferably two."

"Have you got enough?"

"Half maybe."

"All your extra money is going toward your mom?"

"It's expensive. After tonight, I'm thinking I should take out a second mortgage on my house or maybe a personal loan. If I can convince her to go."

"Can't she cover some of the cost?"

Another fear tumbled out. "I don't think she can afford the house anymore, and her car is falling apart."

"She could downsize and pay for her own rehab."

Her laugh held no humor, only an inescapable irony. "You're too logical. Nothing about my mother is logical. She's an emotional creature. It's why she ends up with manipulative men. And it's why I won't be manipulated. By anyone."

"I'm not trying to manipulate you. I want you, but I want to help you, too. Will you let me?" He tucked a lock of hair behind her ear, letting his fingertips barely brush down her neck.

She did want to lean on him, lay her troubles bare, share the burden. Except, after a decade gone, he had blown into town like a tornado and would blow right back out, leaving everyone else to survive the damage.

It didn't seem to matter. She would take him any way she could get him, which was scarily reminiscent of how her mother approached relationships. Monroe felt full of emotion and bereft of logic. A dangerous combination.

She tried logic anyway. "You're not sticking around Cottonbloom long enough to help me."

"Monroe." The way he breathed her name opened another door between them, but he didn't make any promises to the contrary or offer up a platitude.

She appreciated his reticence. It was better to accept the destruction that awaited at the end of the path she tread. With the acceptance came the knowledge she would continue as long as she could. She wasn't sure how long they stood in an embrace that was sexual and comforting at the same time.

"I had a chat with Sam Landry at the party tonight. How long has he been back?" His voice was soft, almost hypnotic, and a moment passed before tension wound tight in her stomach.

She pulled away from him and plopped on her bed. How could she put into words her doubts over what was real and imagined? She toyed with her skirt and stared at the carpet.

"Since last fall. He got divorced, moved back, and restarted his insurance business."

"Has he been hassling you?"

"Why would he hassle me?"

"He's under the impression you had a crush on him and went running off that night to get him in trouble."

"It was a long time ago. It's not important." The lie squatted between them like a living thing, but Monroe didn't know how to take it back. The ugliness colored the silence.

"Liar," he said softly but with no judgment.

"What else did he say?"

"Thought you'd called the cops on him the other night at the Tavern."

Her head shot up. "I didn't." She took a breath, blew it out, and forged on. "What if I exaggerated the threat that night?"

At the lengthening silence, she raised her gaze to Cade's face, afraid of what she might see. Lightning flashed, casting him in sinister tones, but only curiosity shaded his voice. "Why do you think that?"

"He only touched my cheek."

"Because you ran."

She pressed the heels of her hands against her forehead and closed her eyes. "I did, but he said—"

"Hold up right there. Did you let him feed you a bunch of bull?" His anger permeated the room accompanied by a roll of thunder. Her knees liquefied.

"What if I misjudged the situation because I was young and inexperienced? What if I was wrong?"

"His hand was in his pants and you think he wanted to read you a bedtime story that night?" The incredulity in his voice cast more doubts.

"When he moved back, he seemed different than I remembered. He set up an insurance agency, got elected to town council. He was right about me not wanting him to marry my mom. Maybe I really was jealous."

Lightning flashed and the cracking thunder made her jerk. He sat next to her. The old mattress dipped, and she slipped closer, her thigh against his. "So you've convinced yourself your memory is faulty? Tell me what you remember."

She closed her eyes and eased her hand toward his, needing his touch but unable to explain why. He threaded their fingers, and she ran a thumb up and down the scar on his palm, the motion somehow anchoring her in the present even as she cast backward.

"I was scared. No, terrified. He was standing over me, his pants undone. At first, I didn't understand."

"What did he say?"

"I don't remember."

"Yes, you do." His voice was soft but commanding. Light flashed behind her closed eyes. "Trust yourself. You remember every detail about that night. Just like I do." Another roll of thunder nearly masked his whispered confession.

Their meeting had been important to him, too. A warmth sparked in her chest. Trust. She needed to trust in her instincts. Ironic that was exactly what she preached at her girls as she'd spent the last few months wallowing in her doubts.

"He called me sweet thing. Told me Mother was passed out and he wanted to tuck me in. Take care of me."

"But he made you uncomfortable before that, didn't he?"

"The way he looked at me. I wasn't sure what he wanted. I'd never even been kissed, but he made me feel dirty."

"I should have punched him tonight."

His anger grew her confidence, the image tapping into a well of dark humor. "That would have been gossiped about for years."

"I don't mind a little gossip and neither do you or you wouldn't have danced with me. Am I right?"

She only smiled and squeezed his hand.

"You climbed out the window and ran to the river. Found my boat. Then, I showed up. Were you scared of me?"

"No," she said with a decisiveness that startled her.

"Why not? I was a strange man in the dark."

"I felt . . ." She burrowed into him, dropping his hand and wrapping her arms around his chest. "Safe. I knew I could trust you. With everything."

Years had gone by, but she still trusted him, bone-deep and illogical though it was. Somehow, they ended up reclined on her narrow, sagging twin bed, stretched out and face-to-face.

"You remember what we talked about that night?" His Adam's apple bobbed, his jaw tensing.

"Every word."

"Then why are you doubting your memory when it comes to Sam Landry?"

Because you weren't here. The words shot through her. Thankfully, she stopped herself from speaking them aloud. With a whisper Cade had blown down the walls she'd spent over a decade erecting. Walls that no other man had come close to breeching. She wanted him, but even more, she needed him. The realization was sobering and scary and only made her hold on to him tighter in spite of it.

A weak voice down the hall called her name. The jolt of reality had her scrambling up and running down the hall. Her mother was on the floor by her bed, moaning.

Monroe fell to her knees beside her, ignoring the carpet burn, and pushed her mother's hair back. "What happened, Mama?" She reverted to the babyish name.

"Bathroom. Help me." Her sentences were clipped like a toddler's.

Cade slipped his hands under her mother's arms and pulled her up.

Monroe hadn't even heard him follow her. She should tell him to leave. She could handle her mother alone. She didn't want to. Cade supported most of her mother's weight on their shuffle to the bathroom. Her mother fell to her knees in front of the toilet like worshiping an idol.

Monroe slipped back out to lean against the bedroom

wall. He joined her, standing in front of her with his hands braced on either side of her shoulders as her mother retched. Tears stung at the backs of Monroe's eyes, and she blinked.

She could accept the unexplainable bond between her and Cade, but no way was she going to literally cry on his shoulder. That was something reserved for her pillow in the middle of lonely nights.

She kept her gaze on her bare feet notched between his fancy square-toed dress shoes. He settled his chin on top of her head. She wasn't sure how long they stood, listening to her mother, but when the noises stopped he kissed the top of her head.

"Let me get her cleaned up."

Monroe let him go, feeling weak and thankful at the same time. Water ran and his murmuring made its way out the bathroom door, but she couldn't make out what he said to her mother. He helped her shuffle back to the bed.

"I got her face washed and teeth brushed. Thought I'd let you handle changing her shirt." He settled her mother on the edge of the bed, her torso weaving in a semi-circle, her eyes blinking but unfocused.

He retreated toward the door, but Monroe caught his hand. "Thank you . . . for everything."

He chucked his chin up and disappeared.

She got her mother changed and tucked back into the bed. At least she hadn't thrown up all over the sheets. Sitting on the edge of the bed, Monroe tucked the covers around her mother's body and dropped a kiss on her head.

Her hair reeked of stale smoke, her body of alcohol. How many nights had she leaned over to give Monroe a good night kiss and smelled like a bar instead of face lotion? Too many times. She stayed until her mother's restlessness eased and her breathing deepened.

Monroe returned to her bedroom. The storm had

settled into a soft, plinking rain against the window. Cade's jacket was gone; the only traces he'd been there were the rumpled sheets where they had lain together.

It wasn't surprise but disappointment that tumbled through her. She couldn't blame him. Any man with half a brain cell would run from the ugliness he'd uncovered tonight. Pulling out the combs and pins, she finger combed her hair out of her face and fumbled the clasp of her pendant necklace open.

Her mother would have one hell of a headache come morning. Monroe headed downstairs for ibuprofen and to check the locks. Halfway down the stairs, she registered the low hum of a sitcom laugh track on the TV.

Cade was sprawled across the couch in the den, the remote in his hand, his bare feet propped up on the ottoman. "How's she doing?"

"She's going to be hating life tomorrow."

"No doubt. Uncle Delmar was a bear after his binges."

Her steps stuttered on her way to the couch. Cade remained relaxed, his face impassive. "Delmar drinks?"

"When I was a kid, he would go on a bender now and again, not show up for work for a few days, get fired. Daddy used to take care of him; then afterward I did."

"I didn't know."

"I did my best to cover for him. He was officially our guardian. If the state got wind, we'd have been shuttled to foster homes. Sawyer says he's better now." Questions pinged, but before she could put any to voice he asked, "You staying here tonight?"

"Yeah. In case she needs me."

"Want some company? I cued up a movie."

"Sure. Okay."

His brows rose as if he had expected a fight, but polite protests were beyond her ability. She wanted him to stay.

"Which movie did you pick?"

"Picked one I'd never seen. Figured you'd watched all of them. *Dead Poets Society*?"

"You've never seen it?"

"Didn't have much time for movies growing up." His voice took on an edge she recognized.

The same edge had cut her when she was left to take care of her mother when it should have been the other way around. Life hadn't been fair to either of them in different ways.

"It's excellent, but not very happy." She sank on the edge of the cushion, tension holding her straight and still.

As the opening credits rolled, he snagged his arm around her shoulders and pulled her into him. Her head settled onto his shoulder, her hand on his chest. She had needed him to force her to lean on him. So many years she had been adamant she would never depend on a man for anything—not for money, not for protection, not for happiness. But around Cade her staunch independence felt more like an aching loneliness.

At first, the movie was background noise, her focus on his hand playing with her hair, the caress of his smooth chin along her forehead, his clean scent. As the movie progressed and her body grew comfortable with his so close, the sad story pulled her in like it always had.

The ending always made her misty-eyed, but with her emotions exposed like severed wires tears flooded her eyes. She tucked her head down, hoping he wouldn't notice, but it wasn't long before her nose got into the act and she snuffled.

He shifted, his hand cupping her chin and tilting her head up. She closed her eyes, but a tear trickled out. Instead of questioning her or, worse, laughing at her, he pulled her fully onto his lap and hugged her tight, her face mashed into his neck. She cried. Not manipulative tears or sentimental tears, but a full-on ugly cry.

All he did was rub her back and hold her tighter, even when she had to wipe her nose on the collar of his shirt. Finally, the storm abated, leaving her exhausted. The anxiety, the worry, the resentment, had been washed away.

She pushed up off his chest. He was frowning, the crinkles around his eyes deep with his squint. "I'm not a crier."

His lips twitched. "Obviously."

A giggle snuck out followed by a hiccup, which made her laugh even harder. "I mean, not normally a crier. I must look terrible." She rubbed at her eyes and patted her cheeks.

"You look . . ."

"Don't say beautiful, because I know you'd be lying."

"Red and swollen." His mouth drew into an apologetic grimace-smile, but the way he spoke didn't make her feel self-conscious.

She pushed off him, but he caught her waist, pitching them both forward. She wiggled and he shifted until they lay face-to-face, her back pressed into the cushions. The soft fabric of his pants caressed her skin. He kissed her cheek, and her eyes drifted shut with the sensations.

"But still beautiful. Nothing can mask that."

"When did you turn into such a smooth-talking hero?"

Chapter Eighteen

Her words pried themselves into Cade's consciousness. He levered himself to an elbow. "I'm not a hero."

Her eyes opened, still glossy from tears. "All right, what are you then?"

The intimacy of the evening set off tornado sirens. Pursuing a goal of sexual satisfaction for them both was one thing; holding her while she cried for her mother was another. And the ache in his chest and the need to wipe all her childhood pain away and replace it with happiness wasn't even on the table for discussion.

Afraid his answer would give too much away, he kissed her. Her lips were soft and salt tinged from her crying jag. Her fingers played in the hair at his nape. Maybe having sex would sever the odd bond born of the past. Maybe memories of their full moon nights together only confused the lust that had bloomed between them as adults. Sex would clear the air so he could see clearly again.

He skimmed his hand up her waist to span her rib cage, an inch below her breast. His thumb followed the path of her bare skin, hooking under the edge of her dress and glancing across her already-peaked nipple.

Her inhale stole the air from his lungs. He slipped his hand under the fabric to cover her entire breast, her nipple pressing into his palm. Like studying Sawyer's engineering books, Cade had studied the mechanics of pleasuring a woman, but in the past bringing a woman to orgasm had been about ego and his body's goal of its own satisfaction.

Her soft skin under his fingertips was like a tonic to his confusion. The scary truth presented itself like a flashing neon sign in Times Square. Sex would only strengthen their connection. The need to lay hands on her was more than he could deny.

Light from the muted TV flickered. She arched, pressing her breast farther into his hand. Her fingers left his hair to wrap around his wrist, but she only pressed his hand tighter against her body. When he moved his hand away from her breast, a sexy whimper emerged from her throat and her fingernails dug into his wrist.

He pulled the dress off her shoulder and pushed the fabric aside, baring one of her breasts. She loosened her hold. The juxtaposition of his tanned hand against her pale skin and his rough calluses against her softness made him achingly aware of her femininity.

Her breast wasn't large but was perfectly shaped for his hand, the nipple small and pink. He thumbed the point, drawing it even tighter before pinching it lightly. She writhed and moaned, her eyes squeezed closed. Was every part of her as sensitive?

"Look at me," he said in a hoarse voice.

Her eyes shot open, huge and blue and still swollen from her crying jag. She looked innocent. Hell, she was innocent compared to him. Or was she? She'd dealt with a different set of demons growing up, but they rampaged through her dreams. He understood that.

He shifted down to lick over her nipple. Her pelvis

circled against his erection. The pressure wound tighter and ached for release. He'd been battling the damn thing since he'd stepped into her room earlier. Outlined by the lightning of the storm raging outside her window, the swaths of her pale skin had glowed.

He pushed her deep into the cushion and sucked her nipple into his mouth. Her hips bucked, and her leg snaked over his.

"Cade, please." The desperation in her voice spoke to him more than her words.

"Let me take care of you," he whispered while his tongue flicked at her distended nipple. Although he'd meant sexually, deep inside him a seed he'd thought had shriveled and died took root with the words and flourished.

True to form, her hand came between them and tugged at his pants. He took her wrist and pressed her hand into the back cushion. Slower and harsher than he intended, so she wouldn't argue with words or spirit, he said, "Let me take care of you, dammit."

She tossed her head back, her neck working with her swallow, her hair fanned around them. The tension threading her had faded, although her body strained toward his with a different purpose now. Her pose was one of supplication.

A primal sense of ownership went hand in hand with the need to protect her. How many men had she allowed to take control of her pleasure? None, if he had to wager.

He let go of her wrist and her hand stayed put, neither encouraging nor denying his access to her body. He pulled at the other side of her dress, baring both breasts. While he licked and sucked and kissed one, his fingers played with the other, pinching and rolling.

Rubbing his cheek across the soft slopes brought her hand to his shoulder; she grasped at the fabric of his shirt as if she wanted to pull him inside of her. He situated her flat on her back and levered himself over her, careful not to put all his weight on her.

She spread her legs to accommodate his hips, and he pumped in a mockery of what his body screamed for. The position was too much of a temptation for him, and he shifted to her side, keeping a leg draped over hers.

While he caught her closest nipple between his teeth, he trailed a hand up her thigh, bringing the voluminous fabric of her skirt with him. Blue fabric bunched at her waist. A tiny G-string made a weak effort to hide his ultimate destination.

He plucked the side string where it made a slight indentation into her soft hip. "This is quite possibly the sexiest, most useless item of clothing I've ever seen."

She hummed and wiggled her hips. He took his time, trailing his fingers along the strings. When he finally pulled the scrap of fabric to the side, he found her smooth and wet.

He pressed his erection into her hip, the contact satisfying him enough to keep his focus on her. For long moments, he stroked and explored, discovering what she enjoyed and what drove her crazy.

He eased his middle finger partway inside of her, trying not to let his mind imagine what the tight hold would feel like around his erection. His thumb rubbed her slicked apex while he sucked her nipple into his mouth.

Without warning, she went off in his arms like fireworks. Her movements forced his finger deep, her walls pulsing in rhythm to her circling hips. He raised his head to watch her in her climax. Her breasts and cheeks flushed pink.

The blue of her eyes lasered into him. He wanted to look away but couldn't. Her vulnerability rocked something deep inside him. He removed his finger as her body went lax.

The intensity turned to tenderness. She stroked fingers down his cheek and across his lower lip. He kissed the tips. He broke eye contact first, gathering her close and hiding his face in the hair at her nape.

Her hands moved down his back and over his buttocks. "Your turn," she whispered in a dazed, husky voice.

He wanted his turn, but more than that, he wanted tonight to be about her. He wanted her to trust him with her body and her soul and her dreams . . . with everything. Her earlier accusation pealed in his head. He wasn't staying in Cottonbloom. Was it fair to ask for everything and walk away? "Not right now. Later maybe."

He turned them on their sides and held her close, his hands caressing up and down her back, one shoulder of her dress still down, the skirt bunched around her upper thighs.

He didn't know how much time passed before her body went limp and her breathing deepened. Sleep eluded him. Eventually, he slipped out of her embrace and off the couch, looking down on her. Her dress only half-covered her, the curve of her bare thigh and one perfect breast exposed. She was the picture of innocent and sensual, guarded and open, strong and vulnerable.

He lifted her into a cradle hold, and she emitted a throaty hum but didn't wake. After laying her on her girlish twin bed he pulled the pink flowered comforter over her body, but the devil in him left her dress in disarray.

He hoped she'd wake in the morning with no regrets, but in case she did harbor them, he didn't want to be around to see them cloud her blue eyes.

Monroe's mother was asleep and snoring and not likely to wake anytime soon. He retreated to the den to put on his shoes and shut everything off. Taking the rusty key, he let himself out and relocked the door. The rain had stopped, leaving everything washed clean and the air cool. He stared back at the house wishing he had X-ray vision.

Since he'd left Cottonbloom, he hadn't invited complications into his life. He didn't do complicated. He'd kept things simple. Nothing about Monroe was simple. Nothing about the feelings roiling in his chest was simple. Cottonbloom seemed to inspire complications.

Chapter Nineteen

Cade spent Sunday morning searching for a distraction in the intricate, logical workings of an engine. His thoughts stole to Monroe so many times, he was lucky the motor's fix was simple. With Sawyer at church—a necessity when you were an elected official—he had the house to himself, which meant no awkward currents to navigate. Tensions between them had only seemed to grow after their disastrous trip upriver.

After a quick, cool shower, he pulled on a pair of cargo shorts and grabbed a Coke out of the frig. The crunch of wheels on gravel drew him to the front window. Monroe. She climbed out in Sunday summer garb—a yellow sundress and strappy high-heeled sandals that did something spectacular to her legs. He flashed to the evening before and the feel of those legs clamped around his hips.

A long drag on the icy Coke did little to stem his sudden arousal. He had a feeling only one thing would alleviate his need and that was to bury himself inside of her.

His tuxedo jacket was draped over one of her arms, and he reined in his more primal urges. She was circling to the back and he met her at the kitchen door. She wasn't here to finish what they'd started last night.

"Hi." Her voice was probing, her smile tentative, and her gaze on his chest. A sharp pain twisted in his gut. She was uncomfortable.

"Hey yourself." Shifting on his feet, he wanted to force her to look at him, wanted to ask hard questions about regret, but he didn't, afraid of the answers.

"Do you think maybe" she swallowed hard, and he tensed as if expecting a blow "you could put a shirt on? This is all very, very distracting." She waved toward his chest, her gaze finally rising. Instead of regret or awkwardness, amusement lit her, and like the sun banishing the clouds a warmth flooded through him that had nothing to do with sex.

"I think I like you distracted." He took a step closer, and she pushed the tip of her index finger between his breastbones.

"Cade Fournette, if you come one inch closer I might throw you over the kitchen table and take wild advantage of you."

His breath got caught somewhere in his windpipe, making his words come out hoarse. "Yep, distracting you is the best." He tried to move closer, but she spun around him, the skirt of her dress brushing his knees.

"Nope. Not in your brother's house with him due home any minute."

"All right, fine." He retreated for a T-shirt but didn't pull it on until he was back in the kitchen. Her gaze seemed to devour him and he couldn't recall a woman who had ever been so blatant in her desire. Although there were undiscovered depths to Monroe, she didn't play games, and he appreciated that about her. Along with about a hundred other things.

"How's your mama?" he asked once his shirt was on.

"Feeling about as crappy as you'd imagine. Full of apologies and promises as usual." Her worry cleared quickly. "You left your jacket last night."

"Thanks." He took it from her outstretched arms and hung it over a kitchen chair. Only a ticking clock and the faint tap of her heels as she shuffled her feet broke the silence. She was right, Sawyer would be home soon, and Cade wanted her to himself. "You got plans for lunch?"

"None."

"How do you feel about a picnic on the river?"

"The river?" She spoke the words cautiously.

"You scared of the water?"

"Of course not." Her gaze skated away from his, and hidden meaning lurked behind her denial. Was she afraid of the river? The thought was somehow unbearable, as if he and the river were somehow joined and fear of one would lead to fear of the other.

"Would you go out on the river with me?" It was a question of trust and grew in importance. He stilled.

"I'm not really dressed to go tramping through marshes." She gestured down her dress.

"No tramping necessary, scout's honor. I'll bet Tally even has a pair of water shoes you could borrow."

"Were you even a Boy Scout?" She glanced at him under her lashes, the gesture flirty, already slipping her strappy heels off.

"I was a Cub Scout for three months. Quit once I figured out they weren't going to teach me how to start a fire or survive a zombie apocalypse." Her laughter relaxed him. "I'll pack some sandwiches. There's sunblock in the medicine cabinet, and Tally keeps some things in the middle bedroom."

She walked past him muttering about poison ivy and snakes and sunstroke but with a smile on her face. He packed the cooler with BLTs, chips, a Baggie full of Oreos, and two grape Nehis. A meal worthy of the most elite elementary-school lunch box.

She came out of the back wearing a pair of flip-flops with big, plastic daisies between her toes and stopped in a patch of sunlight from the window. He stared. She was sweet and wholesome and sexy as hell.

"I'm assuming these are Tally's unless Sawyer's cross-dressing these days," she said.

"Definitely Tally's. Let's hit it." He zipped the cooler closed and led the way outside. "We're going to take a boat with one of my first engine designs."

"What will it do?"

"Nothing exciting like fly or hover. It's quieter. Will save on gas."

"Sounds perfect." She slipped her hand in his and the sensation of plugging into something electric coursed through him.

As they took the pine needle–strewn path together a numbing realization washed over him. Was this a date? An honest-to-God date? He glanced over at her. She was concentrating on where to put her feet. The yellow of the dress made her skin glow and her hair shine.

It was. He should have taken her to a fancy restaurant on the Mississippi side. Put his signature on the claim he'd staked last night on the dance floor.

The river peeked through the trees, the soft cadence of running water like an old, familiar song he knew by heart. The river. A sense of inevitability unknotted his stomach. It had all started on the river so many years ago. The circle was complete.

The flat-bottomed two-person skiff was pulled up the bank. It was perfect for maneuvering through the narrow channels extruding from the main river like capillaries.

He stowed the cooler and pushed the boat out into the water. He kept one foot in the bow of the boat, one foot on ground, and held out a hand. She stepped over his foot and stood in the middle of the boat.

To get to the stern, he wrapped his hands around her upper arms and shuffled by her. The scent of sunscreen mixed with the river reminded him of summers before his parents died when he and Sawyer would tie themselves to the bank to drift and pretend to fish for hours, the sun stealing all their energy.

She darted her tongue over her bottom lip, and he nearly kissed her. Before he could act on the compulsion, he sat down on the sun-warmed metal seat. He didn't want her to think this was about getting her in bed—although he wanted in her bed in the worst possible way, especially after getting a taste of her last night.

He wanted more. For as long as he was home.

A melancholy wove through his sense of possession. Temporary. This was all temporary. The river, home, Monroe. Why did he have to keep reminding himself of that?

Reluctantly, he transferred his attention from her to getting them going. Turning away from him, she settled onto her seat, crossing her feet at the ankles and knitting her hands together in her lap like she was sitting in a church pew.

He cranked the boat engine; the whisper-soft technology he'd created meant he didn't even need to raise his voice to be heard. "You ready?"

She looked over her shoulder and nodded as the engine worked them slowly backward. He idled in the heart of the river. Where should he take her? A hundred childhood destinations scrolled. Only one held any significance. A slight jerk as he shifted forward had her hands curling around the sides.

He hadn't realized how much he'd missed the river until he came home. The pulse of his blood seemed to match the flow of the current. In all the times he'd climbed a rock face or hang glided or heli-skied, he'd never felt the same connection to nature he had when he was on the river. He'd done all that other stuff for the rush and to conquer his fear, not to appreciate the majesty of the world.

"It's so quiet." She cocked a leg up and shifted to be able to see him, her hair streaming around her neck.

"It also handles shallow, reedy water better than anything else on the market. Nothing worse than having to get all wet and untangle your motor. Especially in an area thick with gators."

"Seems like a pretty specific market."

"You'd be surprised. Recreational fishing is a huge industry." He veered onto a wider stream. The breeze coming off the water was enough to keep the bugs and heat at bay.

"Do you fish?" She turned around to face him and tucked her fluttering hair behind her ears.

"When I was a kid Sawyer and I used to take a boat out, but we threw back what we caught because we were both too lazy to fillet them. Mama always lamented our lack of fishing prowess." He laughed, but it trailed into nothing as he added softly, "We never got the chance to tell her the truth."

"I'll bet she knew exactly what you two were up to." Her soft smile did funny things to his organs.

"Maybe. I hope so. After they died, fishing was no longer recreational; it was a necessity."

"I used to . . ." She glanced toward the bank.

"Used to what?"

"Lie in bed at night and wonder if you were out looking for food. Worry if you had enough. Don't laugh, but . . . I prayed for you every night."

He didn't feel like laughing. It had been a long time since he believed in some higher power. A long time since harsh reality had destroyed the fantasy of a benevolent god who would provide for them.

Whether her prayers reached heaven or not, the knowledge someone had worried about him, had thought about him, had understood him, lightened a weight that he'd dragged for too many years.

They stared into each other's eyes, the few feet separating them too far. The river narrowed, the trees on either bank reaching for one another and forming a tunnel of green-filtered sunlight and shadows. He slowed them, the boat puttering against the swifter current and keeping them still. The beauty surrounding them was his church, the flow of the water his hymn, the peace his prayer.

Words were beyond him.

"It's beautiful." Her voice was reverent. "I know where we're going."

"How do you know?"

"You told me about this stretch of the river once. Do you remember?"

He didn't, but they'd talked about nothing and everything their nights together.

"After you left, I waited for you. Every full moon." A thread of heartache weaved her words.

"Why?" His voice croaked like a bullfrog.

"You were the only one who knew everything. Who understood. I was . . . so alone. So lonely."

No one would have guessed a rich Mississippi girl with a big house and a pool and a multitude of friends was as lonely and alone as a poor Louisiana boy trying to survive.

Her slight laugh was full of self-deprecation. "Anyway, you never came back."

Her words pierced him like an accusation. His own truths poured out as they had that night under the cottonwood tree. "I didn't want to leave. I had to."

She tilted her head and waited.

Telling Tally had weakened the dam and the words flowed easier. Monroe listened, the expression on her face never changing.

"Did you want to get caught?" she asked after he fell silent.

"Of course not. Why would you think that?"

"You needed help, Cade. You were exhausted and desperate and hopeless. It got worse every time I saw you."

He blinked and kicked the engine into a higher gear. His heart matched their acceleration upriver. She stayed facing him, her hair whipping around her face. Was she right?

It didn't take long before the shadow of the cottonwood tree emerged around a bend. He'd never been this far upriver in the daytime. Old prejudices born from the men who'd split the town kept the 'Sips on their side and the swamp rats on theirs.

He ran the skiff aground close to where he'd hidden it the first time they'd met. In the bright sunlight and with birds trilling, the dark magic he'd found there at night was muted.

He hopped into the shallows and secured the boat. She stood, rocking from side to side, her hands out for balance. The bank was steep, the path they'd used so many years ago carved away. Without warning her, he set his shoulder into her stomach and lifted her up.

She squealed his name, equal amounts of surprise and laughter in her voice. It had always been that way with them, the easy veering from serious to light. One minute they'd be talking about another one of her mother's binges, and the next she would have him laughing about a trick someone had played on a substitute teacher.

He climbed the bank, using his free hand to grab at exposed roots for leverage. She grabbed the waistband of his shorts and laughed harder.

He crested the top but didn't put her down. He stared at the tree, surprised at how much bigger it appeared. The leaves rustled in the wind racing over the field of cotton that stretched as far as he could see on the opposite bank. White bolls dotted the landscape.

"Are you going to put me down?" She pushed up from his back.

"In a minute." He slipped his hand under her skirt, the skin of her thigh like silk against his rough palm, the nerve endings firing along his scar. She went limp, her arms coming around his waist from behind. He removed his hand and gave her bottom a smack.

Her outraged, "Hey!" had him chuckling, and he bent to put her down. Her face was flushed from either arousal or hanging upside down or both.

"I wanted to throw you over my shoulder and haul you out of the party last night."

"I kind of wish you had." Her eyebrows waggled. "Maybe next time?"

The implication tempered the happiness in her smile. Would there be a next time? He caressed her cheek and whispered, "Maybe." Attempting a normal tone, he continued. "I'll unload the boat."

He tossed an old quilt into her waiting arms. She disappeared, and he manhandled the cooler up the bank. She had set up camp in their spot, leaning against the trunk.

He dropped the cooler nearby and joined her, not against the tree but lying on his back and staring into the branches. It was both familiar yet almost unrecognizable in the light of day after so many years. Like the connection he shared with Monroe.

"What would have happened if you'd stayed, do you think?" She played in his hair, the sweetness of the feeling indescribable.

"I'd have ended up in jail for sure."

"No. With us."

He shifted so he could see her face framed against the sun-dappled leaves. "What do you mean?"

"Did you ever . . . think about me as more than a little girl back then?"

He blew out a long, slow breath as if preparing for someone to rip off a bandage. "Not at first. Not for years even. I kept coming back for the same reason as you needed me, I suppose. Someone to talk to. Someone to lean on."

"If not at first? Then eventually?"

He smiled at her hopeful lilt. "I swear one full moon I showed up and you had changed."

"Like a werewolf?"

A laugh burst from his chest. "Something like that. You went from all skinny edges to curves. I couldn't help but notice, but I would never have touched you. You were too young, going to college, making a life for yourself. I had nothing to offer. The only place I was headed was trouble." He brushed her hair back. "But I thought about it. Thought about you."

"I thought about you, too." She moved next to him, laying her head on his chest, and he closed his eyes. "I used to pretend my pillow was you and practice kissing it. Mostly, though, I would just hug it and pretend you were hugging me back."

The intensely vulnerable feeling that shot through him was something he'd never experienced. He'd done crazy things before—some downright dangerous—but he'd never been stymied by fear. He was a risk taker by nature.

"You're a much better kisser than my pillow."

"Am I?"

She hummed an affirmative and lifted over him. Her breasts pressed into his chest and she slid her smooth leg between his. Her hair fell forward and tickled his cheeks. Kissing Monroe under the cottonwood tree had been an unattainable fantasy a decade earlier. The fact that it was happening, and in the light of day no less, was mind-blowing.

It was like a first kiss, *his* first kiss. Soft and sweet and colored with a wealth of sensuality. She set the rhythm, the give-and-take, the devastating invasion and retreat.

He recognized Monroe as both a stranger and a part of himself. A part he'd tried to forget yet was integral to who he was. How had they come so far, so fast? Her kisses picked apart any defense he might mount, and he surrendered.

Chapter Twenty

A rumble welled from his chest and throat, vibrating her body. Or maybe those trembles were entirely of her making. Being in control was a heady feeling. She delved her hands into his hair and skimmed her tongue along his lower lip, slowly, sensually, enjoying the soft pliancy of his mouth under hers.

But her control was fleeting. He cupped the back of her head and pressed a hand along her back, rolling them until he was on top and bending her to fit his will. Passion replaced the slow exploration. Aggressive and demanding, his kiss devastated her senses.

She lost all concept of time or space. Nothing mattered except their kiss. He continued to grapple her closer with rough hands as his tongue toyed with hers. His stubble rubbed at her chin and cheeks.

He pulled away, his lips feathering along her jaw. She tilted her head back, and his mouth trailed down her neck. Breaking away, he propped himself up on his elbows. His eyes were cutting and intense. So different from their childhood meetings when the darkness had tamped down his fierceness.

She played with the hair at his nape. "What's wrong?"

"Nothing. Everything feels perfect." He didn't sound happy about it.

He rolled off her and reached for the cooler. Her body missed the weight of his. Her dress was bunched around her upper thighs, her body on fire.

He handed her an ice-cold can. The shift from rolling around on the ground together as if they couldn't get close enough to calmly eating lunch was disconcerting. Why did it seem he was completely unaffected by their epic make-out session while she was left reeling and trying to establish some kind of mental balance? She pushed up to sitting and pressed the can against her neck to cool herself down in more ways than one.

"I haven't had a Nehi in forever." She popped the top and took several swallows. "Dear Lord, call nine-one-one if I go into a diabetic coma."

"This'll help offset the sugar."

She lifted the top piece of bread off the sandwich. "BLTs. My favorite."

"Stole the tomatoes from Regan's mama."

Monroe froze with her mouth around the corner. He laughed, his head back, his throat working. "Your face. You'd think I'd confessed to stealing the Crown Jewels or something. Rest easy; I got them at the grocery. They're probably from California."

She took a bite, and sure enough, the tomato wasn't sweet enough to be Mississippi grown. "You're the boy who cried wolf, considering you were out trying to plant rabbits in her garden."

He shrugged and took a bite of his sandwich, his lips still upturned. "I honestly didn't know what Sawyer was up to until he handed me the first rabbit out of the trap."

She finished her sandwich, skipped the chips, but couldn't deny the lure of an Oreo. "How do you eat yours?"

"With my mouth," he said dryly.

"But do you twist it apart and lick the cream?" She demonstrated her preferred method. Halfway through the second lick, she slowed. The intensity of his gaze was focused on her show-and-tell, his Oreo hovering halfway to his mouth. She touched her tongue to her top lip, leaving some sweetness behind. Who knew eating a cookie could be so sensual? Maybe she could provoke him to finish what they'd started before lunch.

His phone buzzed.

The curse he muttered was tinged with regret and not rancor. He checked the screen and answered. "What's up?"

A male voice garbled words like Charlie Brown's teacher on the other end. Cade checked his watch. "I wasn't expecting it until tomorrow. I'll explain everything when I get back up at the house."

His gaze clashed with hers, his lips quirking. "Messing around out on the river. See you in a bit."

He slipped the phone back into his pocket. "We're going to have to head back. My new project arrived and Sawyer is hopping mad."

She adjusted her skirt and licked the residual cream off her top lip. "Why is he mad?"

"Probably because I'm a bossy cur who's taking over his garage."

"Have the two of you been fighting a lot?"

"We've been stepping on each other's toes some." He repacked the cooler while she shook out the quilt.

They walked side by side to the bank. While she waited for him to load the boat, she turned and looked at their tree. The safety and security it had represented had been false. It was a tree like any other along the river. Cade climbed back up the bank, and she transferred her attention to him.

It was Cade. It always had been. The safety and security

she'd craved was in him, not a part of the tree. Her smile beat back the tears she didn't want to explain. He picked her up again as if she weighed nothing and slip-slid down the bank to deposit her on the seat.

She expected him to gun the engine and fly them back downriver. Instead, they puttered with the slight current, going in and out of shadows and bright sunshine.

Kicking off the flip-flops, she turned sideways and let her feet drag in the water. The water was never clear, but in the summer the dry conditions and teeming plant life provided a greenish-brown cast to it. Tall reeds encroached into the water, narrowing the navigable section to the very middle.

The small dock at the back of Sawyer's house came into view. She pulled her feet out and slipped her flip-flops back on. Arms crossed, Sawyer stood at the top of the rise like a parent ready to discipline them for stealing the boat.

Cade stepped into the shallow water, the mud sucking at his boots, and pulled the boat half onto the bank, tying it off to a pine tree. He circled her waist and lifted her to dry ground. Instead of making her feel vulnerable, his strength made her feel feminine.

"I didn't plan to spend my Sunday dealing with your special delivery, Cade." Sawyer's voice rang with more ire than the situation seemed to call for.

"Sorry about that. Wasn't expecting it to arrive until tomorrow."

"You're planning to take over my garage, are you?"

"I'd like to use your garage while I'm here." Cade didn't seem to be asking for a favor. "Told you I was getting a project shipped down."

"Sure, shove my stuff aside. It's certainly not as important as *your* designs."

Monroe looked back and forth between the brothers. No one could mistake the territorial battle brewing between them. Cade took a step forward. "You're not even working on anything. What's your problem, little bro?"

Cade's jab sent them spiraling further, and Sawyer's shoulders bowed up. "I had my eye on an old Camaro and was thinking about fixing her up, but now your shit is in my way."

Monroe wrapped her hands around one of Cade's biceps, surprised to find it taut and thrumming with static energy. "I have an idea. Divide the garage right down the middle with a long strip of tape. It worked on *The Brady Bunch*."

Her forced teasing diffused the tension. Sawyer rolled his eyes, but the edge of aggression in his voice dulled. "Could you at least get that motor Delmar dropped off back to him?"

"Sure. I'll take it over right now."

Sawyer walked back to the house, his hands shoved into his pockets and his head down. She watched Cade watch Sawyer. As the distance between them grew, Cade's muscles relaxed under her grip.

"You want to ride along with me?" He didn't look at her.

"Why not." She wasn't sure whether he even wanted to talk about Sawyer, but he spoke before she came up with a question.

"You ever been out to Uncle Delmar's?" He stepped out of her hands, leaving her to walk at his side.

"Can't say that I have."

"Well, are you in for a treat." While his voice retained shades of his confrontation with Sawyer, his mood lightened, and she decided to follow his lead.

She sat on the metal desk while he backed the old truck into the garage and used the hoist to maneuver the engine into the bed. She enjoyed watching him work, his ease in the environment obvious. Yet he hadn't seemed out of place in a fancy tuxedo circulating with Cottonbloom's finest.

He opened the passenger door and helped her in as if it was a date. Maybe it was? If so, it was the most unusual date she'd ever been on. And definitely the best.

The truck bounced over the lightly graveled path to the main driveway in front of Sawyer's house. As they picked up speed, the wind whipped her hair around her face and she gathered it in her hand as best she could. Between the boat ride and truck, she was going to be a windblown mess.

"Haven't fixed the AC. Sorry about that," he said over the loud growl of the engine.

She scooted to the middle of the bench seat to escape the worst of the wind. Duct-tape patches caught the cloth of her skirt. "No problem."

His hand came down on her knee, easing underneath the cotton to touch her bare skin. She froze as if any movement from her might scare him away like a wild animal. His thumb caressed the underside of her knee in slow, light arcs of sensation. Tingles trailed up her leg, sparking a sexual response that caught her off-guard in its intensity.

They'd made out under the cottonwood tree. He'd touched her much more intimately after the cocktail party, even during it, but this touch held promises and portents.

Neither of them spoke, and when he removed his hand to turn onto a narrow track with grass growing between the rutted tire tracks she missed his touch desperately. Pine trees rose on both sides, offering flashes of respite from the sun.

The summer heat, the tang of pine sap, the feel of his body next to hers . . . Seemingly insignificant, the moment carved itself as a new memory.

They pulled up beside a small, square house, dark-green paint flaking off the clapboards. The porch was narrow and short and supported a single rocking chair. Several empty beer bottles sat on a side table, flies buzzing around the rims.

She grabbed Cade's sleeve as he was sliding out of the truck. "Do you think Delmar gets lonely out here? His place seems a little . . ."

"Run-down? Ramshackle?" Cade smiled, but it was full of a resonating melancholy. He folded his arms on the top of the cab and rested his forehead against them, peering in at her. "I offered to buy him something nicer and closer to town. Sawyer's offered him a room at the farmhouse. He's turned us both down. This is where he wants to be. He grew up here."

She swallowed and looked back at the little house. It seemed too small for one man, much less a family.

"I don't remember Daddy talking about it much. He worked to get out of this kind of poverty. And he did. Got married, bought a nice house, had a family." Cade's eyes closed and his lips thinned. "Makes you wonder why good men die while men like Sam Landry are allowed to live. It's not fair."

"No, it's not fair." She slid closer and cupped his cheeks, caressing his cheekbones with her thumbs.

He turned his head to lay a kiss in the palm of her hand, his eyes still closed. She wanted to pull him close and kiss the pain of his childhood away, kiss him because of what he'd done for her, kiss him for the man he'd become. The path they were on felt inevitable.

The knowledge was both a comfort and a curse, made her feel both strong and weak. Whether he knew or not, he would be taking a piece of her with him when he left Cottonbloom. Maybe he'd always had a piece of her. Maybe that's why she'd never been able to give her heart to another man. She had been waiting for Cade to bring it back to her. Only problem was he'd claimed an even bigger chunk in the process.

Her throat felt scratchy with tears and the burst of

emotion that came with the sudden, life-skewing realization. "Cade, I—"

"Cade! Monroe! Well, I'll be. What're you two doing out here?" Delmar's yell cut her off.

Cade pulled away, the moment lost. "I've got your motor all fixed up. Where do you want me to put it?"

"Over by the shed would be good."

Monroe slid out of the truck and wandered to stand under a mixture of evergreens and hardwoods in front of the little house. What had she been ready to admit? She wasn't even sure. Less than three weeks he'd been in Cottonbloom. Yet even as her logic paced and lectured, her heart accepted that they were irrevocably tangled.

She picked at the bark of one of the pine trees and stared out into the dense woods. A flash of man-made white caught her eyes. Without the benefit of a hoist, Delmar and Cade were busy heaving the engine out of the truck bed.

She stepped through the woods, zigzagging around clumps of undergrowth. The tallest trees thinned and she stepped into what used to be a clearing, overgrown now with weeds and the sprouts of trees, some as tall as she was.

An old trailer on cement blocks stood in the middle. Sunlight reflected off the single remaining disc of a home-made wind chime, silent and twirling in the light breeze. There was something achingly sad about the lonely piece of metal. Kudzu had engulfed a quarter of the trailer, and left it sagging in that direction as if in a slow, painful surrender to nature.

This was Cade's trailer. The one he'd lived in after his parents' death. He'd told her about it, but nothing could prepare her for the reality. She tiptoed closer feeling as if she were disturbing a sacred spot.

On the ground under the former wind chime were

several more pieces of metal that had given up the fight. She reached up to touch the last disc, and the rotted twine snapped, the disc lost in the tall grass. The sight was heartbreaking in a way she couldn't describe.

A branch snapped behind her and she startled around, scratching her leg on a nearby clump of thorns. Massaging his bad hand, Cade walked out of the woods toward the trailer, not glancing in her direction. He seemed hypnotized by the sight, and waves of his agitation shot her heart into a faster rhythm.

He stopped at the foot of the rotted-out steps, not six feet away from her, yet he hadn't acknowledged her in any way. As she opened her mouth to speak, his voice rumbled. "If I had a gallon of gasoline in the truck, I'd burn this hellhole to the ground."

Chapter Twenty-one

Delmar had presented the trailer to Cade like it was nirvana. It had been old even then, and so starkly different from their cozy two-bath, three-bedroom brick ranch-style home, it was laughable. He'd wanted to cry and give up. The first of many times he'd almost given up.

Instead, he cleaned it up as best he could before he brought Tally and Sawyer out to see it, putting on a happy face and telling them how much fun it would be to live next to Delmar. Somehow, they'd made the rotting, buckling trailer a home.

"After Mama and Daddy were killed, I tried to hang on to our house, but they hadn't planned on dying. . . . No life insurance. The drunk driver that hit them died with nothing. They left a few thousand in savings and most of that went toward the funerals."

She shuffled closer to him as if he were a wild animal she wanted to trap—slowly, quietly, as if she worried he might balk. He longed for the comfort of her touch yet couldn't reach for her.

"We made it about six months in the old house before

the bank repossessed it. Uncle Delmar offered up this place. I did the best I could." His voice hoarsened.

She took his hand. He squeezed too tightly, but she didn't protest or pull away when he brought her hand to his chest, somewhere over his thumping heart.

"You kept your family together. You made incredible sacrifices for them."

He closed his eyes and shook his head. "I wonder sometimes if I should have let the state put them in foster care. They might have had a decent place to live. A decent meal on the table every night. A better start."

"What are you talking about? Sawyer went to college and Tally owns a very successful business. You've obviously done all right for yourself." A fair amount of tease lightened her voice. But something else, too. Something important that rang false.

God, she sounded proud of him when the truth resided in the dark parts of himself he rarely examined. He swallowed hard and squatted down in the tall grass. With her hand still in his, she was drawn down, too.

"I was so goddamn jealous of Sawyer." His voice dropped to confessional tones.

"Why?"

"He breezed through high school, popular despite our circumstances, dated a rich 'Sip, headed to LSU on a scholarship. I was smart enough to go to college. Instead, all I got was a GED and a job as a mechanic in a boatyard, making jack, covered in grease, while Sawyer . . . I sound like the biggest prick on the planet."

He wouldn't be surprised if she shoved him down and stalked off. His bad hand tingled. He spread his fingers wide and put his hand down on the sun-warmed ground. She tugged free, and he finally looked over at her. No horror clouded her eyes, only pity. He wasn't sure which was worse.

She looped her arms around his shoulders, her mouth close to his ear. "You sound human."

He couldn't stop himself from leaning into her, their foreheads touching.

"I'm happy at how well Sawyer's done; I swear."

"I know. He's proud of you, too. But this does explain a lot."

"What do you mean?"

"The tension between the two of you. You need to talk to him. Does he know why you left?"

"Not yet, but if I tell him everything, he'll think . . ."

"What? That you're normal? You tried to be everything to Sawyer and Tally—father, mother, brother, friend—and left before you could find a different footing with them."

He shifted to his knees, wrapped her in his arms, and laid his cheek at her temple.

"I wish I could have given Sawyer and Tally the things you had."

She tensed and pushed off his chest. "Yes, I lived in a big house with an awesome pool. Between my mom and dad, I got almost anything I asked for—clothes, shoes, ballet lessons—I could've had a stupid pony if I wanted one."

"Sounds pretty damn good to me."

"You seriously don't get it, do you?" She cupped his cheeks, forcing him to look at her. "What I didn't have was a real family. Safety. Protection. Those are the most important things you gave Tally and Sawyer. I may not have gone to bed hungry, but I went to bed scared. You were jealous of Sawyer? Yeah, well, I was jealous of Tally. She had you to take care of her and I had no one. So don't tell me what you gave them wasn't enough. It was more than enough."

Tears glimmered in her eyes even as determination steeled her features. He'd been so caught up in his pity party, he'd discounted the emotional scars she bore from her own childhood. Even more than that, her words resonated, tempering the guilt that had steadily grown over the years of self-imposed isolation.

He wasn't sure what to say, how to apologize, so instead he kissed her, leaning in with a desperation that shocked him. She murmured something unintelligible before she pulled him close, her hands in his hair and pulling at his neck.

What started as a simple kiss of comfort morphed into something that threatened to spark a forest fire. It turned languid and sensuous, almost as if the heat around them slowed their movements. She rubbed her tongue against his, her throaty moan driving his arousal higher.

He ran his hands from her shoulder blades through the dip in her waist to cup her backside. Pressing her close, he rotated his hips into her, knowing she could feel his growing erection.

Delmar's whistle cut through the trees, startling a covey of birds. Part of Cade wanted to curse his uncle for interrupting them, while part of him was relieved. Over the past few weeks, the wavery image of her from his dreams and memories had coalesced into a flesh-and-blood woman. A woman who knew and understood him better than anyone. Maybe even better than himself. It was madness.

Still he held her close, didn't answer his uncle's call. He dipped his head for one last kiss, this one sweet, tugging her bottom lip lightly between his teeth. He raised his head and watched her eyes flutter open, a dazed arousal blurring her features.

What would happen when he went back to Seattle? Richard's impatience was bleeding through his e-mails. He thought shipping Cade's current project down was a waste of time and money.

"Where're you at, boy?" His uncle's voice snaked through the trees.

"Coming, Uncle Delmar."

He helped her stand and led her back through the dense woods, holding back branches and stepping on thorny brambles so she could cross without getting scratched. The track he'd driven on so many years ago had been erased by time. They were both silent.

He put on a smile for his uncle, who thanked him over and over for his help. Cade owed Delmar a thousand favors for everything he'd done over the years. Even if Cade had hated the trailer, it had been a lifeline.

Monroe climbed back into the truck, but before Cade joined her he grabbed his uncle around the shoulders for a hug. Delmar gave a surprised jerk but returned the hug wholeheartedly. Cade pulled away even as Delmar continued to pat his shoulder.

"It's good to have you back, boy. I've missed having family around that understands."

"Understands what?"

"Life out here." Delmar gestured behind him, toward the river.

Cade wasn't sure what his uncle was getting at, but it seemed important. "Sawyer likes to go out on the river."

"Fishing to Sawyer is fun. Fishing to us is survival. The bond we have with the river is different from Sawyer's."

His heart kicked up a gear, knowing deep inside what his uncle meant. That's why Cade had stayed close to water after he'd been forced to leave Cottonbloom. Mobile, Alabama. New Bern, North Carolina. Maryland. Connecticut. And finally Seattle.

"I'm not staying in Cottonbloom. I can't."

His uncle cast a glance over Cade's shoulder to the truck. "You love Seattle that much?"

"It's amazing. How many times have I offered to fly you up there for a visit?"

His uncle made a scoffing sound. "You'll never find anywhere else like Cottonbloom."

"That is most definitely true," Cade said dryly. "Listen, I've got to get Monroe back. I'll come by soon and we'll go fishing, all right?"

Delmar turned away and waved two fingers over his head, redneck sign language for "Let's do it."

Cade slid behind the wheel of his truck, unaccountably restless. The road noise and the blowing wind made conversation next to impossible. A blessing. She sat close to him again, but he didn't touch her this time. Too much of his past had been unearthed over the course of the afternoon. The swirling ambivalence toward Cottonbloom on top of the deepening connection with Monroe made for an uncomfortable bramble of emotions.

He parked behind her SUV in front of the farmhouse. He slid out and she followed. Shifting on his feet, he looked anywhere but at her, afraid she would see more in his face than he was willing to admit.

"Okay, well, I guess I'll see you later?" she asked even though he heard a different question in her tone.

"You still need me to play dummy at your next class, right?" He risked a glance in her direction.

The corner of her mouth was drawn back, a spark animating her eyes. "Yeah. You're still a dummy."

"What?" He took a step toward her, but she yanked her door open and climbed in.

"Nothing. I'll see you around." The wheels spun gravel up, pinging the bumper of his truck on her exit.

Chapter Twenty-two

Monroe juggled two paper bags of groceries, the wind whipping her yellow sundress around her legs. Her wrap-around porch offered respite from the coming storm. Normally, this time of night in the summer children rode up and down the sidewalk followed close by hovering parents ready to prevent tears. Tonight it was deserted.

Her street was charming, the houses solid. Twenties-style Craftsman-built, they were set farther apart than the houses in the cookie-cutter neighborhoods popping up around the college. A mix of widows, retirees, and young families jumbled into a vibrant mini-community within Cottonbloom. She loved it.

The chimes hanging from an overhead beam held an off-key, haunting concert accompanied by the squeak of her swing being pushed by the invisible hand of the wind. Summer storms alternately filled Monroe with excitement and fear.

She loved watching the trees bend to the will of the winds that rolled off the plains of Texas, through Louisiana, and across the Mississippi River. But at the same time, those winds could coalesce into the swirling mass of a tornado. From her earliest memory, tornadoes had been the monsters in the night her mother had warned against.

The storm brewing from the southwest wasn't the stuff of nightmares. It had the feel of Mother Nature relieving the heat and tension that had built around them like a pressure cooker. The winds blew straight across the trees lining Monroe's street. Dark clouds snuffed out the fading orange rays like an inkblot spreading across the sky and bringing with it an early gloaming.

She unloaded her groceries and took a quick shower. The afternoon outside with Cade had left her sticky and off-balance. In shorts and a T-shirt, she stepped back onto the porch with a glass of iced tea. The wind seemed to speak to her. The swirling chaos matching the turmoil Cade incited. A different sort of storm, but no less destructive. After the layers of the past they'd peeled back, he could still flip a switch and turn distant.

She huffed a laugh. Hadn't she herself recognized his defensiveness long before now? Why did she think she was special? She wasn't; she was foolish. It was better this way. Better if they left things murky and unexplored. She would duct-tape the cracks of her heart back together before he could inflict any more damage.

Streetlights flickered like beacons up and down her street. Lightning flashed behind the darkness followed by a rumbling thunder, as if the gods were hungry. Another flash of light zigzagged its way from sky to ground. A loud crack made her flinch.

The night dimmed further. The streetlights no longer lit a path and the beckoning lights in the windows of her neighbors had been extinguished, giving everything a surreal, abandoned feel. A shiver ran up Monroe's spine, and she chafed her arms. The air had dropped several degrees in the few minutes she'd been standing there.

The first raindrops on her tin-roofed overhang joined

the wind chimes in an off-key duet. Drops plopped faster and faster until a solid sheet of water obscured the houses around her, lending her a sense of isolation.

When the wind tangled her hair and surged rain onto the porch, misting her legs, she retreated to her house. The power might be back on in a few minutes or it might be out for hours. Holding a small penlight between her teeth, she riffled through her junk drawer for a box of matches. As she was lighting the last candle on her mantle, a hard rap on her front door had her jumping and dropping the match.

A shot of adrenaline coursed through her body triggering trembles. But it wasn't a debilitating fear she faced. It was something darker, more dangerous. Exactly what she'd been yearning for even as she'd tried to talk herself out of it. Her heart knew who was on the other side of the door, and her body knew it was time.

She threw the door open without checking through the peephole. One of Cade's hands was propped on the doorjamb; the other held the heels she'd left at the farmhouse. Rainwater dripped down his face and had soaked his white T-shirt. At the curb, his rusted-out truck peeked through the rain.

The moment was heavy with unspoken promises. Her destiny had intertwined with Cade's from the moment he found her on the river.

"Brought your shoes." His voice slid through her like thick honey even as his excuse registered as thin.

"You drove out here in a torrential rainstorm to bring me my shoes?" She tried to inject some tease in her voice but failed.

He was static, waiting. She touched his arm. That was all the invitation he needed. He swept inside her house, so fast she could only process his body pulling hers close, his rain-soaked T-shirt wetting her. He banded his arms around her so tight she lost her breath. Or maybe it was his kisses—intense, deep, possessive—that made her breathless.

The shoes clattered to the floor. He glided his lips down her throat and nipped at the skin, sending tingles through her body. Her nipples were hard, painfully so, and she squirmed against him. He reached behind him, grabbed a handful of his T-shirt, and ripped it over his head.

Could he read her mind? His hard, warm chest eased the ache in her breasts. She ran her hands up his biceps and over his shoulders and back. The muscles jumped and shifted under her explorations. "You're beautiful."

He raised his head from where he'd been tugging on her earlobe with a huffing laugh. "What?"

She had no room for embarrassment. "You're beautiful. Perfect."

A serious cast came over his face like blinds being pulled. "I'm neither of those things. Especially not perfect."

When would he drop the chip from his shoulder and believe he was good enough? "You're perfect for me."

He shook his head, his eyes still somber, but didn't contradict her this time, only dropped his mouth to claim hers for another kiss. This one spoke of tenderness and yearning, and she rose on tiptoes to return it with everything she had.

"I've wanted you so damn long." His lips moved against hers as if he couldn't bear to break the kiss.

Now it was her turn to smile, their lips still touching. "You've been back less than three weeks."

He pulled back, the seriousness of his expression cutting her smile away. "It seems like a lifetime."

She wasn't sure if he meant it in a good way or more like a life sentence in prison. He stole rational thought with his lips, his hands inching her V-neck shirt up. His movements accelerated and her shirt was gone, a puddle of pink at their feet. Next he worked on the button of her shorts, and they fell to her ankles.

The power outage had forced an unintentional romantic vibe. Candles flickered, and a variety of scents wrapped around them. Pine combined with lavender, the combination earthy and arousing, but it couldn't compare to the clean, wild scent of man.

He walked her backward and lifted her to sit on the heavy antique desk in the corner, the wood cool against her skin. She parted her legs, and he pressed against her, the fit as easy and natural as if they'd done this a thousand times.

She propped herself on her hands, the position highlighting her simple lace bra that screamed outlet mall instead of high-end lingerie store. He didn't seem to care. His hands moved from the dip of her waist to cup both breasts. When he brushed his thumbs over her peaked nipples, she moaned and let her head fall back.

He snaked his good hand around her back. Her bra loosened. A shot of self-consciousness flooded her, heat burning up her chest, and she splayed a hand over the front of her bra in a fit of modesty.

She raised her eyes to meet his. Everything about Cade Fournette induced an instinctive trust. Always had. He waited like he had at the door for her to make the move. She drew her bra off and tossed it aside.

A rumble came from his chest. He forced her to lean back on her hands, one of his arms supporting her around her waist. Her arching back put her breasts on display, and he took full advantage. He dropped his lips to one nipple, while his hand tormented the other.

She chanced a glance down, the sight nearly sending her over the edge. His eyes were closed, his lashes casting crescent shadows in the candles' light. His face was a mask of pleasure overlaid with determination.

As if sensing her stare, he looked up, his mouth slack and her nipple gleaming. "You are beautiful. Perfect."

Had he repeated her earlier compliment on purpose? An automatic denial formed in her head but was swept away by his eyes and mouth and hands. He made her feel perfect.

Desperation overtook her like a fever. She straightened, forcing him back, and grabbed the waistband of his jeans. The damp denim made working the button free a challenge. The distraction of the ridge pressing against the zipper didn't help her concentration, either. With a mind of its own, one of her hands kept falling to rub the length of him.

His good hand joined hers to tug at his pants. Finally, the button gave way and she worked the zipper down. He had gone commando. His heavy erection slid into her palm. She tightened her grip and stroked him. Hard and soft and mouthwatering. She tried to push him back so she could fall to her knees, but he made a small sound of denial in the back of his throat.

"I know this is our first time, but I need to be inside of you. Now."

His words thrilled and terrified her. He grabbed her panties and roughly pulled them down, the giving of a seam sounding unnaturally loud. He curled his hands under her knees and pulled her legs apart, but instead of pushing into her, he looked. It was almost as if his gaze were physically licking her, up and down, over and over.

"Cade, please. I need you, too."

Her declaration seemed to light a blaze in him. He clutched her legs and spread her even wider, but this time he stepped into the void, the head of his erection brushing her. She bit the inside of her mouth to stop from climaxing at the light contact.

"Do I need a condom?"

She hummed, his voice barely registering. He took her chin and forced her to look at him. "Do I need a condom? Will you get pregnant?"

"N-no. I'm on the Pill."

It was all he needed. He pressed forward inch by inch. She gloried in the stretch, and when he was halfway home she flew apart in a white-hot blaze. As if in a dream state, she heard his curse, felt him slam deep inside of her, was dimly aware she moaned and writhed in his arms.

He lifted her off the desk, his hands scooping under her butt, his erection still inside of her, hard and hot. Her back hit the cushions of her couch, and he came over her, his jeans hanging around his thighs, his boots still on.

He grabbed her wrists, pressed her hands over her head, and hammered into her. She felt neither used nor trapped by him. His gaze stayed locked with hers, even as the build to pleasure became more intense.

He groaned, his eyes closing. She pressed her heels against his flexing backside to keep him in place. Whatever this thing was between them, it went deep. Deeper than merely dating and more meaningful than a hookup. At least to her.

He fell over her, his chest heaving against hers, his face buried in her hair. His hands still circled her wrists, but his grip had slackened. She pulled free and let her hands wander up and down his back and over the taut curve of his butt. Turning her face, she kissed his cheek and jaw and felt his lips brush the shell of her ear.

After an eternity, he heaved himself to his elbows, nose to nose with her, his erection still semi-hard and inside of her. The moment seemed important, bordering on sacred.

Chapter Twenty-three

Artificial lights flicked on with a blinding intensity. Rain continued to pelt her windows, but the hum of her AC kicking on brought him back to reality with a thud. Even though what they'd done had seemed inevitable, now they were on the other side he wasn't sure what to do.

She squinted against the harsh overhead light, hiding the clear blue of her irises. Her blond hair cascaded over his arm and down the chocolate-brown cushion of the couch like silk.

He hadn't been throwing a smoke show to get in her pants. She was the most beautiful, perfect woman he'd ever seen, and it was for that very reason he needed to leave.

He pushed all the way off her to stand next to the couch. Jesus, he hadn't even managed to get his pants and boots off. At least his getaway would be quick. He yanked his jeans up and zipped them, but between his bad hand and the wet denim the button proved too difficult.

He made the fatal mistake of looking down. She blinked up at him in a daze, her lips soft and red and swollen, her nipples little points that begged for his mouth, her bare legs spread in welcome.

"What are you doing?" she asked.

"I don't know," he whispered truthfully.

She rose and notched herself into his side, her arms around his waist, her breast against his bare chest. "You weren't leaving, were you?"

"Maybe?"

Instead of throwing a hissy fit or getting teary-eyed, she pulled back and shook her head, her blue eyes soft. "Nope. We're going to cuddle. In bed."

Her tone reminded him of the way she talked to the girls she trained—this was the take-no-shit Monroe. He couldn't help it, he smiled, but he forced a warning into his voice. "I don't cuddle."

She harrumphed, grabbed his hand, and led him toward a dark hallway, blowing out candles and flipping lights off as she went. She led him to her bedroom. Honestly, he would have followed her sweet little ass into an alligator-infested swamp.

"I need to clean up. Why don't you shuck the boots and jeans and wait under the covers?" She popped up on tip-toes to brush her mouth across his and sashayed toward the hall bathroom, shaking her hair out along the way.

Off-balance and fumbling around in the dark—literally and figuratively—he did exactly as she'd commanded and slipped under her cool cotton sheets naked.

The fury of the storm had passed, rain falling in the aftermath. He'd never slept over with any woman he was seeing. He was the jerk who rolled off and grabbed his pants. He wasn't the chump who took off his pants to cuddle.

When the rain stopped, he would leave. The argument between his brain and his heart quieted with the compromise. She was back, her hips and hair swinging, her breasts small but full and perky, her legs long and lean. He silently thanked his gene pool and the ability to see every glowing curve of her body.

She slipped under the sheet and pulled at his far shoulder, forcing him on his side to face her. Then, she scooched closer and wiggled until their bodies were pressed together from chest to feet. "There now. Cuddling isn't so difficult, is it? Even you can learn to do it, Cade."

He smiled into her hair and breathed her in. Under the vanilla scent of her soap was the smell of sex. He smelled good on her. No, more than good—perfect.

He roamed his hands over her back and down to her butt and up into her hair while her hands were performing a similar trek over his body. She nipped his neck and his pulse jumped.

"You smell so good I could eat you." The words were out before the double entendre registered, or maybe it was a Freudian slip, because his assessment was perfectly accurate.

"Cade." The way she whispered his name cast her back into the shy Monroe.

He loved she could be genuinely sassy and sexy and shy all within a few minutes and sometimes at the same time. He laughed softly and hugged her close. Thank God the rain still fell outside her window, because he wasn't ready to leave. Not quite yet. He'd definitely undervalued the act of cuddling.

He closed his eyes when one of her hands threaded through his hair and massaged his scalp. How long had it been since anyone touched him without wanting anything in return?

He cast back to his childhood, when his parents had been alive. His days and nights had been full of a freedom he'd tried hard to replicate after he'd left Cottonbloom. Freedom from having to worry about food, keeping his family together, keeping a roof over their heads. Freedom from responsibility.

Feeling as close to that freedom as he'd been in a long

time, he drifted into a state of limbo, the sound of the rain in his ears and her hands on his body performing an ancient alchemy. Time became irrelevant. Everything was laced with her scent and touch. He might have dreamed.

He was hard again, maybe harder than he'd ever been. Painfully so. Restless, he shifted, the night air cooling the heat building in the core of his body. A warm, wet mouth closed over him.

He lifted his head off the pillow. Monroe's hair was spread over his thighs, her hand around the base of his erection, her tongue circling the tip. This was a dream. He let his head fall back with a groan and raised a hand to cup her hollowed-out cheek. Bold, sexy Monroe was back.

"If I'd known cuddling involved this I would have taken it up years ago." He'd tried for teasing, but his voice was harsh.

Her mouth left him, and his hips bucked up, seeking her warmth. "Consider this cuddling with benefits."

He pressed the side of his face into the pillow and smiled. Their bedroom banter was as foreign to him as the cuddling was, but he liked it. A lot. And while the Cade Fournette who didn't cuddle or tease would have selfishly let her finish him, the one in her bed wanted to drive her as crazy as she made him.

In an athletic move that had her squealing with laughter, he pulled her up his body and rolled her over, his body on top of hers. The darkness was too deep to see the color of her eyes, but he could see her smile, easy and accepting. A warmth spread from his chest.

He kissed her. She wound her arms around his neck and opened for him. It was her nature to give and expect nothing in return. It was his nature to take. Or at least it had been the past few years, but he hadn't always been a selfish bastard. She brought out something in him he'd tried to leave behind. Maybe he'd had to come home to find it.

All he knew was he didn't want to take from her. He wanted to give, to hold, to protect.

He broke their kiss and stared down at her, both of them breathing hard, all tease gone. Words swirled in his head but didn't assemble themselves into a coherent thought. Past, present, and future coalesced into a single moment.

Fear had him sliding down her body. Pleasure was simple, and something he could give without losing part of himself. Everything about her was sweet and welcoming. He could have stayed between her legs until the sun rose, her body writhing against his mouth, hearing her chant his name and tug on his hair.

Her climax was sudden and intense, and he held her hips down to ride it out. He stayed to play long after she'd stopped shivering against him. She pulled at his hair, the tingling pain only intensifying his need. He shook off her hands and knelt. Her legs were spread wide, and her back arched, begging him without words.

Part of him wanted to take her face-to-face again. He wanted to see what secrets she held close, but in turn she might see his, and he wasn't ready for that. He might never be ready for that.

"On your hands and knees." His voice was too rough, too commanding, for the tenderness they'd shared, but he couldn't help it.

He thought she might argue or tease him, but as if he'd snapped a whip she moved to her hands and knees, wiggling back until she cradled his erection. He fit himself to her and pushed forward, the tight pull of her body even more amazing than before.

He'd planned to close his eyes and chase his pleasure. Instead, he curled his body over hers, his mouth at her temple. Words compressed from his lungs with each hard thrust. They barely registered.

He needed her to come with him. Her pleasure heightened his own. He snaked a hand between her legs and stroked. He wasn't a beginner in knowing how to bring a woman to climax, but with Monroe it was effortless. She was completely in tune with him and incredibly responsive.

As soon as the shudders took over her body, he bucked into her until he too came in a rush that left his body weak. He collapsed on top of her, driving her flat to the bed, his face buried in her hair. What was supposed to be detached doggy-style sex had turned intensely intimate.

Some of what he'd whispered in the dark rolled back through him, firing an embarrassed heat. He'd told her she was beautiful and sexy. True. Sweet and strong. True again. The word "love" hadn't passed his lips, but the word "forever" had. As in he'd wanted her forever, wanted to stay in her bed forever.

Less than three weeks, she said earlier. He'd been back mere days. His years in Seattle seemed a dream. He'd been living the life of a ghost, leaving his soul to wander Cottonbloom. The steamy heat must be driving him crazy.

He rolled to her side and more cuddling commenced. She nuzzled his neck, pressing kisses against his damp skin. The rain had turned to a drizzle, only the occasional ping against the window breaking the silence. He should leave. He would leave.

She took his bad hand and pulled him over to his side so she could massage it with both her hands. "Everything still feeling tingly?"

The question surprised him. He expected her to bring up his runaway tongue. "Even my toes. I haven't come that hard since I was a teenager."

Her laughter bubbled out and she leaned up to kiss him, her lips curved in a smile. "I meant the nerve damage in your hand, silly, but you made me feel pretty tingly, too."

Silly. No one had called him silly since he was a kid. "I'm learning to ignore my hand."

"Grip my wrist."

He did, and even he could feel the improvement he'd made even though his fingers sometimes refused to cooperate. His knee barely even twinged now. It was time to head back to Seattle. Instead of relief, dread with a fair amount of irony bit him in the metaphorical ass.

She continued to minster to his hand. Her warm, soft, naked body sent him sneaking toward sleep again. He'd rest his eyes for ten minutes, let her drift off, and tiptoe out. Facing her in the light of morning seemed too daunting. . . .

The clang of a pan startled him awake. Filtered sunlight traced dust motes through the air. Clutching the sheet to his chest like some virtuous maiden, he sat up. There was no sneaking out in the light of day with Monroe awake and between him and freedom. He was screwed.

He pulled on his still-damp jeans and his boots. His shirt was somewhere on her den floor. He sidled out of her bedroom, but the open floor plan put him in view before he made it a handful of steps.

"Morning," she said in a too-chipper voice considering the time. "I've got pancakes and bacon ready."

He turned slowly. Her blond hair tumbled down her back, messy and sexy as hell. His white T-shirt hit her mid-thigh, and she wore nothing else if her pert shadowed nipples were any indication.

She slid a plate piled high with steaming pancakes onto the bar, melting butter spreading over the top. He took two steps toward the kitchen as if expecting a booby trap.

The flash of a memory rocked him. Waking up in his childhood bedroom to the smell of bacon and the murmur of his parents' voices punctuated by the occasional laugh. How different would his life have been if they'd lived?

A loss two decades old suddenly felt immediate. His

parents gone in an instant. The trajectory of his life skewing like a satellite out of orbit, spinning out of control. He mourned what might have been.

Monroe's smile fell, and she stepped from behind the counter. "What's wrong?"

He had spent years turning himself into a fortress, impenetrable. Yet she could tell something was wrong in two seconds without a single word. Panic and claustrophobia heated him.

"Thanks, but I have to go help Sawyer. I didn't mean . . ." He swallowed and backed toward the door.

Her face clouded, but he couldn't tell whether she was hurt or angry. She had a right to be both. The door turned into his enemy. The injured fingers of his left hand couldn't maneuver the chain lock.

Her hand covered his, her warmth at his side, her scent winding around him like a caress. She flipped the dead bolt and slipped the chain free, their hands brushing. He hoped she put his trembling hand down to his injury and not the emotional deluge swamping him.

The door swung open, and he gulped in great breaths, making a run for his truck. It felt cowardly and wrong all the way around, but he couldn't help it. He drove off with her standing on her porch in his T-shirt. He watched her in his rearview mirror until he made the turn off her street.

Chapter Twenty-four

"Ohmigod, you had sex?" Regan's voice veered high and loud.

Monroe shushed her and glanced around Regan's interior design studio. The only customer was Nash's aunt Leora, who had the hearing of a hawk even into her seventies. Monroe hadn't meant to tell Regan anything, but the anxiety that had built over the past few days with no word from Cade needed an outlet, and she needed advice.

"You would not believe how awkward it was in the morning. First of all, I'm pretty sure he planned to leave two minutes after we did it the first time."

"The *first* time? You go, girl!" Regan held her hand up for a high five.

Monroe slapped her hand absently. "Yeah, well, so the next morning I'm feeling pretty awesome, wearing his T-shirt, making pancakes, and here he comes out of the bedroom doing the walk of shame. As soon as I put the plate down, he tried to bust out my door like the Kool-Aid Man. He left without a shirt on."

Regan held her fist against her mouth. Monroe wasn't

sure if she was stifling shock or giggles. "I'm sorry. I know that sucked. How mad are you?"

"Honestly, I'm not sure. Kind of upset, but then his face . . . Something was upsetting him. He tries so hard to stay impassive, but it was almost like he wasn't even there with me. He was somewhere else."

"Are you sure he doesn't have a girlfriend in Seattle? Or a *wife*?"

While Monroe knew little about his life in Seattle, she almost wished the problem were another woman. Whatever had sent him running was even scarier. A flesh-and-blood woman was less intimidating than the host of demons he fought.

"Regan, dearie, can I get your opinion?" Ms. Leora's voice wavered to them. She held up a floral upholstery in blues and greens. "Wouldn't this make lovely pillows?"

Regan cocked her head. "Indeed, and they would go well with the upholstery we had your living room couch covered in last fall." She led Ms. Leora to the counter to write up a ticket.

"Hello there, Monroe. I heard your fund-raiser did well." Ms. Leora plunked her pocketbook down on the counter.

"It did, thank you, Ms. Leora." Monroe pasted on a smile.

"And how is planning for the tomato festival going, Regan?" Ms. Leora clutched her pocketbook close, her fingers thin.

"It's great." To anyone else Regan's smile appeared sunny, but Monroe recognized the strain.

"I hope it won't end up being a waste of time and money. Who's paying for the fancy gazebo in the meadow?"

"The lumber came wholesale, and Nash is kindly donating his time to help frame it."

"So he informed me. At least he'll get outside. I worry he's not making friends now he's back."

Monroe couldn't help but smile over the coddling statement. "Nash is doing fine. We all hung out the other night, as a matter of fact."

Ms. Leora flashed an assessing gaze over Monroe and hummed before turning distinctly lemony and returning her attention to Regan. "You're aware, of course, the city is reassessing the properties along River Street and raising taxes. Poor Martha is feeling the strain. Elizabeth, bless her heart, didn't leave the Quilting Bee in the best shape for her daughter."

Martha was a generation younger than most of the women who gathered and shopped at the Quilting Bee. Her mother had a fatal stroke in the middle of a stitch, leaving the shop to her only child. Martha had never married, and as the years passed the Quilting Bee seemed more a burden than a joy, her mother's legacy in Cottonbloom a yoke around Martha's neck.

"It's been a decade since the last assessment, and with the revitalization of downtown everyone's businesses are worth more. It's a good sign for owners and the city."

"Cottonbloom does not need revitalizing. It's perfectly fine."

"You're more than welcome to voice your opinion at the next council meeting, Ms. Leora." Regan concentrated on the order form. "Let's see . . . the pillows will be ready in a week or so. I'll call you."

While Regan finished with Ms. Leora, Monroe retreated to Regan's office, moved a pile of fabric samples off an armchair to the desk, and plopped down. The screen of her phone didn't show any missed calls or texts. Her confusion and worry was skidding into angry territory. She got that men didn't usually call after a one-night stand, but that's not what they'd had, was it? Too much had been said. It had been too intense.

The front door bell tinkled and a few seconds later Regan walked in and went straight to a wooden filing cabinet. "I closed up a little early. There are no more appointments on the books and it's too hot for much foot traffic." She pulled out a bottle of Black Label Jack and two glasses.

"Is that filed with the *J*s or *W*s?"

"The *M*s for 'Medicinal.'" Regan flashed a smile and waggled her eyebrows. This was her real smile, not the one she used to trot out for pageants or during her job as mayor.

"I really shouldn't."

"You have to. You can't let a friend drink alone." Regan's voice was teasing as she poured.

Monroe stared at the glass filled with an inch of brown liquor. Hadn't she been as closed off as Cade in her own ways? She pushed the glass back toward Regan. "Actually, I don't drink."

"Since when?" Regan took a sip, her lips curled slightly, her eyes on Monroe.

"Since forever."

Regan put her glass on the desk in slow motion. "You've never turned down a beer or glass of wine."

"No, and I don't know why I didn't." Monroe tipped back in the chair, focusing on the pocked ceiling tiles. "That was a lie. I never turned down a drink because I didn't want anyone to guess the truth."

"The truth about what?"

"I don't drink because Mother's an alcoholic. I've spent years holding full bottles of beer and glasses of wine so no one would ask any questions." Monroe raised her head to gauge Regan's reaction. A pensive seriousness settled a frown on her face.

"So it's more than her going out and having fun?"

"Much more. Has been since we were kids. I tried to talk her into a rehab in Jackson, but she's afraid of the gossip."

"Is there anything I can do?"

"Not a thing. Mother drinks to escape, but you can never escape yourself."

Regan twirled the glass, uncertainty in the movement, hurt feelings in her voice. "Why didn't you tell me? Lord knows, I'm the last person who would judge you on your mother's behavior."

Monroe sighed. "Habit. Shame. You're my best friend, Regan, but for too long the secret's felt too big to face and if I'd told you . . . Please don't be upset. It seems like the longer you keep a secret, the harder it is to talk about."

Regan turned her face to the far wall, but seemed to be looking beyond it. "That I can understand." She turned back. "I could help."

"I don't need help. I'm just tired of pretending."

"I can't believe you fooled me for so long." Regan shook her head and raised her glass to her lips but stopped an inch short. "Do you mind if I have a drink?"

"Of course I don't. Drink up."

The tension between them eased, and Monroe relaxed into the chair, feeling lighter than she had since Cade had run out of her bed. They spent the next few hours talking about everything and nothing. Celebrity gossip, their crazy families, Cottonbloom politics, Sawyer Fournette's idiocy, Cade Fournette's foolishness.

Monroe ended up on the floor, her feet propped up on the chair with fabric samples over her bare legs like a blanket, an AC vent blasting in her direction. Regan had kicked off her heels and sat with her legs hanging over the side of her leather armchair.

Monroe covered her face with her hands, her fear surfacing. "I think I was Cade's booty call. The one man I—"

Her heart accelerated. Cade Fournette was the one man she could love. Might already love. Maybe had loved forever.

"You know what we should do?"

Monroe recognized the zealous enthusiasm in Regan's voice. It was the same tone she'd used to talk Monroe into skinny-dipping in the neighborhood public pool at midnight and into buying fake IDs and into spending five excruciating minutes kissing Kit Wannamaker in a closet in ninth grade. None of those endeavors had turned out well. She and Regan had gotten caught in the pool and with the fake IDs, and Kit had come out of the closet the next year—literally.

It was also a tone Monroe was unable to deny. Anyway, one of Regan's harebrained schemes might distract her from thinking about Cade. "Dare I ask?"

Regan was up and riffling through a box in the corner of her cramped, messy office. She came up with two cans of spray paint and an evil smile. "We should have a little fun, and what's more fun than showing the Fournettes up?"

Regan had finished off her drink and the one she'd poured for Monroe and at least two more. While she was far from sloppy drunk, her thought process was obviously impaired. She slipped on her heels, but her shirt was untucked over her pencil skirt and her French twist had come half-untwisted.

Monroe caught her arm before she could get the front door unlocked. "This is a terrible idea."

"You don't even know what I'm thinking."

"You're tipsy with two cans of spray paint. Nothing good can come from that combination."

Regan made a *phish*ing sound and got the door open. Darkness had fallen while they'd talked. Monroe debated a moment before running to catch up with Regan. At the very least, Monroe would keep Regan from doing something dangerous.

They crept toward the footbridge that led to the Louisiana side. It was a popular place for graffiti. "How're you going to reach the side of the bridge?"

"We're not painting the bridge." Regan crossed over.

Streetlights reflected off the newly painted yellow wall. Regan pulled the cap off one of the cans and shook it. Monroe grabbed her arm. "Are you serious?"

Regan answered by drawing an enormous letter *T* on the wall, red rivulets trailing down like blood. Monroe looked around, waiting for someone to pop out, point their finger and yell, *Aha!* While not dangerous, what Regan was doing was certainly foolish and not mayoral in the least.

Monroe tried again. "You're going to regret this in the morning."

Regan continued with her message. She dropped her spent can and took the one hanging uselessly in Monroe's hand. When Regan was finished, they stood back to take in the wall in all its glory. Written in huge block letters was "Tomatoes Rule, Crayfish Drool. Labor Day."

"I'll have to admit, the red on yellow is a standout combination," Monroe said.

The whine of a siren sliced through the humid air. Adrenaline rushed her body, and she took off at a run back across the footbridge. Unfortunately, Regan couldn't keep up in her heels and tight skirt. A spotlight caught her halfway across the grassy common area on the Mississippi side. Still mostly in the dark, Monroe could have made the corner of the buildings and ducked back into Regan's studio, but she couldn't leave Regan hanging.

Monroe walked back over to where Regan was talking with the Cottonbloom Parish sheriff, her hip jutted out and her arms crossed over her chest.

"Wayne, it wasn't me," Regan said as sweet as pecan pie.

"Then why do you have a big red paint streak on your cheek?" The fortyish-year-old veteran officer pointed with the pen he was using to make notations on an electronic tablet.

Regan gave herself away by rubbing even more paint across her cheek with stained fingers. Wayne turned to Monroe, tutting. "You're part of this, too, Monroe? Have you ladies been drinking?"

The threat of a ticket or worse had Monroe shifting and chewing on her lip. "I don't suppose you'd let us loose and we'll make sure the wall is repainted as soon as possible?"

"Repainted?" Regan put her arm around Wayne's shoulders and turned him toward the wall. "I think it looks fabulous. What do you think, Wayne?"

"A work of art," he said with a hint of amusement as he made more notations. "Look, I need to give Commissioner Fournette a call and see how he wants to handle the situation. That is town property, you know." Wayne slipped into the driver's seat of his squad car.

Regan groaned. "If it's up to Sawyer, he'll have us sent off to the state penitentiary for defacing his perfect little wall."

Monroe looked over at Regan's message. If she weren't on the cusp of getting in trouble, she might have laughed. As it was, her stomach was in the middle of a performance of *Riverdance*.

Wayne came strolling back over, readjusting the gun belt that hung low on his narrow hips. "Well, ladies, you're going to have to come down to the station with me." The Cottonbloom, Louisiana, police department was responsible for the entire parish, while Cottonbloom, Mississippi, had its own small police department.

Wayne opened the back door of the squad car and gestured them inside while reading them their rights. The moment took on the farcical quality of a *Cops* episode.

"Sawyer didn't demand you cuff us?" Regan held out her wrists.

Wayne didn't answer. The history between the two elected officials was a story people loved to dredge up and discuss over coffee or cocktails. Regan plopped down on the bench seat and scooted to the far side, staring out the side window.

In a more respectable voice and before ducking into the back, Monroe asked, "Can I use my phone to make a call?"

"Sure. Why not."

She pulled her phone out of her back pocket. She hesitated over Cade's name but scrolled past to *Tarwater* and hit the button.

"Monroe. Well, this is a surprise." Pleasure warmed Andrew's voice and Monroe cringed, knowing he probably hoped she had changed her mind about them.

"Hey, Andrew. Sorry to skip the pleasantries, but I need a favor."

"Anything." The earnestness in the word squeezed at her throat.

"Regan and I are in a pickle. Could you meet us at the Louisiana police station?"

A ruffling sounded over the phone as if he was already on the move. "What have you two gotten yourselves into? No, don't say anything over the phone. I'll be there in ten. And for God's sake, don't talk to anyone."

By the time she disconnected, they were pulling up to the ugly concrete box built for function and not aesthetic purposes. At least Wayne was inclined to let them walk into the main door and not the one in back for criminals. He escorted them to the front desk.

"You're not going to book us, are you? Andrew Tarwater is on his way. Surely this isn't more than a misdemeanor, if that." Monroe tried to smile.

"I have to follow protocol, but we don't mind taking our time, do we, Gloria?"

The middle-aged black woman sitting behind the desk wore a standard brown uniform, but pink streaks in her hair matched her long bedazzled fingernails. She grinned. "I'd be happy to mosey."

"Thanks, Gloria. How's Emmett's hip?" Monroe had rehabbed Gloria's husband over the winter.

"He's out playing golf and fishing like a twenty-year-old. And he can't get out of his chores anymore." She winked and they chatted a few more minutes.

A flurry of sound and movement heralded the arrival of Andrew, Sawyer, and Cade. Andrew and Sawyer argued their way up to the desk. Cade, however, was silent and shot a glare in Monroe's direction. He looked furious.

What right did he have to be mad? Wasn't he the one who walked out after their night of mind-blowing sex? He hadn't called or texted. In fact, she was only spilling her guts to Regan because he'd acted like the biggest dillhole in Cottonbloom. *He* was the reason she was in trouble. Her looping logic seemed to make perfect sense, and she glared right back at him.

While Andrew pulled Wayne aside for a low conversation, Sawyer's deep voice boomed in the small room, the level of vitriol startling. "What is wrong with you, Regan?"

"Just doing a little advertising, is all." In contrast, Regan's voice dripped with saccharine sweetness, although her smile had nothing to do with humor or good will.

Sawyer's gaze roved from Regan's messy hair to the scuffed, pointy toes of her heels before he turned to skewer Monroe. "How were you dumb enough to get pulled into Regan's foolishness?"

Regan took two steps toward him. "You shut your mouth, Sawyer Fournette. Monroe had nothing to do with it. All she did was hold a spray can, so you can aim your petty little insults at me if it makes you feel more like a man."

Wayne stepped away from Andrew, who gave her a thumbs-up and a wink, and leaned against the desk. No doubt the Cottonbloom police station hadn't seen fireworks like this in forever.

"What'd she paint on the wall, Wayne?" Even though Sawyer directed his comment to the officer, his gaze never left Regan. The air around them thrummed. If Monroe didn't know any better, she'd classify it as sexual.

Taking great relish in the drama, Wayne scrolled through his tablet, cleared his throat, and as if delivering a Shakespearean line said, " 'Tomatoes Rule, Crayfish Drool. Labor Day.' "

Now that Andrew had taken care of matters, a burst of relief bubbled out of Monroe as shaky laughter. Sawyer turned his ire back on her. "You think this is funny? Well, maybe I'll press charges and have the two of you locked up for a night."

Finally, Cade did something besides give her the death stare. He laid a hand on Sawyer's shoulder. "Bro, seriously? You're not putting Monroe in jail."

Sawyer shook his hand off. "You're going to defend her?"

"I'm going to protect her." Cade planted his feet wider. He and Sawyer were locked in a battle that seemed to dwarf the situation.

Andrew stepped into the fray. "No charges will be filed, gentlemen. And if the ladies agree to paint over their artwork within two business days, then no harm, no foul."

"Nice of you to ride to their rescue, Tarwater," Sawyer said. "If it's not repainted by start of business on Friday, I'll be back down here to file charges."

Regan's hand rose with the middle finger extended.

Monroe caught it in both of hers before Sawyer caught sight. "You betcha, Sawyer. We'll take care of it."

Sawyer strode out of the building. Cade followed more slowly, throwing a glance over his shoulder that she avoided. There was too much tension and animosity and hurt feelings ricocheting around the room. Now that the threat of being charged or going to jail had passed, a headache knocked on her temples.

Andrew gestured her and Regan toward the front doors. "Come on, ladies. Let's get you two home."

Regan led the way, her head high and her stalk huffy. Unfortunately, her disheveled appearance did not lend to an impression of calm confidence. Monroe hoped she didn't look quite as crazed.

She matched Andrew's stride and stuffed her hands in her front pockets. Cade was leaning against a light post next to his beat-up truck, his arms crossed and one booted foot crossed over the other in a seemingly casual pose that was ruined by the stony look on his face.

"Thanks for coming down. I really appreciate it. Could you get Regan home? I need to talk to Cade."

Halfway down the steps, Andrew caught her arm. "Are you sure you don't want a lift, too? He seems upset."

Monroe patted Andrew's hand, inducing him to let her go. "I'll be fine with him."

Andrew's mouth tightened, but he didn't argue and headed to where Regan leaned against the side of his Mercedes. Monroe took a deep, steadying breath and walked toward Cade. No matter how angry or frustrated Cade was, he would always protect her. It was something she understood, bone deep.

"Why didn't you call me?" His words stopped her in her tracks.

"Wait, what? Why didn't *I* call *you*? You walked out of my house. You couldn't escape fast enough. I freaking made you pancakes, and all I got was crickets. I've got the T-shirt you were in too much of a hurry for. Feel free to drop by and pick it up at your convenience."

His stance of aggression changed into something more defensive. All of the hurt and anger and betrayal had built like storm clouds inside of her since he'd walked out. She unleashed.

"I am not your booty call, Cade Fournette. I don't do one-night stands." She stepped closer and poked him in the chest. "Was it just about sex? Because if it was then I—"

"Slow down, woman." He put his hands on her shoulders and squeezed. "It was not just about sex. But can we leave that for a minute? I want to know why you called Andrew Tarwater instead of me."

"Because he's a lawyer. And sort of a friend. And, to be honest, after you walked out, I have no idea what you are. What *we* are."

"I'm your . . ." He looked toward the halo of light above them.

"See, you don't even know. Are you my lover? My boyfriend? My booty call?"

"I thought you were *my* booty call?" The hint of a smile crinkled his eyes.

"No. You don't get to be all cute and charming. I'm seriously trying to define us here."

He ran his hand down his face taking all amusement with it. "Don't you get it? We are indefinable. We always have been. I don't know what we are, but it goes beyond being lovers or friends, and it scares the hell out of me."

His words struck a chord inside of her. They moved at the same time, coming together in a fierce hold, his arms holding her close, her fingers biting into the muscles of his back.

Their lips collided in a kiss at once sensual and desperate. She wasn't sure how long they would have stayed making out in the parking lot, but the piercing siren of a police car cut them apart.

He tore his mouth away from hers but dragged her body closer. Into her hair he whispered, "Can I take you home?"

"You can take me anywhere," she whispered back.

At first she wasn't sure he even heard her, but eventually he loosened his hold and opened the driver's side of the old truck. She slid to the middle of the bench seat.

He started the truck but didn't get them moving immediately. Shifting toward her, he circled his hand around her neck and kissed her again. Slower this time, their lips giving and taking. More. She needed more.

She threaded her fingers through his hair and made a fist, pulling him closer and sliding her tongue inside his mouth, taking charge of the moment. He groaned and gave her what she craved. One hot kiss followed another until she was cutting her legs against each other, bordering on uncomfortable in her arousal. She grabbed his closest hand and drew it between her legs.

"I love the fact you look all sweet and innocent yet detonate in my arms." He spoke against her lips, the husky, sexy vibrations traveling straight to her nipples.

He squeezed her upper thigh with his bad hand, his fingers slipping under the hem to trace the elastic of her panties. She was close to shattering.

He pulled away, putting both hands on the steering wheel and sounding like he was practicing deep-breathing exercises. "We are in the parking lot of the police station. You don't need to be hauled in for defacing property and indecent exposure on the same night. I'm not sure Sawyer would come bail us out."

He put the truck in reverse and got them headed toward her house. She squirmed on the seat, the break only growing her arousal. She leaned over and nipped his ear. "I swear, if my house was farther away I would totally go down on you while you were driving."

He tapped the brakes, throwing her forward a few inches, her breasts rubbing against his biceps.

"I'd be happy to cruise up and down River Street a few times."

She laughed. God, she loved his teasing, questioning tone. If she gave him the green light he would totally drive around. "Another night. Right now, I need you to get me home as quickly as possible. Without getting pulled over by the cops."

This time it was his turn to throw his head back with a husky laugh. He drove fast and parked in her garage. Her car was still in front of Regan's store.

He slid out and grabbed her around the waist, pulling her close. They stumbled up the porch steps and into her house. Once inside, he pressed her against her front door with his big body. The crinkles at his eyes and the lines bracketing his mouth weren't from laughter. A desperate intensity had replaced his tease.

She didn't need him to tell her what he needed, because she needed it, too. Slipping her hands between them, she went to work first on her pants, pushing them down with her panties. His jeans were next. After loosening them, she curled her hands around the curve of his hip bones before pushing his jeans and underwear far enough down to free his erection.

There was no preamble necessary. He hiked her leg up and around his thigh, fisted the base of his erection, and pushed inside of her. They exhaled in synchronicity. It was about more than pleasure—at least for her.

He grabbed her hips and ground himself deeper. Their hands brushed, both working to get her shirt off. She unclasped her bra, needing to bare herself to him.

The cotton of his shirt was a soft caress against her

breasts as he pushed her against the door, taking a small thrust in the process. Based on their ride, she'd expected something quick and dirty, yet he seemed to be in no hurry, and she was glad for it. The longer he took, the longer he would be inside of her, part of her. A dangerous way to think.

He set his forehead against hers. "You're beautiful. And funny. And strong. And sexy." Each compliment was punctuated by a long, slow thrust.

Words were beyond her, so she kissed him with all the emotion she'd kept pent up since he'd come home. Maybe since he'd left home. No man had ever measured up to her memories of him. And while her old memories were colored by childhood and innocence, she was making new memories of him, not better but different, deeper, shaded by a woman's experience.

His hips moved faster to mimic the franticness of their kiss, the grind like nothing she'd ever experienced. She wanted to wait, savor him, but the friction drove her into a blinding orgasm. He followed soon after, his groan echoing in her entryway.

Thank God he didn't move, or she might have tumbled to the floor. Her entire body trembled. She didn't feel strong at the moment; she felt weak and vulnerable.

Wrapping her arms around his shoulders, she kissed his neck, slightly damp, the pulse jumping against her lips. For better or worse, she loved him. She'd always loved him in her childish way, but now she loved him as a woman loved a man.

The words battering around her heart didn't come out. She didn't know if she'd be strong enough to handle the fallout if he turned and walked out the door again.

Chapter Twenty-five

Cade hid his face in her hair, searching for words. Anything he thought to say sounded either too trite or too revealing. His tongue had developed the habit of running away from his brain while they were having sex. He couldn't seem to stop it. She was beautiful and funny and strong and sexy, and dammit, she deserved to hear that every day.

He could have stayed leaned up against her and the door for a while longer, but her trembles were growing more noticeable by the second. He pulled away. Her head lolled back, her eyes closed, her lips puffy and red from the hottest kisses he'd ever experienced.

Slowly, he withdrew, his body fighting him every inch. Being inside of her offered a comfort and solace that went beyond sex. To a place he'd never been, had never cared to go, but now that he'd experienced the wonder he wasn't sure he could ever leave.

"That was hot," he said, and immediately felt like a crass adolescent. "I mean, it was more than hot; it was amazing. Surreal. Unbelievable." He tucked his tongue in back of his teeth to stem the flow of words.

"It was all those things, but especially hot." Her voice was sweet and sexy at the same time.

"That's twice now I haven't gotten my pants off." He pulled his jeans up but didn't fasten them. Her palms were flat on the door as if still needing the support. She was naked while he was clothed, and the contrast was turning him on in a major way.

His gaze wandered up and down her body, enjoying every slope and curve. Her arm came up to hide her breasts, a flush spreading from her chest up into her cheeks. He could almost feel the heat of her embarrassment.

He took both her wrists in his hands and pressed them over her head. "The woman who offered to go down on me in the truck and let me fuck her against the door is suddenly feeling shy?"

"That was in the heat of the moment. This is . . ." She turned her face into her arm.

She didn't have to say it. He understood. This wasn't about being physically stripped but about being emotionally bared to him.

"Are you staying or going?" The vulnerability in her voice made him want to gather her close. So he did.

"Staying, if you'll have me."

"I'll have you." A trust he didn't deserve lit her face.

He loosened his hands but didn't entirely let her go. "I don't suppose you have anything to drink?"

"Water, tea, or there's a bottle of wine a client gave me for Christmas in the frig."

"You realize it's June."

"I thought wine got better over time. Feel free to open it. I won't ever drink it."

He dropped his hands, and she sashayed toward her bedroom, her confidence restored. Had he done that?

Her refrigerator was only half-full. Lots of healthy fruits and vegetables, but also leftover pizza. He grabbed the pitcher of tea and the bottle of wine that was tucked into the back. Muscadine wine. The bottle was a screw top. He found a glass and poured, swirling the wine and sniffing.

Another memory rocketed him backward in time. His parents drinking wine and slow dancing in the kitchen. The music or maybe their muffled laughter had awoken him. It had been before Tally was born, and Sawyer was a baby. His mother rarely drank, but muscadine wine was her favorite, and Cade remembered the same sweet smell on her breath when she'd tucked him back into bed.

He closed his eyes and took a sip, grimacing as the overly sweet tartness hit his tongue and burned the back of his throat. It was terrible. He spit the rest of his mouthful out in the sink.

"What's wrong?" The T-shirt she'd thrown on was the one he'd left. It slipped off the curve of one shoulder and hit the top of her thighs so he couldn't tell if she'd pulled on underwear or not.

"That is the worst wine I've ever tasted."

"Really? Let me see?" Instead of taking the glass, she covered his hand with her own and lifted the rim to her lips. He watched, mesmerized, as she wet her lips and then licked them.

"Tastes fine to me, but what do I know?" Her teasing smile only drew him closer to her mouth. The urge to taste the wine on her lips was undeniable.

With their hands still wrapped around the wineglass, he captured her lips, the sweetness of her and the wine nearly undoing him. If he could drink the entire bottle off her lips then he would award it a blue ribbon.

A cold wetness on his chest had him pulling back. The wine had spilt on him, the aroma more appealing than the taste.

She wiped at the spot. "Goodness. You should get out of that wet thing."

His laugh was spontaneous. "Isn't that normally the man's line?"

Laughing, she took his hand and tugged him into her bedroom. The light from a candle lent romantic overtones. The scent that wove the room wasn't a flowery one but a combination of pine trees and the sea air.

In his previous life, he might have felt trapped and boxed in, but none of the familiar restlessness came over him. He didn't barter with himself this time about staying. There was no question he was waking up in her bed.

Still wearing his T-shirt, she slipped under the covers. The flash of little white panties was more erotic than the entire Victoria Secret catalog. Taking his cues from her, he stripped off his shirt and jeans, leaving his boxer briefs in place.

"Why did you run off the other morning?" Her question lilted in the peace.

He propped his head up on his hand and played with a piece of hair that tickled his chest. "That morning—" He cleared his throat, the remnants of emotion still raw. "The last time someone cooked for me like that was my mother."

"Are you saying none of your previous . . . girlfriends," the word seemed painful for her to say, "cooked you breakfast or dinner or made you a sandwich?"

"I pay people to cook and clean for me." It was a non-answer, and she deserved more. "I've never allowed a woman close enough to cook for me."

"Were you worried one of them might slip you some rat poison?"

"A couple of them probably thought about it." He brought the piece of hair to his nose and inhaled.

"Does Cottonbloom seem provincial compared to Seattle?"

"In some ways it feels like time has stood still, but in

others I barely recognize the Cottonbloom from my memories."

"Everything is changing. The town is growing—both sides—and most people don't care if you're a 'Sip or a swamp rat. The college has opened up all kinds of opportunities. You could move your business from Seattle to Cottonbloom and not miss a beat."

"That's never going to happen, Monroe." He injected a warning into the words, but even as he said them something resonated. Deep in his subconscious, the thought had taken root days ago.

Everything he had worked for was in Seattle. It was complicated. It was insanity.

Yet he hadn't missed that life. Not for a second. Not with Monroe circling his thoughts and his brother and sister inserting themselves back into his worries.

"Fine. But you should make things right with Sawyer before you leave." She notched herself into his side and laid her head on his shoulder; his arm automatically went around her and pulled her even closer. The thought of leaving was unbearable.

She yawned. "If I fall asleep are you going to skedaddle in the middle of the night? Don't make me wake up in an empty bed."

"No. I'm done running." He wouldn't run away from Cottonbloom again, but he wasn't sure he could stay, either. Pushing the uncertainty out of his mind, he tucked her head under his chin and vowed to hold on to her as long as he could.

Light burned against Monroe's closed eyes, and she jerked awake. She blinked against the blinding sunlight streaming through her window, the drapes pulled wide. Something was different. Cade.

She rolled to her back and ran her arm over the expanse

of deserted mattress. The sheets were rumpled and the pillow mashed. The smell of coffee drifted from the kitchen.

She pulled on a tank top and yoga pants and freshened up. When she popped around the corner of the kitchen, he startled, splattering batter from the whisk.

She put on her sweetest drawl. "Why, Cade Fournette, are you makin' me breakfast?"

"Trying. Coffee's brewed."

She poured herself a cup while studying him through her lashes. He'd pulled on his jeans and T-shirt. Unfortunate for her viewing pleasure but probably safer for all his bits and pieces while cooking. He ladled batter onto the griddle, the sizzle and smell filling the silence.

"I used to get off third shift and make breakfast for Tally and Sawyer before getting them to the school bus. Pancakes were their favorite." His voice rumbled between them, his tiny admission dispelling the morning-after awkwardness.

She put her coffee down, wrapped her arms around him from the back, and laid her face against his shoulder blade. "You did a good job with them, Cade. The struggles and sacrifices were worth it."

He was stone against her, tense and hard. In an instant he turned from a statue into flesh and blood, spinning in her arms and capturing her mouth. Thank the Lord she'd brushed her teeth. It was her last rational thought.

He pushed the pan off the eye and flipped the stove off. Somehow, she ended up with her legs around his hips and his hands under her butt. The cold wood of her kitchen table shocked a gasp out of her, her lips still on his.

He pulled away, staring into her eyes. "I want you to come to Seattle."

It took a long moment for the words to make sense. "I've never been, but people say it's beautiful. When it isn't raining." She tried on a teasing smile, but his expression didn't lighten. She let the smile drop and swallowed hard. "I'll have to give Bartholomew some notice. Even taking off a few days throws the schedule into chaos."

"I'm not talking about a vacation, Monroe. I'm talking about something permanent."

She pushed him away, unable to process the implications with her legs around his hips, his erection against her, his hands on her body. She half-sat on the table, her knees weak either from his kiss or his offer. "Hold up. Are you asking me to move to Seattle with you?"

"Yes." He said the word as if throwing out a gauntlet as he backed up and leaned against the wall, crossing his arms over his chest.

His offer landed on her heart with the force of a slap. "Where would I live? What would I do?"

"You'd live with me, of course. You could take time off, hang out."

"Hang out? Like as your kept woman?"

The hint of a smile crossed his face, but it was gone before she could be sure. "Or get a job. PTs are in demand everywhere. Whatever you want."

She'd never considered leaving Cottonbloom. It was her home. Unlike Cade, she'd embraced the quirky, divided nature of the town and accepted her memories—good and bad. But a town and a life were nothing without people, and there were too many people who depended on her.

Without Monroe, her mother might spiral further down the rabbit hole. Bartholomew depended on her and had already spoken to her about buying him out when he retired. Kayla and the other girls counted on her to be a stabilizing, supportive force in their lives. The thought of leaving Cottonbloom felt like offering a limb for amputation. The thought of losing Cade felt like donating her heart.

"You could stay here. Tally and Sawyer would love that." She threw out her own challenge.

"I have a state-of-the-art workshop in Seattle. Sawyer's garage won't cut it long-term."

"Build a better workshop. You have the money."

"My business is based out of Seattle. My partner is there."

"So you expect me to pick up and move my life?"

"It makes more sense."

"Does it? What do you have up there besides a bunch of engines? Family? No. Friends?" He hesitated, and she answered for him. "I'm taking that as a no. No one loves you up there, Cade."

"What are you saying?" His eyes narrowed on her and she squirmed, her palms growing damp, her fingernails biting into the wood.

Anticipation stretched the seconds, fraying her nerves. "Your brother, your sister, your uncle, and . . . *I* all love you."

He moved faster than she thought possible, his hands gripping her shoulders, his fingers pressing hard into her muscle. "Say that again."

She knew what he wanted from her, and now that the moment was upon her the words felt as natural as if they'd lived inside of her for a long time. "I love you, Cade Fournette. Maybe I always have."

"I'm not the same boy who came to your rescue."

"I'm not the same girl who needs rescue. We've both changed, but you understand me like no one ever has. That much has stayed the same, hasn't it?"

His grip loosened. He laid his forehead against hers and shuddered out a long, slow breath. "Then you'll come to Seattle." It was more statement than question.

"That's not what I said," she whispered.

He leaned back, slid his hands up to cup her cheeks, and forced her to look at him. "But you love me."

The satisfaction and relief that threaded his words was not the same as a return declaration of his feelings. "Yes, but I love my mother, too, and she needs me here. I love the girls in my program. They need me here, too. I have no doubt you want me, but do you need me? Do you love me?"

His lips parted on an intake of air. A hard knock on the front door startled them apart. Whatever he was going to say was lost as he stepped away. The knock came again. "Doesn't sound like they're going to give up anytime soon." His voice had already grown distant, like that of a man given a reprieve.

Her knees felt like they had been injected with Novocain, her walk more than a little shaky. She peered through the peephole, seeing a distorted Regan on the other side. Casting her eyes heavenward, she unlocked and opened the door.

Regan pushed big, round sunglasses to the top of her head and swept inside. Her face pale and dark circles under her eyes. "We'd better get that dadgum wall painted before chicken-headed Sawyer Fournette has us arrested. I swear—" Her chatter shut off like someone hit the mute button.

Cade emerged from the bedroom. His shoes were on and his shirt was tucked. "Regan."

"Hey, Cade." A blush had suffused Regan's cheeks. "I'm sorry. The wall was all me and I'll take care of it. You guys continue whatever you were doing. Or not doing." She backed toward the door. "Whatever the case may be."

"No. I'm leaving." He brushed by Regan and opened the door, pivoting around with one foot in and one out. "Will you at least think about my offer?"

Monroe nodded. "Of course."

He shoved his hands in his front pockets and walked

slowly down the porch steps. Before disappearing into the garage, he turned back. Something potent passed between them, but it had the feeling of an ending and not a beginning. Tears blurred her eyes as she closed the door and rested her forehead against the place they'd been joined so intimately only hours earlier. When she heard the sound of his old truck fading, she turned around.

"Oh, sweetie, what happened?" The caring and kindness in Regan's voice sent a few tears down Monroe's cheeks. She wiped them away, sniffed, and shook her head, banishing them through sheer force of will.

"Cade asked me to move to Seattle."

"Whoa. Is that the offer you're supposed to be thinking about?"

"Sure is."

"You two have moved pretty fast. Could you convince him to stay in Cottonbloom a while longer so you could make sure that—"

"I love him. I can't imagine I'll ever love another man. It hasn't happened quickly at all; it's been forever."

"What are you talking about? He's been back less than a month."

Monroe pressed her hands against her cheeks, a smile threatening in spite of everything. "You want some coffee? Because I have something to tell you."

Regan sipped on her coffee while Monroe's story poured out. Once she was done, she sighed, another weight of her past shed.

Regan turned her coffee cup on the kitchen table. "There's so much you never told me. Your mother, Sam, Cade."

"I've never told anyone except for Cade. You're the best friend I've ever had, but I was young and scared and ashamed. I didn't want you or your parents or anyone at school to know what was going on."

"I'm so sorry I wasn't there for you. I feel terrible." Now the tears were in Regan's eyes.

"Please, I didn't tell you so you could feel bad for me or guilty. Even back then, I knew I couldn't tell anyone about Cade."

"I would have understood."

"If anyone would have it would have been you, but if I'd told you about Cade, then I would have had to tell you everything. I wasn't ready then, but with Cade back I finally feel able to talk about it. Does that make sense?"

Anger superseded Regan's tears, and she banged her fist on the table, sloshing coffee from both their mugs. "I'm going to get Sam Landry's butt off the city council and then personally kick it down River Street."

"Are you going to have him stoned to death, too?"

"This is not funny, Monroe. He almost—he could have—I can't bear to think about it." Regan closed her eyes and blew out a long breath. When she reopened them most of the anger had ebbed out of her face. "That's why you got a black belt and why you work with those girls, isn't it? So it doesn't happen to them."

"Most of them won't have a Cade Fournette to run to. Fate was smiling on me that night whether I realized it or not."

"Tally doesn't know?" Monroe shook her head, and Regan sat back in her chair. "Are you going to follow him to Seattle?"

"I'm honestly not sure." She ran a hand through her hair. "Let's go get our community service over and done with. What do you say?"

"Sure." Regan didn't sound as ready to let the matter go, but Monroe didn't give her a choice, heading into the bedroom to pull on an old T-shirt and shorts.

Chapter Twenty-six

Sawyer wandered into the garage, keeping to the edges. An air of expectation followed him as he picked up and put down various tools. Cade sat back, his bad hand tightening on the handle of the socket wrench. He waited.

"Sorry I was kind of a jerk last night." Sawyer clinked two screwdrivers together in a syncopated, grating rhythm. "With everything going on with Regan and the festival . . . Plus, they're talking layoffs at the plant."

Sawyer still hadn't made eye contact. Cade slipped his hand into the tight space between hoses, letting his fingers guide him to the correct bolt. "Your job at risk?"

"Nah. But I'm not looking forward to giving out the pink slips. Most of those people live from paycheck to paycheck. Not to mention, they're my constituents."

Cade's fingers lost their agility. The wrench slipped and his knuckles busted against metal. He muttered a few curses.

"Let me help. I'm pretty handy, you know?" Sawyer pulled a stool next to Cade, and they sat side by side tweaking parts and discussing the mechanics behind the engine Cade had designed. The common ground they trod settled an ease that hadn't existed between them for years. They brainstormed ideas for driving the modifications even further as Cade furiously sketched and made notes.

He hadn't been this energized in a long time. The last year especially had seen his enthusiasm ebb drastically, which went a long way toward explaining his itch to climb El Capitan.

Sawyer helped tighten bolts and check seals. All the animosity and resentments that had flared since Cade had come home seemed dampened. A smudge of grease lined Sawyer's face and his brow was furrowed as he tightened a bolt.

The older Sawyer got, the more he looked like their father. Sandy blond hair, hazel eyes, humor never far from breaking free. Although his laughter had been absent of late. Dark circles ringed his eyes, and his face held the hint of strain. Cade hated to think he was the cause. The drive to make things better for his siblings hadn't died.

"I have a question . . . or rather, I need your advice," Cade said.

Sawyer sat back and slowly turned to face him. "Did I hear you correctly? You want my advice? Mine. As in you require a portion of your little brother's wisdom."

"Let's not go crazy. 'Wisdom' is probably stretching the realm of credibility." Cade jiggled a hose to have something to do to occupy his hands. "I'm toying with the notion of moving my operations to Cottonbloom."

"Why would you do that?" Sawyer's voice reflected shock but also a fair amount of suspicion, amplifying the doubts creeping around the edges of Cade's mind.

"You think it's a bat-shit crazy idea?" He glanced over at his brother. Sawyer had crossed his arms over his chest, and his face looked so much like their father's Cade couldn't look away.

"Not necessarily." Sawyer ran a knuckle over his bottom lip as he considered Cade. "Is this because of Monroe?"

"Maybe?" The uncertainty in his voice unsettled him.

"You've only been back a few weeks. I'll admit, I'm floored you would consider doing something so drastic for a woman."

"What Monroe and I share . . ." He chuffed a laugh and shook his head. "I guess I should tell you all of it."

And he did, only glossing over the reason Monroe had fled to the river in the first place. That was her story to tell.

"Wow. I had no idea." Sawyer shuffled a hand through his hair.

"It was better no one knew. We both would have gotten into trouble." He kicked at the dusty floor. "You're the first person I've ever told."

"Thanks for trusting me." Sawyer cleared his throat, his voice less husky sounding when he continued. "Wouldn't it be easier to ask her to move to Seattle with you? There are PT jobs anywhere. Your company is based out of Seattle. I've seen your setup. It's world-class. Down here what do you have? My garage?" He made a grand gesture around them. "This is not exactly what I would call posh. Not like the life you have up there."

"I already asked her, and let's just say, she wasn't as receptive as I'd hoped to making a change." He couldn't see her uprooting her life in order to date him. Anyway, she was only one reason for wanting to move back here. There were others, but if he tried to articulate them he would sound like a sentimental fool, and he'd never been either. But instinctively Cade knew he had to try, no matter how foolish he sounded.

"Coming back . . . it's not just Monroe. I miss you and Tally. I want to be part of your lives."

"You are part of our lives," Sawyer said gruffly. "I'll never fully understand how much you sacrificed for us,

Bro. When I imagine what would have happened if the state had taken us I want to puke, but it felt like you abandoned us as soon as you could."

Cade swallowed down the automatic apology. It was time for more truth telling. "I didn't abandon you. I got caught stealing by Chief Thomason. It was either leave or go to jail."

"Why didn't you tell us?" Shock lifted Sawyer's voice.

"I was ashamed and disappointed in myself. I let you down."

"We would have understood, supported you." Sawyer clapped him once on the shoulder and squeezed.

"By that time you were in college and Tally had decided to pursue her personal trainer license. Neither of you needed me anymore." Clarity born of distance cleared the fogged glasses through which he'd viewed the past. Going from having a purpose—protecting and providing for his siblings—to nothing had left him floundering. Maybe Monroe was right. He'd wanted to get caught stealing that engine.

"I didn't stop needing you because I was in college. You were my big brother. I looked up to you, tried to be half the man you were."

Cade blew out a long, slow breath, knowing what needed to be said but dreading it. "Seeing you go off to college, make the Dean's List . . . I was crazy proud of you, but I was also a little jealous." He winced as he said the last word but forced himself to continue. "I already felt old and stuck and I was only twenty-three. I wanted to go to college and party and have fun, but . . ." He shrugged.

"I'm an idiot for not realizing," Sawyer said softly.

"What? No. *I'm* the idiot."

"Does everything have to be a competition with you, Bro?" He popped Cade's arm and flashed a smile, triggering laughter.

The ugliness Cade had carried around for too long seeped into the red clay dirt under his feet. An embarrassing sting of tears had him blinking. "Thanks for bullying me back down here. I needed you, and you were there for me. That means more than you know."

"It's what you do for family. You did more for me than I could ever repay," Sawyer said. "If you decide to move operations down here, I'll support you one hundred percent, but don't do it and change your mind six months later. You have to stick."

The words resonated with him. Monroe deserved a man who could stick. If he uprooted his life in Seattle, he had to grow deeper and stronger roots in Cottonbloom. He would have to accept there would always be people who looked down on him because of where he came from, because he'd done what had to be done to keep his family together. To the Tarwaters of Cottonbloom he would always be the Louisiana swamp rat or the high-school dropout.

Sawyer continued, unaware of Cade's swirling, confused thoughts. "Anyway, what will your partner think? I can't imagine him moving down here."

"Richard is not a country boy, that's for dang sure. He'll give me pushback no doubt." Cade ran a hand through his hair, ruffling the back. "I don't know. Maybe it's too complicated. Impossible."

"Impossible was keeping the three of us together after Mom and Dad died. If you did that, you can handle Richard."

"I appreciate your confidence." Cade tried on a strained smile. "You want to go out on the river tonight?"

Sawyer's ready smile wiped away a portion of the exhaustion and worry Cade had observed since he'd been home. "Sounds fun."

The years peeled away and instead of Cade feeling as

if he needed to keep things from Sawyer to protect him, he and Sawyer talked as equals. Sawyer's work with the machinery was second nature. A stray thought inserted itself. If Cade did move back to Cottonbloom, maybe he could convince Sawyer to quit the factory and make Fournette Designs a family business.

After Sawyer headed to the house to grab them drinks, Cade did a final check of the engine connections. His hand was ninety percent better. The nerves still tingled at times, but the dexterity and most of the strength had returned thanks to Monroe. He couldn't work as long at anything that required fine motor skills, but he could do his job. Develop and build and test new engine technologies. He snaked his right hand between the outlet manifold and a stiff hose to tighten a bolt.

The current design was almost ready to be tested, but with Sawyer's help and insight he planned to upgrade and modify it further. The current design was meant for a boat, but it could be translated to cars. If their suppositions were correct, the efficiency gains would be significant, which would reduce gas usage, which would in turn reduce emissions without losing power. It was every car manufacturer's wet dream.

He sat back and twirled the wrench around his palm. He'd found working in Sawyer's garage invigorating. Surrounded by nature, honest sweat dampening his shirt, knowing people he cared about were a stone's throw away. He could walk down to the river. The source of what motivated him all these years even though he'd sometimes cursed the muddy waters.

His work space in Seattle, much like his apartment and his life, was sterile and uninspiring but tidy and uncomplicated. His life in Cottonbloom had been none of those things and coming back hadn't changed anything.

* * *

Monroe drove like a granny to Sawyer's farmhouse, dreading the coming confrontation. Cade's truck was out front, parked in the grass near the huge willow tree. She parked beside it and ran her hand down the rust-pocked bed. He would leave his truck and leave her to weather life without him.

She'd skimmed through the profile from the business magazine again and hardly recognized the man they'd described. His life in Seattle was so far removed from Cottonbloom, she felt an alien-like displacement even thinking about moving there.

She continued around the back, finding him bent over a huge crate, the engine he'd been working on packed inside. His face was stern yet achingly handsome. This man had turned from protector to hero to lover.

She said his name on a croak and cleared her throat. He looked up, his smile automatic, which only made her stomach spin faster. She took a few steps closer, her ankles and knees like poorly set jelly.

His lips uncurled and drew a straight line across his blanked face. "I can already guess why you're here."

She swallowed and opened her mouth, but no words came, dread muting her.

"You don't want to come with me." It was a statement and not a question.

"I can't."

"I thought you loved me," he said accusingly, and tossed the wrench he was holding toward a tall red metal toolbox, the clang jarring.

"I do. Of course I do. Do you love me?"

His eyes flared. At his non-answer, she continued. "If you need more time, I get that, but I have a life here. A good life full of good people who love me."

"I-I do love you, Monroe. Really." His tripping words were hardly convincing.

Pinpricks of anger helped camouflage the deepening pit in her stomach. "I'm not moving to Seattle so you can test-drive a relationship with me."

"Is that why you think I asked you to move with me?"

She looked toward the river, gaining solace from what she couldn't see but knew was there, before turning back to him. "In some ways, leaving Cottonbloom would be freedom. No one calling me to stop tomato marauders or to clean up after one of my mother's bad nights or to rescue a scared teenager. I could do what I wanted. Which is to be with you."

Hope flared in his face, but it was as quickly extinguished. "You won't come even with all that?"

"As much as I love you, my place is here in the middle of this crazy town and all the messiness of life. You have a place here, too. Please stay in Cottonbloom, Cade."

"I want you to come with me." Emotion hoarsened his voice. He reached for her, but she stepped back and his hand fell to his side. If he touched her, the electric arc of their connection would only make her question herself and add to her devastation.

"Will you think about staying?"

"The first iteration of the engine is done. I've got to head back to see to its installation in the test chamber." It was an evasion.

Reality stamped out her foolish dreams. Once he was away from her, from this place, he would never find his way back. "I'll wait for you, Cade, but I won't wait forever."

The ultimatum was a lie. She would spend forever pining for him. She walked away anyway, forcing her shoulders back and her spine straight. She wouldn't beg him to stay in Cottonbloom, stay with her. It was his decision to make.

He didn't run after her to stop her like in the movies, and she drove away, heartbroken.

Chapter Twenty-seven

Cade spun a pen in his right hand while he worked the fingers of his left like Monroe had taught him. He checked the clock. She would be at work, sending some poor soul through their paces. Who was the lucky recipient of her smile and the focus of her attention?

He missed the way her smile lit her from the inside out. If he was making a list, he also missed the way she chewed on her lip when she worried over his hand and the sexy confidence she exuded when they made love and the way she cuddled with benefits.

He missed everything.

"You look like your dog got run over." Richard stood propped against the doorjamb, his hands tucked into the pockets of his dress pants, a sheaf of papers under his arm.

Cade hadn't even noticed him, every part of him except his body back in Cottonbloom. He sat up straight and shuffled papers around his desk in a weak pretense of working. "I'm fine."

Not waiting for an invitation, Richard wandered farther inside and dropped into one of the chairs across the desk, crossing his legs and draping an arm over the back of a neighboring chair. Cade envied his friend's casual sophistication. Well-fitting tux or not, it was a façade with Cade, whereas it was bred into Richard. Like the river and Cottonbloom and his childhood had been bred into Cade. Not just the bad, but the good as well. He had forgotten that until he'd returned.

Richard sat still and waited, his face serious and assessing. Cade relented, slumping back in his chair and giving up the illusion of working. "What?"

"I know I encouraged—well, 'bullied' might be more accurate—you into coming back to work, to your life here. But . . ." Richard leaned forward and braced his forearms on his knees, holding on to the papers. "I think I was wrong."

Richard was full of unabashed confidence. He never admitted to being wrong. Misinformed maybe, but never wrong. Cade looked around with an attempt at humor. "Am I being pranked?"

Richard sat back and resumed his position of elegant nonchalance. "We've had lovely weather since you've been back."

The abrupt change of subject set off alarms. Cade recognized the tactic Richard employed during their patent-leasing negotiations and squirmed. "Three days with no rain is always welcome."

"You've not taken advantage. Normally, you'd be making plans to hang glide or climb or bike."

"My hand." Cade clenched his injured hand into a fist. Tingles shot down his pinky and ring fingers. His hand was a convenient excuse. Whether it was his injury or something to do with the last weeks in Cottonbloom, the obsession to throw himself off cliffs had vanished.

"You're more a son to me than my flesh-and-blood one, Cade." Richard ran a hand over his face, a weariness edging into his usual high-energy animation. "You came back from Louisiana different."

Different. Was he? Or had he fundamentally shifted back toward the boy he'd been? The man who had shed the stifling, suffocating ties of his youth now longed to bind himself tightly to his old life. Perhaps more accurately, a new life in an old place.

Three days gone and he missed his brother and sister desperately. Even worse, Monroe stalked his every thought, waking and sleeping. He'd never gone in for gooey, love-sick thoughts, but he finally understood what it felt like to have part of his soul ripped away. It hurt like hell.

"I love Monroe Kirby."

"She's the woman from your past? The one I shipped your tuxedo down for?" At Cade's curt nod, Richard continued. "Easy enough. Ask her to move up here. Your condo is luxurious. Wine and dine her. Show her how the other half lives. She'll never want to leave."

"She wouldn't care about any of that. She doesn't belong up here. Neither do I. Not anymore. I miss her. I miss my family. I can't quite believe it myself, but I even miss Cottonbloom. I don't want to disband the company, but I can't live here anymore." Cade blew out a slow breath. The feelings had been weighing on him since before he stepped off the airplane in Seattle.

Richard looked down and fingered the edges of the papers before tossing them on the desk. Contracts. Cade almost laughed. Richard always could anticipate the twists and turns of a negotiation.

"It's like you read my mind," Cade murmured as he flipped through the top document.

"That's my job." Richard's smile cut through the chains binding Cade in Seattle. "We'll scale down to a simple business office here, which I'll man. You can set up shop in Louisiana like you want."

He took what felt like his first deep breath in days. "What about bringing Sawyer on board?"

"Is that wise?"

"My instincts are better, but his technical grasp is unparalleled. We worked together some on the Wallamaker design. I described the concept, and he suggested the nuts and bolts to make it happen."

"I don't doubt he's as smart as you are. I'm thinking more of the family dynamic. Can you work together and get along?"

"A hundred percent of the time? Not a chance. But we'll work it out even if we have to take it to the toolshed. Our blood is thick."

Richard pointed to the stack. "Second set of contracts is a job offer for your brother. If things go well, we'll offer him a partner position in a year."

"Sounds more than fair." Cade stood up, the malaise of the past days gone. His body thrummed with the same energy as before a jump off a cliff or out of an airplane. This might be the biggest, boldest leap of his life.

Richard had aged over their conversation. The skin of his cheeks sagged with his frown, and his shoulders slumped.

Cade slowly regained his seat. "When we met, I aspired to be like you in every way, Richard. My father was a good man, happy with his life from what I can remember. I would never have achieved a hundredth of this without you."

"I appreciate the sentiment more than you can imagine, but don't emulate me. I gave up my family to succeed, and I'm not sure what I've gained is worth it." The regret in Richard's voice highlighted one possible path in front of Cade. The one he wasn't choosing.

"You'll always have a home in Cottonbloom; I hope you know that."

A sliver of a smile quirked Richard's lips. "I'll come visit. Just not in summer."

"Fair enough." Cade laughed and pushed up again. If he hustled, he could sort things out by lunch and then head home. He paused. Home. Not his sterile high-rise condo, but Sawyer's old farmhouse. Or maybe Monroe's little house, if she would let him in. Strike that; he would camp out on her doorstep until she did. Prove to her that he was back to stay.

Richard meandered to the door as if Cade had stolen all his energy. Before he made it into the hallway, Cade took three steps and pulled him in for a hug. Not a manly bump of chest and shoulder tap but an honest-to-God father-son hug.

Richard broke away, but not before Cade noticed his teary eyes. Neither of them mentioned it as Richard walked away and turned the corner, out of sight. Cade looked over his shoulder and into his office, already feeling like an interloper.

Everything was changing. He would miss Richard, but without a doubt Cottonbloom was where he belonged, and thoughts of his future with Monroe stamped out any lingering melancholy.

Three days he'd been gone. A lifetime. Monroe stared into her refrigerator, knowing she needed to eat but seeing nothing that invoked a semblance of an appetite. Very briefly she considered pulling the bottle of muscadine wine out and killing it. On an empty stomach it would get her drunk, and fast. But she didn't. She was stronger than her mother.

Anyway, Monroe didn't want to drink away her memories of Cade. They were all she had left. Tears stung. She should be dehydrated considering the amount of crying she'd done over the last three days. Lying on the couch, she closed her eyes and allowed her mind to wander into her recent memories—the press of his body over hers, the pleasure they'd shared, the intensity of feeling that bound them.

Exhaustion swamped her. Sleep had been elusive, and when she'd managed to find it her dreams had been populated by Cade as a boy, as a man, as a protector, as her lover. Her heart was scattered around her in pieces without instructions on how to reassemble it.

The buzz of her phone shot her straight up, her heart knocking. Not Cade, but her mother. She gritted her teeth and answered.

"Monroe. Sweetheart." Her mother's words were slurry.

"Are you drunk?" The background noise confirmed Monroe's fears. Her mother was out somewhere. "Do you need me to come pick you up?"

"No. I mean, maybe I'm a little buzzed, but . . . that's not why I'm calling."

Monroe pushed off the couch; the freedom of chucking it all and running off to Seattle to wallow around in Cade's bed was looking like the smarter choice. "Where are you?"

"The Tavern. Sam is here, and he's hitting on one of your girls fierce."

"My girls?" Accelerant shot through her body. She grabbed her keys and ran out the door.

"The pretty one with long, dark hair. Looks young." Her mother's voice dropped to a near whisper. "She's been drinking."

Monroe's stomach bottomed out. Had Kayla learned nothing from her last visit to the Tavern? "Why are you calling me?" she asked even as she fumbled the key in the ignition. "Is he doing something besides acting a fool?"

"He *is* a fool." Bitterness laced her words. "I don't trust him."

Had she guessed something? No time to dwell on the

past now. "That girl's name is Kayla. Don't let her leave with him. Do you hear me, Mama?"

After getting her mother's vague assent, Monroe disconnected and tore through town and over the bridge. Gravel sprayed on her turn into the parking lot. She ran up to the front door as her mother pushed through, a wild look in her eyes.

"Are they inside?"

"I turned my back to order another drink and they were gone. Poof. Disappeared."

Monroe spun around and searched the parking lot for movement. Nothing. She took her mother's hand and pulled her back to the door of the bar. Butch, the same bouncer who had been there last time, held up a hand as they approached. "I'll need to see—"

"No you don't." No matter the man was a foot taller than her, Monroe got in his face. His eyes flared, but he retreated without another word.

Monroe quick-stepped through the room, her gaze pinging from clusters of people to the lonely individuals at the bar. It was a weeknight and not too crowded. No sign of either Kayla or Sam.

Her mother had stayed on her heels, and Monroe led the way to the kitchens. If Sam had already driven off with Kayla, there was no telling where they went.

"Have you seen—"

"They went out the back." The cook chucked his head and flipped hamburger patties on the grill.

With dread topping off her worry, Monroe busted out of the alley door. Two people grappled a few feet away against the rough, grungy brick wall. The relief of seeing Kayla's dark hair was short-lived. Sam had his hand up her skirt while she tried to push him away, a litany of "nos," "stops," and "pleases" falling on top of one another.

Monroe ran over and hit Sam's shoulder. He didn't release Kayla, only glanced behind him, his mouth slack and his eyes bloodshot.

"Get the hell away from her, Sam." Monroe grabbed the back of his shirt and yanked. This time Sam stepped away and faced her. Hatred burned from his eyes, along with something else she recognized from her dreams. A determination to hurt her.

It wasn't fear but cold, calculated fury that spurred her. Kayla didn't stand a chance against someone like Sam. Physically or emotionally. If she pressed charges, he would humiliate and destroy her in the court of public opinion. Monroe wasn't weak, and she wasn't scared of him. Not anymore. Cade had left her that at least.

"You like them young, don't you, old man." She stepped closer but didn't touch him. Not yet.

"She's at least sixteen. Nothing illegal about messing around."

"She's also drunk, and doesn't much look or sound like she was wanting to mess around." She spit in his face.

"You little bitch."

She sidled within arm's reach of him. "How about you finally come clean with my mother? How about you tell her why you broke things off and moved out?"

Her mother was pressed against the bricks as if she were single-handedly holding the wall upright or vice versa.

"Because she was getting too clingy and boring." Sam didn't take his eyes off Monroe.

She returned his stare with an equal amount of hate. "One night while you were passed out, Mother, Sam came into my room to try to mess around with me."

Sam's face flushed and he jabbed a finger in her face. "That is a goddamn lie."

"No, it's not. I remember everything. If I hadn't run, you would have sexually abused me. Maybe raped me."

"Please. You wanted it. You were asking for it."

"You're delusional if you think a thirteen-year-old girl wanted to mess around with a nasty, old middle-aged man." She baited her words with as much scorn as she could muster.

The intent flashed in his eyes an instant before his fist made contact with her cheek. She did nothing to block him. The hit dazed her, the intensity of the pain surprising. Her legs wobbled and gave out. She landed on her butt, rocks biting into her palms. Her face throbbed in time with her heartbeat.

She marked the passage of time by her gasping breaths. No one moved. Her mother's mouth was slack, her face pale. Kayla stared at her, eyes huge and dark and filled with a fear Monroe recognized intimately. She turned her focus back to Sam. His face was mottled, his hands clenched into fists at his sides.

Strength surged through her body, propelling her to her feet and forward. She spun with a roundhouse kick, putting everything she had into it. Her heel made solid contact with some part of his face, and he went down.

Had there been other girls? Guilt and responsibility weighed her down. "If onlys" scrolled like ticker tape. She couldn't undo the past, but she could do something about it now. She stood over him as he rolled on the ground, his hand covering his mouth.

She kicked him in the ribs twice, hard. Something to remember her by. He curled in like a worm trying to protect itself. If she'd been a better person, she wouldn't have gotten such satisfaction in the beating. But seeing him writhe in pain was very satisfying indeed.

She stepped back and pulled her phone out of her back pocket. The screen had shattered. Her mother was still huddled against the brick wall with Kayla. "I need your phone."

"Sweetheart . . . did he touch you?" Her mother raised trembling fingers to brush along Monroe's jaw. She wasn't asking about the punch but about another night.

"He would have."

"I should have protected you, but I was useless, wasn't I?" She paused. "I'm an alcoholic."

It was the first time her mother had admitted it. Monroe wasn't sure whether it was the relief of reaching a turning point with her mother or the pain in her face making tears rush to her eyes.

"Yes," she said on an exhale.

Her mother nodded, looked away, and handed her phone over.

Monroe dialed the police and with as few words as possible explained the situation. "Send Wayne, would you, Gloria?"

Only minutes passed before the sirens cut through the night. Sam pushed to sitting, the sound triggering an inherent flight impulse. Monroe moved into his field of vision, and she was gratified to see fear mask his face.

"Don't move unless you'd like your balls busted, too." She stood straddling his thigh, her foot close to the threatened target. He froze.

The jangling of a utility belt drew her gaze up. Wayne and one of his deputies jogged toward them. "What in heaven's name happened?" Wayne's voice echoed off the bricks.

He came straight to her, took her forearms, and guided her to lean against the wall next to her mother. Now that help was there, the pain in her face crescendoed and an insistent hammering took up in her temples. Her stomach crawled up her throat, and she had to swallow hard to keep from throwing up.

The deputy was on his haunches talking to Sam. He would lie. She had to talk. Slowly, haltingly, she got the story out. At some point, Kayla had come to her and held one hand while her mother clasped the other, and she gained strength from both women. They corroborated her story with slicing interjections.

"You want to press charges?" Wayne asked.

She didn't spare Sam a glance. "Hell yes. Whatever you can hit him with."

She was sure she didn't imagine the resolute satisfaction in Wayne's eyes. "You got it." Over his shoulder, he hollered, "Cuff Mr. Landry and get him loaded in the back of the squad car. Read him his rights." Turning back, he said, "I'm calling an ambulance for you."

"I'm fine." She pushed off the wall, but a wave of vertigo had her listing into Kayla.

"Your face is already starting to bruise and you might have a concussion. Anyway . . ." He grimaced and looked down. "We need photo evidence. Irrefutable. Landry will hire the best lawyer around. Probably Tarwater Senior, and he's a mean cuss in the courtroom."

"Of course. Evidence."

Her mother and Kayla led her to the parking lot in a turnaround of her last night at the Tavern.

"Thank you, Monroe." Kayla's whisper barely registered through the throbbing pain.

She didn't want Kayla to blame herself. She didn't want this incident to define Kayla's life. The pain made it impossible to get the words out, and when the ambulance pulled up she submitted gratefully to the EMTs' care, letting Wayne, Kayla, and her mother speak for her.

Her mother rode in the back and held one of her hands in both of hers. Sleepy, she was so sleepy. Before she drifted off, she whispered one word. "Cade."

Chapter Twenty-eight

Cade steered the rented Mercedes over the Cottonbloom Parish line. He'd decided to come home in style. A last day of luxury before he traded it in for his daddy's truck for good. His anxiety grew with every mile. Monroe hadn't answered any of his calls. Either she was away from her phone or she was ignoring him. He didn't want to entertain any other possibility. His phone buzzed and he tensed, before Sawyer's name popped up.

He answered the call through the state-of-the-art dash. "You're not going to believe—"

"You need to come home. Now." Sawyer's tone dried Cade's mouth and had him clenching the wheel. Visions of the police standing at the door and imparting the news of his parents' accident flashed.

"What's wrong?" his voice croaked in the small space.

"Monroe and Sam Landry got into a set-to at the Rivershack Tavern. He punched her. She's in the hospital getting X-rays for a possible fractured cheekbone and under observation for a concussion."

A fury like Cade had never experienced built during the short pause.

"She asked for you."

He mashed the accelerator to the floor. "I'm going to rip Sam's arms off and shove them down his throat."

Sawyer's chuckle was full of dark humor. "No need. Monroe already handed his ass to him. He's being treated for a broken jaw and several cracked ribs. Then, he's going to jail. Monroe was adamant about pressing charges."

If he hadn't left, she wouldn't be in the hospital right now. Whatever had happened he would have been by her side so she didn't have to face it alone. Tears stung the backs of his eyes, and he had to blow out a deep breath. "I'm on my way."

He disconnected and utilized the full capacity of the Mercedes's engine and handling. He pulled into the hospital parking lot in a time that would have made Mario Andretti proud. Desperate to lay eyes on Monroe, he ran to the entrance, the leisurely opening of the automatic doors ticking his impatience higher.

A knot of people in one corner drew his gaze. Sawyer had an arm around Tally. Regan Lovell paced in front of them. Kayla and two other girls from Monroe's class sat in red vinyl-covered chairs.

"Where is she? I need to see her." His voice cut through the heavy silence of the room and everyone swiveled toward him.

Sawyer shook his head as if clearing his vision. "Did you teleport?"

"I'll explain everything later." He pulled Sawyer and Tally into a group hug. "Can you get me in?"

Sawyer shook his head. "They're only letting family back. Her mama's in there now."

"I'll get you in." Regan marched to the nurse behind the desk. He followed and listened as she performed a Jedi mind trick on the nurse. Any argument the nurse tried was futile, and within three minutes Cade was pushing the security doors open.

Wayne Pearson and Police Chief Thomason stood outside Monroe's door drinking steaming cups of coffee and talking quietly. Unease from his previous run-ins with Chief Thomason slowed Cade's steps.

Wayne spotted him first. "Cade Fournette. Well, I'll be. Thought you'd left us for good."

Probably what Monroe had thought and Thomason had hoped. "Nope. Just tidying up matters. I'm moving home. I need to see her."

Chief Thomason's brows rose, but he didn't comment. Wayne pointed toward the door. Cade hesitated and turned back. "I've got an investigator digging into Sam Landry's life in Georgia. I'll make sure you both get a copy of the report."

Wayne and Thomason exchanged telling looks, and Thomason said, "That'd be a big help. He's already retained Tarwater as counsel." As Cade turned away, the chief said, "Hey, Fournette."

Cade glanced over his shoulder, his hand on the door.

"Your mama sure would be proud of you."

Cade nodded, another piece of his past settled where it belonged, and turned back to the door. It was time to think about the future. Monroe's mother stood and shifted on her feet, but he didn't spare her more than a glance.

The beep of a heart monitor set a steady, comforting rhythm. A purpling bruise on Monroe's cheek was stark on her pale face. Her blond hair was fanned out on the pillow, the sheet pulled up under her arms. An IV was taped to the inside of her left arm, so he approached from the right and took her pliant hand in his. She felt cold.

"X-rays came back negative." Her mother's whisper sounded unnaturally loud and grating. "All she's got is a heck of a bruise and a slight concussion. I'll give you some privacy."

He heard the door open and close. Without letting go

of her hand, he pulled up a chair. Pressing his lips against the soft skin on the back, he mouthed a brief prayer even though he'd given up on religion the day he'd buried his parents.

"Cade?" Her voice was raspy and disbelieving. "Dear Lord, how long have I been out?"

His laughing sigh expelled a good portion of his worry. She sounded like his Monroe. "Not long. I was already on my way when Sawyer called me. Had already crossed the parish line heading home to you."

"Home to me?" Her blue eyes swallowed him in warmth. He wanted to reach out for her and never let go.

"I've been a fool."

"A dummy?" Her mouth twitched.

"No, don't let me off the hook. You deserve to hear this." He swallowed. Besides his pathetic, fumbling try earlier, he'd never told a woman he loved her. Had never loved a woman. Not in the bone-deep, primal way he loved Monroe, but he lacked the vocabulary to express himself. He tried anyway. "Nothing is more important than you. Nothing. Not money, not my company, not jumping off cliffs, not some ghost life I was living."

His reconnection to the town, to his family, but mostly with Monroe had made him recognize the void inside of him couldn't be filled with material things or thrills. It could only be filled with love—selfless and powerful.

"I love you, Monroe. Can you forgive me?" He pressed his lips against her hand again, needing to feel her warm skin against him in any way possible. "God, I've missed you."

She didn't respond immediately yet didn't pull her hand away, either. He would count his victories, no matter how small.

"You've only been gone three days, Cade."

"Three days and fourteen hours. I've been miserable.

Told Richard I was moving back. Told him we could disband the company or we could keep it going with me in Cottonbloom."

"What did he say?"

An ironic huff popped out. "Already had the contracts drawn up moving the R and D to Cottonbloom while keeping the business office open in Seattle. He's not keen on our summers or the wildlife apparently."

She pulled her smile up short and touched her cheek.

A protective fury and a feeling he'd failed her battled for dominance. "I'm so sorry I wasn't here. I threatened to beat the crap out of him, but I heard you already did. I'd do anything to take that hit away from you."

Now she did tug her hand free, but only to grab his wrist and pull him closer. He rose and braced his hands on either side of her shoulders, careful not to jostle her. As he brushed a kiss over her forehead, she whispered, "I wasn't scared of him, Cade. In fact . . . I wanted him to hit me."

Cade pulled back and looked at her as if she'd spoken gibberish.

"I goaded him into a punch. Called him a nasty old man. Spit in his face." A frantic sort of laughter threatened, but she tamped it down. Cade might call in the doctor. Or a psychiatrist.

"Why in God's name did you want him to hit you?"

"Because Kayla's not strong enough to go through a trial with him. It would break her. Define her life. I needed him to hit me, so I could be the one to file charges." Cade's green eyes were full of questions, and she turned her face to the side to escape having to answer. Yet she couldn't escape the truth.

"I needed to take him on by myself, or he would have continued to define *my* life. Can you understand that?"

"Like my parents' deaths defined mine?"

She turned back to face him. "Yes. Exactly."

"I've let the past go to come home. Or maybe I've embraced the best of my past to come home." A strong ribbon of emotion threaded his philosophical words. "I can't live without you, Monroe Kirby. Do you still love me?"

From any other man the declaration might veer toward melodrama. Coming from Cade and with her understanding the bond they shared, his admission made perfect sense. His face reflected the same despair she'd felt at their separation.

"I've loved you since I was thirteen. Three days won't change that. Nothing will." She ran her hands up his biceps, curled them around his neck, and pulled him down. His lips brushed hers, but she could feel his resistance.

"I don't want to hurt you any more than I already have." His lips moved to her good cheek.

She'd protected herself for a long time, but loving him didn't feel like a weakness. She felt stronger than ever.

"If you ever walk away from me again, I'll . . ." somewhere, somehow, she found a smile ". . . take you out into the swamps and feed you to the gators."

His laugh rumbled through her. "After hearing what you did to Sam, I'd be too scared to leave."

With the weight of sadness cut away, her mood shot into the stars and she laughed, nuzzling her lips along the stubble of his jaw. "Where are you staying?"

"Hadn't gotten that far. I was headed to your place when Sawyer called."

She chewed her bottom lip before making her decision. "Is it too soon to think about living together?"

"I only know one thing for certain: I'm going to be in your bed every night." He leaned up and brushed the hair back from her forehead. Something was troubling him.

"Wh-h-hat?" She drew the word out, worried she wouldn't like what he had to confess.

"Since I'm going to be moving operations down here, I'm going to need to build a garage. I was thinking we could eventually build a house. Something bigger maybe." She'd never heard him sound anything less than a hundred percent confident, but there was no mistaking the note of hesitancy.

"What'd you have in mind?"

"There's a plot for sale next to Uncle Delmar's place."

"On the river?"

"Yep."

A house with Cade on the river. It was a future she hadn't let herself dream about. "Gracious, are you trying to convert me from an uptown 'Sip to a Louisiana swamp rat?" She employed a thick, fake Southern accent reserved for TV shows. Only when he relaxed did she realize how tense he'd become.

"We could stay in Mississippi, although I'm not sure Sawyer would ever forgive me. Anyway, I like the thought of you wandering out to keep me company while I work. Me being able to walk up to the house for a kiss."

"Or a quickie?"

He dropped his face into the pillow at her neck. The breath of his laughter sent shivers through her body. "How did I live so long with you only in my dreams?"

"This is what you want? To build a life in Cottonbloom? With me?"

"It's what I want and probably more than I deserve, but I'm going to hang on with both hands." He gently touched her lips with his.

Her face was too sore to participate in a make-out session. The pain medication had cut her headache to a dull throb. The past nights of sleeplessness in combination with the stress of the evening, her concussion, and the relief of having him beside her had exhaustion pushing her toward sleep even as she fought it.

"Will you stay?"

"I'm not sure—"

"You said you'd be in my bed every night." She scooted over as far as the bedrail would allow. He climbed in beside her and gathered her close. Gingerly, she laid the hurt side of her face against his heart and drifted to sleep, safe in his arms and in his heart.

Epilogue

ONE WEEK LATER . . .

A vibrating buzz woke Monroe. Without opening her eyes, she threw a hand out toward her nightstand and grappled for the phone. She blinked, clearing the sleep from her eyes. The backlit screen displayed Regan's name and the time—a quarter past midnight.

Cade's phone rang as she answered. "Regan. What's wrong? Are you okay?"

"The gazebo is on fire." Emotion strung Regan's voice high and thin. The sound of sirens and shouts provided background noise.

Sleep slowed Monroe's thought processes. Cade answered his phone with a growling, "What?"

"Do you need me?" she asked Regan.

"It was Sawyer, Monroe; it had to be."

"I can't believe—"

"Ohmigod, he's here." Regan disconnected.

Monroe let the phone drop and shifted toward Cade.

"Dude, don't do anything crazy. I'm on my way." Cade was already swinging his legs off the side of the bed. "We'd better get down there."

They dressed in relative silence and pulled up to the

common area by the river less than ten minutes later. The fire truck's twirling red lights lent the scene an ominous, eerie feel. The fire was out, the gazebo a giant smoking former bonfire, the grass in all directions scorched.

Monroe and Sawyer were in a heated discussion with Police Chief Thomason. The chief watched the two like a spectator at a tennis match. Cade slipped his hand into Monroe's on their quick walk up to the trio.

She squeezed and leaned into his arm. They were a united front. Taking sides wasn't an option. Regan was in a tank top and tiny cotton pajama shorts, fuzzy cow slippers on her feet. The halo of righteous outrage emanating from her like pulses of energy kept Monroe from smiling. No matter how she was dressed, Regan Lovell was a force to be reckoned with.

Regan spied her and waved both arms around like a crazed monkey. "Look what he did. Of all the low, detestable acts, Sawyer Fournette. Not to mention illegal. Isn't this illegal, Keith?"

"Well, technically, yes, but we don't—"

"The shoe's on the other foot now, isn't it, Golden Boy, and I hope it's about three sizes too small. I'll have you arrested and sent to spend the rest of the night in a jail cell with a man named Bubba who'll treat you *real* nice. Don't think I won't." She pointed a finger toward Sawyer like she wanted to skewer him.

"How many times do I have to tell you that I had nothing to do with this?" Sawyer ran a hand through his already-rumpled hair, sending pieces sticking straight up. He wasn't looking much more mayoral than Regan. His cotton pajama pants were covered in LSU emblems, and the Mardi Gras T-shirt he wore was from the year he graduated from high school and a size too small.

"How did you know about it then? Huh? Huh?" Regan jutted her chin in emphasis and propped her hands on her hips. Sawyer's gaze drifted down. Not only had she not bothered with real shoes; she also hadn't stopped to put on a bra.

"Same way you found out. I got a call from Chief Thomason." He gestured toward the police chief, who was making notes in a small notebook.

"Why did you call him?" She shifted toward Keith and thumbed toward Sawyer.

The man took a step back. "Now, Regan-darlin'—"

"Don't you darling me, Keith Thomason. I'm acting as Cottonbloom mayor. Why did you call him?"

"I usually do if something big happens that could affect both sides of the river. I let Wayne know, too. Common courtesy. If there's an arsonist running loose—"

"He's not running loose; he's right here." She emphasized the last two words with a jabbing finger toward Sawyer.

"He was sound asleep when I called." Keith gestured up and down Sawyer in a look-at-him way. Sawyer stood with his arms over his chest and a half smile on his face.

"He could have been faking it. His hair was always ridiculous. I mean look—" Regan stepped forward and finger combed the pieces sticking up. Sawyer didn't move except to drop his clenched hands to his sides. She froze for a moment with her hands buried in his hair before stepping back and holding her hands behind her back. "See, I fixed it." Her voice had lost a good amount of its vitriol.

Monroe exchanged a glance with Cade. Without dropping her hand, he stepped forward. His voice was low and commanding, the tone Monroe guessed he used in boardrooms. "Is there any evidence that points to Sawyer?"

Keith shook his head. "None."

"Except for motive," Regan interjected.

Cade spared her a brief glance. "Flimsy motive. Will torching the gazebo stop you from putting on the festival?"

"Heck no."

Sawyer crossed his arms over his chest, the sleeves of his too-small T-shirt riding up his flexing biceps. "You don't think I know what a muleheaded, crazy woman you can be? This will only galvanize you to make your festival bigger, am I right?"

"Darn tooting it will," Regan shot back.

"You just blew my motive apart." He turned back to Keith. "Have you found any evidence at all?"

"Not yet. I'll get the fire marshal out here once the sun is up. Maybe we'll find something then." He already sounded resigned to finding nothing. "No witnesses this time of night, of course."

"You've driven around and checked all the businesses? In case we do have some arsonist on the loose?" Regan narrowed her eyes on Sawyer, obviously not convinced of his innocence.

"Course, Regan. And we'll keep up extra patrols. Wayne is doing the same on your side of the river, Sawyer. There's really nothing else either of you can do tonight."

Regan stepped away to stare at the billowing smoke, chafing her arms. Monroe met Cade's gaze and chucked her head. He gave her hand one last squeeze and broke away toward his brother.

Monroe put her arm around Regan's waist. "You okay?"

Regan shot a look over her shoulder. "You don't think Sawyer had anything to do with it?"

"I don't."

"Is that because his brother has brainwashed you with his you-know-what? Or do you really believe it?"

"I really believe it."

"Then who would do this and why?"

Both sides of town sat quiet and expectant. "It could have been teenagers. A prank that went too far. Who called it in?"

"Wayne noticed the smoke from his side of the river and called our fire department. At that point, there wasn't anything left to save. Someone doesn't like me. Or doesn't like what I'm trying to do, anyway."

"What are you talking about? You've been the best mayor Cottonbloom has ever elected. Look at what you've done with downtown." Monroe waved a hand toward the rows of businesses. A few years earlier, owners were moving out to strip malls closer to the university or to bigger towns. Without Regan's progressive, aggressive plans, they would be staring at empty storefronts.

"The letter told me to stop the festival. Or else."

With everything going on, Monroe had forgotten about the letter. "Or else what?"

"It was vague on specifics. Probably whoever made it got tired of cutting out the letters and gluing them down."

"Do you have any culprits in mind?"

"You haven't been to a town council meeting lately, have you? A few businesses, like the Quilting Bee and McGee's Hardware, are getting hit harder with the increased taxes. The boom hasn't done them any favors."

"I seriously doubt Ms. Martha was out here with gasoline and a match."

The image of the petite, gray-haired, fiftyish spinster as an arsonist sent them both into giggles, lightening the mood considerably. Regan held her hands out and looked down her body, sticking one foot in the air. "How ridiculous did I look just now going off on Sawyer in fuzzy cow slippers?"

Monroe steered them toward the street where Regan had left her red VW Bug parked, the driver's door hanging open, the interior light flickering. "I'm not going to lie. Pretty darn ridiculous. Although I swear Sawyer was checking out your boobs at one point."

"He was not. The man can't stand me." Regan tugged

at her tank top, a blush racing up her fair skin. Her voice was more breathless than flinty.

"Only reporting what I observed, ma'am."

Regan slid behind the wheel, one fuzzy slipper in and one out. She grabbed Monroe's hand. "I know your loyalties are divided now, but thanks for having my back."

Monroe leaned in and gave her best friend a half hug. Since Monroe had finally confided in her, they'd become closer than ever. "Always, Regan."

She backed away and watched until Regan's taillights disappeared. Hands in her pockets, she returned to where Cade and Sawyer talked, their heads close, their difference in coloring more pronounced in the artificial glare of the fire truck. But their bodies were cast from the same mold.

She looped her arm through Cade's. "Everything okay?"

"Hey, babe." Cade put his arm around her shoulder, hauled her close, and sighed, as if a missing part had been returned. She pressed her still-sore cheek into his chest and breathed deep. She could smell the love they'd made earlier, slow and deep and uniquely satisfying.

Sawyer shifted to watch the firefighters roll up their hoses. "You don't really believe I did it, do you, Monroe?"

"Of course I don't." And she truly didn't. The bad blood between Sawyer and Regan might manifest itself in jabs and pranks, but not in something as destructive as arson.

"Regan thinks I did."

"She's not a hundred percent convinced you didn't do it, but she's also entertaining other motives."

"Like what?" He swung his head around.

"Like a few of the old-school business owners haven't been happy that property taxes are on the rise now that everything is worth more."

With grass sticking to his feet, Sawyer paced, stopping every few steps to rub one foot over the other. "Has she received any direct threats?"

Was it her place to tell Sawyer about the letter? "The city council meetings have been fiery. And you know Regan. . . ."

Sawyer harrumphed. "That red in her hair is no lie. I can't argue with the fact she's done a bang-up job on her side." He would never have admitted that with Regan in earshot, which cemented her belief Sawyer was innocent. "What if this is a warning shot and some nut job comes after her next? Maybe starts a fire at her house?"

"She got a suspicious letter."

"When? What did it say?" Sawyer stopped pacing, a restless energy thrumming.

"I haven't seen it, but she got it earlier this month. She dismissed it as a prank, but now . . ." Monroe gestured to the smoking remains.

"That is not good." Sawyer looked toward the heart of Cottonbloom, Mississippi.

"What're you thinking?" Cade rumbled. "She's not yours to protect, thank the Lord, and after tonight she probably feels like you're the one she needs protection from."

Sawyer kicked at the air. "You're right. I don't know why I let her needle me. She's a big girl and can handle things on her own."

"Exactly." Cade's voice was knife-like, and Monroe narrowed her eyes on him. He cleared his throat and slipped out of her arms. "I'm going to see if we're free to go."

Sawyer and Monroe stood in silence for a moment. Things between them were more comfortable than they'd been in a long time, but she still felt a little like she was betraying Regan when they hung out.

"Listen. I know I'm putting you in an awkward position, but . . ." Sawyer didn't look over at her and his voice approached a whisper, forcing her to step closer. "If

Regan mentions anything else, if she gets another letter, will you let me know?"

Their conversation had the feel of a clandestine meeting between two spies, passing information that could get them killed. Monroe's mouth opened and closed. "Why?"

"I know she has you, but you know her parents are useless. If she needs help, I can be there. For old times' sake. At least until whoever did this is caught."

Pieces of the past shifted and realigned. Whatever Regan thought, Sawyer still cared about her in some fashion. "Sure. I'll let you know. Might be a good idea to drop by a Cottonbloom, Mississippi, town meeting."

He rubbed his jaw, still not making eye contact with her. "Maybe so."

Cade returned, clapping his hands together once. "We're free to go. Thomason doesn't think you're at all involved, Sawyer, so rest easy."

Her gaze crossed Sawyer's. He wouldn't be resting easy tonight, but it wouldn't be himself he was worried about. Sawyer and Cade exchanged a brotherly hug and promises to talk in the morning. Sawyer strolled toward the footbridge, his truck sitting on the Louisiana side of the river.

"You ready?" Cade grabbed her up in a loose embrace, his hands roving over her hips. She hummed, and they walked arm in arm toward the old truck.

"I'm not sure I'm going to be able to go back to sleep. I'm too keyed up. Too much to think about," she said, her mind on Sawyer and Regan and the fire.

"Good, because I wasn't planning for us to go back to sleep." The naughty rumble of his voice turned her blood to molasses. "How do you feel about driving around?"

Suddenly the fire seemed inconsequential in the big scheme of things. All that mattered was the man whose smile was brighter than the coming dawn. The man who had filled in all the missing pieces of her life. The man who loved her and, by the look in his eyes, planned to love her the rest of the night.

"Race you to the truck." With joy and love and lust battling inside of her, she grabbed his hand and pulled him along, his laughter weaving with hers.

Read on for an excerpt from Laura Trentham's next book

Then He Kissed Me

Available in July 2016 from St. Martin's Paperbacks

Tallulah Fournette sat at the bar of the Rivershack Tavern, debating whether to head home. Three episodes of *The Bachelor* waited on her DVR. Even under the threat of torture, she'd never admit to watching the show, but the desperation oozing from the contestants fascinated her.

Her phone beeped and she glanced at the incoming text, muttering a curse that would have her mother clutching her pearls in heaven. A small amount of fear shaded the edges of her frustration, and she flipped her phone facedown as if that could shut her ex-boyfriend up.

She nursed her beer, feeling a little in limbo, not wanting to stay, but not wanting to go home to an empty apartment, either. Cade and Monroe were probably somewhere making googly eyes at each other, and Sawyer was so busy getting the newly named Fournette Brothers Designs set up and planning the Labor Day crayfish festival, he didn't have time to hang out with her.

She swiveled on the bar stool and exchanged smiles and waves with several men and women who were members of her gym. It was Friday night and all she had waiting for her at home was accounting work for the gym and episodes of *The Bachelor*. She might as well adopt a litter of cats.

The heavy wooden front door opened as she was turning back to the bar. From the corner of her eye, she saw a man enter. She glanced over her shoulder and whipped her head back around to stare down at the scarred bar top. It was Nash Hawthorne. Her heart skipped like a third-grader seeing her crush. Under the guise of taking a sip of her beer, she stole another glance.

She'd seen him at Cade's welcome-home party a couple of weeks earlier, and the same shock and zing of awareness stripped away the restlessness that had plagued her all evening. She'd beat a hasty retreat from Cade's party, the reasons as murky as the river.

When he'd moved to Mississippi when they were young, it was like he'd hopped into a different river that had taken him in the opposite direction from her. While she'd barely squeaked through high school, he'd gotten a Ph.D. and would be teaching history at Cottonbloom College come fall.

Unable to help herself, she looked in his direction again. He still stood inside the door. Calls from a pool table in the back went up, and he smiled and waved. Not only was she surprised to see him at the Tavern at all, apparently he'd become a regular. Tonight he fit right in with his olive-green cargo pants and black T-shirt.

If she'd known professors like Nash existed, she might have attempted college after all. He had an old-school Indiana Jones vibe. Although scholarly with his black-rimmed glasses and perpetually rumpled brown hair, danger permeated the air around him nonetheless, like he would risk his life to save some ancient scroll or might rappel into a tomb seeking the Holy Grail.

It didn't hurt that the man was jacked. Not in an

artificial way like some of the men who lifted weights in her gym, but in the lean, defined way she much preferred. She had no idea what happened to the brilliant, skinny, short, acne-covered kid of her childhood. It's like he'd been in a cocoon and emerged as a brilliant, built, tall, handsome man. Nerdy Nash Hawthorne had turned into Cottonbloom's most eligible bachelor—and that included both sides of their peculiar little town.

His gaze swept the room. Maybe he had a hot date. She'd heard rumors the single-ladies Bible study at Cottonbloom Church of Christ had nearly come to blows trying to decide who was going to take him a "Welcome to Cottonbloom" basket.

She turned back to her beer before he could catch her staring and watched the foam bubbles pop around the edges. A warm body took the seat next to her, and she was enveloped in a wholly masculine scent that muted the haloes of cigarette smoke around them. Seeing his big hands link together on the bar and the dark hair that peppered his forearm settled a weird knot of nerves in her stomach.

Nash had never made her nervous when they were kids. She'd trusted him above all others back then, even her brothers. But that had been a lifetime ago. In fact, those days seemed to belong to someone else. The days before her parents had died. Before things got hard.

Nash had been gone a long time, and once he'd moved to Mississippi after his mother had died, they'd barely seen each other. His aunt Leora had kept him close, claiming his asthma made it difficult for him to be outside. Although it hadn't seemed to bother him all the time they'd spent wading and exploring the river as kids. She fingered the end of her braid.

She screwed up her courage and turned to him. "Hey, I don't know if you remember me, but I'm—"

"Tallulah Fournette. How could I ever forget you?" He swiveled toward her. His carefree, charming smile struck her mute.

She had the tendency to hang out with rough-and-tumble men who'd followed the same path she had. Street-smart and tough, the difficulties of life forcing them to be serious and defensive. Those were her people, the ones she felt comfortable around.

Nash's optimism and easygoing nature were in his smile and in the way he held himself. His body language was foreign, yet unusually appealing, and she found herself smiling back. "Everyone calls me Tally these days. Except for my brothers when they're trying to annoy me. I'm not sure what my parents were thinking saddling me with a name like Tallulah."

"Maybe they were thinking, here we have this unique baby girl who is going to do great things in the world, so we should give her a great, unique name." His voice had matured along with the rest of him. Deep and a little husky, it projected like a professor's should.

"Or maybe they were thinking, let's pick the most embarrassing name possible so our daughter learns to deal with bullying at a young age."

The bartender stopped in front of them, wiping his hands on a bar towel, a smile parting the hair of his long dark beard. "What'll it be, Nash? The usual? Or would you like something special?" He leaned in as if imparting a secret.

"Special? I'm intrigued. Surprise me, Clint."

"You want another beer, Tally?"

"No, I'm good. Thanks." She waved Clint off while still staring at Nash. "You've been hanging out here a lot, I take it?"

"Little bit." He pointed to where Clint had disappeared through a short curtain into a storage room. "We discovered a common appreciation of Scotch whiskey."

Clint returned with a heavy tumbler and an inch of amber liquor. Nash went for the side pocket of his cargo pants, but Clint waved him off and stayed to watch Nash take the first sip. He closed his eyes, leaned his head back, and hummed. Tally couldn't tear her eyes away from the happiness on his face. "Perfect."

Looking extremely pleased, Clint rattled off the name and vintage before being called away to the opposite end of the bar.

"Scotch whiskey, huh? Is Jack not good enough for you?" The amount of flirt in her voice surprised her. Flirting was not in her wheelhouse.

"I did my postdoctoral work at the University of Edinburgh and developed a love of their whiskey. Jack will do in a pinch, though." He winked, and something fluttered around the nervous knot in her stomach. She did her best to ignore the feelings, but found herself smiling at him nonetheless.

"As in Scotland? Are you kidding me? That is so cool." Now that he mentioned it, a foreignness lilted through some of his words. A Scots brogue mixed with a Southern drawl was intriguing and surprisingly sexy.

"I'm not going to lie. It was cool. My research emphasis is medieval history. Americans think anything from the Civil War is old. That's nothing compared to Hadrian's Wall, for instance. Built a hundred and twenty years or so after Christ's crucifixion."

"And it's still there?"

"Miles and miles of it. You can touch stones placed by hands that are long gone."

His enthusiasm was intoxicating. Her heart was pounding a little faster, and she leaned closer. Close enough to see the shaving nick on the edge of his jaw, close enough to see the yellow flecks in his brown eyes framed by the black rims of his glasses, close enough to see the tattoo that peeked out of the sleeve of his black T-shirt.

Before she could stop herself, she pushed the sleeve up a couple of inches. His biceps flexed, and she pulled back as if bitten. Geez, you'd think she'd never touched a man before. She cleared her throat. "What's your tattoo of?"

He pulled his sleeve to the top of his shoulder, exposing a stylized cross on a shield. "The symbol for the Knights Templar."

"Oh my God, are you on the hunt for the Holy Grail? In Cottonbloom?"

He threw his head back, his laughter coming deep in his chest but morphing into a cough that had him hunched over and covering his mouth. Finally, his laugh-cough subsided, and he took a sip of the whiskey. "No Holy Grail in Cottonbloom to my knowledge. The Knights Templar stood for bravery and discipline. I guess that's what it means to me."

"Bravery and discipline, huh? Not bad things to stand for." She took a sip of her warm beer to have something to do besides stare at his defined arm.

"Would you like to dance?"

"Dance?"

"There's a dance floor in the corner." He pointed somewhere behind her. "And music playing. Dancing's not so far-fetched an activity, is it?"

She looked over her shoulder. The corner consisted of a small square of planked flooring she'd never noticed. Maybe because she'd never seen anyone actually dancing in the Rivershack Tavern, unless it was a drunk girl's mating call in the middle of the pool tables.

"Yeah, I don't dance."

"That's not what I remember."

"What are you talking about?"

"You used to take ballet. You put on a recital for me in the middle of your backyard."

"I can't believe you remember that." She turned toward him.

He looked into his whiskey as if he could divine the future, a half smile on his face. "I've not forgotten a minute that we spent together. Don't you remember?"

Emotions she didn't understand grew a lump in her throat. Of course she remembered. Every second. Next to her parents, Nash had been the most important person in her life. Above even her brothers back then. The fact he remembered filled her with hope and despair.

"Why in the world did you come back to Cottonbloom, Nash?"

Nash suppressed another coughing fit. All the cigarette smoke hanging in the room like fog was making his usually well-controlled asthma act up. Friday and Saturday nights were definitely the worst as he had discovered over the past two weeks of coming in regularly. He took a too-large sip of the excellent, aged Scotch to soothe his throat. Not the way such fine liquor should be savored.

He wasn't at the Rivershack Tavern for the Scotch or the company—although he'd surprisingly enjoyed both—he was sitting in the smoky bar for Tallulah Fournette. As soon as he'd heard she was single again and a semi-regular, he'd found himself there night after night, waiting.

It's not like he'd moved back to Cottonbloom for her. A multitude of reasons drew him back to his hometown. His aunt was getting older. Cottonbloom College, while not as prestigious as an Ivy League school, offered something none of those schools could. The chance to build an outstanding history department from the ground up and the promise of early tenure. He was excited for the challenge.

But more than familial obligations and a job drew him home. Cottonbloom lived in his memories like an old tome he struggled to translate and interpret. When he dreamed of Cottonbloom, the negative recollections leaked out as if his memory were a sieve, saving only the good stuff.

The days before his mother got sick, catching lightning bugs in the summer, the walks along the river with Tally. He ignored the bad stuff—his mother dying, bigger boys pushing him down, calling him a freak and later Nerdy Nash, the constant ache of loneliness.

If reconnecting with Tally had crossed his mind more than a few times while he had been debating the job offer and move . . . well, it wasn't something he was willing to admit to her.

"Is Cottonbloom not on *Conde Nast*'s top destinations list?" He kept his voice light, hoping to coax out another of her smiles.

"Not yet, but it will be if Regan and Sawyer have a say."

"Ah, yes. Regan is rather passionate about her tomato festival."

"Try obsessed. My brother has bought stock in antacids. Not that he's any better. He wants to win the competition so bad, he might have sold his firstborn to the devil." Her smile was a combination of tease and sarcasm.

"You don't think—" he cleared his throat and side-eyed her "—Sawyer had anything to do with the gazebo fire?"

Her smile thinned and her eyes narrowed. "Absolutely not. Who said he did?"

"No one. Well, no one besides Regan thinks he did it." Nash had a hard time believing someone as smart and level-headed as Sawyer would torch the gazebo, but then again, the man had planned to drop a half-dozen rabbits into Regan's mother's prize tomato garden. Regan had caught Sawyer in the act.

"Regan's motivations are more personal than professional, if you ask me," she said with more than a hint of antipathy.

Nash would have said the same of Sawyer, but he kept his opinion to himself. Tally looked ready to defend her brother to the death. "Say what you will, but the woman can get things done. Businesses on the Mississippi side of River Street are booming. And she has a solid plan for the contest money from *Heart of Dixie* magazine if she wins."

"So does my—" A text buzzed her phone on the bar between them. She glanced at the screen, her forehead crinkling.

"Is that your escape text?"

She set the phone back on the bar, facedown. "What are you talking about?"

"I thought all girls had some system in place if some weirdo dude was hassling them. You know, your friend calls or texts you and all of a sudden something very important requires your attention somewhere far, far away."

"Are you a weirdo?" The worry cleared from her face, her smile making her green eyes sparkle.

"I do get ridiculously excited about *Star Wars*."

"Really? I pictured you as more of an Indiana Jones fan."

"Why's that?"

She raised her eyebrows and harrumphed. "Knights Templar, Holy Grail. I can only imagine what percentage of your classes are female."

"Professor Jones was an archaeologist." He took another sip of his Scotch and shook his head. Now that she mentioned it, a good eighty percent of the classes he'd taught as an associate professor at Edinburgh had been female. He stilled. Was she insinuating women signed up for his classes because they might find him attractive? Did *she* find him attractive? Embarrassment followed by a wave of longing incinerated his insides and triggered another spate of coughing.

Her eyes flared before she burst into laughter. This was the laugh he remembered, and he tumbled back twenty years.

"Ohmigod, you don't even realize, do you?"

"Realize what?"

"Better if you don't know." She grinned.

Her cheeks were flushed, and dark hair that had escaped her braid wisped around her face. Unlike most of the women in the bar, she wasn't wearing a skirt or heels. Her simple blue T-shirt emphasized lean curves, and her dark-wash jeans were tucked into a pair of black motorcycle boots. Smudged black eyeliner emphasized the only thing about her that was soft. In her laughter, her intense green eyes shed their wariness and turned warm and welcoming.

He smiled back and propped his chin up on his hand, leaning in closer. "I can assure you I am stodgy and boring."

"Really?" Her voice dripped sarcasm, but she mimicked his stance, so they were only a few inches apart, their elbows nearly touching on the bar. "What do you do for fun?"

"I like to explore creepy, cobwebby catacombs full of dead people."

Her smile faltered. "Are you serious?"

"Yep."

"I'm pretty sure Cottonbloom is fresh out of dead-body-stuffed catacombs. How are you keeping yourself entertained? Are you dating anyone?"

"Nope. How about you?"

She glanced at her phone. "Not at the moment."

Even though she'd voiced a denial, his spidey sense tingled at her slight hesitation. A woman as tough and beautiful and smart as Tally probably had men crawling all around her. Had he missed his window already? Or had she and Heath Parsons gotten back together? He forced his voice to stay light and teasing. "What would you suggest for entertainment?"

"You could pull up a chair with the rest of us to watch these festivals unfold. Ten-to-one odds that they'll get us on the national news—and not in a complimentary way. More like a point-and-laugh-at-the-rednecks kind of way."

"That's not good. I'll be implicated if someone starts digging for dirt."

"How so?"

"I might have been involved in the bunny kerfuffle last month."

She blinked at him a couple of times before bursting into husky laughter. He couldn't help but smile back. She'd turned into a beautiful woman, if an intimidating one. He'd had to screw up his courage to walk across the bar and take the seat next to her. She seemed to have some sort of force field around her that repelled men. The vibe alternated between "back off" and "you are beneath my notice."

He held his hands up. "Are you laughing at me?"

"I'm not . . . Yes, I am, but not in a bad way. I like the way you talk. It's cute."

"*Cute?* Geez, next you'll be putting ribbons in my hair." "Cute" was the word any man of legal age dreaded hearing from an attractive woman.

"I didn't say *you* were cute, you're . . ." Her gaze drifted over him.

"I'm what?"

"Definitely something other than cute."

The way she said it made him think it was meant as a compliment. "What else is there to do?"

"Let's see . . . Uncle Delmar and some of his buddies play bluegrass out on River Street the occasional Saturday evening in the summer. Turns into a kind of block party. They built that new movie theater up by the college. An ice cream shop opened this spring on the Mississippi side. And there's this charming establishment." She presented the bar like a game show host presenting a prize.

"Wow. You're really stretching for entertainment."

"God, I know. You're going to regret moving back."

"I doubt that," Nash said before throwing back the last of his Scotch.

The front door opened and a breeze gusted around the bar, curling smoke around them. Bands were tightening around his lungs, and he forced himself to breathe slowly. Call it prideful or just plain foolish, but he didn't want to pull out his inhaler in front of her.

"You could come down to the gym. You look like you're in good shape. Do you spar?" Her eyes flashed over his body again. Was she checking him out? Or assessing how easily she might kick his butt? Deciphering the ancient scrawls of monks was effortless compared to reading women.

"A little." Gaining early admittance to college at sixteen had made him an easy target for teasing. The fact he'd been a gawky late bloomer who looked closer to twelve than sixteen put a bull's-eye on his back, and he'd taken a martial art class at the urging of his counselor.

Martial arts had given him friends and confidence—two things he'd never had in abundance. When he'd moved to Scotland for graduate school, he'd taken up boxing, finding the workout and regimen more suited to his energy levels. It was an outlet for his generally sedentary work and a way he kept a handle on his asthma.

"Why don't you come down one day after your last class and I'll put you through your paces."

"I'm not teaching this summer, actually."

"You're not working?"

"I didn't say that. I'm finishing up a paper on Charlemagne for publication in a trade magazine and catching up on my reading—both academic and for pleasure—and planning for my fall classes."

Her gaze dropped to the floor, and she sat up straight on the stool, swinging her legs back around to face the bar. She toyed with her still half-full beer glass, but didn't take a sip. An awkwardness had descended, but he wasn't sure why.

His nervousness grew in the silence. He'd worked hard over the years to control his ingrained shyness when it came to the opposite sex, but Tallulah was different. He wanted her to like him, dammit. He didn't want to take her home—not yet anyway—he just wanted a chance to get to know her now that they were grown. The closed-off look on her face made him wonder if he'd already blown it.

"Do you still go down to the river?" He choked off another coughing fit.

She side-eyed him, but didn't turn to face him again. The connection that had been knitting itself together had frayed. "Not so much anymore. Sawyer bought a house that backs up to the river farther into the parish, but"—she shrugged—"it lost its magic somewhere along the way."

He coughed again and his hand slipped into his pocket. He wasn't going to make it much longer. "Listen. I have to head out." He stifled more chuffing coughs as he slid off the stool. "I'm going to take you up on your offer though. When's a good time to drop by the gym?"

"Right after lunch is our slow time. Hey, are you all right?"

Squeezing his lips together to stem another round of lung-scraping coughs, he backed away, nodding. He hit the front door and launched himself outside, taking big gulping breaths of humid air. Not caring who saw him now, he fumbled with his inhaler and took a hit.

The medicine coupled with the clean air offered

immediate relief. He slid into his imported Land Rover Defender and banged his forehead against the wheel a couple of times. No doubt, Tallulah Fournette thought he was the biggest weirdo on either side of Cottonbloom.